# *The* Challengers Aero Club

*To Pam -*
*Best wishes and hope you*
*enjoy the read. Remember the*
*Marlins!    Severo*

## Severo Perez

### SCRIPT & POST SCRIPT
### LOS ANGELES

*Library of Congress Cataloging Data*

*Severo Perez*
*The Challengers Aero Club / by Severo Perez -- 1st Ed.*

*ISBN: 0979088100*
*ISBN 13: 9780979088100*

1. Willa B. Brown--Cornelius C. Coffey--Colonel John C. Robinson--Chauncey Spenser--1930s--Chicago--Fiction. 2. African Americans--Aviation--The Great Depression--segregation--U.S Army--Fiction. 3. National Airmen's Association of America--Harlem Airfield (Chicago)--Tuskegee Airmen--Fiction. I. Title.

*For Judy*

# Preface

The *Challengers Aero Club* is a fictional work based on the
lives of three remarkable aviators: Willa B. Brown, John
C. Robinson, and Cornelius C. Coffey. The setting is Depression-
era Chicago during the critical years before the Second World
War.

While researching a documentary about the pioneer aviator Willa Brown, I was fortunate to interview seven individuals
who had been part of the activities at Chicago's Harlem Airfield
and the Coffey School of Aeronautics. Harold Hurd, Chauncey
Spencer, Lola Jones Peppers, Marie St. Clair, Quinton Smith,
Walter Sedgewick, and Glenn Cartwright shared their recollections. I also interviewed two of Willa's brothers, Simeon and
David Brown, and a cousin, Dorothy Brown. Because they were
the last living link to that important period, I asked them to tell
me about their personal experiences. They related colorful anec-
dotes and memorable details, but significant gaps remained
in the history. No one had been alongside Willa, Coffey, and
Johnny all the time.

Amateur historians and distant relatives were eager to
tell me what they knew. None of these sources, however, had
been part of the aviation craze in the 1930s. The few published

memoirs tended to ignore the contributions of others. And finally, there were often repeated tales that were more urban legend than fact.

From the firsthand interviews and news clippings, I was able to discern what our main actors were doing and when they were doing it. Undisputed are the facts that they faced enormous racial and financial obstacles, and through intelligence, training, and perseverance, they managed to succeed beyond their own expectations. Naturally, no success can exist without unexpected detours and consequences, and for me, fortunately, the lack of a neat narrative arc allows for storytelling latitude. That is why I have chosen to set the novel free and allow it to become its own fictional work.

I extend heartfelt gratitude to Connie Gibson for sending me on the journey to produce the documentary film, *Willa Beatrice Brown: An American Aviator.* My sincerest thanks to Carlos Rene Perez, Dan Bessie, Adrienne Mayor, Marcia Ober, Carol Perez, and Sara Bleick for their extensive and supportive notes.

And of course, I am profoundly indebted to my wife, Judith Schiffer Perez, for her love and encouragement and for editing far too many drafts of the manuscript.

Severo Perez

I

*Friday after Thanksgiving 1928, Terre Haute, Indiana*

illa Brown pushed open her parents' front door and stepped out on the stoop. "It stopped snowing," she called to everyone inside, her breath condensing in the frigid air. "Come on. We've got a long drive." She cinched the belt of her chic dove-gray overcoat and touched her ears through her matching cloche hat.

She and her fiancé, Jim McClellan, were driving back to Gary, Indiana, that evening, a five-hour drive, and as was customary for African-Americans making a road trip through the South, they dressed in business attire. While technically they weren't driving through the Deep South, Southern Indiana bordered Kentucky and state lines didn't confine narrow minds.

Stepping out on the stoop, Willa's boyfriend paused to button his suit jacket. He ran his hand across the thin fabric on his sleeves and glanced warily at the sky. Two days earlier, the temperature had been in the seventies. He hadn't anticipated the cold snap. Willa hastened down the narrow stairs and waited by Jim's dark-green Plymouth roadster.

They'd planned to leave earlier, but with friends and relatives dropping by to meet Willa's tall, handsome beau, it was 3:30 before they had a chance to break away. The overcast skies made it seem later.

Hallie Mae, Willa's mother, and Reverend Eric Brown, her father, squeezed onto the stoop behind Jim, causing him to slip on the icy cement. He steadied himself and gingerly descended to join Willa by the car. Following Hallie Mae and Reverend Brown down the stairs were their four sons, an aunt, and a girl cousin.

An icy gust of wind rattled the bare branches of the neighbor's elm.

"Will you be warm enough?" Hallie Mae asked. Her long braid slipped from her shoulder onto her chest as she leaned forward and crossed her arms against the chill.

"We'll be fine, Momma."

Reverend Brown looked up at the sky. "Could be a hard freeze if the clouds lift."

Willa gave her brothers, father, aunt, and cousin quick hugs. Hallie Mae wrapped her arms around Willa, nearly knocking the hat from her head.

"Momma, I'll call person-to-person collect for myself when we get to Gary. You know what to do?" she said, straightening her hat.

"I'll say, 'Willa's not here,'" answered Hallie Mae.

"Why would you be calling for yourself?" asked Simeon.

Willa grabbed her slender fourteen-year-old kid brother around the neck and ground her knuckles into the top of his head. "Simeon Ulysses, think. Why would I be calling Momma collect after driving five hours?" She kissed the spot where she'd rubbed her knuckles and turned him loose. The brothers laughed at Simeon's expense.

2

"Oh yeah. So she knows you're there safe and it won't cost," Simeon replied, regaining his composure.

"Okay, that's it. It's time to go," Willa insisted.

"I'll wait for your call," said Hallie Mae. "And, Jim, it was a real pleasure meeting you."

"Thank you, Mrs. Brown," answered Jim. "I had a fine time."

Six-foot-tall Jim McClellan dwarfed the entire family. The tallest of Willa's brothers barely cleared five foot six. Jim had bunked with them the night before, and for a high school math teacher, they found him a good sport with a great sense of humor. The brothers crowded around to shake his hand and silently admire the new green roadster.

"Jim, Jim," Simeon raised his voice above the others. "Jim, how's my big sister doing at Roosevelt High?"

"You'll have to ask Willa," Jim said, turning up his coat lapels. "But I'll say this…" He cupped his hand to his mouth as if he were sharing a secret. "She gives the old biddies the vapors." The brothers roared. "She's has her students working in the school office typing, taking shorthand, doing bookkeeping, and I don't know what. They run the school."

Willa's brothers looked at one another, beaming. They knew as much and were pleased to hear it from someone other than family.

"She also makes the girls read about that lady pilot who died. What's her name?" asked Jim.

"Bessie Coleman," Simeon answered quickly.

Jim winked at Willa. He knew Bessie Coleman's name, and everyone else present knew about the famous black pilot. "Willa would teach the boys auto shop if they'd let her."

Again, everyone laughed because they knew it was true. It was apparent Jim loved their sister. At twenty-three years old,

Willa was the first of her family, and one of the few individuals from her community, to graduate from college and become a schoolteacher. They were proud of her.

No one was a bit surprised when Jim handed her the car keys. "Willa, please drive. You know the roads," he said, opening the passenger side door. Willa kissed her index finger and touched his lips.

"Mrs. Brown, the sweet-potato pies were delectable." Jim reached out his hand to Hallie Mae.

"Thank Willa. She made them." Hallie Mae took Jim's hand. "Goodness, your fingers are freezing."

"Look at you, Jim! You with only a suit coat." Papa Brown glanced around at his family. "I don't think any of us have a coat that will fit you."

"I'll be fine, sir. The car has a heater."

"You just wait right there." Hallie Mae rushed back into the house and emerged moments later with a faded crazy quilt. "You might want to put it around your shoulders."

"You didn't have to, Mrs. Brown. I'll be fine."

"Take it," coaxed Willa, sliding into the driver's seat. "Or we'll never get out of here." She started the car.

"Thank you," said Jim, taking the blanket and placing it next to him.

An hour out of Terre Haute, snowflakes melting and refreezing as sleet glistened in the headlights. Jim opened, closed, and opened a vent under the dashboard.

"This car doesn't have a heater, does it?" asked Willa.

"No, but the salesman said if I open the vent down there, heat from the motor is supposed to warm the cabin. That's probably as good as it's going to get." He rubbed the palms of his hands together under the vent. "That white professor who dropped by yesterday, what was his name?"

4

"Dr. Miller," said Willa, her eyes on the road.

"He put me through a grilling. I thought your parents might be tough to meet, your father being a minister, but they turned out to be sweethearts. Dr. Miller wanted to know if I was good enough for you."

"Don't take it like that. He thinks highly of you. He told me so. He's recommending me for a master's degree program at Northwestern University. He thinks I should eventually leave teaching and become an administrator. And this master's program could lead to that."

"Are you going to consider it?"

"Maybe. I don't know. Would you be interested?"

Jim laughed. "If I wanted to become a school administrator, my name would be Coach."

"Be serious. Do you want to teach math the rest of your life?"

"Seriously? I like teaching, but I don't know if I can do it for five more years." He leaned back and blew his breath into his palms. "I learned last week that old man Jenkins, our esteemed city alderman, isn't running for reelection...and--"

"Of course, you should run," Willa interrupted.

"I didn't say I was running. I have a year before I have to make a decision. I think...well, I believe...I could win that seat, considering population changes and church congregations. On paper, the numbers add up. I'm thinking about it."

"That's a year away. It's a start. After three or four years as alderman, you could run for Congress! I'll be your campaign manager."

"Before you elect me president, I nominate that blanket your momma loaned us as my running mate." He threw the quilt over his shoulders as if he were a musketeer donning a cape. "How do I look?" he asked, arching his eyebrows like a silent-movie idol.

Willa glanced over and chuckled. "That's my baby blanket, by the way." Seeing a turn in the road ahead, she pressed on the brake and the car skidded sideways.

"Whoa." Jim released the quilt and put both hands on the dashboard.

"There's ice on the road," Willa said to herself and managed to recover. At thirty-five miles an hour, the Plymouth was approaching the turn too fast. She downshifted to second gear and tapped the brake gently. When that didn't slow the car, she pulled back hard on the hand brake. The tires locked but failed to grab on the ice-slicked pavement. The roadster drifted through the turn, tore out a fence, and crashed brutally into an irrigation ditch.

The car horn blared for several seconds and then went silent as Willa slumped from behind the steering wheel onto the seat where Jim should have been. Her bobbed hair was flecked with bits of glass. Deep gashes to her jaw and cheek began to fill with blood.

Outside of the car under the open passenger side door, Jim lay motionless. He held Willa's cloche hat in his hand as light sleet continued to fall and darkness overtook the country road.

A white police officer held a flashlight between his teeth while lifting Willa's stretcher into an ambulance. The rookie driver slammed the van's back door shut and nodded anxiously toward the icy pavement. "Damned ice. I nearly cracked up on Beaton Road," he said, clapping his gloved hands. "I don't know what to do. Can I take her to Hillsdale and see if they'll make an exception?"

The officer flicked away frozen saliva from the flashlight. "They ain't gonna accept her."

"But county hospital is twenty miles away, and Hillsdale's only three," figured the driver. "She probably won't make it either way."

"You'll add more 'an six miles to your trip. All Nigras go to county, no exceptions." The officer's flashlight beam swept from the sleet-mottled quilt covering Jim McClellan's body to the wrecked Plymouth. "What a shame. It's a really nice car."

# 2

In the yellow light of sunrise, a motorcyclist stopped at the edge of a field in the rural outskirts of Chicago. John Robinson steered his red Indian motorbike through a weathered wooden gate, fishtailing on the slick spring grass as he drove toward a ramshackle tractor barn and oak tree at the opposite end of the field.

Through a crack in the door, he could see his friend Cornelius Coffey working by the light of a kerosene lamp.

Twenty-three-year-old Coffey looked up. "About time," he said, turning off the lamp and hurrying out of the barn to look up at the sky. It was going to be a clear, sunny day. "You ready to do this?" he asked.

"I've already done it in my mind," answered Johnny. "I saw myself flying, and I knew I could do it. It's a motorcycle with wings."

"Well, it's an airfoil with a motorcycle engine," Coffey muttered to himself. Normally, he would have made a point of correcting his friend. Today, however, he was too proud and excited to contradict. He dragged the barn door open, revealing an ultralight homebuilt single-winged airplane, painted white with red trim.

Johnny unbuckled the motorcycle's saddlebags and retrieved a leather flight jacket, gloves, and an aviator's cap with earflaps and goggles. "I borrowed them from Mr. Mack," he said, putting on the jacket. "They've been in his office for as long as I've worked there. I don't think they've ever been worn." The flight jacket and cap gave the tall, broad-shouldered twenty-four-year-old Johnny an air of confidence that ignored a crucial reality. He'd never flown before, nor had he had a lesson.

Johnny and Coffey lifted the tail section and pushed the monoplane like a wheelbarrow to the center of the field. For the two young mechanics, the plane represented the culmination of a two-year-long challenge. Soon after they'd met on the job at Mack Chevrolet, the only licensed black mechanics in the shop, they discovered their mutual interest in flying. Of course, owning an airplane was akin to owning a luxury yacht for two guys making seventeen dollars a week.

It was about that same time Coffey learned of a local businessman, Edward Heath, who was selling airplanes in do-it-yourself kit form. For the well-heeled aviation enthusiast, Heath sold a fully assembled, ready-to-fly Heath Eagle for just under a thousand dollars. For less than seven hundred dollars, he sold a version without the engine. For the truly adventurous, he sold the plans for the Heath Parasol Ultralight for five dollars. Heath's plans were not for hobbyists, but those with professional mechanical skills and experience in making models could assemble one.

Johnny teased Coffey about wasting five whole dollars on what seemed like a quixotic whim. "Coffey, if you build an airplane, I'll fly it." Of course, at the time, he didn't know Coffey that well and had assumed he'd never have to live up to that dare.

The enterprising Mr. Heath also sold propellers, engines, seats, cables, and smaller kits for the wings and other parts of the plane's design. Coffey purchased the wing kit and began assembling it in the barn. Eddie Heath allowed Coffey to scrounge through stock returns, discards, and wrecks because the young man paid two bits or a half dollar for something he might just toss in the incinerator.

As construction continued, Johnny realized that the slight, serious-minded Coffey was determined to build an airplane. He sacrificed his evenings and weekends to gluing and clamping an intricate framework of wooden frets and struts that formed the wing and then the body of the Heath Parasol monoplane.

Johnny wasn't about to back out of his dare, either. He read everything he could about flying. For his part, he acquired the Ace motorcycle engine and the lightweight motorcycle wheels.

Johnny had to admire the attention to detail and craftsman-ship Coffey had put into the Parasol. The finished aircraft stood five feet high and seventeen feet long from propeller to tail and weighed two hundred and fifty pounds. The fuselage looked like a one-person kayak with the Ace four-cylinder motorcycle engine mounted in front and the stabilizer and vertical fin in the back. Suspended above the pilot, the wing was joined to the fuselage and wheels by an undercarriage of welded motorcycle tubing.

"Okay, this is it," he said, running his hands over the tightly stretched canvas that formed the skin of the aircraft.

Climbing into the cockpit, he saw that the Parasol wasn't entirely finished. A sturdy apple crate served as the seat, and there was no windshield to protect the pilot. To keep Johnny from falling out of the plane, an extra-long leather belt was fastened to the frame from under the crate. Cinching the belt around his waist, he marveled that Coffey had even punched extra holes in the leather, making sure it fit him.

"Start her up," Johnny said, his voice cracking.

Coffey had tested the motor dozens of times as it sat clamped to sawhorses. Out in the middle of a field, Coffey gave the propeller a hard spin, and the motor started instantly. The plane lurched dangerously forward. Startled, Coffey stumbled back, brushing the back of his hand against the spinning propeller. A fraction of an inch closer, and he could have lost fingers. Except for a small, painful scrape, his hand was fine. He laughed nervously and wiped his face with his palms.

"You know, we don't have to fly today!" Coffey shouted over the engine noise. "We can just taxi around and get a feel for her."

"Sure," called Johnny, though he'd only heard the last part about taxiing around. Johnny hadn't seen Coffey's incident with the propeller, and the engine noise made it impossible to hear. Coffey checked the flaps, the rudder, and the ailerons, using hand signals to communicate.

Johnny taxied the craft around the field several times, getting a feel for the speed and lift. After a half hour of practice runs, Coffey needed to check the gasoline level. He signaled for Johnny to idle the engine and bring the plane to a stop. The Parasol had no brakes. Coffey grabbed onto the tail and dug his heels into the sod, a futile stumbling effort that left him flat on his face. As he looked up, the monoplane rolled to a stop on its own.

Coffey refilled the gas tank and tightened the connectors to the rudder. Satisfied that all the cables were in working order, he nodded at Johnny.

"Let's do it," said Johnny.

Coffey tore off a handful of grass blades and held them above his head, allowing them to slip through his fingers. He pointed in the direction of the breeze, picked up the rear of the plane, and positioned it for takeoff.

Johnny waved off any last-minute instructions. He couldn't hear Coffey in any case. He revved the engine and pulled back on the throttle. The plane sped across the field and started to lift. An instant after becoming airborne, it flipped upside down. Johnny grabbed the frame and pulled himself into a ball inside the cockpit. The plane flopped onto the field with a thud. The Parasol and Johnny's head bounced off the soft earth. Coffey stood frozen. His pal—more important—"My plane!" he screamed.

As he raced toward the Parasol, Coffey saw Johnny hanging upside down, waving.

"Let's do it again," Johnny grunted. He undid the seat belt and fell out of the cockpit. He scrambled to his feet. A red smear of blood streaked his forehead. "Let's do it again," he repeated, his heart pumping. "The ailerons went from zero to ninety degrees like a flash. Loosen them up, and let's see. I can do it. I had it."

Together, they righted the plane as if it were a large box kite. Johnny dismissed the scrape on his forehead, wiped the grass and dirt from his goggles, scrambled back into the cockpit, and buckled the seat belt. Coffey's inspection revealed no major damage. He loosened the tension on the aileron cables.

"Feels better," Johnny said, testing the ailerons. "There's no telling how they're going to work until I'm in the air."

Coffey found two rocks and placed them in front of the wheels. He approached the propeller cautiously, gave it a timid spin, and jumped back. The engine sputtered and died.

He shrugged off his fear and gave the propeller a forceful spin, making sure his hands were clear when he finished his motion. The engine caught immediately. Coffey lifted the aircraft by the tail and backed it away from the rocks.

On the second attempt, the plane made three hops and became airborne. Johnny shrieked an adrenaline-spiked *"Whoooiiiee!"* Banking into his first turn, he felt a new sensation caused by the centrifugal force of the turn. The exhilaration lasted until he realized he wasn't breathing. He gasped with excitement. He was flying, and it felt better than anything he could recall.

Coffey's eyes welled with tears as his airplane banked and circled the field. They took turns flying until every drop of fuel was shaken from the gas can. Johnny even siphoned a half gallon from his motorcycle.

On the last flight of the day, as Johnny circled the field, the engine sputtered and went silent. The Parasol was heading in the wrong direction for a landing. Considering his speed and altitude, Johnny somehow intuitively knew he had one chance to position himself for an approach. He calmly forced the plane into an extra-tight turn, putting the Parasol in the right direction, but much too low. His trajectory pointed him at the tractor barn and the oak tree next to it. He waited until he was twenty yards from the tree and pulled back on the ailerons and elevators. The Parasol lifted just enough to clear the top branches and make the field. The moment the Parasol coasted to a stop, Johnny leaped from the cockpit.

"Yes, yes, yes, and *yes, siree!*" he shouted. "Did you see that?"

Nothing that day bothered Johnny. The experience of flying gave him a glow. It didn't occur to him that he could have cracked his skull or killed himself several times over.

"Let's go. I'm starving!" Johnny called out.

"We can't just walk away," said Coffey. "Except for refilling her--which we can't do--I want to leave her ready for the next time. Otherwise, I'll forget what I did or didn't do." They pushed the Parasol back to the barn. Coffey took down a logbook and wrote that they'd used two and a half gallons of gas, while spending thirty minutes taxiing on ground and fifty minutes in the air.

Coffey couldn't muster the same excitement as Johnny. He felt responsible for not anticipating the near-fatal disasters. He would never make those mistakes again.

On the way home, they ran out of gas two miles from Indiana Street and had to push the Indian motorcycle the rest of the way in the dark.

# 3

As attendants wheeled Willa into the Chappie Indiana County Hospital emergency room, her arms flailed, pushing the doctor and nurses away. They heard her repeat a slurred, "Aki, aki..."

"What's she saying?" asked the doctor.

"Dun't know," the attendant shrugged.

"She's going to hurt herself. Hold her arms. Now!" barked the doctor.

The nurse and attendant held her while the doctor swiftly prepared a syringe and administered morphine. Four seconds later, Willa's body relaxed. She'd suffered a severe concussion, a fractured jaw, a cracked hipbone, and injuries to her liver, bladder, and uterus––as well as lacerations of her face, of which several required multiple stitches.

For the next forty-eight hours, Willa couldn't hold a thought in her head. She drifted in and out of sleep. Her first recollection came three days after the accident. Opening her eyes, she saw an image of someone obscured by gauze. Her hand rose to her face, and the figure gently restrained it and lowered it to the bed.

"Don't," Willa heard her mother say. "Don't touch the bandages."

"Mmumm…Mmmm." She tried to speak but couldn't open her mouth. She knew she was in a hospital. She couldn't see but could feel a cast on her hips and left leg.

"Good morning, baby girl." Willa heard her mother's voice next to her ear.

"Willa woke up." Hallie Mae spoke to a new person entering the room. "Nurse Pettaway is here," she told Willa.

"I spoke to you before," said the nurse. In her cloudy state of mind, Willa found the dark resonance of Pettaway's voice as comforting as clover honey.

"You can't talk, because your jaw is wired shut. If the world is a little distorted, it's because we've given you morphine for the pain. Today, the doctor lowered your dosage, and we'll lower it every day from now on. You should be hungry. You'll be taking your nourishment through a glass pipette."

Willa must have fallen asleep. She didn't remember anything else. When she woke again, she had a glass tube pressed to her lips. She sipped chicken broth that tasted like a copper penny.

The bandages covering her eyes were removed early the next morning. Finding no surprises in her darkened hospital room, she fell back to sleep. She awoke later to the sound of her mother's voice. "David and Charles are going to sign on to do farm labor with a crew out of Farmington. They'll be gone most of the spring and summer."

Willa assumed that her mother was talking to her. Had she been awake and fallen asleep again? She didn't remember; she only knew that the world around her felt and sounded different, as if the laws of gravity had been restored. She felt pain. Her cast chafed, and her head hurt.

"And yesterday, your professor, Dr. Miller, tried to visit you, but they're only letting your father and me in," her mother continued.

Willa motioned to her mother to stop talking. She asked for paper and a pencil by miming writing on the palm of her hand.

When paper arrived, she wrote, "Jim?" and handed it to her mother.

Momma Brown's silence told Willa the answer.

It took several deep breaths before Hallie Mae could continue. "Jim was buried today. Baby girl of mine, I'm so sorry. Your father went to the funeral."

Perhaps Willa's lack of sensation was due to morphine residue, or maybe she was still in shock. She felt vacant, like an empty room in an empty house. The one image she had was of Jim tossing the quilt over his shoulders. Willa also remembered her baby-word name for that crazy quilt, *aki*.

Head Nurse Pettaway, a formidable woman in a stiff, starched uniform, took an interest in the young teacher. Willa had sensed the nurse's presence from the beginning. Her voice had the familiar deep timbre of someone who sang contralto in the choir.

After the wires were removed from Willa's jaw, Nurse Pettaway noted that she wasn't much of a talker and didn't ask for anything to read. She sat in bed staring out the window at the dark, barren trees. The bouquet of flowers and notes from her students didn't cheer her. When her hip cast was removed on Christmas Eve, a cause for celebration for the hospital staff, Willa gave them a polite, "Thank you," and that was that.

Nurse Pettaway didn't work on Christmas Day, but she dropped by with her gospel group to sing for the staff and patients. She found Willa much the same. The Christmas decorations, the carolers, the gifts and visits from her parents and brothers had had no effect. While alone, Willa sat in bed staring out the window.

The day after Christmas, Nurse Pettaway entered the room, sat on Willa's bed, and took her hand. "How are the headaches?" she asked.

"They're fewer," Willa replied.

"That's good," she said, massaging Willa's palm. "After thirty-two years of nursing, I know a little about healing. Now that the cast is off, you need to get up and walk around."

"I will," said Willa, "but I can't right now."

"You were lucky. Can you imagine me saying that?" confided Pettaway. "Very few people survive what you went through. You're lucky because your spine is perfect and your hip is mending. You're going to walk. But in order to live, you need to get active." She leaned closer and whispered, "If you don't get on your feet, you'll die here. And I don't want to see that."

Willa didn't respond. Nurse Pettaway punched up the pillows and helped her patient readjust herself on the bed.

"You haven't talked much. Most folks want to get their scary-accident stories off their chest and tell them over and over. How about you? You want to tell me about the accident?"

Willa shook her head.

"Then, what about your young man? What was he like? Was he kind?"

Willa again shook her head. "I can't," she said softly.

"That's all right," Pettaway said, squeezing Willa's hand. "I've seen lots of folks lose loved ones. It's different for everyone. I'll look in on you this afternoon. We'll get you on your feet."

As the nurse stood to leave, Willa grasped her hand. "I was driving," she blurted; a painful sob broke from deep inside. Willa clutched the nurse's hand and wept. Pettaway lifted her and held her in her arms. Willa cried for what seemed a quarter of an hour before the nurse felt her patient's grip loosen.

"Here, let me help you lean back," said Pettaway. She moistened a towel and wiped Willa's face.

# 4

At six forty-five in the morning, Johnny and Coffey entered the Mack Chevrolet dealership through the back driveway off East Monroe Street and went to their lockers to store their lunches and coats. They changed into uniforms provided by Mack, who deducted a steep seventy-five cents a week from their salaries for laundry.

Unless the streets were covered with six feet of snow and a blizzard was bearing down full force, Emil "Red" Mack expected his mechanics to punch the clock and be standing in a fresh uniform next to their open toolboxes at 7:00 a.m.

Johnny and Coffey had their stations near the entrance. Customers had to pass them when bringing in their cars for service. Each stall had its own pit, which allowed work on the car from underneath. Mechanics had to supply their own hand tools. Big tools like jacks and winches were provided by the dealership at a price.

Red Mack came out of his office and walked down the line of ten repair stalls. A tall, barrel-chested hulk with curly red-hair, Mack survived successfully in the shady world of late 1920s Chicago. His best customers included numbers runners, liquor smugglers, bootleggers, racketeers, cops, and politicians.

If Silky, a well-known Irish Northside bootlegger, needed a quick repair job on his Buick, Red could count on Johnny. Not that Johnny had mob contacts, but he was an excellent mechanic and knew how to keep things on the "down low;" and because he was black, he was as good as invisible.

However, if the police chief's new Oldsmobile needed work, it was Coffey's assignment to make it right. Red recognized that Coffey had a gift for engines. He'd seen this young mechanic approach a car, start it up, shift through the gears, and after a few seconds of listening to the engine, diagnose what was wrong. Time and again, a disgruntled customer drove away relieved that the colicky car he'd brought to the dealership was humming when he left.

As Red neared the garage door, he saw one of his mechanics sleeping on the floor behind a car. The man was still wearing street clothes. Red kicked at the man's feet.

"When did you have your last drink?" bellowed Red, his voice reverberating off the walls of the garage.

"Red, it was last night, not late," begged the employee, staggering to his feet.

"Go home. You're drunk," Mack ordered. "I can smell you from here."

"I'm solid, Red."

"How long have we known each other?"

"Long time, Red."

"I don't care if you're married to my cousin. You show up like this again, you're fired."

"I know. It won't happen again. No, sir, Red. I need this job, sir." The mechanic picked up his toolbox and backed away to the exit.

Mack turned to Coffey. "You ready to get to work?"

"Yes, sir."

Mack motioned to Johnny. "Okay, open it up." Johnny put his shoulder to the heavy sliding garage door to reveal a row of cars lined up for service.

"Coffey, you take this first one." Red motioned for the car to pull into Coffey's stall. The driver came out of the car surprised to find a black mechanic.

"I can see your problem," said Coffey, examining the radiator. "How'd it happen?"

The driver craned his head looking for Mack, but the red head was already out of the building and five cars down the line. He turned back to Coffey. "A rock fell off a truck and hit the radiator. Now it has a leak. I had to put water in it twice just driving here."

"Let's have a look," said Coffey. He filled a pitcher with water and topped off the radiator. "Start her up," he said.

The driver started the car, and Coffey could see the extent of the damage immediately. "Turn it off," he signaled. "We're going to have to replace the radiator."

"Can't you fix it?"

"Fixing a radiator is expensive. We don't fix them unless they're rare or one of a kind. We've got your radiator in stock, and we'll have you out of here by noon."

"How much will it cost to fix it?" the driver persisted.

"Sir, I have to pull the radiator and send it to a shop next door for some very tricky welding. It may work; it may not. You pay either way. It's going to cost more, and you'll have a nasty-looking weld mark on the radiator grill. A new radiator will cost about fifteen dollars, and you'll have your car as good as new."

"Fifteen dollars! No, sir! I just want to fix it."

Mack returned to the shop, and the driver reached out to him.

"Look, Mr. Mack, can you put me up with another mechanic, somebody not...you know...I just want to fix the damn thing." His head tilted toward Coffey.

"What's the matter?" asked Mack.

"I just want to fix the radiator; I don't want to buy a new one."

Mack looked to Coffey who nodded, confirming the appraisal.

"You want to fix it?"

"Yes, sir."

Mack glanced down the line of cars entering the shop and signaled for the next one to stop. "Coffey, you take this blue sedan. Harris will take the radiator job." He motioned for Harris to move his toolbox to Coffey's station.

Coffey picked up his toolbox and made eye contact with Johnny. Coffey shrugged as if to say, "What can you do?"

Johnny laughed.

"How much will it cost to fix it, and how long will it take?" the driver asked.

Mack pointed to Harris. "This man will take care of you." He walked away motioning for the next car to move up.

"About thirty dollars," said Harris. "And it'll take two days."

"Thirty dollars! In that case, just put in a new one," blurted the driver.

"A new one, sure. That's twenty-five dollars."

"But he said fifteen," said the driver, gesturing to Coffey.

"That's Coffey's rate. He's trying to build up clientele. The shop rate for a new radiator is twenty; labor is five — maybe more if we have to change hoses. It'll take two days. And let's hope there's nothing wrong with the mounts."

"There's nothing wrong with the mounts." The driver's panicked eyes flew to Coffey, who opened the hood of the blue sedan.

"You want a new one or do you want to fix it?" asked Harris.

"A new one," said the driver.

Harris stepped away to the parts department and was quickly collared by one of the other mechanics.

"What was that all about?" asked the mechanic.

"If a customer doesn't want Coffey or Johnny as mechanics because they're colored, we're supposed to charge the customer five dollars more than the shop rate. Red calls it the Jim Crow markup. If this ever happens to you, do it. You get a piece of the action, so keep it under your hat."

# 5

On January 2, Willa walked slowly out of the hospital followed by Nurse Pettaway and an orderly. She pulled her coat tightly around her neck against the cold and didn't let on about the pain in her stomach. The orderly placed a paper sack with Willa's belongings in the backseat of the Model A Ford and climbed in on the passenger side. Pettaway handed Willa the keys.

"Thank you for letting me drive. I appreciate all you've done for me," said Willa. She gave Pettaway a tender embrace, patting her shoulder as they separated. "I won't wreck your beautiful car."

"I know. Joe here won't let you," said Pettaway. "If at any time you think you can't drive, just pull off the road, and Joe will take it from there."

"I will," said Willa. She started the car and stared at the steering wheel for a long moment.

"Are you going to be all right?" asked Pettaway.

"I think so," said Willa and put the Ford in gear.

With four brothers, Willa expected the family homestead to be crowded. It wasn't. David and Charles had joined a migrant farm crew and were in Florida picking oranges to help pay off Willa's hospital debt. They wouldn't be back in Indiana until May to pick raspberries and strawberries for Indianapolis and Chicago confectioners and ice cream producers.

Her older brother, Eric, had married and moved to a small house behind Reverend Brown's church. He worked at the local Coca-Cola bottling plant operating the bottle-washing machine. Simeon, her youngest brother, lived at home and attended junior high school. He didn't have a job that winter.

With three of her four sons out of the house, Hallie Mae Brown had more time on her hands than she'd had in almost thirty years. And so she doted on Willa, expecting an accounting of her whereabouts at all times, as if she were still a teen.

At the first opportunity, Willa visited Dr. Miller in the Commerce Department of Indiana State University. She had known Dr. Miller since she was fourteen, when she'd taken a job caring for his elderly mother.

Seeing Willa standing outside his office, Dr. Miller rose quickly, tripped on a box of books, and half-hobbled over to open the door. An overweight fifty-five-year-old bachelor, Dr. Miller came from one of the wealthier families in Terre Haute. He opened the door with a wide smile, his shirt tucked unevenly into his trousers.

"Please sit. I'm so relieved to see you," he said, taking her hand. "What a terrible loss. You have my condolences. How are you doing?"

"Thank you, Dr. Miller. I'm doing better. I'm glad to be here, too," she answered, laughing nervously.

"Just thinking that you might have died in a senseless automobile accident..." Dr. Miller's eyes moistened.

"I'm going to be all right."

"Thankfully, yes," he said, dabbing away tears with his handkerchief. "You and my mother. Ha! What a pair you made. Before you came to work for her, a series of women, all licensed and professional, passed through the house. None lasted more than two weeks. They couldn't stand her, or she couldn't stand them. You gave her the best years she had in her old age."

"She could be a handful," Willa replied, smiling. "Your mother had such trouble with the language. Since your name is Miller, people assumed she spoke English."

"It was all part of her performance. She could speak English but hated how people reacted to her strong German accent. She thought the locals were uneducated boobs. She didn't think that about you, though. She wanted a daughter, and you were as close as she was going to get. She loved to dress you and drive the local society crazy with envy. What a show you two put on when you drove her to Herz's Department Store. She insisted you sit with her in the Camellia Tearoom — and they served you. You broke the color line."

"She asked me to accompany her," Willa said. "I didn't know she was going to take me to the tearoom and break any color lines. It wasn't comfortable. I was only sixteen."

"My mother claimed she was the second cousin of a minor German baron. Who knows if it's true? Frankly, I don't want to know. Here, she pretended she was royalty. Our name was Mueller until the beginning of the Great War," he said. "In 1914, we became Miller."

"She could get feisty, so at two every afternoon, I'd pour her a glass of pear schnapps and she was fine."

"The nurses never gave her schnapps. That's probably why she remembered you in her will. I hope that helps with the medical expenses." Dr. Miller reached into his desk and handed Willa an envelope.

"Five hundred," Willa said, genuinely surprised. "That was very generous of her. Thank you. It will help a lot. Thank you."

"Willa, it's January 1929. The economy is robust, and you're going to mend. You took so much of the pressure off my shoulders in those years you took care of Momma, I feel I owe you. I'm a white man who probably shouldn't be offering advice. You were one of my best students, by far. Looking down the road, there will be a need for more schools for colored children and more administrators and principals. If you're prepared, if you earn a master's degree and a doctorate, you'll be one of the leaders. You could be the superintendent of a school district."

"Dr. Miller, that's very kind of you. Right now, I hope I can get my job back at Roosevelt High."

"They'll hire you back. Don't worry about it. I've already spoken to Principal Broussard."

"I need to find a job around here, something to take care of basic things. I have to be careful and not reinjure myself. I hate to have to rely on my parents. They've already done too much."

"I have an offer. I can pay you ten dollars a week to work in the commerce library."

"Is there a commerce library?"

"There will be a commerce library. You can start Monday if you want. You want to see?"

He led her to a classroom, where she was shown dozens of boxes crammed with books, lining one entire wall, floor to ceiling.

"After Mother died, I was alone in our big house," said Miller. "I sold it and leased an apartment near campus. President

Wallace gave me this space for my collection of books. Here, students and researchers can use them."

"Did you read all of these?"

"Many of them. Some I collected because they dealt with economic theory. That's what interests me. These boxes over here contain the *Congressional Record* dating back to 1873, which probably should be in the history department. However, these are mine. Most books and texts I purchased because they belong in a commerce library. The rest of the collection includes the standard reference works. It will be light work, something you can do at your own speed. The head librarian is sending over old bookshelves and card catalogs, and he'll teach you the Dewey Decimal System. We'll call it the Ursula K. Miller Commerce Library. Are you interested?"

The ten dollars a week was about the best Willa could have hoped for. Her parents had borrowed money for the hospital expenses, and Dr. Miller's mother's gift repaid most of the debt. Her brothers could have quit their migrant farm labor jobs and come home, but they chose to stay with the crew and keep their earnings.

At the end of her first day of work at the library, Willa found Simeon waiting for her when she exited the building.

"What are you doing here?" she demanded.

"Momma sent me to walk you home."

"You don't have to walk me home."

"I know, but Momma will skin me if I don't. Anyway, I like coming here and looking at all these purty girls." He spun around to watch a group of white coeds walk to their dorm.

Willa grabbed him by the arm and gave him a sharp jerk.

"Simeon, you don't have the sense God gave a gopher," she said and popped him in the shoulder with her fist.

"Ouch. Okay, I'll stop. I won't do it anymore," he replied, secretly sneaking a peek at the coeds.

"You better not."

As soon as she got home, Willa went directly to the kitchen. "Momma, I don't need an escort to walk me home from the library," she said. "It's humiliating. Simeon is fifteen. I should be taking care of *him*. Besides, the days are getting longer––and it's daylight."

Momma Brown took a meatloaf from the oven and set it aside. Wiping her hands on her apron, she turned to face Willa. "Baby girl of mine, I almost lost you. I couldn't stand to lose you again," she said, her voice wavering.

"Yes, Momma," Willa said and never mentioned it again.

On Monday morning, musty-smelling oak card-catalog cabinets, bookshelves, and used library tables and chairs were delivered to the room. Starting in February, every weekday morning right after breakfast, Willa escaped to the solitude of the commerce library. She worked at a library desk, a thermos of coffee close by, as she opened the boxes and typed the book's title, author or editor, publisher, year of publication, the number of pages, and any other pertinent data on three-by-five index cards. There were books on accounting, advertising, banking, economics, entrepreneurship, statistics, and trade; the subject matter went far beyond the simple double-entry bookkeeping, typing, and shorthand she'd taught the girls at Roosevelt High School. The two-inch thick guide to the Dewey Decimal system had a number for almost every book she touched. And when there wasn't an exact number, she created one.

Willa occasionally cataloged a book that caught her interest and took it home to read. She finished *The Advent of Commercial Aviation* in two days. However, *The Wealth of Nations*, a book recommended by Dr. Miller as highly readable, put her to sleep.

By late August, Willa completed cataloging all the books. Dr. Miller's collection, which had appeared huge in the winter, now filled only a quarter of the shelving.

"It doesn't rival the Library of Congress, but it's a start," said Dr. Miller with a proud grin.

"I'll be returning to Gary on Monday," said Willa.

"Oh, *wie jämmerlich*," said Dr. Miller.

"It's not sad. I'm going to be all right," replied Willa.

"My mother endowed the position of librarian. I wish you could stay and run the library," he said sadly.

"You know I can't accept. I learned a lot this summer because of you. Thank you. But the one profound lesson I take from this experience is that—and please don't take offense—I cannot spend the rest of my life in a library."

They both laughed.

"And you won't. Look into Northwestern University. They've started a new master's program in vocational education. You'll stay in touch and let me know how you're doing?" asked Dr. Miller.

"Yes, I will."

"You won't," he snapped back. "*Praxis versus theorem.*"

# 6

On the second Saturday in September, a United States Department of Commerce inspector parked alongside the road, opened the weathered gate, and walked across the field to the shed where he found Coffey working on an engine part. The inspector held a clipboard with Coffey's application for a license for the Heath Parasol.

"Dennis Schoolcraft," he said and held out his hand. He had the look of a retired Marine sergeant, with close-cropped hair, a straight-back posture, and a lean waist.

"Cornelius Coffey. Pleased to meet you." Coffey had been waiting for the visit, and now that the inspector was finally there, his mouth felt dry.

"What you got there, son?" asked Schoolcraft.

"It's a carburetor heating experiment."

"What's it supposed to do?"

"If it works, I'll be able to start my engine in zero degrees. Of course, I won't know if it works until it gets that cold."

"That's not a carburetor I recognize. Is it European?"

"No, sir. I milled it myself. It'll fit on an Ace motorcycle engine."

"You make that here?" Schoolcraft looked around the shed, incredulous.

"No, sir, the shop where I work has a lathe. I made the mold myself and had a fella at one of the forges cast it for me."

"Well, young man. If you've got the noodle for that kind of thinking, I hope it works for you. Is this what you want me to license?" asked the inspector, indicating a plane covered with a tarp.

"Yes, sir," said Coffey, pulling back the tarp to reveal the Heath Parasol monoplane.

Schoolcraft reacted with a guffaw. Thinking he might be the victim of a practical joke, he turned to Coffey and asked, "Are you serious?"

"Y-yes...sir," he stammered.

"Well, I've seen the finished kits sold by Eddie Heath, but I've actually never seen one like this," he said, squatting to look underneath. "The undercarriage is more bicycle than aircraft."

"It's not, sir. It's motorcycle-grade tubing."

"You do all the welding? That's a pretty fine bead you laid down."

"Yes, sir."

The inspector stood and studiously examined the cockpit, fuselage, tail, and rudders. He gave the entire plane a shake, hoping something would fall off.

"You've flown this. You patched some tears here and here." He looked at Coffey, who was slow to respond.

"Yes, sir," Coffey admitted.

"You're not the first. You haven't hurt yourself, have you?"

"No, sir."

The apple crate had been replaced with a real seat and a seat belt. The windshield was also new. While still looking like a kayak on bicycle wheels with a long beach umbrella overhead, the Heath was in perfect working order, built to specifications.

"I want to see you taxi and then do a takeoff and landing exercise."

"Yes, sir," said Coffey, a grin spreading across his face. "Just a takeoff and landing?"

"That will be fine," he confirmed and followed the eager young man as he pushed the Parasol into the center of the field. He watched as Coffey held up a bandana that fluttered east.

"The Parasol is the lightweight version of the Heath Eagle," Coffey said, as he lifted the tail and positioned the plane for takeoff.

"Your Parasol is nothing like the Heath Eagle," Schoolcraft chuckled.

Coffey climbed aboard and nodded toward the inspector. The quick ignition of the engine startled Schoolcraft. After two taxiing passes, Coffey took off. The headwind lifted the Parasol almost vertically, so much so that Schoolcraft imagined he was watching a june bug take flight.

Coffey then turned back and landed in exactly the same spot.

"Well, hell, I hate to say it, but it passes," said the inspector. "You'll get your registration and tail numbers in the mail. Get some proper instruction, son. And don't kill yourself!"

"Yes, sir, I'll do that."

They both knew Coffey would ignore the advice. No one locally would teach Coffey to fly. Johnny and Coffey continued to practice on their own and found a man with an inspector's rating who, for a significant gratuity, agreed to sign their flight logs.

For both of them, the written exam was the easy part. They studied the book that the licensing test was based on and memorized it. Their exam scores were perfect—not all that unusual for aviation fanatics in 1929. Without any fanfare or publicity, Johnny Robinson and Cornelius Coffey became the first black men in the United States to become licensed pilots.

# 7

On the hot days of late August, the plumes of gray-yellow smoke from the steel foundries dulled the sky above Gary, Indiana. The few remaining trees within the maze of railroad tracks and smokestacks were soot-laden and exhausted. Gary was a company town. Anyone who didn't work in the steel plants supported the community of those who did.

In the nine months since Willa's accident, the neighborhood had changed. Downtown storefronts teemed with the foot traffic of migrants from the South. Along Broadway Street, a barbershop, two hair salons, a diner, and a music store catered specifically to the new clientele.

Willa moved into a boardinghouse for women, where the residents were single teachers and nurses living away from their families for the first time. As the landlady led Willa to her room, she recited by rote, "No men in the rooms, ever. No men in the lobby after six. No smoking, no alcohol, no cooking, and no pictures or knickknacks on the walls. Breakfast is provided as part of the fee. All other meals must be ordered and paid for in advance. Curfew is eight. No exceptions." A hand-lettered sign in the hallway read, "Leave Bathroom Clean." The word "Please" had been boldly added in pencil underneath.

The house rules, thought Willa, were more rigid than Momma Brown's.

"This is your room. That will be three dollars and fifty cents in advance," said the landlady, opening the door. "You're lucky you have a window."

The tiny room had a single bed and a stand-alone piece of furniture the landlady called a chifforobe. The window faced south, away from the lake and foundries, and overlooked drab apartment-building rooftops and the tallow-colored sky.

Willa paid the landlady and sat on the bed, taking it all in.

This living situation was temporary, she hoped. Only nine months before, she and a teacher friend, Millicent Carter, had shared a room in a house converted into several apartments. They had their own entrance and could come and go as they pleased. After Willa's accident, Millicent couldn't afford the apartment by herself and had to let it go. That fall, due to the influx of the migrants, good situations for single women were hard to find.

On the Friday night before school was back in session, Constance Hardaway, daughter of Gary's leading black dentist, Doctor Gordon Hardaway, invited Willa and two of her schoolteacher friends for dinner. That night, Willa experienced another side of life in Gary, Indiana. The Hardaways owned a large, two-story Victorian only a block from the white neighborhood where the managers of US Steel lived.

Dr. Hardaway, a large bear of a man, and his wife, Clarice, opened the door. "We're so glad to have you back in Gary," said Clarice, greeting Willa, along with her friends Millicent and Teresa. "Thank you for coming into our home."

Embracing Willa, Constance added, "I'm so glad you're here. And I'm so sorry about Jim."

Willa drew her closer, patted her shoulder, and whispered, "Me too, Connie."

"Let me introduce you to my sisters," said Constance. "Hortence is a senior at Roosevelt High School, and baby sister Rebecca is a sophomore. My brother will be down in a bit. He just got off work. He graduated from Wilberforce College last May and is Gary's first colored fireman," she added proudly.

In the dining room, the guests included Reverend Lorenzo Hutchins, the minister of the Mt. Zion Colored Methodist Episcopalian Church, and his wife Zenia.

As her brother entered the room, Constance smiled and then announced, "And Willa, Teresa, and Millicent, this is my brother, Wilbur."

Having bathed, shaved, and dressed in a new sports coat with a tie, Wilbur politely addressed the group. "Good evening, everyone. So good to see you, Reverend Hutchins and Mrs. Hutchins." He turned to Willa and her friends. "Please, tell me your names," he said.

As Teresa introduced herself, Millicent leaned toward Willa and raised a cupped hand to her mouth. "Get a load of those eyelashes."

Silently, two female servants in uniform entered the dining room and began serving dinner. Even though she'd performed the same duties in white people's houses hundreds of times herself, Willa wasn't accustomed to having someone put asparagus tips on her plate or fill her water glass. She acknowledged each serving with eye contact and a nod, or a quiet, "Thank you." For Millicent and Teresa, the servants were invisible. Dishes came and went, and they didn't miss a beat of the conversation.

After dinner, Doctor Hardaway pushed his dessert dish away and turned to Reverend Hutchins. "Reverend," he began, "I wanted to ask you about Asa Randolph. When I was in New York in 1920, I saw him perform in *Othello*. Do you think an actor can lead a union like the Brotherhood of Sleeping Car Porters?"

"Do you have something against the man, Gordon? I have church members who work as sleeping car porters," said Reverend Hutchins. "They have great respect for the man."

"I don't have anything against him. It's that acting seems a frivolous profession." Turning to his son, "Wilbur, what do you think?"

Willa interrupted. "Doctor Hardaway, I'd like to know, was Mr. Randolph any good as Othello?"

"He was quite good," said Doctor Hardaway.

"It's clear that Mr. Randolph isn't playacting when it comes to leading the union," Willa went on. "I think there's something to be said for knowing how to project oneself in public. He's gotten thousands of Pullman porters to join. I see that as proof he's effective. What does anyone else think?" Willa asked, glancing around the table.

Mrs. Hardaway hid a smile, pretending to cough and covering her mouth. Mrs. Hutchins looked to her husband and said nothing. Millicent and Teresa looked down at their plates, and the three sisters' eyes darted from their father to Willa.

"What do you think, Wilbur?" she continued.

"About acting or Randolph? Acting is harder than it looks. I tried out for a play in college. They told me to stick to sports. And I don't know what's happening with Mr. Randolph."

Having grown up with three sisters, Wilbur was at ease in the company of women. He didn't mind that Millicent couldn't keep her eyes off him.

"Does anyone know what's happening with the alderman's race?" Willa asked, looking around the table. "I understand Jenkins is retiring after this term."

Constance shook her head ever so slightly, as if to say to Willa that women didn't talk politics.

"I just don't know about those things. It takes all my time to prepare for classes," added Millicent.

"I'd like to know who really decides who runs for office," said Willa.

"The powers that be will make a selection," said Doctor Hardaway.

"Why does it have to be the anonymous 'powers that be'?" asked Willa. "Why can't it be someone from the Fifth Ward? With the change in population, I think it's possible to elect a race candidate to city government."

"Who would you run?" asked Reverend Hutchins.

"I don't have the name of a person, but anyone who qualifies," replied Willa. "Anyone twenty-one years old and a citizen of the Fifth Ward can run. Someone educated and knowledgeable about community needs — someone like Wilbur could win. He's the first race fireman. Why not the first city representative?"

"The potential voters are there," agreed Reverend Hutchins. "But turning them into real votes is the task, isn't it? And frankly, today, there's no one — and I apologize to Wilbur ahead of time — no one is prepared for this. It would require money and an organization."

"Someone like Doctor Hardaway could run and win," said Willa.

"Stop, right there. I'm a dentist. I don't need more headaches than that," he said firmly and stood up. "That's enough politics. Let's listen to Constance play the piano."

The party moved to the living room where Constance took her place at a black Bosendorfer grand. She began playing a slow, tender rendition of Liszt's "Liebestraum." Less than a minute into the short piece, Reverend Hutchins closed his eyes and nodded off. Four minutes later, when Constance finished playing and everyone applauded appreciatively, Mrs. Hutchins shook her husband.

"Dear, wake..." she said softly. "He's had a long day," she explained.

Reverend Hutchins opened his eyes. "That was beautiful, quite soothing, Constance. I wasn't asleep, it was a deep reverie. I knew when you started to play that I was in very good hands. However, I think it's time we say good night."

After escorting Reverend and Mrs. Hutchins to the door and bidding them good-bye, Doctor and Mrs. Hardaway thanked Willa and her friends for coming, excused themselves, and retired for the evening.

As her parents left the room, Rebecca stealthily crept to the bottom of the stairs and listened. Constance played Beethoven's "Fur Elise."

The moment Rebecca heard the door close upstairs, she signaled, and Connie slapped out the swinging intro to Eubie Blake's "Charleston Rag."

"Dance?" Millicent asked Wilbur. He shook his head. "Come on! Come on," she teased, taking his hand and dragging him to his feet. Clownishly, Wilbur made broad jerky moves, not at all in tempo.

Constance scolded from the piano, "If you're going to goof around, Wilburton, sit down. You're making me make mistakes."

"Wilbur knows how to dance. He's being silly," said Rebecca, pushing him back onto a Victorian loveseat. Rebecca turned to Willa. "You know, no one has ever interrupted father in his after-dinner conversations. Did you notice how he bolted from the room when you mentioned that he could run for office? You probably got him to go to bed early, too."

Constance and Hortence laughed.

"I'm sorry," said Willa. "Should I apologize?"

"For goodness sakes, no," said Constance, not missing a beat on the piano.

"Isn't it true, Wilbur?" asked Rebecca.

"It's true," he said. Right out of college and as Gary's first black firefighter, Wilbur was the most eligible bachelor in town. That night he found himself surrounded by five dancing women, three of them attractive and eligible. He wanted nothing more than to sit back and enjoy the view. Millicent, hoping to attract his attention, danced with her eyes fixed on him. He acknowledged her, but with his hands joined and forefingers to his lips, Wilbur's eyes were focused on Willa.

Aware he was staring at her, Willa stopped dancing and looked squarely at him, "Is your name really Wilburton, like Wilberforce?" she asked.

With a mockingly pained expression, Wilbur closed his eyes as if he'd been sucker-punched and nodded.

# 8

After every outing, Johnny returned the leather flight jacket, helmet, and goggles they used on weekends to the office of Emil "Red" Mack, owner of Mack Chevrolet. The items had hung in Red's office next to a picture of Bessie Coleman for years, until Johnny asked to borrow them. It was common knowledge that Mack had been one of Coleman's sponsors in 1920 when she went to France to learn to fly.

The nickname, "Red," was often used for mixed-raced men. The rumor was that Emil Mack might be part black, though no one dared ask.

"Johnny, come here a sec," called Red.

"Yes, Mr. Mack."

"Did you get to fly this weekend?"

"No, sir, it was too cold."

"Come into my office. I've got a deal for you. It pays real well—if you're willing. I've ordered two milk trucks for Silky McDougal. They're going to need regular service. Come rain or shine, those trucks need to be on the road Monday mornings at 4:30. He needs someone like you, but he's willing to pay two guys to make sure the job is done."

"I don't know. It's night work."

"Yes, it is. And it pays twenty-five dollars apiece—for one night's work. Let me know."

"Yes, sir. I'll think about it." Johnny knew that if you owed Red money, and he asked you to do something, you pretty much had to do what he asked.

"Ask your friend. It's a good deal," said Mack.

Later that morning, Mack brought out a new employee to the garage floor, and the new hire saw Johnny working on a car. "I didn't know they let niggers work here," he wisecracked.

Mack took the man by the collar and lifted him six inches off the floor. "Do you want to work here?" he asked.

"Yes, sir," the man replied, nearly choking.

"Then you're going to be this man's assistant," said Mack pushing the man in Johnny's direction.

"Can you use a deadbeat like this?" asked Mack.

Johnny glanced down at the new hire. The young man looked more scared than mean. "Can you change the oil on this car without me having to show you how?"

The new hire nodded.

"Maybe," answered Johnny.

"Then you can have him," said Mack, turning to leave.

"What's your name?" asked Johnny.

"Deason, Paul Deason. What do you want me to do?"

"Anything dirty I don't want to do," said Johnny. "Keep my tools clean and ready; wipe up any spills. You can start by changing the oil on this one," said Johnny, closing the door of the car he was working on.

The white mechanics snickered as the new hire stepped down into the pit under the car.

For all his open-mindedness, Mack knew that Johnny and Coffey couldn't find work anywhere else, so he paid them eighteen dollars a week, while the white mechanics averaged twenty-five dollars doing the same job. Johnny was several paychecks in debt to Red, having taken advances against his salary to pay for his Indian motorcycle.

Whether freezing weather or summer scorcher, Johnny and Coffey ate their lunch outside at an unused loading dock two buildings away. If they ate in the dealership lunch area, they'd invariably be called back to the floor.

Coffey always ate a sandwich he'd made himself, spreading the wax paper wrapping on the concrete dock next to him. He opened the latest issue of *Aero Digest* as usual; he tried to read an article a day—which was how he came across the ad in the latest issue for the Curtiss-Wright School for Aeronautics.

Johnny bought a sausage sandwich from Elsie's Lunch Hut across the street and joined Coffey on the dock. He flopped down next to him and took his sandwich from a sack. "We got to get back," he said. "Red caught up with me at Elsie's."

"Might as well; it's freezing out here. What's with the new white kid?"

"Deason? I don't know…He's strange. He apologized and said Red put him up to making the nigger remark."

"I believe him…Look-it here," said Coffey. "The Curtiss-Wright School is offering a course certifying aircraft engine mechanics for jobs in the 'growing field of aviation.' Read." He handed the magazine to Johnny.

"The tuition of nine hundred and seventy-five dollars can be paid in installments in advance, for a class beginning in September 1929. You have to be eighteen years of age and have ten years of school and an auto mechanic's certificate," Johnny finished reading. He looked at Coffey, surprised. "There's no racial covenant!"

"I know. I'm going to sign up," said Coffey.

"Nine hundred and seventy-five dollars is a lot of money to put together."

Coffey fished half a pencil from his breast pocket and wrote on his lunch bag. "If I send ten dollars a week between now and September, that's two hundred and forty." I can get five hundred by selling the Parasol. That's seven hundred and fifty. You could sell your bike."

"Stop! You're driving me nuts. Let's not go off the deep end here," said Johnny.

Coffey carefully refolded the paper lunch bag and put it in his back pocket.

"You're not selling the Heath, and I'm not selling my Indian," said Johnny, standing up. He began pacing on the loading dock.

"What are you doing?" asked Coffey.

"I'm thinking. What if we could make that much money in let's say six months and not two years?"

"I'm not robbing any banks." Coffey laughed, as he wadded up the wax paper.

"Once in a while, I do a night job for Red. It's big stuff...a broken axle; I replaced a clutch...big stuff. I do it at night here. He asked me if I wanted extra work on a steady basis. I told him I'd think about it, but I have to do it. I owe him. But he's made this offer for the two of us. We would each make twenty-five cash for one night's work."

"We won't be arrested, will we?" asked Coffey. "I don't want anything to do with some of your sporting friends."

"Arrested for what? We'll be fixing milk trucks in a garage on Clark Street in Lincoln Park."

"That's on the North Side."

"That's right; it's safe. I want out of here as much as you," Johnny replied, slapping the magazine with his hands. "With what we make here and one or two nights a week there, we can do it. Where else can we make this kind of money doing what we're good at?"

"Are they really milk trucks?" Coffey asked dubiously.

"No, but we don't have to know that," answered Johnny, clapping his friend's shoulder.

# 9

On the first day of school, Willa carried a cardboard box filled with books and supplies into Roosevelt High School's main entrance. Wilbur Hardaway, intent on catching Willa by surprise, ran up behind her with a bouquet of roses. "Mother always said the best way to get the teacher's attention is to bring flowers," he blurted out.

Willa turned, indeed surprised. "Thank you, and thank your mother," she said. "What are you doing here?"

"The flowers are from me. I'm crazy about you," he said loud enough for anyone nearby to hear.

"Wilbur, hush," said Willa, taken aback. "We just met."

"I wanted to wish you luck on your first day back."

"Thank you. This was very thoughtful, but I have to get to work."

"I thought over what you said about running for alderman. I'll do it, if that's what it takes. That along with my fireman job, I can support both of us."

Willa was dumbfounded. "Wilbur, are you *proposing?*" she asked. "I don't know you. I was talking hypothetically, that maybe someone like you, could be elected alderman. I wasn't suggesting you go out and do it. It was an after-dinner conversation. And I believe I upset your father."

As Wilbur was about to speak, Millicent, Teresa, and a group of teachers and students came out of the main entrance to welcome Willa back. "I'll be right there," she called out and motioned for her colleagues to wait inside.

When everyone was out of earshot, she said firmly, "Wilbur, I like my job. I'm getting my life back together again, and you being here is …well…inappropriate."

"I've come off too strong. That's not the impression I want to make. I was going for 'sweeping you off your feet.'" He grinned and cocked his head like a puppy. "Get to know me. What do you say?"

Willa smiled. "You can have any single lady you want. Why me?"

"Because you're not like any of the other girls," Wilbur said. "It's been nearly a year since your accident. It's time to move on, don't you think?"

Recognizing that he had simply repeated what she had said seconds before, Willa replied, "You're right, I'll think about it." Wilber simply stood there grinning. "Don't you have to put out a fire or something?"

"It's not my shift, and I'm free until Thursday morning."

"Well, I'm not. Thank you for the flowers. They're beautiful. You have no idea what kind of explaining I'm going to have to do to those people inside. Good-bye." She took the flowers and hurried into the school building where her teacher friends and excited students gathered around.

Willa liked Wilbur well enough. He was well mannered, charming, and housebroken. She could take him anywhere.

Wilbur's family was his best feature. Doctor Hardaway, for all his huff and puff, and Mrs. Hardaway, were loving, generous people. And to Willa, having grown up with four brothers, Wilbur's three sisters felt like instant best friends.

The Hardaways were proper churchgoing folk as well. Mother and sisters wore similar dark-colored clothing and matching prim hats. When Willa joined them at Mt. Zion or at public functions like the fire department equipment demonstration, she stood out in her colorful dresses and sprightly hats.

From the first time Wilbur made his surprise appearance on campus, Willa's students were obsessed with her private life. If Willa and Wilbur were seen together in downtown Gary, no matter how accidental, the sighting set off a wave of gossip. Several girls approached Willa in the hallway. A ginger-haired teen with green eyes asked boldly, "Miss Brown, are you going to marry Wilbur Hardaway?"

Willa was taken aback. She felt her face flush. "No. We're just friends. That's it; there's nothing else." Somehow, in the students' minds, Willa's denial was confirmation of a spicy romance.

When Willa mentioned the incident of the ginger-haired girl to the Hardaway sisters, Rebecca spoke up, "Oh, that's Sonya. She has such a crush on Wilbur. She told me so."

"Well?" asked Hortence.

"Well, what?" asked Willa.

"Are you going to marry Wilbur?"

"Didn't I tell just tell you what I told the redhead? We're just friends. We're…just…friends."

The sisters looked disappointed. They were fascinated by everything Willa, even if they didn't understand what enchanted them about her. No one else they knew read the

*Chicago Defender* and the *Chicago Chronicle*, kept current with fashion, could make her own clothes, talked about learning to fly a plane, read every issue of *Vogue* and *Collier's*, and just as avidly consumed *Aviation*, *Aero Digest*, and *Popular Mechanics*. To the sisters, she was a wonder.

In October, Willa found an apartment she could afford. A "decent" unmarried woman living independently was unheard of in 1929, so when Willa made the move, the sisters saw it as an incredibly daring act. For her part, Willa wanted privacy. For the first time in her life, she had her own place--and her own bathroom.

While decorating the apartment, she found an ad for custom-made flight gear. The ad featured an attractive woman about to pilot a plane, wearing a stylish leather jacket, helmet, and goggles. The boots were a steep sixty dollars extra. Willa cut out the ad, framed it, and hung it next to the bathroom mirror.

On their second date, Wilbur muscled himself into Willa's apartment. "Why do you read *Popular Mechanics*?" he asked, picking up a copy of the magazine.

"I could get fired for you being here," Willa said, trying to push him out of her apartment. She couldn't budge him.

"I'm not staying, am I?" asked Wilbur.

"No, you're not," she asserted, snatching away the *Popular Mechanics*.

"I have to use the bathroom. I'll leave right after. Leave the door open and stand out in the hall, if you want."

Willa pointed in the direction of the bathroom.

Standing over the toilet, Wilbur saw the framed ad for the flight suit.

He came out of the bathroom and returned to the front door. "I'm leaving, see? Here's what you need to know. I don't care what you want to do. If you want to learn how to pilot an aircraft, you do it. As long as I'm there to watch."

The remark caught her off guard. It was sweet of him to say so. Willa gave Wilbur a kiss on the cheek and pushed him out the door.

Over the next few weeks, she rode a relentless wave of public approval for Wilbur--even though somewhere deep inside, Willa felt all was not right. There were, after all, many little things that were vague irritants about him. When their conversations waned, he would tap his fingers on his knees. When she noticed, he would shrug as if to say, "I can't help it."

The practical reasons for marrying Wilbur were financial. He brought by extension his solid family and his promise to support her personal objectives. *Do I love him?* she wondered. After Jim McClellan, that part of her heart felt numb. Wilbur didn't stir an intellectual kinship; however, if sexual tension was love, they had plenty of that. Strong and lean, Wilbur was a good date and a great kisser.

His negatives were significant, she thought. He wasn't interested in any of the things that mattered to her. He knew very little about car engines, even though he pretended otherwise, and he firmly believed that his two years of college was all he needed to get ahead in the world.

Before Christmas, he laid out his proposal. They would get their own place. He agreed to support her through graduate school and buy her a car for the commute. Even with her continuing doubts, on Christmas Eve 1928, Willa relented and consented to marry Wilbur Hardaway, but with several caveats — no big wedding, no expensive trousseau, and the wedding had to take place right away.

"Won't people think you're...you know...with child?" asked Wilbur.

"With child? How Victorian of you. Even if it were possible, people will think what they will. You and I know I'm not. In six months, when I'm not showing, they'll forget about it."

# 10

"**S**o you need some extra dough to get into that aviation school?" Red asked, as he looked up from his paperwork and appraised Johnny and Coffey, one happy-go-lucky and the other no-nonsense. *Quite a pair,* Red figured.

"Yes, sir," replied Johnny.

"Silky, you both know Silky McDougal?" Mack looked straight at Coffey.

"Yes, sir, I know who he is," answered Coffey.

"I've sold him two new milk trucks that he's going to need serviced," said Mack. "The deal is…you provide weekly maintenance. Those trucks must be on the road by four thirty Monday morning, no matter. If you do have major repairs, if an engine needs an overhaul, dump it. It'll be faster to drop in a new one. Same with clutches, transmissions — anything taking more than four or five hours to fix, dump it. You'll each get twenty-five dollars for the night. I'll only take a small piece, five bucks each."

"Where are we going to get parts at midnight?" asked Coffey.

"We stock everything here. Except for the frame, we can rebuild the trucks five times over. If there's a busted fender, we'll supply you a new fender, and the Clark Street garage will paint it. One phone call and you've got whatever you want within a half hour. The garage on Clark Street has every piece of equipment you'll need."

Coffey and Johnny nodded.

"The trucks are in the lot. Here are the keys. You're driving them over there this morning. You enter through the alley behind the garage. Guys, keep this on the quiet, all right? Now, go punch in your time cards. Stay in your street clothes and leave your toolboxes here behind my desk. I'll keep an eye on them. Remember, you're on the clock, so get back as soon as you can."

Coffey and Johnny followed Red's orders and clocked in.

Everyone knew the milk trucks were covers. Instead of milk, these two trucks delivered beer kegs and a variety of smuggled alcohol.

Only a hundred yards from Lincoln Park and Lake Michigan, the Clark Street address was a white working-class neighborhood with a mixture of businesses and residential apartments. Two milk trucks pulling up in the alley behind the garage didn't draw anyone's attention.

Coffey and Johnny blocked the rear alley and went inside to inquire about where to make their delivery. In a front room, they could see several men in long dark coats, not unusual for February in Chicago. Expecting to find the manager, they nearly walked into what looked like an arrest in progress. Two policemen stood with their backs to them. They couldn't tell, but possibly five men, maybe more--Red's associate Silky among them--were facing the wall with their hands on top of their heads.

The men in the long coats were holding guns. As Johnny and Coffey quietly backed away, two shotgun blasts and repeated bursts from a Thompson submachine gun sent them diving for cover. Silky McDougal, dressed in a dark suit and tie, turned from the wall and made a break for the alley. Before he could take a step past the inner doorway, three shots to his back spun him around, and his head hit the concrete floor with a thud.

Coffey grabbed Johnny's coat sleeve. "What the hell you gotten me into?" he whispered hoarsely.

Johnny couldn't speak. He tried, but nothing came from his throat. One of the police officers spotted them, walked over, and motioned for them to stand. Terrified, they came to their feet.

"You're Red's boys, right?" asked the cop. "Plans have changed."

Johnny and Coffey stared back.

"Drive the trucks to this address and go about your business." He handed Coffey a slip of paper. "You were never here, and you ain't seen nothing. Right? Nod, yes."

They nodded.

"Your trucks are blocking the alley. Move them, quietly. Now, get the hell out of here."

Both turned and half ran out of the garage.

They drove the trucks to the South Side address, a processing plant for a popular brand of dairy products. The sign over the entrance read, "Brook View Dairy, Chicago's Finest Milk, Cheese, Butter, and Ice Cream."

Inside the Brook View plant, an agile young man in a dark suit and tie met the trucks and waved them into a garage. As Coffey climbed out of his truck, he noticed this was a first-rate truck garage with a hydraulic lift, engine hoists, and overhead winches.

"I'm Marcus Lipsky," the man in the suit told them. After a careful once over of both trucks (and Johnny and Coffey), he said, "Whatever deal you had with Silky, you have here, if that's good for you."

Johnny looked at Coffey.

"That's fine," replied Johnny. Coffey nodded.

"Good. Red says you're the best," said Lipsky, taking out a roll of cash two inches thick and peeling off two twenties and two fives. "Here's for your first day of work."

꩜

Back at Mack's Chevrolet, Coffey sat on the floor with his head between his knees. "I'm nauseous," he said. "I don't want any part of this. Look at me. I'm still shaking."

"I'm sorry," Johnny apologized. "How was I to know that was going to happen?"

Looking up from behind the car where they'd been talking, they saw Emil Mack appear. "I hear there was a change of plans," said Red.

"Yes, sir," answered Johnny. "But, sir––"

Squatting to their level, Mack laughed. He put a large hand on each of their shoulders and lowered his voice. "Silky, Bugs Moran and the North Side mob are out of business. We're dealing with the South Side now. It's all been arranged."

"What about what we saw? Silky was––" asked Coffey.

"We don't know what happened to Silky, do we?" Mack looked them in the eye. "How could you know? You've been here all morning. The time clock says so. I'll tell you what I'll do for you fellas. You keep my five-dollar bite and show up at Lipsky's place on Sunday night, or whenever he needs you.

There won't be any more problems; I can promise you that. And your hours here are whatever you can give. That's how important this is to me."

"Will you raise our salaries to what white mechanics get?" asked Johnny, aware he was pushing it.

Mack sighed. "If I pay you what they get, then they'll want more. I'm trying to get you some equanimity here. You'll make three or four times what the white guys make."

"I'm against it," said Coffey. "For a moment there, I thought we were going to die. I fix cars, Mr. Mack."

"Coffey, that wasn't supposed to happen. The South Side made a big move. I don't know why. But I have to play ball with them. I need you to help me out here. You're the best man I have, and I don't want to see you hurt. Lipsky is protected, if you get what I mean. His word is good, and so is mine. I'm asking you to do me a favor, Coffey. A really big favor."

Coffey knew better than to turn down Red's request, but the resigned expression on his face said he felt trapped.

The Sunday night job became routine. The trucks were run continuously and hard, with occasional run-ins with rogue cops and double-dealing robbers. Coffey and Johnny were often at Brook View Dairy three and four nights a week, replacing tires, axles, clutches, and engines. The well-lit garage was soundproof and equipped with a fair selction of tools. Lipsky made certain a pot of coffee and sandwiches waited for them when they arrived. On nights they needed additional help, they brought in Paul Deason.

If Coffey needed a special tool, something the shop didn't have, Lipsky asked him to write it down. And in less than an hour, no matter the time of night, it would appear. They could swap out an engine in half a night. By four thirty Monday morning, the trucks were tuned up, broken taillights replaced, and bullet holes filled, sanded, and painted. The trucks were ready to roll. Lipsky stood nearby with his ready roll of cash.

Every Friday for the next six months, they sent a US Post Office money order to the Curtiss Wright School of Aeronautics for their paid-in-advance tuition.

The wedding was held at the Mt. Zion Colored Methodist Episcopal church in Gary and performed by Reverend Hutchins. Willa's relatives were poor people and brought her simple gifts, such as kitchen towels, homemade blackberry jam, and a colorful log cabin quilt. Her father's congregation gave the wedding couple a lovingly handcrafted linen-and-lace tablecloth. Willa couldn't help feeling overcome by the time and care it took to make these gifts. Her eyes welled with tears.

Wilbur completely misinterpreted her sentiments and whispered, "It's okay. You should see what we got from my parents and friends."

The Hardaways gave elegantly wrapped presents from Marshall Fields Department Store. Willa opened three large boxes containing an entire crystal dessert set with goblets, coffee cups, cake, and pudding dishes. Each gift received a chorus of "ahhs" from the guests. From the Hardaway friends came a twelve-place set of china, a silverware service for twelve, highball glasses (rather, water glasses), a silver-plated punch bowl, and a gilded clock for the mantel.

Willa knew Wilbur's family meant no offense. The look on Dr. and Mrs. Hardaway's faces showed that they loved this bright young woman who had apparently tamed their restless son. Wilbur beamed at the gifts, and to Willa's surprise, her relatives were not humbled at all by the expensive gifts.

"We're so happy for you," her brother Eric's wife said. The thought entered Willa's mind that she was expected to become Gary, Indiana's new social director, and everyone was invited.

~

As newlyweds, intimacy was never a problem; a strong physical attraction bound Willa and Wilbur together without many words. And because the first two months of married life were taken up with the campaign to elect Wilbur alderman of Gary's Fifth Ward, they really didn't have that much time for any other kind of communication.

Doctor Hardaway's social connections and Wilbur's complete lack of a political track record made him an excellent candidate. To get the vote out more efficiently, Willa organized committees by church affiliation, school zone, and business. Constance, Hortence, and Rebecca were constantly at her side, answering phones and handing out cards and posters.

Wilbur's job was to stay out of their way, dress well, and show up on time where he was needed. At gatherings, Willa warmed up the crowd and essentially gave the campaign speech. When he took center stage, all Wilbur had to do was be his amiable aw-shucks fireman self and recite a few scripted lines. By Election Day, the voting public was solidly behind the handsome, personable young man. At the close of the polls, he led six other candidates with 39 percent of the vote and easily won the run-off.

~

With Wilbur's pledge of financial support, Willa planned to finish summer school at Roosevelt High School and enroll in the master's degree program in vocational education at Northwestern University in the fall of 1929. As promised, Wilbur agreed to buy her a car.

At Mack Chevrolet, Red himself took Willa out for test drives. After trying out three cars, she settled on a two-year-old green Chevy coupe. But her arduous shopping style was too much for Red. He hadn't intended to spend three hours answering questions from a married schoolteacher from Gary. Finally, just to get rid of her, he caved and gave her a significant discount.

While she was at the dealership, two of Red's mechanics couldn't help noticing this attractive, well-dressed woman slip behind the wheel and drive expertly off the lot.

"Who was that?" asked Coffey.

Johnny shrugged. "She's not from around here," he answered.

Wilbur had only the most superficial idea about how his campaign was organized behind the scenes. From his point of view the campaigning was effortless. He liked the VIP treatment and the flirty eyes that followed him everywhere, though most of the time he was a good husband. His problem as a political player was that he couldn't remember which donor had given him money and for what reason. When backers expected him to know their interests, he dodged their questions. The funeral home owner wanted the street paved; constituents with children wanted signal lights at intersections near schools; and everyone thought colored police officers would be a good addition to the city.

Most of his life, Wilbur had relied on his good looks and manners to get by, and he was hardly prepared for the everyday life of an alderman. To complicate matters, politics in Gary, Indiana, were as rough and tumble as those in nearby Chicago. Wilbur fell under the spell of two crusty, white aldermen who welcomed him with Cuban cigars, free smuggled single-malt liquor from Canada, and frequent poker games. These "enlightened" aldermen were fully aware of how Wilbur's campaign had been run—and who ran it.

Making sure his tumbler was full, they lectured about how women had no head for politics. Aglow with alcohol, Wilbur naturally agreed that politics was a man's profession. His vanity also made him a sucker at poker. The aldermen let him win a few hands and flattered his card-playing skills. By the end of the first evening, he'd lost thirty-eight dollars—more than his monthly fireman's salary.

Wilbur understood what was happening to him. He knew the good ole boys were taking advantage, and somehow, he believed he could outsmart them. They let him win—just never enough for him to erase his growing debt.

Embarrassed by his gambling losses, Wilbur became a different person from the genial guy Willa had known while they were dating. Though he didn't explain his actions or whereabouts, he expected Willa to do his laundry, iron his clothes, prepare his meals, clean house, and hold down a job.

When the silverware went missing, Wilbur insisted his mother had borrowed it for a reception. The story was fishy from the moment he opened his mouth. If any social event were in their plans, Willa would have known about it first.

When community appeals to Wilbur went unattended, the complaints got back to her. At one point, a group of parents wanted to address the council because a child had been injured crossing the street near the grade school. A traffic signal was desperately needed. And the potholes on Cleveland Street were ruining car transmissions. When Willa approached him about these concerns, Wilbur waved her away. "I know what I'm doing," he said and was out the door.

Willa wasn't about to be dismissed. "Wilbur!" she called after him, but he was in his car and gone. Surely, they would talk about this later. In the following days, Wilbur made himself scarce. He came in late and left early. Intimacy disappeared. By the middle of August, he told Willa he was thinking of quitting his fireman's job.

"Quitting your job? What? You can't quit your job!" she insisted, standing face-to-face with him.

"You just don't understand politics," he protested, turning away. "Women aren't cut out for this kind of thinking. I have to be there making decisions. You don't."

"Wilbur, what the hell are you talking about? I know how the city works," she replied, staying in his face. "I got you elected." Wilbur took several steps back.

"You know what the other aldermen ask me?" Wilbur shot back. "They want to know when you're going to have a baby like a wife's supposed to."

He might as well have slapped her.

Wilbur stalked off to play poker with his aldermen friends. If there was a moment when Willa had no further doubt that the marriage was over, this was it. A divorce was inconceivable, of course. She'd made the decision to marry, and that was a vow taken before God, her parents, and the world. What hurt her most was that Wilbur knew she could never have children.

The following morning, as she was about to leave for work, Willa discovered her Chevrolet coupe missing from the garage. "Wilbur, the Chevy's been stolen!" she cried in a panic, running back into the apartment.

"What?" blurted Wilbur, waking with a hangover. His head ached miserably. He squinted at Willa and averted his eyes from the sun pouring through the window.

"I'm calling the police. They couldn't have gotten far." She picked up the phone and dialed the operator. "What's the name of the sergeant in charge? They'll recognize my little green coupe anywhere."

"Hang up," Wilbur said, collapsing back into the bed.

"What's the name of the sergeant?" she urged. "I have the operator on the line."

"The Chevy wasn't stolen. Hang up," he repeated, pulling the covers over his head.

"What?" Reluctantly, she hung up the phone.

After a long pause, Wilbur answered from under the covers, "It was repossessed."

"Repossessed?" she repeated the word several times.

As Wilbur got up and dressed, Willa started going through the house. Nearly every expensive wedding gift had gone missing: the china and glassware, the gilded mantel clock, and the silver-plated punch bowl. Even her relatives' handmade gifts were missing. The log cabin quilt and the linen-and-lace tablecloth had disappeared.

"What kind of money could you possibly get for the quilt?" she asked Wilbur.

"Fifty cents," he replied, tying his shoes.

"And the silverware?

"My parents borrowed that. They--"

"Wilbur, shut up," she cut him off. "I talk to your sisters every day. They've said nothing about hosting anything. So, shut up about that."

Wilbur sat on the bed, lost. He'd run out of excuses.

"What's going on here?" she demanded. "When do I have a say in what we do with our lives? You said we were going to afford this."

Wilbur's shoulders sagged. "I've lost a lot of money."

"How much?"

"Two...three thousand," he admitted in a much lower voice.

In 1929, the amount was staggering. Three thousand dollars could have paid for a very nice house. It could have bought six green Chevy Coupes like the one that was repossessed or a plane she'd seen advertised in *Aero Digest*.

"Why didn't you sell the dessert set?" she demanded, holding up a small crystal bowl.

"I couldn't sell those. They're from my parents."

"You can sell my family's gifts, modest as they are, but you can't sell your parents' gifts?" she shouted, tossing the crystal bowl in Wilbur's direction. He fumbled the catch, and the bowl smashed near his feet.

"You might as well take these with you," she continued, throwing a dessert cup at him. "I don't have any use for them."

Wilbur backed out the door, batting away flying goblets and saucers.

Furious and in tears, Willa broke every piece of crystal. She then packed a suitcase and walked out the door.

# 12

O n Friday, August 23, 1929, Coffey and Johnny punched the time clock for the last time at the Mack Chevrolet dealership. That payday, news around the shop was that Coffey and Johnny were mailing off their final money orders for their tuition to the Curtiss Wright School of Aeronautics. They were to report the following Monday for registration.

In the changing area, a mechanic called out to them, "Hey, fellas, Red wants to see you in his office." Johnny flinched. Red had a way of keeping people under his thumb—except for Coffey. Coffey had never asked for favors or borrowed money. In fact, it was Red who was in debt to Coffey for coming through for him when the South Side took over the bootleg business earlier that year.

"What should we do?" asked Johnny.

"Let's go see him," answered Coffey, handing Johnny the flight jacket and goggles they'd borrowed from Red. "Give him whatever he wants, and let's get out of here."

Red waved them in. "Fellas, I'm sorry to see you go. You and I are caught up, aren't we?" he asked, glancing toward Johnny, knowing full well that all advances had been paid in full, with interest.

Johnny nodded. "Yes, sir." He had worked his butt off six-teen hours a day to get free of Red's loans.

"So, who's taking over the Lipsky operation?" Red asked.

"We trained Deason," said Coffey. "He's Lipsky's choice. He's good, has his own crew. He'll keep it on the down low."

"So, we're all set. Good. You know, fellas, I got a special place in my heart for flying. Once upon a long Goddamn time ago, I thought I might learn to fly and sell aeroplanes instead of Chevrolets." He chuckled good-naturedly. "I don't know. Maybe flying will never be more than a circus show, but you guys have got the bug. Like my friend, here," he added, gesturing toward the picture of Bessie Coleman. "That little Texas lady was gonna teach me to fly. That was part of the deal. Then she got herself killed…a real shame."

"We want to return your jacket and things," said Johnny, handing over the coat, cap, gloves, and goggles. "We thought they belonged next to her."

"Are you crazy?" guffawed Red, waving away the gar-ments. "What am I going to do with 'em? Besides, you earned the stuff. And ya know, fellas, maybe I'm the crazy one. I'm buying a radio license."

"Radio license?" asked Coffey. "You mean, like for the crys-tal radio I built?"

"Totally different. Radio, it's a real thing." Red leaned back. "A company called Westinghouse is making this box, and you'll hear my voice coming from it."

"What will you say?" Johnny asked.

"People say I have the gift of the gab. I'll talk. I might play master of ceremonies and have musicians perform like they do at the Drake Hotel ballroom. Who the hell knows? I'll tell people about Chevrolets." Red laughed heartily at his own far-fetched musings.

"Does it cost a lot to put your voice in the radio?" asked Coffey.

"That's the whole deal, fellas; after I buy the transmitting machine and turn a room in here into a studio and pay some guy who calls himself an engineer less than I pay you, it don't cost a damn cent. Electricity is cheap, and the airwaves are free. What I figure is that people will pay me to tell about whatever they've got to sell." Red laughed again. "By the way, what did your course end up costing?"

"Almost a thousand for a two-year course," said Coffey.

"That's a lot of money, boys." Mack winced. "You could have bought a Cadillac. How are you going to live?"

Johnny grimaced. "We'll be okay. We have enough to keep us fed and sheltered for a few months."

"Beyond that, we'll be all right," said Coffey.

Mack held out his hand. "Good luck, boys. If you need money, there are always jobs that need to get done overnight. Just give me a call. And don't get yourselves killed."

# 13

With less than forty dollars in her purse, Willa caught a bus to Chicago, where for the first night, she slept on the sofa at her friend Millicent Carter's apartment. Two days later, she took a room on Indiana Avenue in South Chicago. Her parents sent Simeon to live with her, ostensibly to study drafting at Wilson High School, but also as a semi-chaperone. Her father was a minister, after all. And even though this meant losing her privacy, having Simeon stay with her meant that her father sent a dollar-fifty a week for his meals and other needs.

Willa missed her friends in Gary, especially Connie and her sisters. She was grateful not to have a telephone, because when she was near one, the calls from the sisters usually turned into long, drawn-out pleas for her return. "Please, give him another chance," Connie begged. Willa could hear Hortence and Rebecca in the background.

"It's over," Willa told them. She didn't want to speak ill of him. She left it with, "Wilbur will explain."

Whether or not he explained, Wilbur did contact Willa once. "I'm sorry," he apologized. "Mother and Father are really upset. I'll try to do better."

"Wilbur, I don't hate you," she admitted. "I just don't love you enough to trust that you won't do it again."

"You're my wife," he pleaded. "What about the vows?"

"Don't talk to me about vows or broken promises. The marriage was a terrible mistake." After several seconds of silence from him, she hung up.

Willa accepted full responsibility for the breakup. That didn't keep her from agonizing over how things might have come out differently. What if Wilbur had been more forthcoming? More honest? The "ifs" didn't matter. What upset her most was her own humiliating self-delusion. She had entertained a fantasy that Wilbur, with a little work, could become another Jim McClellan.

In addition to all the people she'd hurt, Willa had another heavy price to pay: a divorced woman could not work as a schoolteacher in Chicago. Consequently, convincing the manager of Walgreen's Drugs to hire her as a cashier/waitress to work only the breakfast and dinner shifts was quite a coup. Of course, the hours she negotiated matched her school schedule. Classes at Northwestern University began in a week.

At first, the other waitresses resented Willa because they assumed the attractive competition would siphon off their already meager tips. Surprisingly, they discovered that when Willa worked peak hours, more customers came in and everyone's tips increased.

⁓

On the Friday in August that Johnny and Coffey resigned Mack Chevrolet, they found themselves at the Walgreen's counter admiring a beautiful waitress. They'd seen this attractive woman before but couldn't remember where. Johnny flirted, and Willa ignored him until it was time to take their orders.

For his part, Coffey was content to simply look. He knew he didn't have the time or money to date an attractive waitress like this. That didn't stop him from admiring how her slender neck bent slightly when she wrote down the order, or how her shapely hips moved when she walked past.

"What's your name?" Johnny pestered.

"That's not on the menu," Willa bantered.

"Hamburger, Coke, and an apple pie," ordered Coffey.

"Same except, no pie for me," said Johnny. When Willa turned her back, he pulled up his collar, pretending that a chill had swept the room.

"Stow it," Coffey growled. "Why can't you just enjoy the view?"

Johnny laughed.

After a six-month diet of beans and peanut butter, when the burgers arrived, they dove in and didn't speak until they were through.

Johnny pushed away his empty plate first. "Deason is bringing some family out to see the Heath on Sunday," he said and having eaten too fast, belched. "What if I put on a little show?"

"What do you have in mind?" asked Coffey, finishing his burger.

"I can do a barrel roll, a loop. I'm working on a climb and stall."

"The Heath is made of bicycle parts," warned Coffey.

"It's an airplane. It's supposed to fly," Johnny reminded him.

Willa placed the apple pie in front of Coffey, along with a clean fork. "You own an airplane?" she asked skeptically.

"What's your name?" asked Johnny, again.

Willa took a moment to inspect these two guys in Mack's Chevrolet uniforms. "Willa...It's Willa Brown...You got a plane or not?"

Johnny leaned forward confidently. "We have a plane."

"Well, what do you have?" she insisted, crossing her arms and leaning back against the service table.

"We have a Heath Parasol monoplane," bragged Johnny, glancing at Coffey for confirmation.

Willa thought a moment. "Did you get the twenty-seven horsepower Henderson engine recommended for the Heath kit?"

Johnny laughed and stopped abruptly. "Ah, no. We have an Ace engine." He turned to Coffey for support. Coffey swallowed a bite of pie, looked up, and grinned shyly.

"The Henderson is recommended. We have an Ace engine with four in-line cylinders, similar dimensions, and almost equal horsepower. I made some modifications." He shrugged. "It's what we have. It flies." His fork sliced off another precise bite of pie.

"You interested in planes?" Johnny jumped in.

"I'd like to learn to fly," replied Willa, clearing away dishes.

"Whooweee, she wants to learn to fly!" Johnny teased.

"Yes, and I'm going to learn," she answered tersely, handing him the check and starting for the kitchen.

"Are you married or something?" Johnny called after her.

She turned to face them. "If you've got a plane, I'd like to see it. Otherwise, thank you, come back, and see *us*. I make the pies myself."

"Why don't you come out Sunday and watch us fly?" Johnny called.

Willa paused halfway through the kitchen doors. "What time and where? Write it down." She was through the doors and gone.

Johnny wrote an address on the back of the check.

"Really good pie," said Coffey.

⚘

That Sunday afternoon, Willa took the bus to the end of the line and walked a half mile along the two-lane road leading to Coffey's field. A car passed her, drove through the open wooden gate, and crossed the field to the shed. Dressed in an ill-fitting suit and wearing an oversized tie, Paul Deason stepped out of the driver's seat. An older black man and two teenagers with caramel complexions accompanied him. They too were dressed in suits.

"Johnny and Coffey," said Deason. "This is my father and my two brothers."

"Pleased to meet you," said Johnny, now realizing why Red Mack had handed Deason over to him as a helper and trainee.

"Johnny, I told Bernie Coco I was coming out here, and he's invited himself. He wants to see the plane, too," said Deason. "He'll be here any minute. He was right behind me."

Johnny and Coffey looked at each other. Bernie Coco was the local numbers runner connected with the South Side mob. They also knew Bernie reported to Lipsky.

Just then, Bernie came bouncing across the field in a gleaming new Buick. He stepped out of the car looking like the Leyendecker man from the Arrow shirt ads; his entire appearance—from his slick hair to his crisp, blue pin-striped suit and down to his black, wing-tipped shoes—was perfection. Bernie's three passengers were fashionably attired strangers, two women and a man. As introductions were made, Coffey spotted Willa approaching on foot.

Two crowds had formed. The one Willa approached included Johnny and Coffey and their mob guests. The other gathering, fifty yards away, appeared to be made up of curious passersby and people who lived in the houses down the road; some were black, but most were white.

"Hi, I'm Willa," she said, approaching the plane.

Johnny immediately recognized her from Walgreen's. He held out his arm, and the crowd parted to let her approach. She glanced at the Parasol, not the least bit impressed.

Coffey climbed into the cockpit, and the Parasol roared to life. Taxiing the plane out onto the field, he made a turn, followed by a brisk takeoff; circled the field twice; and landed as delicately as a finch landing on a twig. Willa was duly impressed, even though no one else in the crowd could have known that Coffey had executed aviation perfection—not a wasted motion in the takeoff or a bump in the landing.

The moment Johnny took up the Parasol, Coffey's routine was forgotten. He flew in four tight circles above the field, went into a barrel roll, straightened out, and made a wide loop-the-loop, pushing the Parasol far beyond its limits. The jarring maneuvers dislodged the windshield Coffey had installed. Johnny was forced to land. Coffey quickly repaired the windshield, using a hand drill and two screws with bolts.

Willa's heart beat so fast she could hardly breathe. "Do you think I could sit in the plane?" she asked.

"I'd like to do that, too," said one of the women with Bernie's entourage.

"Sure," answered Johnny. "Be my guest," he said, helping the pretty young woman step up to the cockpit. Putting her foot on the bicycle tubing, she quickly realized that climbing in would require her to lift her flapper skirt so high that she'd reveal garters and underpants. Embarrassed, the young woman politely declined and stepped down.

Willa wasn't deterred. She reached between her legs, grabbed the back of her skirt, pulled it forward, and tucked it into her front waistband. She stepped on the frame, swung her right leg into the cockpit, and climbed in. Once seated, she looked like she belonged there.

"What's this for?" she called out.

Johnny and Coffey came over. "That's the foot control for the ailerons."

"Can I try it?"

"The steering wheel controls the rudder," said Johnny.

"And this?" she asked.

"That's the ignition switch," said Coffey.

Johnny and Coffey were both taken with her and a little taken aback by Willa's directness, as well.

The rest of the crowd quickly bored with aviation stuff. Bernie waved to everyone. "Let's go."

"Johnny, we're taking off," called Deason. "You wanna come to the house? Coffey? And you too, Miss?" He beckoned to Willa.

Johnny looked wistfully toward Willa, who was still in the cockpit peppering Coffey with questions. "Yeah, I'm coming," he answered.

Bernie and his entourage waved and were gone.

"Coffey, I'm heading out with these folk," Johnny said. "I have my bike. Does anyone need a ride?" he asked, looking hopefully at Willa.

"It's only a short walk to the bus line. I'll walk. Thank you," she said, waving good-bye.

"I'll take the bus, too," answered Coffey. "I have to refuel, check the oil, and leave the Parasol ready to fly next time."

"Then, I'll see you in the morning," said Johnny. He started the motorcycle and followed after Deason's car.

Intrigued that Willa was still waiting and watching him finish his work, Coffey locked up the shed and joined her on the walk to the bus stop. After an awkward silence, Coffey asked, "Why are you so interested in flying?"

"I don't know. Maybe because everything around us, you know, all professions, industries, and trades have a history of exclusion," she said. "But not aviation; it's new. It's a clean slate. Up there in the sky, there are no fences, no ditches, no whites-only water fountains, no male-only barriers. I want to get in on the ground floor. And you and your friend are pretty close to the ground," she teased, nudging him in the ribs with her elbow.

"Thanks," he grunted. "You talk like you have an education."

"I'm getting a master's degree at Northwestern University."

"A master's degree? So, why do you work as a waitress?"

"What's wrong with being a waitress?"

"Nothin,' just...You have college degrees."

"My classes are in the morning—and the waitress job lets me work dinner hours. Besides, I need to work. I don't have a choice." She stopped walking so Coffey had to pause and look directly at her. "Does it bother you that I have an education?"

"Well, no. You're a different kind of lady. That's all," said Coffey.

"What do you do?" asked Willa. "Do you work at Mack Chevrolet, like your uniforms said?" she asked.

"No, we quit on Friday. We start classes at the Curtiss Wright School on Monday."

"The master mechanics class advertised in *Aero Digest*? That's...that's....well...that's really...good," Willa said, getting animated.

"You know about that?" said Coffey surprised that she'd even heard of *Aero Digest*.

"Do I know about it? If I weren't going to Northwestern... I'd want to go there, except I could never afford it. You guys must be loaded."

"No, we worked pretty hard," said Coffey.

"You mean working for the likes of the fellow in the Buick?"

"No," insisted Coffey, resentful of being lumped in with the mob or most of Johnny's pals. "I mean, I'm a mechanic, and I'm good at it."

"Cornelius, I want to learn to fly," said Willa. "I'm willing to start whenever you're ready to teach me."

"I don't have an instructor's ticket. I'll have to think about it."

"Please do," she said earnestly. "How many people were there today?"

"Maybe ten, fifteen," guessed Coffey.

"Twenty-five. We certainly could have used something to drink. Would it be all right if I sold Cokes and frankfurters next Sunday? I'll split whatever I make with you, so you can pay for gas." She slipped her arm through his and stood very close.

"Yeah, sure," said Coffey.

Three hours earlier, he didn't even know this beautiful woman, and now here they were, walking arm in arm, and she was offering to pay for gas for his plane. His quizzical shrug prompted Willa to stop for a moment and pat his cheek as though he were a little boy. The gesture embarrassed him. He liked it.

# 14

The registration table was the only furniture in the cavern-ous lobby of the Curtiss Wright School. Seated there shuffling through applications were two women, clearly secretaries, and a man cross-checking names to paperwork. As Coffey and Johnny approached, the three ignored them as if they weren't there. The man finally looked up and took off his glasses impatiently. "I'm sorry, we don't hire laborers here. You might want to check the warehouse district, two blocks over on Thirty-Fourth Street."

"We're not here to apply for work. I'm Cornelius Coffey."

"And I'm John C. Robinson. I have the documents the school requested, as well as my letter of acceptance and receipt for tuition."

There were cold stares from the three registration clerks. The man jumped to his feet. "Come this way," he said, leading them to the janitorial basement. The janitor, an elderly black man, didn't know what to make of these two clean-cut young men, except he knew something wasn't right.

"What should we do?" whispered Coffey.

"I don't know," answered Johnny, frustrated. He'd spent five years in Alabama, and this felt like Jim Crow.

"Mr. Mack...Maybe he can tell us what we can do," suggested Coffey.

Johnny hesitated. "God, no. I can't call him. I don't want to owe him any more."

"Would you gents like some coffee?" asked the janitor.

"No, sir," said Coffey. "Can I use your phone?"

"It's a pay phone," said the janitor pointing to the hall.

As Johnny listened, Coffey called Red Mack and explained where they were and what had happened. He hung up. "Mr. Mack told us to sit tight."

A few moments later, a tall man in a tweed sport coat appeared.

"I'm Paul Edinger, the school's director. I want you to know there's no problem. We're going to refund your money in full. As I said, there's no problem. We'll give it to you in cash or check—nine hundred and thirty-four dollars. Just wait here, and my secretary will be down to take care of you."

"Sir, we don't want our money back," said Coffey.

Edinger nervously cleared his throat. "The Curtiss Wright School doesn't have colored students," he explained. "We're not equipped...you understand? And we wouldn't want to put you in any situation that might...you understand...be embarrassing to you," Edinger intoned solemnly, as if he were doing them a favor. "Aviation mechanics can be very hard. Look, I realize you paid for money orders and postage. I'll throw in another five dollars for your trouble. How about that? I bet you never thought you'd see that much cash at once."

"Mr. Edinger, Cornelius Coffey and I meet all your requirements," said Johnny. "We have training. We're both certified auto mechanics. We're high school graduates. We have pilot's licenses."

"That's excellent, just excellent. When we start a colored program with ten young men just like you, we'll have classes right here," said Edinger.

The pay phone rang. The janitor hustled out to the hall, answered, and motioned to Coffey. Coffey took the phone and listened and then motioned from the doorway for Edinger. "It's Mr. Emil Mack from Mack Chevrolet. He'd like to speak with you."

The director took the receiver. "Paul Edinger here," he said crisply. He listened and then explained, "Well, sir, you see, some of our students are from the South, and they might get upset if they have to attend classes with colored boys." Edinger held the phone away from his ear. Though nobody could hear Red's words, his invective was loud and clear.

After a pause in the shouting, Edinger replied, "There's no reason to sue. No, sir, there's no problem...Yes, we did accept their money. That's correct...Of course, the young men have to understand they're on their own."

After hanging up, Edinger paced the hall, visibly irritated. He returned to the janitor's room and faced Coffey and Johnny. The situation was still prickly. "Yes, you're admitted, but if you drop out, there will be no refunds."

Coffey and Johnny suppressed their grins and shook hands with the director of the Curtiss Wright School of Aeronautics. Not far from Johnny's thoughts was what he might owe to Red Mack.

# 15

The very next week, Willa set up a concession stand with two of Coffey's sawhorses and an old door he used as a worktable. Covering the door with butcher paper, she sautéed onions on a grill made from a fifty-gallon oil drum borrowed from a local church. The two groups of spectators Willa had observed the previous week returned and converged around the smell of the cooking onions. She added frankfurters to the grill and along with the five-cent Cokes, everything sold out quickly.

"If God really intended for you guys to fly, he would have given you more money," Willa teased Coffey as she served up the last German sausage and onions on a six-inch Kaiser roll.

As the crowd moved away from the shed to watch Johnny fly, Coffey joined Willa by the grill. "How do you know about all this?" he asked, indicating the sausages and soda pop.

"My papa's a minister, and we're used to putting on Sunday picnics for a hundred folks," she replied. "This is nothing. After I got back my two-dollar-and-eighty-cent investment, we made about seven dollars and fifty-five cents." Her brother, Simeon, was standing among the spectators about ten yards away. "Simeon," she called out, motioning for her younger brother to join them. "Come over here a second." Simeon reluctantly pulled himself away from the crowd.

"Simeon, meet Cornelius Coffey, and Coffey, this is my youngest brother."

"Pleased to meet you," said Simeon, hurriedly. "Can I go watch the plane?"

"Pleased to meet you, too," replied Coffey. "Yeah, you go watch. We'll talk later." As Simeon ran back to join the crowd, Coffey turned to Willa. "Do you have a lot of family in Terre Haute?"

"My mother and father, and three of my four brothers. Then there are uncles, aunts, and lots of cousins. My mama's Shawnee, so I'm related to half of Western Kentucky," she added, opening a bottle of pop she'd saved for herself.

"I have a mama and an aunt in Detroit," said Coffey.

Willa didn't respond; she was watching the Parasol perform a corkscrew spiral. After a long silence, Coffey spoke. "If the plane survives, I can teach you on Saturday afternoons. I can't let you do the stupid, crazy things we did when we learned to fly. But you can learn the plane and taxi and such. It's harder than flying."

"It's a start," replied Willa gratefully. She moved closer to Coffey and offered him a drink from her Coke.

After the show, Coffey invited Simeon to stay awhile and offered him twenty-five cents to help with a wing repair. Delighted with the pay, Simeon showed a knack for the detail work of gluing and clamping struts. Unlike his big sister, however, he was a compulsive talker.

When Coffey asked, "Why is Willa so interested in flying?" he got more than he bargained for.

"Willa loves anything with engines," Simeon began. "Cars, motorcycles, you name it. She can tell you anything you want to know about motors. That's no lie. She wanted to be a racecar driver when she was in high school. Then she wanted to be a pilot like Bessie Coleman. When Miss Coleman died, you'd think it was her own mother who got killed. She cried and cried. Nobody could console her."

Coffey said nothing as Simeon went right on with, "Yeah, she can drive anything, too. She drove a tractor back in Terre Haute. She said she did it because one of her professors hurt his back and needed help plowing—but I know she wanted to drive that tractor.

"She liked going fast, too. She got into an accident and killed her fiancé. It was awful, Coffey. He was a really nice guy. Then she married this guy who was a fireman and divorced him just like that. They weren't married more than five or six months," Simeon concluded.

Coffey busied himself so he didn't have to respond. He raked up scraps of canvas left over from the wing repair. He stopped abruptly and reached into his pocket. "Here's your two-bits. You're a quick learner. Go ahead and take off."

"Thanks," said Simeon, cheerfully stepping away unaware that he had said anything untoward.

The following Saturday, Willa's first flying lesson consisted of starting the plane and taxiing around the field.

Later, as they pushed the plane into the shed, Coffey asked haltingly, "I understand you were engaged to a fella who died and then married a guy you divorced?"

Willa frowned. He had just named her two relationships with men that only one person could have told him about. She stopped pushing. "That Simeon, I'm going to wring his neck," she mumbled, letting Coffey muscle the plane into the shed by himself. He set about checking the oil and preparing the Parasol for its next outing.

"Look, you want to know about the auto accident?" she asked. Willa couldn't see, but it appeared as if Coffey nodded. "I was driving back to Gary, Indiana, after a Thanksgiving visit to my parents, when the road iced up. There was no warning— I lost control of the car, and the last thing I saw was a fence. They told me Jim was dead when help arrived. We were going to get married. I should have died, too, but instead, I woke up several days later unable to talk and with my face swollen like a pumpkin. I spent five weeks in the county hospital."

Coffey closed and locked the shed door. "I don't know if I want to hear all this," he grumbled.

The field was in twilight as they walked toward the bus stop. Coffey reached out to her and tried to take her hand.

"I don't want any ghosts between us," she said, turning away and refusing to take his hand. "I can't have children," she added candidly. "The accident took that from me, too."

Coffey looked at her partly stunned, partly awed—much like the expression he'd had the first time he saw her scramble into the cockpit of his plane.

"And yes, I was married," she continued. "Wilbur Hardaway was a solid prospect, a fireman. Long story short, I'm not cut out to be a homemaker, but I'm no flapper party-girl, either. So you and your friend don't get any ideas."

Coffey laughed uneasily and then realized she was dead serious.

Willa stopped walking. "Gary, Indiana, is a small town," she said. "In the eyes of some, I killed Gary's most eligible bachelor and married and ruined the second most eligible. It was time to go. I was accepted to graduate school, and I figured I might as well continue with my plans."

The sun slipped below the horizon. As they arrived at the bus stop, the lone streetlight came on.

"I have some 'experience,'" she said. "Does that bother you?"

"Umm, no," answered Coffey.

"You and Johnny are the best-looking men anywhere east of the Mississippi—you really are. But if you aren't what you say you are, I have no use for you." Both fell silent as the bus appeared in the distance.

# 16

Students enrolled at the Curtiss Wright School to complete a two-year program that would qualify them as certified aircraft engine mechanics. While most of the students had the same passion for aviation as Johnny and Coffey, three Southern boys couldn't get beyond their racial blindness. The main culprit, Jesse Batchlor from Georgia, reacted like a pit bull conditioned to bark at the postman. He became irrational at the sight of a black man.

Confronting them on the first day, Batchlor ordered Coffey, who at the time was down on one knee sorting the tools in his toolbox, "Fetch me that toolbox!" Without thinking, Coffey handed him the box. "Now, boy, go fetch me a cup of water," Batchlor added.

Coffey looked up at Batchlor's grin. "I think you're mistaken," he answered. "I don't fetch."

Batchlor's grin disappeared. "If you don't fetch, then what good are you, boy?"

Coffey stood, towering over the shorter white man. Batchlor stepped back, surprised.

Stepping quickly between the two, Johnny leaned toward Batchlor. "You don't want to fight," he said in a voice only the Southerner could hear. "Not here."

Unused to being challenged by a black man, Batchlor glanced over his shoulder looking for support. Everyone knew that Curtiss Wright's rules called for expelling all parties in a fight. When no one stepped forward to back him up, Batchlor could only blink and stare back.

Johnny scanned the room. The men were curious, but they didn't move. "If you, or any of you here want to fight," Johnny said loud enough for all to hear, "Coffey or I will meet you at the YMCA on Michigan Avenue with gloves and a referee. Then you can have at us all you want, or…I could knock you into tomorrow." There were no takers.

Batchlor backed away from the much taller Johnny.

Over the next several weeks, ink spills appeared on Coffey's and Johnny's assignments.

After the first series of tests, Niels Hoffer, a Norwegian engineer and Curtiss Wright instructor, held up the top grades. "If you plan to successfully complete this course," Hoffer announced to the class, "you'd do well to ask these gentlemen to help you. By their grades, Mr. Coffey and Mr. Robinson are already first-class mechanics."

Batchlor abruptly left the room, the only one to do so.

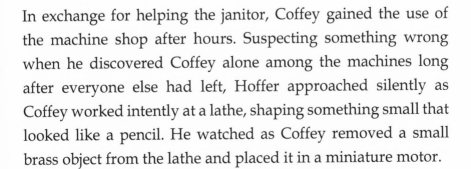

In exchange for helping the janitor, Coffey gained the use of the machine shop after hours. Suspecting something wrong when he discovered Coffey alone among the machines long after everyone else had left, Hoffer approached silently as Coffey worked intently at a lathe, shaping something small that looked like a pencil. He watched as Coffey removed a small brass object from the lathe and placed it in a miniature motor.

"Does that work?" Hoffer asked.

Coffey turned around, startled. "Sir?"

"Will the motor work?" Hoffer asked again.

"Well, the tolerances are a joke." Coffey laughed nervously. "I can't make some parts to scale. They'd be too small. If this did work, it would shake like it needed an overhaul." Coffey held up the model. "It's the new Wright Cyclone engine. It's a beautiful thing, don't you think?"

Hoffer put on a pair of glasses and took the model. He saw that the brass object Coffey had placed in the engine was a crankshaft. He turned it with his fingers, and to his amusement, the pistons moved. Smiling, he looked up at Coffey. "Why would you do this?" he asked, intrigued with the model. "This is not a class assignment."

"No, sir. I'm doing it on my own time. The engine fits the model for the new Douglas design. It's over there behind the door, if you want to see."

By the rear door, Hoffer found a model of a Douglas DC-2 frame, one-sixteenth scale, propped on a pallet. "The DC-2 isn't scheduled to debut until spring of 1933," he stated. "You had to do your own scale work. Will this fly?"

"If I balance out the weight, it will glide. I didn't make it for that. If I want to know how something works, I have to build it."

"What have you done before?" asked Hoffer.

"I built a Heath Parasol kit, with an Ace motorcycle engine. And I've built small model planes with working engines. But they make so much noise they're not fun to be around."

Hoffer picked up Coffey's notes. Written in pencil in a painstaking all-capitals style, each page was filled with detailed drawings and measurements. Coffey had drawn from several perspectives every engine Hoffer had referenced in class.

"You could be an instructor," said Hoffer.

"Someday, yes, sir." Coffey smiled shyly.

⊷

Though Johnny and Coffey were Curtiss Wright's star pupils, the harassment didn't stop. Someone put a brick through Coffey's Douglas DC-2 model. Hoffer took the vandalism personally. He could see how crestfallen Coffey was as he picked up the fragile remnants.

On another occasion, Johnny walked away from his toolbox, and when he returned, an expensive set of wrenches was missing. When he reported the theft, Hoffer threatened to expel the person found with the tools and anyone who might have known about it and kept silent. The following evening, the janitor found the tools in a trash bin where they had been hurriedly dumped.

After the next exam, except for Coffey and Johnny, half the class struggled with the assignments.

Soon after, a white student, Virgil Bentley, approached Coffey. "I don't know who sabotaged your work," he began. "But I didn't say anything and for that, I apologize. My parents were missionaries. I grew up in China and Japan. They would be ashamed of me, and I'm ashamed for myself." He held out his hand to shake. He was much younger than Coffey. He looked sixteen but was probably twenty-two. Bentley had an earnest and guileless face. Coffey shook his hand.

"I don't really want to fix engines," admitted Virgil. "I need this certificate to qualify as an inspector for the US Department of Commerce. I'd appreciate your help. I build models, too. I do a fair job with the painting and got an award from my French Spad S.7 model."

Along with Virgil, Coffey and Johnny rebuilt the damaged DC-2 model. When completed and painted in the official blue and green company colors, Hoffer put it on display in the school's lobby.

After failing three exams in a row, Jesse Batchlor washed out from the Curtiss Wright School. With his departure, the school's atmosphere changed. Not all students warmed up to Coffey and Johnny. However, those who remained worked side-by-side with them.

# 17

The Wall Street "Black Friday" Crash in October 1929 was big news at the time, though no one, certainly not the average working person, expected the widening collapse that followed. By the summer of 1930, dozens of out-of-work men loitered on street corners hoping for a day's work. Warehouses, foundries, and factories that only the year before seemed destined to run forever now had their gates chained and locked. Not everyone was affected in the same way. The Depression didn't cost Coffey and Johnny directly. As freelance mechanics with good reputations, they found a line of auto and motorcycle repairs waiting outside Coffey's tractor shed every Saturday morning. By nightfall, they had at least one live chicken, enough potatoes for the week, and cash for lunches and bus fare.

By September, because of the city's massively diminished tax base, the Chicago school board fired nearly two thousand teachers and closed scores of schools. As 1930 came to a close, jobless, aimless teens were at a dead end. Thousands rode the rails looking for unskilled work in the West. Soup kitchens drew hundreds of desperate people.

As spring of 1931 arrived, Willa kept her job at Walgreen's by taking her pay in overstocks of napkins and ketchup and leftover meals. The one bright spot for Willa was the prospect of resuming her flying lessons. Hoping to get in a little practice, she took a bus out to Coffey's field and entered the shed carrying a box she plopped on the dirt floor. "They're paying me in supplies," she told Coffey. "Are you ready for me to taxi a little?"

Coffey shook his head. "I can't. Not today. Don't go away, though. I want you to stick around a few minutes."

"Why?" asked Willa, disappointed.

"I got a surprise for you. You heard of Willie 'Suicide' Jones?"

"The lunatic wing walker?"

"Yes. That's him now," said Coffey, pointing to the horizon, where a World War I vintage Jenny biplane was approaching from the west. The blue wings featured white stars, and horizontal red-and-white stripes ran the length of the fuselage. The plane circled the field, sputtering and leaving a trail of blue smoke as it landed. As the Jenny pulled up near the shed, the engine coughed and shut off abruptly.

Coffey looked at Willa. "That didn't sound right," he said, "and it sure doesn't smell right."

Suicide Jones climbed out of the cockpit. "What did I tell you on the phone. Isn't she a beauty?" At twenty-six, Suicide Jones looked like a boy. Only five feet three inches tall, he couldn't have weighed more than a hundred pounds.

"The paint job is eye catching," Coffey replied.

"It was painted this way when I got her."

"Suicide Jones, meet Willa Brown." Coffey approached the plane, sniffing the air.

"Glad to meet you," said Jones.

"Do we call you Willie, Jones, or Suicide?" asked Willa.

"That's a show name. I'm William Jones. Call me Jonesy." He turned to catch up with Coffey. "I know Baby here needs work; that's why I brought her to you," Jones continued, curious about what Coffey was doing. "I heard about you in Los Angeles. You're supposed to be a first-rate aircraft mechanic."

Coffey opened the engine cover and poked around at the motor like a dentist examining an open jaw. "She's got some miles on her," he said and closed the cover. Going over the plane carefully, he pulled at cables and checked the fuselage. He climbed into the cockpit and took his time examining and testing the controls. He started the engine and taxied around the field for several minutes, while Jones ran behind the plane. Coffey revved the engine, and the motor coughed again and died. As he climbed out and put his feet on the ground, he gave the jenny a hard push. The entire plane wobbled.

Willa laughed. "I'm sorry," she said, watching the plane shiver like a bowl of gelatin. She couldn't help herself and laughed again.

"All right, don't rub it in," Jones said, glaring at Willa. "What's the damage?"

"I think you should have had it fixed before you had it painted," answered Coffey.

"You already said that. This is the way she came. Can you fix her?" Jones said, getting a bit testy.

Coffey opened the engine cover. "Jonesy, you flew in on a death trap. I can smell the oil you're leaking fifty yards away. The block is cracked. Your cables are worn. I couldn't get air speed. I don't know how the heck you got here."

"Very funny. It's not that bad. What will it take to fix her?"

"It's that bad. You need another engine."

"A new engine! I thought a spark plug wire was loose."

"That's probably true, too. Whoever sold you the Jenny made the engine look clean. They covered the crack in the block with a bead of solder, which was fine until your engine heated to 450 degrees."

"You're right. I know. Baby's got a long, mostly sad story. I flew her in the shows. But when she needed serious work, the owner painted her black and used her for smuggling. Do you know what they do to planes used for smuggling? They torch them! Luckily, that didn't work out because liquids are too heavy, and her heart wasn't strong enough. They tried to sell Baby for crop dusting, but with those huge tanks, she couldn't get off the ground. A paint shop owed them eighty bucks, so they had her painted like this and then jazzed up the engine to sell. With the economy like it is, they couldn't get rid of her. So instead of giving me the money they owed, they paid me off with Baby. She's mine."

"That's some story, but it's still a death trap," said Coffey.

"Can you fix Baby?" replied Jones.

"I can get ahold of an engine I rebuilt myself pretty cheap. But we're talking a lot of hours. Your frame needs work, and that means recanvassing and repainting. I'll replace all your cables. One hundred and seventy dollars for everything."

"I don't have that much money, Mr. Coffey and Miss Willa. I can't pay, not right this minute." With that, he climbed on the wing, reached into the cockpit, and drew out a stack of handbills. "We're going to have an air show," he announced, smiling. "If you'll put a new heart in my baby here, I know how to make us all some cash." He climbed back into the cockpit and pulled out a long, rolled canvas that unfurled into a six-by-ten-foot excellent job of circus art. In the center was the Jenny biplane in a dramatic nose-up moment. The text read: "Willard

Suicide Jones—Dare Devil Pilot and Wing Walker. Motorcycle stunts. Bring the Children." There were three vignettes painted in compositionally appropriate circles. A motorcycle leaped through a ring of fire in one. A person dancing on the top of a Jenny biplane was in the next, and a strong man holding a motorcycle over his head was in the last.

"I thought your name was William," said Willa.

"It is. The painter made a mistake, and I needed the sign the next day. It works for me, though. If a copper asks me if I'm Willard Jones, I can honestly say, no sir, I ain't. So's here what I propose: tomorrow, you're having an exhibition of your little plane here."

"My little plane?" asked Coffey. "What do you have in mind?"

"We'll park the Jenny next to your barn and place this sign right next to it. And we'll nail up the flyers around the neighborhood. We'll make three hundred dollars easy the following Sunday."

Coffey looked at Willa.

"How will you make three hundred?" she asked.

"We charge fifty cents to get in. And after, I take people up for rides. Five dollars for five minutes."

"We have no setup for people to pay. Your sign says wing-walking and motorcycle stunts; we don't have any of that," said Coffey. "I know how to fix your plane. I don't know about shows."

"Most people will pay. You'll see. And I'll take care of the rest."

"Unless you have some collateral, I don't think Coffey should do it," Willa cut in.

"Ma'am, I'm good for it. Believe me. It's a sure thing."

"I believe you. But Coffey's right. We don't know anything about putting on an event like you say. However, I'd like to see your show, and you need your plane fixed. You give the title of the plane to Coffey here, and he'll fix your Jenny. When he gets paid for his work, you'll get the title back."

"No," protested Jones.

"If it's a sure thing, there shouldn't be any problem, right?"

"Damn," said Jones, looking to Coffey a little surprised. "Is she your manager?"

"She is today."

"We're going to have some expenses," added Willa. "We need extra people to handle the crowd and some kind of security."

"Why don't you handle the money," Jones suggested. "That way, you'll know everyone is paid. I have a fella on the crew that does security. You'll understand when you see him. I'm going to have expenses, too. But after everyone is paid, I split what's left with Coffey."

"That suits me," said Coffey.

"Coffey still gets to hold the title and possession of the plane," said Willa.

Jones looked from Willa to Coffey and then back at Willa. Then, glumly, he stalked to the cockpit and removed a leather envelope and handed it to Coffey, who passed it to Willa.

~

The following morning, Willa set out trays of sauerkraut, ketchup, and mustard next to a hill of six-inch Kaiser rolls she'd brought along to hold the sausages she was grilling with onions.

When a decent crowd had gathered around the grill, Suicide Jones came out of the shed wearing an Uncle Sam costume and began handing out flyers to people standing in Willa's hot dog line. "Next Sunday, come and see daredevil flying," he told the sightseers. "You'll witness fearless motorcycle stunts. Adults fifty cents, kids free. You'll see Willie 'Suicide' Jones next week, a death-defying aviator and wing walker. He'll do the Charleston out on the wing of a plane. People with heart problems are urged to stay home, because these stunts are truly death defying."

He greeted every person who had come out to see the day's free show, making his pitch different each time so people stopped to watch him two and three times. After Johnny taxied, took off, and started his routine, Jones joined Willa by the grill.

"We nearly sold out of the sausages and sold all the Cokes," said Willa.

"Sell me one of your sausages," Jones replied. "You know, getting a crowd's stomach juices flowing by grilling onions is an old carnie trick. Where did you learn it?"

"At church picnics," Willa answered, handing him a frank on a piece of bread.

"I'll pay you next week."

"Of course, you understand that a ten-cent hot dog today is twenty cents to you next week."

"In that case, give me two," said Jones. "Run me a tab."

"Do you know how many people have to show up to make three hundred dollars?" asked Willa.

"Yes, over a thousand," said Jones. "It's about showmanship. This is going to be a busy week."

Over the next week, Willa paid Simeon and his friends a dime each to put up leaflets around Chicago's Southside.

Suicide Jones did a ten-minute radio interview on *Breakfast with Roxanna* broadcasting from Red Mack's radio studio. And the fascinating poster for Willard "Suicide" Jones miraculously appeared and then disappeared at key locations around the Southside.

By Friday, Coffey and Johnny had installed the rebuilt engine, reinforced the frame, replaced hoses and cables, and repatched and retouched Suicide's plane.

Coffey left a message for Willa at Walgreen's to show up at the shed at five thirty the next morning. He had something to show her.

# 18

**W**illa walked the half-mile from the bus stop to Coffey's shed in predawn light. Coffey met her with an embarrassed grin. He nodded toward Suicide Jones's Jenny. "Get into the pilot's seat," he said.

"You mean now?"

Coffey motioned with his head for her to climb aboard.

Before he could change his mind, she jumped onto the wing and climbed into the pilot's seat. Coffey settled into the passenger seat. "Start her up," he said, patting her on the shoulder.

The instant the engine roared to life, the aircraft frame reacted as if it were alive, giving Willa more than an inkling of the difference between the Jenny and the Parasol. "Whoa!" she shouted as she nearly scraped the shed, taking more room to maneuver than she had estimated. She turned and steered down the center of the field. Willa could feel the Jenny wanting to lift as the air flowed over and under the wings. After they had taxied around the field for about ten minutes, Coffey reached over and tapped her head. "Let's switch places!" he shouted.

Coffey made sure Willa was strapped in before taking the pilot's seat. His methodical checking made sure every cable and moving part of the aircraft worked. Willa saw the ailerons go up and down, the rudder wag. Everything appeared ready. Coffey taxied to the end of the field, turned the Jenny, revved the engine, and sped down the hardened earth runaway into the morning breeze. Willa gasped the instant they were airborne. From the sky, the sun had already risen. They flew along the Lake Michigan beachfront to Evanston and then turned south and inland. Outside of the urban areas, the patchwork of farms stretched flat and green to the horizon. Clusters of trees and church steeples marked the small towns.

The skin on her face tingled, and her senses felt sharper, exhilarated. Her heart was racing. After they landed, she waited for Coffey to secure the Jenny. His bashful smile expressed his pride in turning a death trap into a vital flying machine. He approached Willa expecting no more than a thank-you; instead, she backed him into the shed and gave him a deep, long kiss.

Suicide Jones pushed open the shed door, startling them. "I see you got her warmed up," he commented suggestively, nodding toward the plane, but it was clear what he meant.

"She's ready," said Coffey.

Jones winked at Willa. "I've booked some acts who will help us out tomorrow. They do shows with me and can pretty much do box office and concessions themselves. You're going to need two grills and at least six guys. I'll tell the barker to pull an extra grill from his truck."

"I have the volunteers," replied Willa.

Jones climbed into the cockpit and started the Jenny. He shouted over the engine roar, "She sounds real sweet!" He took her out for two hours.

Willa invested ten dollars in Kaiser rolls and couldn't sleep the night before the event. On Sunday morning, three tired-looking carnival trucks arrived at Coffey's field. The first truck pulled a trailer carrying a kiddy merry-go-round with small airplanes suspended on chains.

Jones positioned his Jenny so she could be seen from the road. The second truck had a mural-sized painting of a man balanced upside down on his head riding a motorcycle, arms outstretched, about to jump through a blazing ring of fire. Printed boldly over the rider were the words, "Horacio, The Fearless Motorcycle Artist."

Jones directed the driver of a third truck to angle his vehicle in such a way that the three trucks created an entrance. The driver of the third truck emerged wearing an undershirt and tuxedo pants. The workers were white and mixed-race men.

"This is where we set up!" Jones called out. A giant man stepped out of the back of the third truck and began unloading the podium for the barker, a table for admission, and a second grill. He had long, wavy hair that hung down below his shoulders; a tattoo of a topless Hawaiian dancing girl on each arm; and a solid physique that dared anyone to say anything about tattoos, hair, or size.

"Gather around, everybody. Here's how it's going to go." For a small man, Jones could project his voice. Willa, Johnny, Coffey, Simeon, and the assembled help surrounded him. "We're setting up a table between the trucks for people to pay," he said, pointing to Willa. "Willa, you need to be there. Bruno, the hairy guy carrying that hundred-pound grill over his head? He's going to stand behind you to look like you have security."

"What's to keep people from walking around and sneaking in?" asked Simeon.

"You'd be surprised. Some older kids will sneak in, but we don't charge for them anyway if they lie about their age. Most people want to see and be part of the crowd."

"Do I really need a bodyguard?" asked Willa.

"No, but you're going to have a couple hundred dollars in coins. Bruno only looks scary. You'll need his help carrying the money."

"How much are the trucks and helpers going to cost?" asked Willa.

"The barker gets fifteen dollars, Bruno gets five, the motorcycle artist gets twenty, and the merry-go-round gives us half of their take. They usually get more, but I need to pay for my Baby. This is like a dress rehearsal for us. It's the show we'll take on the road. So, everybody! We're going to draw a line with chalk out there, and it's important to keep people behind that line. The motorcycle ramp and ring of fire will be set up beyond the chalk line. Make sure no kids cross that line.

"We start with an exchange between Bruno and the barker, which leads into the motorcycle skit. The barker will stretch it out to twenty minutes. Then, Johnny, the barker will signal for you to take off with a big red flag. You're eye candy until he sets up my entrance. If he holds the flag above his head, stall. When he lowers it and touches the ground, you land. I do fifteen minutes, and then I land."

Johnny felt a little put off by this pipsqueak being so dismissive of his flying skills.

"Johnny, then you take off again and do what you can do for about ten minutes. Wait for the flag to touch the ground and then land. Coffey, you will fly the Jenny, and I'm going to wing walk. Don't make any quick moves. You need to stay north of the white chalk line so people can see."

Jones sent his men out to the field to start painting a one-hundred-yard chalk line. He turned to Willa.

"Since you're responsible for the concession, you keep your regular deal. Can you remember all this? We start with the motorcycle, go up four times. That's it. When the show is over, Bruno stays at the box office, and you collect the five dollars for the flights I do after that."

"Can people afford five dollars?" asked Willa.

"I'm always surprised how certain people show up and pay for a flight."

Willa was impressed. Jones even looked taller. When he turned and took several steps toward his crew, she noticed he was wearing lifts.

"Are you ready?" Jones shouted to his men. He turned back to Willa's crew. "In about two hours, they'll be here. More people than you ever thought will come out to this field."

"We'll see," answered Willa.

The man wearing the tuxedo pants put on what appeared to be a fake shirtfront with a collar and tie and then donned a tuxedo jacket covering his bare arms, and completing the illusion of a barker with a top hat. Carrying a huge red flag, he went to work near the entrance greeting the early arrivals. As Jones had predicted, two hours later, people began to stream in. Willa was amazed how the presence of the barker and Bruno brought people to the entrance.

Willa and her brother, Charles, who had come in for the day, handled the gate. Bruno, the six-foot-six giant, stood behind them with his arms crossed. Seven hundred and eighty people paid fifty cents to enter, with at least the same number of children attending.

The Jenny and the Heath Parasol were parked near the white chalk line where the spectators could examine them. Johnny and Coffey stood nearby to answer questions and to keep children on the opposite side of the line. The merry-go-round ran continuously with children lined up eight or nine deep all afternoon.

Before hand Willa had wondered if she could sell all six baskets of Kaiser rolls. However, by show time, Simeon and friends had sold four hundred hot dogs. All the breadbaskets were empty and stacked by the shed.

The barker in his black tie, tails, and top hat walked out to the field where a ramp for the motorcycle was positioned in front of a huge ring wrapped in burlap. Lifting a megaphone, he turned to the crowd.

"Ladies and Gents, Children and Aunts, can I have your attention? If you stay on the south side of the chalk line, you will be perfectly safe."

With most of the crowd now ready for the show to begin, Bruno left his post behind Willa and entered the main trailer. He exited seconds later carrying a motorcycle over his head.

The barker immediately focused on Bruno. "Bruno?" He projected his voice with a megaphone. The giant stopped and looked at the barker.

"Bruno? Is that Horacio's motorcycle?"

Bruno nodded.

"Did you ask Horacio if you could borrow it?"

Looking in all directions, Bruno shook his head.

"Did you ride it? You know, Horacio will be very angry if you rode his motorcycle?"

Bruno shook his head, emphatically, no.

"Well, what were you doing with?"

Bruno began to juggle what looked like a hundred-and-twenty-pound motorcycle over his head and then spin it like a twirler's baton. He stood on top of it as if it were a unicycle. At the end of his routine, he returned the bicycle to the main truck, where Horacio pretended he was the victim of an outrageous prank.

The moment Bruno finished his routine, the barker refocused the crowd. "A ring of fire, Ladies and Gentlemen! *The ring of fire!*" When most of the faces were in his direction, he struck a long match and touched the burlap-covered ring. The barker walked away from the ring to his podium, pretending not to notice the ring had failed to light. "Hot, isn't it?" he remarked to a small child. The crowd chuckled.

"Ladies and Gentleman, Children and Great Aunts, the ring of fire and Horacio, the motorcycle artist!" he announced, followed by a long pause. The crowd roared with laughter. Suddenly, the ring burst into flames, and the motorcyclist flew out from the back of the trailer. The cyclist jumped through the ring of fire several times. He did three variations of a handstand on the handlebars. He finished with an acrobatic routine on the moving motorcycle where he jumped from a standing position facing foreword and landed in a sitting position facing backward. He flipped around facing forward. For his finish, he lay down the bike on its side and bowed to the cheering crowd.

Willa observed that almost to a person, the audience was transfixed by the theatrics of the show.

Johnny took off in the Parasol and circled the field. He did a single barrel roll and a wide loop-the-loop. He was about to repeat the routine when the barker touched the red flag to the ground.

Suicide Jones shook his head at Johnny's attempts at stunt flying. He went up, circled the field, and mimicked the Parasol's barrel roll and wide loop-the-loop. The stunts were done while flying back and forth across the center of the field, parallel to the white chalk line. He swiftly did three fast barrel rolls followed by two tight loop-the-loops. He did five barrel rolls in a row, and on the return, three consecutive loop-the-loops. He flew upside down and then sideways, with the wing only inches off the ground. Willie's fearless performance electrified the crowd.

There wasn't much Johnny could do with the Parasol that could match the Jenny's performance. He didn't try. He did a loop-the-loop, turned, and did another. He circled until he got the red flag.

Coffey flew the Jenny straight and steady as Jones climbed onto the top wing. What the public down below couldn't see was that Jones now wore a pair of socks with leather soles that looked similar to the boots he'd worn earlier. To the audience below, it appeared he staggered out of control on the wing. Jones was actually attaching safety cables to the stanchions below. Once he was safely secured, he was free to take a couple of steps and dance.

Willa saw that the barker had a set of prearranged signals for Suicide Jones. If he held the flag to his left and shouted through the megaphone, "Do you want to dance?" Suicide Jones did a couple of steps as if he'd actually heard the barker.

The barker turned to the crowd, "Ladies and Gentleman, Willie Suicide Jones is going to dance the Charleston, going ninety miles an hour on the wing of an airplane. Last week, a wing dancer in Gallup, New Mexico, plummeted to his death doing this same trick. The faint of heart are asked to avert their eyes at this time." He moved the flag to the right. His speech was timed to allow the plane to make a turn and begin its run past the crowd as Suicide Jones performed an exaggerated version of the Charleston. The skit concluded with a bit where Jones pretended to slip and nearly fall off the wing, barely catching himself. The barker shouted, "Oh Lord, he's in trouble!" A universal gasp was followed by a silence where only the sound of the Jenny could be heard. The whole routine was planned, of course. What he was really doing was unhooking the safety lines.

For the next two hours, Jones gave private interviews and rides for people with five dollars.

After the crowd dispersed, Suicide Jones joined Willa, Coffey, and others in the shed as they finished counting money. Willa paid Bruno, the motorcycle artist, the barker, and all the extra help who came out that day.

"After all is said and done, how much did we make?" asked Jones.

"After paying everyone, deducting for Coffey's invoice, you each get seventy-six dollars," said Willa.

"Not bad," said Jones. "Now, can I have the title to Baby, please? When I took her up yesterday, I knew we'd be doing business for a long time. This is a new machine to me, as good as any I've flown before. As you can see, this is what I do. I'll try to bring her in every month."

"You should have somebody check her out before each flight," said Coffey.

"That's hard to do where we're going." Jones turned to Willa. "Sweetheart, if you ever want to leave these stuffed shirts, look me up."

"I might just do that," she said.

Willa was surprised how quickly the crews packed up their trucks and were ready to go. Before he took off, Jones turned back and shouted, "Hide your grill and the money! When the police arrive, tell them you knew nothing about what happened here!" The trucks moved out leaving a field littered with napkins and Coke bottles.

"How did you do?" asked Coffey.

"I took twelve dollars from the gate, and my share of the hot dog concession came to forty-three dollars. I couldn't earn that in a month at Walgreen's."

"Still think Jones is a lunatic?"

"Yes, but he's a damn smart one," said Willa.

# 19

The following weekend, the visitors to Coffey's field numbered over sixty, more than double the normal attendance at the Sunday outings. After the previous week's crush, Simeon had the concession business down pat: Cokes cold, frankfurters hot, no waiting.

Young folks—black and white—arrived on motorcycles and in cars and parked behind the shed. There were strangers and old friends. Virgil Bentley and several other students from Curtiss Wright brought their girlfriends and mingled in the shade of the oak tree. The men wore suits and ties, and the women dressed knowing they were there to see and be seen.

Willa's friend, Millicent Carter, came out, and a childhood friend of Johnny's, Oliver Law, showed up to greet the young pilots. "I wish I had come out sooner. Sorry I missed the big show last week."

"Ollie, you're like Haley's Comet," said Johnny. "You show up every seventy-six years."

"Come on! I saw you when I got out of the army. It's only been two years. I work for the Pullman Porters as an organizer. I'm on the road a lot. If I knew how to fly one of these things, you bet I would spend more time in Chicago."

"In a couple of months, Coffey and I will have our commercial ticket and we can teach you to fly."

"In that?" asked Oliver, pointing to the Parasol.

"No, not in that. It's in the future."

"In the army, I applied for flight training, but they wouldn't accept my application. When you're ready to give classes, I'll be the first to sign up," he said.

A green Buick pulled up behind the shed. A cluster of people had to step back so the driver could nose the car into the shade.

"Well, look who's here," commented Oliver.

The driver, a slender, fashionably dressed woman in her midthirties, emerged from the car escorted by two young men.

"You know her?" asked Johnny.

"I dated her once, but I didn't have the dough-ray-me, if you know what I mean."

The woman's escorts feigned interest in whatever she was interested in, and she was interested in meeting Johnny, the handsome young man in the flight suit.

Willa turned to her friend Millicent. "Who's the dame with the green sedan?"

"That's Janet Harmon. She brought two dates and seems interested in acquiring a third." Millicent laughed, nodding her head toward Johnny.

"How does she rate all that attention?" asked Willa.

Overhearing her question, Oliver Law leaned over and whispered, "She's loaded. She owns properties, apartment buildings, and several nursing homes. She's a registered nurse."

Johnny was ready to meet his new admirer when Coffey shouted, "Let's get going!" Coffey was right; they were already thirty minutes behind schedule. Johnny gave Janet a shrug and a wink, as if to say, "I've got to go, but I'll see you later."

Coffey lifted the rear of the Parasol and positioned it for take-off. He hurried around the plane and stopped Johnny before he could climb aboard. "There are stress cracks where the motor joins the wood," whispered Coffey. "I've reglued and reinforced everything, but take it easy. She's not made for stunt-flying, John."

"I'll take it easy," replied Johnny, looking over his shoulder at the willowy woman.

Johnny took off immediately, circling the field and going into three barrel rolls and a loop-the-loop. He pushed the plane into a hard climb and stalled the engine.

Coffey threw up his arms, exasperated. It was exactly what he'd told Johnny to avoid. When Johnny pulled out of the dive, the engine partially separated from the frame. What sounded like the crack of a baseball bat was the propeller spinning away from the motor, twirling high into the air, returning to earth and shattering splinters in the direction of the spectators. Everyone gasped. Janet screamed.

For a few tense moments, everyone stared silently as the Parasol began a wide spiral descent. Johnny miraculously managed to compensate for the imbalance and crash-landed the plane. The left wheel collapsed the instant the Parasol came to a stop. Johnny stepped away from the wreck without so much as a smudge on his flight suit. Coffey, the first to arrive, shook his head at Johnny and the broken plane.

"Are you okay?"

"I'm okay," said Johnny.

"That's two crashes. You only get three."

"That's superstition," said Johnny examining the damage. "And the first one doesn't count. I didn't know how to fly."

Janet ditched her entourage and raced to Johnny. At the crash site, she clung to him, burying her face in his shoulder.

"I'm okay, lady," Johnny said, trying to peel her off. Janet wasn't letting go.

"I thought you were going to die," she whispered.

Johnny turned to the gathering crowd. "It's not as bad as it looks. I had control all the time. I'm fine," he said. "I can fix this."

"When Hades freezes over," Coffey snorted.

"Johnny, we're so close to graduation, it would be a shame if you went to your eternal reward now," teased Virgil Bentley.

Janet's entourage pretended to be more interested in the wrecked aircraft than her caresses. Johnny put his arm around her shoulders, and she put her arm around his waist.

Millicent looked at Willa. "Looks like she got her prize."

The crowd's focus was on the airplane. No one noticed a US marshal approaching on foot. "Who's that?" called Simeon.

The marshal had blocked the exit gate with his dark sedan. He stopped about twenty-five yards away. "I want to speak with the organizer!" he shouted.

Coffey stepped forward. "That's me."

Willa followed. "I helped put this together."

"In that case, you can both accept this cease operation notice of a rogue airstrip. If you continue to fly and have exhibitions, you will be cited, fined, and have your plane impounded by the local police. Did these people pay to attend today's event?"

"No, sir," answered Willa. "They're here to watch a licensed plane fly." As the marshal surveyed the crowd, Willa stole a glance back at the shed. She smiled. Simeon was quickly dragging the grill and soft drinks inside.

"No food concession or airplane rides? I understand there was a professional show here last week. Probably raked in a lot of cash," said the marshal, angling for a payoff.

"It was the Willard Jones Flying Circus. They said they were going to pay for the use of the field, and no sooner was the show over than they were gone." Willa spoke so earnestly even Coffey could half believe the story. "We had to clean up after them. They left a mess."

"Where are the circus people now?"

"They're in Missouri. I recall they said something about Kansas City."

After the marshal left, the crowd drifted away. A plane crash and a threatening police officer were enough excitement for one day. The Parasol had only one useable wheel. Coffey, Virgil, and Oliver lifted the unsupported wing, as Simeon and Johnny pushed the crippled plane back to the shed.

Coffey and Johnny knew that what they were doing wasn't a crime. In 1931, many pilots stored their planes in barns and stayed clear of major airports. A visit to Marcus Lipsky took the heat off.

"You got away with it. You're lucky," Lipsky told Johnny. "The cops didn't rake off a penny from your air show. They don't like that. By the way, I have a new Brook View Dairy ice cream cart. I could have sent my nephew and sold ice cream cones in three flavors. It's good advertising for me, a few bucks for you, and gets the nephew out of my office. Next time you put on a show, you remember who made a phone call for you."

"It won't be for a while," said Johnny meekly.

# 20

That same year, Johnny and Coffey finished their course at the Curtiss Wright School of Aeronautics. The graduation ceremony was an informal last class held in the lobby. A squadron of model planes hung from the ceiling of the previously bare room. Each model was a one-sixteenth scale replica of the engines and aircraft the students had learned to repair.

Paul Edinger, the school's director, gave out the certificates of completion. The new master mechanics accepting diplomas were only half the number of those who started the course in 1929.

Virgil Bentley came over to congratulate his classmates. He put his hand on Coffey's shoulder.

"The Department of Commerce job came through. I'm leaving for Washington DC this afternoon," he said.

"You're not staying for the rating tests?"

"Don't have to. I have my certificate of completion. That's all I'll need, much thanks to you. I'm supposed to know about engines. I don't have to teach anyone."

"Virgil, best of luck to you," said Coffey.

Virgil reminded Coffey of the gangly, vulnerable Harold Lloyd character from the moving picture, *Welcome Danger*. Like the Lloyd character, Virgil was the son of missionaries and had been raised in China. Both were Americans with a rare outsider's view of the United States.

⊸≋⊱

While graduating from Curtiss Wright was a major accomplishment, in the summer of 1931, Coffey and Johnny also earned commercial pilot licenses.

Willa organized a reception and dance in Johnny and Coffey's honor in the basement of Trinity AME Church. Crepe paper streamers lined the entrance and made a frame around the piano. Chairs were pushed to the walls so guests could dance, and Constance Hardaway played popular songs on the church's upright. Simeon ladled punch into paper cups for Willa, Oliver Law, and an entourage of friends.

Willa tried to get Coffey or Johnny to talk about their achievements, but they were duds. "Come on, Coffey. Say a few words."

"I don't have anything to say," he shrugged and looked at his feet.

"If you want to become teachers, you better start opening up now," she teased.

Johnny uncharacteristically couldn't think of anything to say, either. "We'll probably do the same thing we're doing now," he started. "I'll have to think about it. I've had all kinds of plans, but right now, I can't think of one. Just getting here has kind of worn me out," he said modestly.

Willa looked at Oliver Law who was glad to speak up for his friends. "I think what my friend is trying to say is that they've just flown very high. We can't see what they see, but let me tell you, what they see is a bigger world and more sky. Their work has just begun."

The basement door creaked open, and everyone turned to see who had entered. Janet looked surprised. "Am I late?" Oliver took a moment until Janet stopped greeting her acquaintances and became aware he was delivering a toast.

Oliver continued, "What I admire about Coffey and Johnny is that they've challenged the laws of man and the laws of nature. They haven't asked permission, but somehow, through their incredible determination, they are among the 'firsts.' The first Negro men to earn master mechanics ratings, and the first Negro men to hold commercial pilot licenses, which will allow them to teach other people to fly. Not since Bessie Coleman have we had somebody like this, and now we have two. I wish there was someone here to write about it. I'm proud to say I've known John since we were fourteen. So, to my friends, I drink to you." He swallowed the paper cup full of punch and grimaced. "Where's the kick?" he asked Willa.

"Didn't you hear? There's Prohibition," replied Willa. "And this is a church."

"After such a fine speech, I deserve a reward," grumbled Oliver.

"You'll get what you deserve in the hereafter," Willa shot back.

"That's a long time to wait for a drink."

Johnny knew how to enjoy himself. He danced with Millicent and then Janet. He stood behind the piano and tapped out rhythms as Constance played Scott Joplin's "Maple Leaf Rag."

Coffey felt like a bug in a jar looking out. He stood off by himself and tried to appreciate the celebration in his honor.

Janet steered Johnny away from his friends and out the door into the night air. Since their first meeting, they had spent many nights in her apartment. But with Johnny having to finish coursework and her business obligations, they hadn't seen each other in weeks. She was dying to put her hands on him.

Janet handed him a slender box gift-wrapped in silver and gold paper. "Open it," she said.

She grimaced when he tore away the paper and tossed aside the box. She'd given the wrapping a lot of thought. He fondled a white silk scarf, which she took from him and placed around his neck.

"It's silk. It should keep you really warm," she said. The scarf set off his high cheekbones and strong jaw. He was a delicious-looking man. She kissed his cheek.

"What does a commercial license allow you to do?" she asked.

"It means I can fly certain kinds of planes, and we're certified to teach other people to fly. Of course, we'll need a larger plane, a two-seater," he said. "Right now, we're not finding owners who'll rent us their trainers. That's why Coffey's next plane will be…"

Janet hushed him. "If someone could raise the money, what plane would you buy?"

"You mean if I struck oil, became a millionaire, and could buy a plane? A Stearman Model 85, maybe. The army uses those. A new Curtiss Hawk—most definitely, even a Waco UPF-7, they're all good planes."

"But which would you buy if you could?"

"If I had to choose one for me? The Curtiss Hawk. They're the top training planes, a pleasure to fly. They have excellent range and cruise at a hundred and twenty-five knots per hour."

"Could you make any money with a plane like that?" asked Janet.

"That's what I'm saying. If we owned a trainer like the Hawk or the model 85, people would line up to book flying time at ten dollars an hour and of course, lessons, and on weekends, we could have a real air show."

"I want to learn to fly," said Janet. "If I finance a new Curtiss Hawk, a two-seater, will you teach me?"

That stopped Johnny. "Only someone with a lot of money… I mean…Forget it."

"No, seriously, as a business. We'll use the new plane as a rental to defer costs and make payments. You and your friend will teach the classes and maintain the plane, of course." She matter-of-factly ticked off her logic.

"You can finance a plane? We're not talking a Heath Parasol kit."

"John, you're a damn blockhead," she shot back. "I'm offering you a business proposition, and you're questioning my word. Yes, I can finance a plane. Is that so hard to believe?"

"No, but…understand…a new Curtiss Hawk sells for ten thousand dollars; a Stearman is over twelve thousand. Then you need an airfield. And there isn't an airport around here that will let us put a plane on their tarmac."

"So, we don't buy new. But if we have to, we will. And what do you need for an airfield, a flat plot of land?"

"There's a lot more to it than that."

"Do you think the Curtiss is the best investment?"

"It's a fine aircraft. Coffey and I know it backwards and forwards."

"Then that's what we'll get." Janet grabbed the white silk scarf by the ends, pulled Johnny to her, and kissed him.

# 21

As Janet and Johnny lay in bed, she whispered, "When do I start my classes?" They had closed the deal earlier that day on a nearly new Curtiss Hawk, purchased for eight thousand four hundred dollars from a bankrupt banker. They weren't interested in a yacht on Lake Michigan he also had for sale. Janet put up two properties as collateral and made a down payment of seven hundred dollars. She held the note, and Johnny and Coffey were to make the payments from the rentals and classes. Then, far down the road, when Janet was reimbursed for her down payment and learned to fly, she would sign the title over to Johnny and Coffey.

Johnny sat up, leaning on his elbow, "There are a lot of things we have to do before we can take possession of the plane."

"We better do them real soon. I have to pay rent just having the Curtiss parked where it is."

The new partners had to build a hangar to protect the plane from Chicago's weather extremes, and the facilities had to comply with US Department of Commerce guidelines. The regulations were not that rigorous in 1932, but they had to paint markings on the ground to make the runway visible from the air. The strip needed to be graded and preferably paved.

Through Janet's contacts, the nearby all-black community of Robbins, Illinois, offered an odd-shaped seven-acre plot as a fifty-dollar-a-year rental. Barely qualifying as an airfield, the plot had an east-west stretch of land long enough to accommodate an airstrip. Johnny and Coffey went out to take a look and approved the location.

As her contribution to the new Curtiss, Willa took on the responsibility of acquiring plans that would make Robbins Field meet at least minimally with the US Department of Commerce requirements. She began by calling the engineering firms working on the expansion at Chicago's Municipal Airport, "Muni," as it was called at the time.

"Yes, sir, I'm a graduate student at Northwestern University," she said on the phone. "Mr. Hahn, vocational education is my field. Sir, are you a draftsman or an engineer... Both?...I can be there in hour. My name is Willa Brown. No? Tomorrow morning at ten would be fine, as well." She hung up and made a note of the time.

The following morning, Willa arrived at the office of Hahn Engineering, dressed smartly with hat and gloves as if she were applying for a job.

The office reeked of cigarette smoke. Rolls of blueprints were carelessly stacked on drawing desks. The floor had a trail of zigzag mud trackings, pencil-sharpener shavings, and a heavy sprinkling of paper litter. Stale ashtrays overflowed with butts. Willa had to make an effort to keep a smile on her face as she walked to the back of the room where Mr. Hahn huddled stoop-shouldered over his desk. A cloud of smoke hung over his head. He looked up from the drawings, coughed a raspy smoker's hack and cleared his throat.

"Good morning, I'm Willa Brown. I have the ten o'clock appointment," she introduced herself cheerfully.

"*Ach, eine schwarze Frau!*" muttered Mr. Hahn. Willa was stung for a moment.

"*Nein, wenn sie bitte.*" Willa turned up her smile. "*Eine schwarze Fraulein,*" she lied, but Hahn would never know.

Hahn looked at her over his wire-rim glasses, cocking his head and squinting his right eye to avoid the cigarette smoke. He took the cigarette stub from his mouth and stabbed it out in a pile of butts hiding an ashtray. He immediately lit another. "Where did you learn German?" he asked in heavily accented English.

"From one of my employers," Willa replied.

"You're the student who called?"

"Yes, sir. That's not why I'm here. I want to build a hangar, something that can accommodate two aircraft, a Curtiss Hawk and a Heath Parasol. I thought that you probably have plans like that in your files. It's a basic structure."

"I may have such plans, but I don't have the time to look." He waved her away and returned to his drawings. "I have the Muni people coming over tomorrow, and I have work to finish."

"I don't have any money, but if you have plans like I need, I can take shorthand, do bookkeeping. I type eighty words a minute, seventy-two with no mistakes."

Hahn shook his head.

She looked around the cluttered workroom. "I could put your files in order. How do you want them? By client, by date, by type of structure?"

Hahn studied the smartly dressed young woman in front of him. She was very attractive. He climbed down from his pedestal. His legs stiff from sitting, he stumbled awkwardly. He recovered and motioned for her to follow him to a mountain of blueprints stacked in the corner. He seemed oblivious to his persistent cough. "By client number and the client files by date," he said, waving at the mess as if he wanted to make it disappear.

"They stack over there," he said, pointing to empty built-in shelves. "If you can do that, I'll pay you twenty dollars and I'll give you the plans—if you can find them."

"I'll see what I can do," Willa said, taking in the chaos. As she examined the jumble, she discovered that all the blueprints had sequential contract numbers in common. She opened the windows to air out the place and worked through lunch and dinner. What took hours to accomplish was sorting one by one through a mountain of blueprints. Once she sorted the projects by contract number, the storing and stacking was simple.

At nine thirty that evening, she put away the last plan in the specially designed bins. She wondered how the place could have become such a mess, considering how cleverly someone had planned the workspace.

Willa swept up the litter from the floor, emptied ashtrays, and carried out the trash.

When she reentered with emptied trash cans, Hahn looked around impressed. The desks were cleared, T-squares hung up, and drawing pens put away. The place had been transformed. "Did you find what you were looking for?" he asked, tossing a cigarette butt into a gleaming ashtray. The butt slid out and hit the floor.

"There were three that appeared right," Willa said, handing Hahn the plans. While he studied the plans, she delicately picked up the live cigarette butt and extinguished it in the ashtray.

"Let me see," he said, spreading out all the blueprints. He lit another cigarette and inhaled deeply. "You want simple construction. These are all the same design. It's a basic frame." He tossed the duplicate plans aside. "I drew dozens of these for Muni. You'll need concrete footings for the main structural pieces. The crossbeams above can be used to support a five-hundred-pound engine. If you build where rainwater drains away, the cement floor is optional but always recommended. *Fraulein*, do you want a job? I could use someone to keep this place clean," he said, handing her a twenty-dollar bill.

"Cleaning? No, sir. This was a one-time-only job. Thank you, I have an airfield to build." She pushed the plans in front of him. "Where do you show how much lumber to order?"

"I shouldn't tell you, trade secret," he teased. "If I didn't see with my own eyes what you did today, I'm surprised you didn't discover that at the bottom of the plans, there, in the legend; it tells you everything you need to know."

"You mean here where you're supposed to sign the plans?" Willa asked.

Hahn laughed. "I suppose you want me to stamp and date them, too?" he growled and coughed. He cleared his throat. "You know, I'm supposed to make a site visit and take measurements. How flat is this location?"

"Flat. Flat. Very flat," she responded.

"Map information…where's this hangar going to be?" he asked.

"I have that here." She reached for her purse and retrieved a slip of paper. "Map 19L, parcels 138 to 143, Robbins Field, in Robbins, Illinois," she answered.

Hahn dipped his pen in the ink well and wrote the map and lot numbers. He stamped the Hahn Engineering seal next to the entry and signed and dated the seal, making the plans official.

"You know, *Fraulein*, that blueprint is only for the structure. You need to put that structure on a site map. Besides that, I also have engineering drawings for runways. You will need one for your site to get your certification," he said, cocking his head and squinting his right eye. "I'll come out and take measurements myself. I'll make sure you are legal. The plans start at sixty dollars." Hahn took in Willa's waist and legs. "You're quite the beauty, but you know that."

Willa took a deep breath. "I don't know what you have in mind for sixty dollars, but your files still need a lot of work. For sixty dollars, I'll catalog your contracts and make it possible for you to find anything you want. This is the down payment," said Willa, handing back the twenty-dollar bill he had paid her. "I work for a dollar fifty an hour. I'll need a receipt for the twenty."

Sheepishly, Hahn leaned forward in his desk. "That's what I meant," he said, shaking his head refusing to take the money. "A dollar twenty-five. You do that for me, and we are even. It's late. I have much work to do." He motioned for her to leave with the back of his hand.

"As long as you don't burn the place down, you'll find anything you want. Good night," she said.

⤜⤛

Sixty dollars was three months' pay for a schoolteacher. Cataloging the Hahn Engineering files turned out to be a big job and had to be done after school and after her waitress shifts.

Willa lived off her part-time Walgreen's lunch counter earnings of seven dollars a week, which included the tips, and that was when she was actually paid in cash. With that money, she paid her rent, bus fare, and for whatever meals she didn't get at the lunch counter.

~≋~

Willa turned out to be good for Hahn's business. Because the office was tidy, the Muni executives assumed Hahn was doing well and assigned him additional contracts. Hahn refused to start on the Robbins field plans until Willa finished all the cataloging. Then he only came out with his transit and maps when coaxed with bratwurst and real beer from Canada. As he affixed his engineering stamp, he pointed out that there was a small detail that everyone should know about. "A portion of the field is in another city's jurisdiction. That means two sets of plans and two engineering fees."

"You said these plans would get me Commerce Department and county approval."

"But in the maps you've given me, the runway extends beyond the city limits of Robbins and approximately a hundred and fifty yards into the Crestwood city limits." He bit into the bratwurst.

"We can't afford that. I did my part," insisted Willa.

Hahn took a long drink of beer. "It's what you have," he said, wiping his chin. "If anyone says anything, pretend you didn't know. You have the engineering plans for Robbins; you have legitimate boundaries accepted by Crestwood. All you have to do is supply them a set of plans if you have to comply with their regulations. Maybe nobody will notice."

# 22

**W**illa delivered the plans and permits needed to start construction of the hangar and runway. In the three frugal years since he'd left Mack Chevrolet, Coffey had saved four hundred and twenty-seven dollars from repair jobs and Willa's hot dog sales. He used the money to purchase the lumber, support beams, and nails for the new hangar. That left roofing tiles, two truckloads of concrete, and the loan of a tractor-roller-grader remaining to be located.

For his part, Johnny rode his motorcycle to the Brook View Dairy at sunset. Driving into the plant, he saw the two milk trucks sitting in the yard, disabled. Lipsky immediately ran out and beckoned him into his office.

"Johnny, you must have read my mind. Deason and his helper got arrested Friday night. I need you to fill in until I get him out of jail."

"What did they get pinched for?"

"The bums were selling my stock as theirs. He's lucky he's got an uncle," said Lipsky. "You and Coffey never let me down."

"You were always square with us, Marcus. Maybe we can help each other."

"Name it, Johnny."

"I need two loads of concrete, twenty gross of roofing tiles, and a tractor with a grading blade for two, maybe three days," said Johnny.

Lipsky laughed and pulled Johnny to the door by the arm. "Robinson, I'm in the milk business," he said, pointing outside. "I pay in dollars, not concrete and roofing tiles."

"Yes, sir, but you also have a piece of every construction job in South Chicago."

"You know that for a fact?" snapped Lipsky.

"No, sir, I know nothing." Johnny thought for moment. "In your yard, concrete gets poured in the middle of the truck drivers' strike. I can handle your shop for three weeks. That should give you time to get Deason out of jail."

"Deason will come back to work here when I say he can. Somebody's got to make him pay for his crimes. What do you need?"

"Ten yards of cement on Saturday morning at eight, the roofing tiles on Sunday, and a tractor Monday the following week. I also need brackets and stuff," said Johnny, handing him a list.

Lipsky looked at the request.

"I'll need a mechanic for eight weeks."

"Three weeks. It's only cement. I can mix it myself, if I have to."

"That's a lot of cement to mix by hand. Seven weeks. Johnny, look at my trucks. You got me over the barrel. You need paving gravel? I can get you all you need. Five weeks."

"So, it's Johnny again? Four weeks and the paving gravel," said Johnny.

"Five weeks?" Lipsky stopped himself. "If you do me a favor, it's four weeks."

Johnny nodded.

"I have a friend," said Lipsky. "She needs a plane ride. Can you do that? You promise that for me, I'll take care of the rest. Everything."

"That can be arranged, yes, sir," said Johnny.

⌒≈⌒

On Friday morning, Coffey and Willa, two of her brothers, Oliver Law, and O. C. Pleasant, a contractor friend with a truck, arrived with lumber, hammers, picks, and shovels. Using a transit, Coffey staked out the building's foundation. O.C. and the crew excavated the hangar foundation and made the forms for the major support beams. On Saturday morning, O.C. supervised the two cement trucks pouring the foundation and partial floor.

Lipsky delivered on his promise, literally. Since Johnny hadn't specified a color, the roofing tiles that were dropped off were leftovers from various construction sites. They were all the same type, just not the same color. So rather than have a patch of black, followed by several rows of brown, then a row of white, Willa decided the color tiles should be evenly interspersed as if it were planned that way. O.C. said he had it under control. The framing took several days, and by the following Saturday, the crew had completed the roof.

Willa defended the crazy roof. "We'll only see the design from the air."

On Monday morning, as Johnny and Coffey rode up on the Indian motorcycle, they found a tractor with a grading attachment parked on the property. The hangar claimed the highest ground on the seven-acre plot. Otherwise, the terrain stretched flat with grasses and shrubs to the horizon. The nearest houses were a quarter of a mile to the north. A grove of oak trees two hundred yards to the west was all that remained of the vast American oak forest that had once dominated this expanse.

Over a century before, the trees were cut down and the land farmed until the soil was exhausted. The land had been fallow for at least thirty years.

Using a transit and Hahn's site map, Coffey placed hundreds of wooden stakes, each tied with a red ribbon, outlining the straight lines of the future airstrip.

A truck loaded with road-grade gravel followed. "Where can we put this?" the driver called out.

Before Coffey could answer, O.C. Pleasant, Oliver Law, Willa, and his crew drove up. Willa stuck her head out of the window and shouted, "You're going to let me drive that tractor."

"Take the first turn," called Coffey. He tossed her the engineering plans. Willa studied the field, comparing the plans to Coffey's red ribbons. It wouldn't hurt anything if she went right down the middle and cleared the center.

Coffey hurriedly showed Lipsky's truck driver where to dump the paving gravel and then joined Simeon, Oliver, O.C., and the crew of friends getting ready to watch Willa break ground.

Before any one of her wiseacre brothers could crack a joke, Willa hopped on the tractor, settled in the driver's seat, reached over and turned the key, lowered the blade, and steered down the center of the red ribbons all the way to the end of the airstrip. As she raised the blade and backed the tractor to turn, a police car appeared, bouncing across the uneven terrain and signaling for Willa to stop.

The police car rolled over a dozen of Coffey's stakes before it braked in the path of the tractor, blocking the way. A white officer got out of the car and approached.

"Was I going too fast?" Willa called to him above the noise of the tractor engine.

"Do you have a permit to construct here?" shouted the officer.

Willa cut the engine. "Yes, sir, we do. It's up at the hangar. You want to hop on the tractor? I'll drive you up there."

"No, ma'am," said the officer. "Those markers over there and there." The officer pointed to two distinct white stakes fifty yards on either side of the runway. "That is the Crestwood city limit. Do you have a permit to build in Crestwood?"

"This property is in Robbins, and we've leased it from the city. The city invited us to build here."

Johnny, Coffey, and the rest ran hard in their direction. When they were thirty yards away, the officer pointed.

"No further, that's far enough."

"What's going on?" Johnny demanded.

"Stay where you are," signaled the officer, "or I will have to arrest you for interfering with an officer of the law. Stay on that side of the white flags."

"Officer, there has to be a mistake." Willa jumped down from the tractor. "This man is John Robinson. The permits are in his name and his partner's name, Cornelius Coffey."

"In Robbins," said the officer. "Where we are standing is Crestwood, Illinois. I want to see a permit from Crestwood."

"Officer, we're not building anything out here," said Willa.

"And these stakes with red ribbons are here for what purpose?" The policeman pointed to the stakes that continued at least fifty yards into Crestwood.

"They're beyond the end of the runway. We don't need them, but we thought we'd clear the land anyway, as a fire break," Willa lied. "We'll be doing this in all directions. Look, as you can see, the main structure is far over there, definitely in Robbins. There will be no construction over here."

"If I see anything like foundations or footings, any signs that you're building here without a permit, I'm confiscating your equipment," said the officer. "I'm just letting you know that the city tells me what to do. If you get caught on this side, it's a hundred-and-twenty-five-dollar fine."

"Do we need a permit to clear brush?"

"No, you don't need a permit to clear brush. So, you're saying that this over here has nothing to do with what looks like an airstrip over there?"

"That's correct," said Willa.

The officer smirked skeptically, but since he couldn't find anything more serious than clearing brush, he had nothing.

"A hundred-and-twenty-five-dollar fine," he said. He got back in his car and drove away.

Later that day, Willa spoke with the mayor of Robbins.

"The mayor says we should be okay," she told the crew. "A plane will be off the ground by the time it reaches that part of the runway. He says the city of Crestwood has jurisdiction on the ground, not the air."

"What if we have to take off to the east using that part of the runway?" asked Coffey.

"We'll have to wait and see. It's crazy, I know. I'm sorry," she said, frustrated. She began to tear up.

"Are we all right?" asked Coffey.

"There's a good chance there will no problems. The mayor is going to call Crestwood City Hall and see what he can do," she said.

"Is there any other way to put a runway on this property?" asked Coffey.

"None," replied Willa. "There's not enough room."

"The direction of the wind was the reason we accepted the damn offer," groused Johnny.

"We've gone this far; we have to finish," said Coffey. "Pave to the Robbins city limits, and we'll grade the rest as best we can,"

"We take off to the west and hope for the best," cracked Johnny, climbing onto the tractor.

Over the next few days, the hangar got its first coat of paint and the doors were hung. On Thursday, the much-anticipated Curtiss Hawk landed at Robbins field with Johnny and Janet in the plane. Coffey, Johnny, Willa, Janet, and several friends pushed the plane into the hangar. They closed and locked the hangar doors for the first time.

# 23

The following Saturday morning, Janet stepped from her green Buick wearing a new brown leather flight suit, with matching boots, aviator's cap, and goggles. Ready for her first flying lesson, she strode past a row of cars before finding Willa speaking with a cluster of visitors in the shade of the hangar and no plane visible. Seeing three white men wearing pilot gear and accompanied by friends and spouses annoyed her. Everyone turned as she asked, "Where's my plane?"

Willa turned to her with an exhausted "I-don't-need-this" gaze. "It's ten thirty. The beginning classes are at six in the morning. I thought John explained."

"No. No. I don't get here at six in the morning for my own plane. Where's my plane?"

"He took it up. I don't know, more than five hours ago. I got here at six, and the Curtiss was gone," Willa replied. "And now there are three pilots ahead of you. And they're not together."

"Next?" huffed Janet.

"I was told by Johnny to be here at ten," piped up one of the pilots.

"And I was told to be here at ten," added another.

"I'm sorry." Willa waved for them to stop. "This is the first time the plane will be rented so pilots can get their flight hours. We didn't expect this much enthusiasm."

"Don't you have a telephone?" griped one of the pilots.

"Not yet. This is the first day," said Willa.

"So what are we going to do?" Janet fumed. "I can't hang around here waiting for everyone to finish using my plane."

At that moment, high above Chicago, the Curtiss Hawk sped across a clear blue sky. Johnny glanced at his watch and banked the plane into a wide turn. In the seat behind him, a young white woman snuggled in an oversized flight jacket, her long blond hair flowing loose. Johnny circled Harlem Airfield and began his descent. As he taxied toward the hangar, he could see the cold stares from the waiting crowd. Janet paced in the background, her hands jammed in her coat pockets.

Coffey ran up to the plane and signaled for Johnny to cut the engine. "Where have you been, and who is she?"

"Who? Let's just say she paid for the fourteen loads of paving gravel," he whispered to Coffey. "I took this young woman for a ride. Right, Miss?"

"It was beautiful," gushed the blonde.

"Did you tell all these people you'd take them up today?" asked Coffey, looking back toward the hangar. Willa and Janet were walking briskly in their direction.

"I may have mentioned it. But I didn't expect everybody to show up."

He climbed out of the plane and helped the young woman step out of the seat and onto the wing. Her dress caught on a bolt, and her slender legs flashed up to her flesh-colored silk stockings, garters, and underwear. She grinned, embarrassed, and quickly pulled her skirt down.

"Johnny, I was scared and laughing at the same time." She giggled. Her knees buckled the moment her feet touched the pavement. Johnny caught her in his arms.

"Ooooh, my head is spinning." Her pliable body draped on his.

"Were you waiting for me?" Johnny grinned at the astonished crowd.

"I had to put her, you know, the plane, the Curtiss, through the checklist. This is Roxy Moss. She's an…She has a radio program many of you might know, *Roxanna for Breakfast*. And, Coffey, you'll need to adjust the aileron cables by two maybe three turns, check the oil, and refuel."

The young woman regained her land legs but continued to cling to Johnny. Janet's icy stare didn't go unnoticed. Roxy patted Johnny on the shoulder and took two steps away. Johnny motioned to someone inside the hangar. Roxy kissed Johnny quickly on the cheek before Paul Deason ran out and escorted her to one of the parked cars.

"Who was that?" asked Janet.

"It was a favor for a friend," answered Johnny.

Before getting in the car Roxy turned and waved. "Thank you, Johnny!" she shouted. "Look me up if you're ever in Lincoln Park."

After an awkward silence, Willa turned to the others and said, "Let me take your names and let's book next Saturday."

"How could he do that?" said Janet, still angry at Johnny. "It's my airplane. I want to use it."

"And you will," replied Willa. "It's your plane, but as a business, do we agree that paying customers go first?"

Miffed, Janet looked at the pilots waiting to put in flight hours and reluctantly nodded.

"Coffey? Johnny? Come over here. Listen to me," insisted Willa. She took them aside and motioned for Janet to join them. "If you want people to take you seriously, this can't happen again. Janet has a right to demand her time with the plane."

"Willa, this trip was business," said Johnny's defensively.

"Well and good. Put it in the log so we all know what's going on. Janet has money on the line, and a lot of other people have given time and money to get you up and running. And these pilots over there are willing to pay. You have to tell everyone what you're doing," she said forcefully. "You have to keep logs. I was here at six this morning and no Curtiss. Nothing. You either run this place professionally or you won't last."

"You're right." Johnny raised his arms in mock surrender.

Janet nodded in approval.

Coffey went to work on the Curtiss. The engine was hot, as if it had been flown for hours at top speed. He checked the oil and tapped the gas tank with his knuckles. It rang hollow.

"Where did you really fly?" he asked.

Johnny shook his head. "Let's just say this was a test flight, and I had a guest."

That same week, Willa, Coffey, Johnny, Janet, and fifteen others met at the Michigan Street YMCA and formed a flying club to manage the use of the Curtiss Hawk. They prepared a basic outline defining membership, and how the Hawk could be used. In response to a US Army report made public in 1928, stating that blacks were not suited for aviation because of their natural fear of heights, they called it the Challenger Aero Club. The Challengers' mission was to prove the army wrong.

# 24

Willa made every effort to include Janet in all Robbins Field activities. She wasn't easy to please. Accustomed to buying what she wanted, Janet expected Johnny to fall at her feet like her other suitors and became impatient when he spent hours talking to Willa and Coffey about such boring things as flying regulations.

The following Saturday, Janet arrived at Robbins Field for her lesson to find Willa and Johnny alone in the hangar.

"Willa, why don't you ever give me a tumble?" teased Johnny.

"What? Are you nuts?" she answered shoving him away. "You've got a student waiting."

Janet stood in the doorway, hands on her hips.

"Jan, are you ready?" called Johnny.

"If you're through with whatever you're doing," she replied icily.

"Oh, come on. Wi-Willa and I tease each other. It doesn't mean a th-th-thing," he stammered.

Janet didn't buy it, but she liked that he squirmed. "Are we going to have a lesson?"

"Right now," replied Johnny, reaching for his jacket.

Janet walked ahead until they cleared the doorway and were out of Willa's sight. She stopped abruptly, turned, and kissed him, nearly knocking him off balance.

Janet wasn't concerned with Johnny's other girlfriends. She saw Willa as her only real competition. It frustrated her that she made all the advances and that Johnny simply accepted. He never sent flowers or made any effort to appear grateful. What burned in her mind was that Willa had more access to her own plane than she did. To pay for lessons, Willa kept the Challengers' records for the US Department of Commerce and maintained all the files at Robbins Field. Janet assumed Willa had a hidden agenda and concluded that if she kept digging, she'd unearth the sordid truth.

By the spring of 1933, the Challenger Aero Club had forty-five members and a hangar with two planes. The club was also integrated. Two Jewish members, a high school science teacher, a dentist, and a Native American mechanic had joined and were logging hours at Robbins Field.

That April, the Challengers held a memorial to honor Bessie Coleman. Jointly organized by Janet and Willa, the event drew a crowd of over sixty guests to Lincoln Cemetery. Coffey flew the Curtiss over and threw flowers from the plane.

Johnny rose to say a few words. "Bessie was my great love. If I had ever met her, I would have begged her to marry me — except that I was fifteen and a student at Tuskegee Institute and she was thirty and a famous aviatrix. I didn't care." The gathering laughed. Willa, Janet, and the aspiring female pilots smiled approvingly at Johnny's humorous opening. "The reason we can be here today," he continued, "is because this woman, Bessie Coleman, lit a flame in our minds — the idea that we could soar like eagles."

Johnny was a natural in front of a crowd. He was smart, he knew his subject, and there was a small element of the bad boy in him that women as well as men found attractive.

At Willa and Janet's urging, Johnny became the spokesman for the Challengers. Willa arranged for him to visit local high schools to pitch careers in aviation. New faces at Robbins Field included fifteen-year-old Harold Hurd, seventeen-year-old Grover Nash, eighteen-year-old Marie St. Clair, and twenty-two-year-old Lola Jones. All signed up for flight instruction. Willa's brother Simeon returned and became a regular. Every day, the Curtiss was booked for flight instruction, and every weekend, Robbins field became a gathering place for club activities.

As the second year of operation got underway, the hangar's problems became harder to bear. The dirt floor was tolerable most of the time, but the lack of indoor plumbing and class-room or office space were not. Chicago's winter weather made the drafty, uninsulated hangar miserable. Any serious rain turned the surrounding landscape into a muddy soup.

With paving, drainage, insulation, and additional con-struction, all these drawbacks could have been manageable. The single intractable problem was the runway's overlap into the adjoining town's city limits. The white policeman's warn-ing on the day they began construction of the runway haunted Willa.

Complaints to the Crestwood police about low-flying air-planes held no weight with the Robbins police. However, if a Crestwood officer could nab the plane while it was still on the ground in the small section of runway within Crestwood's boundaries, the aircraft could be impounded and the pilot fined a crippling one hundred and fifty dollars.

On days the wind forced pilots to take off from the Crestwood side of the runway, the teen crew played a cat-and-mouse game with the police. Harold and Grover pretended to cut grass or hid behind strategically trimmed shrubs on the Crestwood side of the runway. When the plane taxied out to the end of the airstrip, one of the young men rushed over, lifted the tail, and positioned it for takeoff. The plane raced down the runway, and the youths sprinted back ahead of the police.

~

In September 1933, a powerful storm swept through Illinois. During the night, someone unknown broke the locks and threw the hangar doors open. The wind gusts smashed the Challengers' two planes. By morning, the planes looked like crumpled butterflies. The Curtiss's wings were broken at critical intervals, and the tail separated from the rest of the body. Willa, Janet, Coffey, and Johnny surveyed the damage.

Janet paced. "Oh Lord. What are we going to do? The payments on the loan have to be made. Otherwise, I'm going to lose two very valuable apartment houses. Who could have done this?"

"The locks were definitely broken," said Coffey. "We can and will repair the planes."

Johnny nodded in the direction of Crestwood. Suspiciously, the police car usually lurking in the oak grove was gone.

"We don't know that for certain," said Willa, even as she suspected the truth. "There isn't an ounce of evidence to prove it."

"It's going to cost," said Coffey. "I don't think we can do anything for the wings. We'll need to make or buy new. The fuselage has tears on the canvas. That we can mend. We'll get to work right away."

❧

Later that week, as Coffey was showing his crew how to salvage all the pieces and separate the good from the bad, a sputtering aircraft circled overhead. The crew ran out of the hangar to see a plane trailing a thick black cloud of smoke approaching for an emergency landing. Coffey grabbed a blanket and fire extinguisher and dashed out to meet the plane.

Harold and Grover helped the choking pilot from the cockpit as Coffey threw open the engine cover and smothered the flames.

"I nearly passed...out," the pilot said, hardly able to get the words out. "I didn't know...runway here. That crazy roof... God sent." He bent over coughing.

When the pilot removed his goggles, Harold and Grover were surprised to discover an aviator with white skin and pale-blue eyes.

Coffey examined the engine. "Oil splashed on the block. There's fire damage and soot. Did you leave this cleaning rag by the oil cap?" He dug out the remains of a burned rag with his long screwdriver.

"No, my mistake. I didn't check the engine and missed finding the rag."

"If you want, I can clean and repair it and get you home today," said Coffey. "You have two cables that look cooked. I can replace those, too."

"If you can do that, please do it, sir," said the pilot, taken with another fit of coughing. The pilot was going to shake hands with Coffey but saw his right hand left a sooty smear on the fuselage. He held out an elbow for Coffey to shake, still coughing.

"I'm Fred Schumacher," he said when he was finally able to speak. He was a portly man, quick to laugh at his own predicament. "I saw that crazy roof on your hangar and the airstrip — and believe you me, it was a moment of joy."

"I'm Cornelius Coffey," said Coffey, motioning for the young men to bring rags.

Harold brought Fred clean rags and a bar of soap and pointed him to the bathroom facilities, an outhouse, and a water spigot twenty-five yards away. After washing up, Fred poked about the primitive airfield. He saw the drafty hangar and the gravel paved runway. Beyond the end of the runway, he saw a police car pulling into the shade of the oak grove.

He continued to the hangar where Harold glued and clamped the Curtiss's broken struts. He then checked on the progress of his own plane. He found that Grover had scrubbed the soot from the fuselage and was now intently looking over Coffey's shoulder.

Coffey threaded the replacement cables as if he were an experienced musician replacing guitar strings. When finished, he closed the engine cover, climbed into the cockpit, and started the engine. There was a backfire and a cloud of black smoke. The engine settled and purred. Coffey taxied the plane around, testing the replacement cables. He shut off the engine and climbed out.

Fred did his own preflight test, running his finger across the place where the leak had started. The engine was immaculate.

"I could have done this job," Fred said. "But, mister, I couldn't have done it better and certainly not faster. You do excellent work. What do I owe you?"

"Five for new cables and a hose, and ten for our time," said Coffey. "Is that all right?"

"Better than all right," agreed Fred. He took fifteen dollars from his wallet and paid Coffey. "Too bad about the storm," he added. He then tipped each young man a dollar.

"Made a mess of the wings, as you can see," said Coffey.

"The Hawk is a fine piece of equipment," replied Fred. "Too bad."

"It can be fixed, but we're grounded for a while. You have about an hour of daylight," said Coffey.

The police car pulled into view from the cover of the oak grove.

"Harold," called Coffey, pointing to the police car. Harold stealthily began making his way toward Crestwood. Everyone knew what to do.

Coffey explained the cat-and-mouse routine with the cops and the need for a speedy takeoff. Fred laughed so hard he hit his head on the canopy.

"Boys, come back a sec," he called Harold and Grover. "Is that the way it is?" Fred chuckled. "Listen, Mr. Coffey, I own an airport over in Oak Lawn, off Harlem Avenue. I've got a hangar you can use and a small house with indoor plumbing you can take over as your office. I have planes I can let you rent until you get your own airworthy. If you have that master mechanic's license, Mr. Coffey, you come work as a mechanic at my field, and I've got room for you and all your crew. I could use bus drivers, too," he said pointing at Harold and Grover. "Think about it."

Fred held out his hand, and Coffey accepted. "I have my own gas pump and two paved runways," Fred added. "You're never at a loss for a headwind at Harlem Airfield."

Harold hitched a ride on Fred's wing into the Crestwood end of the runway. He jumped off the wing, picked up its tail, and positioned the plane for takeoff. As he sprinted back to the Robbins city limits, he shouted, "Next stop, Harlem Airfield!"

# 25

The storm that wrecked the planes at Robbins Field also set back Willa's master's degree plans. For a little over a year, she had managed a survivable fifteen dollars a week by booking, collecting the fees, and banking the proceeds for the Curtiss. She also did accounting and kept record of the all-important pilots' flight hours. With the tips she received at Walgreen's, she had held her life together.

The storm changed everything. She withdrew from the master's program with the hope that she would quickly secure another job and reenroll. Months passed, but she found nothing. The bad economy meant that few people would be taking their meals at Walgreen's. Her hours were so reduced that the only reason she showed up for work was the day-old meatloaf she received in lieu of pay.

Willa searched the want ads. The only listings for "colored" were domestic jobs that paid two dollars and fifty cents a week, plus a room and meals. Though her bachelor's degree qualified her for numerous positions in education, government, and business, the painstakingly prepared letters she wrote went unanswered or her job interviews ended as soon as the employer saw she was "colored."

Willa wrote to Professor Miller from Terre Haute that she was looking for a temporary position until she could return to her graduate studies. Professor Miller wrote back, "My peers don't agree with Roosevelt's New Deal nonsense of throwing money at poor people, but here's a position that might be of help." It was an opening for a social worker in Chicago.

Willa didn't mention in her letter to Dr. Miller the difficult time she was having. She didn't have clothes. Her best outfit's collar and sleeves were threadbare. She washed, repaired, and ironed her blouse and skirt; polished her shoes; and pulled herself together for the job interview. She checked herself in the mirror, and as one last act, she trimmed the tiny frayed threads on her collar.

During the interview, the white supervisor recognized immediately he would never find a more qualified colored applicant and hired her on the spot.

Without training or instructions, Willa was sent out to follow up spousal and child cruelty complaints in "black belt" Chicago, a ghetto filled with row upon row of decaying tenement apartments. Her cases dated back at least six months to a year or more.

Climbing an indoor stairwell on her first call, she saw a girl with wrinkled burn scars on her face and shoulders. The child took one look at Willa holding a clipboard and ran in the opposite direction, disappearing up the stairs and down a long corridor. The child looked like the burn case she was there to follow up. She found the apartment and knocked. An emaciated woman with a fat lip and a bloodspot in her left eye opened the door slightly. For an instant, Willa caught a glimpse of the child scurrying into another room.

"Ma'am, are you Geraldine Potter?"

The woman grunted something that sounded like, "Yeah?"

"This is about a complaint you filed against your common-law husband. I need to ask about your little girl."

The woman avoided eye contact and closed the door in Willa's face without saying a word. Willa knocked again. "Mrs. Potter? Please, can we have a word?" After several attempts, Willa saw she had drawn the attention of the entire floor. Neighbor women stood in their doorways glaring at her. It was going to be like this at most doors she knocked on.

As she made her way down her case list, Willa noted that noisy packs of teens with nothing to do were roaming the streets. Harmless and mostly decent, the teens were simply having boisterous fun. They whistled catcalls and made kissing noises. Willa could see by their clean clothes that most had families and a home.

However, some of the young men and older boys who skulked around street corners didn't look like they had a place to sleep. Their dingy clothes hung loose on their skinny frames. Though she didn't feel threatened, she could see in their bored attitudes that if they could escape detection, they might be capable of doing anything for money or food.

The small children disturbed her most. *What kind of start will they have?* she wondered. She asked a sweet-looking five-year-old boy if he had ever seen an airplane. The shy boy stared back as if she were speaking a foreign language.

"'N'our plame'?" the child replied.

"An *airplane*," she pronounced carefully. "It's like an automobile—but it has wings and flies in the air." The child looked at her as if she were dangerous and ran back into his apartment.

Over the next several hours, going up and down stairs and knocking on doors, she located and spoke with five women.

Two were abandoned with children and had no way to pay for food and rent. One wanted her common-law husband arrested because he beat and raped her. Except for the last woman who claimed she was raped, all withdrew their complaints because they feared reprisals. Willa typed up her observations and handed them to her pleasantly surprised supervisor.

"These are excellent," he said, reading her notes.

"When can these women see some help?" she asked.

"There's no help to be had," responded the supervisor. "If a wife, or woman like this common-law housemate you mention here, files a criminal complaint for rape, then it's a police matter. Though, it's not likely she'll get any satisfaction."

"So, you're saying my job is writing up reports about women who've been beaten by their husbands — they've dared to file complaints with the police that could get them horsewhipped, if not murdered! — and the children who've been burned, starved, neglected, and made ignorant, and there's nothing we can do for them?"

"For the time being. We'll take your reports, and when we have enough cases, we'll petition the city to fund another social worker. Maybe President Roosevelt can find a way to help the children. Right now, it's about creating jobs, and you have a job," he said pleased with his talented new hire.

That night, Willa wrote a letter to the supervisor thanking him for the opportunity. She quit the position and never returned.

# 26

The transition to Harlem Airfield from Robbins Field became Willa's project. Johnny arranged to borrow a flatbed truck from Marcus Lipsky, and one of Lipsky's drivers carted the broken bones of the Curtiss Hawk and the Heath Parasol to a hangar at Harlem Airfield. Willa didn't know Lipsky personally, not like Johnny and Coffey did, but she was sure that any favor from him meant he would expect something in return.

The new Challenger clubhouse was a one-room, twenty-by-twenty wood-frame structure, originally intended for a live-in guard. A potbelly stove dominated the center of the room, and an assortment of used and broken office furniture was stored against one wall. Outside, next to the back door, a four-by-four addition housed a "modern" flush toilet.

Willa found a used blackboard and mounted it on one wall. She drew up a schedule for classes and volunteer sign-ups. She got O. C. Pleasant to move the potbelly stove to a corner, which required punching a new hole in the roof for the exhaust. The stove, no matter the season, gave the room a smoky scent.

While Willa was making lunches for O. C. Pleasant and his men, a lanky young man from the Schumacher School showed up at the back door. Willa could tell he was a farm boy by his distinctively tanned face and pale forehead.

"Miss, kin I buy one of those sausages yore cookin'?" he asked.

"You have ten cents?" she asked.

"I have eight cents," he said and held out a nickel and three pennies.

"How do you expect to buy a hot dog?" Willa chuckled. She waved away the change. "Here," she said, handing him a sausage on a Kaiser roll. "I trust your face; you owe me a dime. Are you a mechanic or what?"

"No, ma'am, I'm studying to become a pilot."

She chuckled at his ambition. "I'm not officially open. Here's a Coke," she offered. "What's your name? I'll start a tab for you."

The young man's face broke into a broad grin. "The name's Ray Boyd."

"Well, Ray Boyd, you tell the boys over at Schumacher's that I sell hot dogs for a dime, hamburgers fifteen cents, and Coca-Cola for a nickel."

By the end of the first week, Willa was selling over twenty meals a day. Over a window facing the Schumacher School, O. C. built a wooden awning, hinged on top. When the awning was propped open with a broomstick, Willa's Café was open for business. The white students dragged over wooden crates and cable reels to provide a place to sit and eat.

A large, friendly man, O. C. Pleasant would rather work on a project than make small talk. He had known Coffey since they were boys and wanted to become a mechanic. To pay for engine repair classes, he traded his time and materials he scrounged from building sites. Willa suspected there was more to it than that, though. Whenever petite Marie St. Clair was scheduled to volunteer in the office, O. C. "just happened" to be working on something nearby.

It took three months to repair the Curtiss. Immediately, the pay phone Willa had installed began ringing with bookings. Johnny was in demand as a flight instructor. Though Coffey also gave flight instruction, his days were consumed maintaining Schumacher's planes. The move to Harlem Airfield proved to be positive for everyone. Schumacher's six large hangers, repair facilities, and paved runways gave the Challengers enormous credibility.

O. C. installed a sink and an indoor counter. The office grill made for a great place to hang out. The potbelly stove constantly wore a coffeepot on top. When Willa couldn't be in the office, Harold Hurd, Grover Nash, Marie St. Clair, and Lola Jones eagerly volunteered to fill in for her.

At six in the morning, Willa took her flight lessons with Coffey. She had practiced takeoffs and landings many times with Coffey sitting in the seat behind. In June, she soloed for the first time. The Curtiss sped down the runway, and the instant the tires left the tarmac, she felt the sensation of lift, defying gravity. A burst of adrenaline shot through her as the plane buffeted through the first thermals. The Curtiss Hawk flew right through the rising currents of hot air and rose higher. Her solo felt exhilarating. There was no other sensation like it—not a car, not a motorcycle. Ideas rushed through her mind. Was she dizzy from the lack of oxygen? She took several deep breaths. She marveled that the same internal combustion engine that powered the earthbound vehicles she saw below also powered her above the fences and ditches. She was free.

Without any fanfare, that following August, Willa earned a basic pilot's license, making her the first black woman in the United States to do so.

That month, she received another letter from Dr. Miller. "More New Deal schemes," he wrote. "The National Youth Administration Act is supposed to provide funds to reopen schools, primarily to get teenagers off the streets and out of the job market." Dr. Miller supported President Franklin Delano Roosevelt, but many wealthy people of his class did not. Willa was aware that his tone was meant to be a parody of his peers.

Wendell Phillips High School in her neighborhood was slated to become one of these National Youth Administration schools. The antidivorcee policy had been dropped the previous year when a successful lawsuit was decided. All through the years divorced women had been excluded from teaching, while divorced men had been allowed to teach. Her marital status was no longer an issue.

At her interview, Willa realized that the two white administrators had not read her cover letter, nor had they seen her curriculum vitae. She called attention to the fact that she was a licensed pilot and would soon earn certification to teach aircraft engine repair. She pitched the idea of providing classes in aircraft mechanics instead of auto repair to the black high school students. The white superintendent and his assistant nodded patiently and offered her a position as a typing and shorthand teacher.

At twenty-one dollars a week, Willa's new job had one immediate benefit: she could finally open an active savings account. Her passbook's first entry, for seventy-seven dollars and fifty-five cents, was entered in ink, initialed by the teller, and dated. She proudly tucked the passbook into a small compartment in her purse.

On warm days, Willa saved twenty cents by commuting to Harlem Airfield on a bicycle Coffey had taken in payment for a car repair. It came equipped with a sizable wire basket in front and had probably been used for deliveries by one of the many businesses bankrupted during the Depression. Willa carried her Corona portable typewriter in the basket. Each day, her post office box held letters from all over the country. She found rejection letters for job interviews. She received replies from Dr. Mary McLeod Bethune, the founder of the Bethune-Bookman School in Daytona Beach, Florida, for black boys and girls, and from William Powell, a pioneering black aviator in Los Angeles. There was also an unexpected letter from Harlem Renaissance poet Anne Spencer.

Back at the Harlem Airfield clubhouse, Willa replied to all correspondence. Anne Spencer had written to introduce her son, Chauncey. "My son wants to become a pilot," she wrote. Could Willa offer suggestions? "He has a degree in sociology," Anne Spencer added.

Willa replied that the Challengers could offer flight instruction and mechanical training at Harlem Airfield and were certified by the Curtiss Wright School.

When Anne Spencer's dapper son, Chauncey, appeared at Harlem Airfield, he wore a dark-blue suit with a fedora rakishly askew on his head. His chiseled features and trimmed moustache gave him the air of a movie idol. He told Willa he'd have to find some kind of work before he could take flight lessons. He fidgeted enough for Willa to see he was broke and hungry.

"Come this way," she said and pointed to the grill. Chauncey surprised her. He took off his coat and hat and put on an apron. He began grilling burgers and wieners for seven dollars a week, even though the flying lessons cost five dollars an hour. His mother had said she would pay for his classes if he had a job. Being a short-order cook qualified as gainful employment, and Willa vouched for him.

Better educated and certainly more sophisticated than any of the white student pilots, Chauncey knew how to parry racist remarks, usually by telling jokes and setting people at ease. With his exaggerated swagger, he quickly became one of the more visible regulars at Harlem Airfield.

Through his mother, Chauncey knew everyone of importance in the colored intellectual world. Marian Anderson was a guest in his parents' home in Lynchburg, Virginia. Langston Hughes read from his own work in their living room. W. E. B. Du Bois published Anne Spencer's poetry. William H. Hastie, the brilliant Howard University Law School professor, was a frequent visitor. Chauncey was the good friend of a young lawyer and Hastie protégé, Thurgood Marshall.

None of this impressed Willa. At twenty-two, Chauncey liked to party far too much for her to take him seriously, especially after he hosted a New Year's Eve party in December 1933, ostensibly celebrating the end of Prohibition.

# 27

etween November and February, winter weather limited activity at Harlem Airfield. In early March, when conditions were finally suitable for resuming classes, the Challengers had their first meeting of 1934. Chauncey worked the grill and engaged the members and guests with stories about the poets, artists, and intellectuals his mother entertained. He was sensitive to social clues and made everyone feel welcome. When Ray Boyd, the young white man who had tried to buy a hot dog for eight cents the previous year, wandered in through the front door and saw all the black faces, he started backing out. Chauncey called out, "Come on in, Ray. Take a seat. I'll get you a burger and a drink."

Ray sat down. Chauncey continued, "I was telling folks about my mother. When I was eight years old, my mother invited a four-feet-tall Baka Pigmy from Cameroon to come live with us. We were the same height, but he was a full-grown, perfectly shaped man."

Chauncey threw another meat patty on the grill.

"Belgian missionaries took him to Europe when he was about ten. He spoke English, German, French, and countless dialects from his country. As an adult, Oko traveled to New York where

P. T. Barnum, the circus impresario, took one look at him and said, 'There's my African wild man.' Oko had scars on his face that made him look fierce, but he was a very likeable fellow."

Chauncey flipped the meat patty.

"P. T. Barnum had Oko wear a wig and a fake bone through his nose, and nothing more than a little-bitty scrap of leather to hide his privates. Now, Oko could read and write in three languages, but the barker told the crowds that he couldn't recognize the written word from a line of ants. As part of his act, Oko did a bow-and-arrow demonstration, and at the end, he held up a shrunken head that drew gasps from the audience. He hated the job, and after a few weeks, he protested that shrunken heads were from South America and that Pigmies were not cannibals or warlike people. So, he quit. But P. T. Barnum wouldn't release him from his contract. Barnum didn't want to lose this incredibly interesting-looking little man. Figuring that running around naked probably embarrassed Oko, Barnum decided to dress him up like a hurdy-gurdy monkey. At that point, Oko'd had enough. He wrote to my mother for help. My mother contacted her friend, law professor William Hastie, and he was able to have Oko released from his contract. He lived with us for five months. He told me that by age three, a Pigmy child can shoot an arrow nearly as well as an adult. He taught me to use a bow and arrow. I can hit a target the size of a nickel at thirty yards."

"I'd like to see that," said Ray Boyd, fully captivated.

"The last I heard, Oko went back to Africa," added Chauncey. But before he left, he made me an honest-to-goodness Baka Pigmy brother." Chauncey paused for effect. "That's how I grew up to be the world's tallest Pigmy."

Harold Hurd and Grover Nash guffawed.

Ray Boyd got the joke, too. "That's rich." He laughed.

"That's an outrageous fabrication," chided Janet.

"Completely true," said Chauncey, handing Ray a hamburger and a drink.

Ray put down his cash on the counter and took his meal to go. As he backed out, he said, "Good for your momma."

Willa smiled at Chauncey's story. "What's not an outrageous fabrication is that we need to get more students taking engine maintenance. Schumacher can use a licensed mechanic right away, but our first batch of students here all want to be pilots."

Chauncey Spencer, Janet Harmon, Marie St. Clair, Lola Jones, Dale White, and others sat nearby. They all took flying lessons with Johnny.

"Schumacher doesn't pay much better than what I make running the café," said Chauncey.

"I'll pay people to fix my plane," chimed in Janet.

"Janet, I wasn't talking about you," said Willa. "And, Chauncey, you don't need to fix planes to make a living. Schumacher pays nineteen dollars a week. I'm talking to all those starting careers. If you want to fly, the best way is to first get as close to a plane as you can. The post office isn't hiring pilots. They're hiring aircraft mechanics."

Willa was right. At the time, the best jobs for blacks were in government, and for those jobs, they needed credentials. Everyone supported the idea; however, there was only one taker for training in engine repair, Dale White. He had come from Indianapolis to study at the Coffee school.

⊗

On Saturday mornings, Janet held court in the clubhouse. The rest of the week, Coffey was responsible for the maintenance of the seventeen planes housed at the airfield. Willa ran the operation and kept everyone on schedule. Johnny had his regular students. The café made a small profit. Simeon and Harold Hurd drove a bus to and from the last bus stop to Harlem Airfield on the hour.

The arrival of a one-of-a-kind aircraft, however, caused a break in the routine. Fred Schumacher directed the delivery, and the plane was swiftly locked away in a hangar with few windows. Curious eyes attempting to get a peek could only see an aircraft hidden under canvas tarps. Schumacher directed Simeon to paint the windows black. Willa guarded entry to the hangar. Only she and Schumacher had keys to the locks. When Ray Boyd asked her what was going on, she shrugged.

"I don't know anything more than you," she said. "They don't let me in there." Entry was restricted to Schumacher, Coffey, Johnny, Simeon, and two strangers, the owners, and none of them were talking.

The owners of the mystery aircraft were two brothers who arrived in a cream-colored convertible Cadillac touring car. Dressed like celebrities in buttery woolen slacks and silk shirts, the white mechanics noticed that the brothers strolled into the Challenger clubhouse instead of Schumacher's office. The taller of the two was in charge, while the shorter one watched with an amused smile.

"What do you have to drink?" the tall one asked Chauncey.

"Cokes and coffee."

"Have any ice?"

"Ice box ice," said Chauncey.

"It'll have to do. Chipped ice, Coca-Cola, and a shot of this." The tall one produced a glass flask and tossed it to Chauncey.

Chauncey knew exactly how to treat these types. He prepared strong drinks and got them to talk about themselves. They played down their own personal worth but bragged about coming into their own financially as legal bootleggers. During Prohibition, they had made "a tidy sum" producing a very smooth medical-quality ethanol, available by prescription. In spite of their showy touring car and expensive sports clothes, Chauncey could tell by their manners that they were old money and not mob types. They were probably connected to the pharmaceutical industry. On their second visit, Chauncey was ready for them and prepared martinis. Over a period of six weeks, they arrived twice a week to check up on the progress of their plane. Chauncey was never able to get the brothers to divulge anything about the mysterious aircraft. The only people who knew the true story were the five who were working on it. The aircraft in the hangar was a one-of-a-kind high-performance racer, known for being fast and highly maneuverable with amazing aerodynamic innovations.

Jimmy Wilkerson, the designer of the Model W-44, was allegedly a semiliterate genius who built racing airplanes intuitively. He reputedly took a carpenter's pencil, drew an outline on the hangar floor, began building, and didn't stop until he was finished. His designs looked more like sharks whose thrust came from within, than birds that flapped their wings. The Model W-44 differed from other racing planes in that those planes were designed to house a powerful engine, while the rest of the plane might as well have resembled a box kite. Even on the ground, Wilkerson's winged fish airplane looked hungry to fly.

When Wilkerson died testing a new plane, the W-44 in Schumacher's hangar was all that remained of the unique design. Wilkerson, afraid that his designs would be stolen, had kept all the details in his head. He left behind no plans or blueprints.

How the bootlegger brothers came into possession of the plane was a secret. When Schumacher asked about its acquisition, the taller brother brushed off the question as if he were shooing away a gnat.

Their intention was to "borrow" liberally from unpatented design innovations and use them to build fast postal and military aircraft. To prepare the technical drawings and schematics needed to patent the design, the brothers hired Efran Landley, a young PhD aeronautical engineer from the University of Michigan. The instructors at Curtiss Wright recommended Cornelius Coffey to Landley as someone who could understand a one-of-a-kind, handmade aircraft.

While the W-44 was in the hangar at Harlem Airfield, it was disassembled and carefully photographed, measured, and blueprinted. When every measurement was completed and documented, it was meticulously reassembled. The carburetor was the final piece of the puzzle. The hand-milled carburetor Wilkerson made specifically for high-speed performance had long ago been replaced with a factory-made carburetor. The factory model caused the plane to stall on extreme maneuvers, the very kind of flying the craft was designed to do. The original carburetor did exist; however, small valves and couplings had been removed and lost.

Coffey, like Wilkerson, could visualize the workings of a carburetor and mill it from soft-grade steel. He made a mold and hand assembled three precision carburetors. But his most critical contributions were the numerous mechanical drawings he made, along with his exacting measurements. After testing the carburetors in the hangar, he selected one. Of course, only an actual flight test would prove if it would function at over one hundred miles an hour.

During this period, activity at Harlem Airfield remained fairly routine. As part of the work on any aircraft, when Coffey finished a repair job, Johnny took it up for a fifteen-minute test. Chauncey hadn't been on hand to witness Johnny fly the day of the Suicide Jones air show, but he spoke of the event as if he *had* been there and exaggerated far beyond what actually took place. The white students pleaded with Chauncey to let them know when Johnny would fly again. In response, whenever a test flight was scheduled, he'd put out a green flag. The Schumacher students came out, bought hot dogs and Cokes, and took them out to the edge of the field to watch. Since the planes weren't his, there wasn't much Johnny could do. But he did manage to sneak in a little something at the end of each test flight, a single barrel roll or flying upside down briefly.

In April 1934, Schumacher, Coffey, and Simeon pushed the much-anticipated mystery airplane out on the tarmac for tests. Chauncey hung out the green flag, and students quickly gathered to admire the W-44. The propeller was part of the nose design. The engine was buried in its shark-like body, and the cockpit looked like a clear aerodynamic bump on the shark's back.

At one hundred and fifty miles an hour, the carburetor performed as expected. When Johnny landed in order to make last-minute adjustments, Landley and the bootlegger brothers, holding empty martini glasses, became animated in anticipation of the big show. Chauncey refreshed their drinks.

The green flag had attracted a fair-sized gallery. He had Simeon filling in at the café, but he wasn't about to miss the final tests. He shut the café window and joined Grover Nash and Harold Hurd on the front row. Janet parked her green Buick as close as she could and raced to join Willa, Marie, and Lola.

Landley signaled for Coffey to step away from the spectators.

"This design is intended for racing," said Landley, signaling to one of the brothers to step forward with an envelope.

"I want you to turn her loose," he said, handing Johnny the envelope. "This is five hundred dollars. I understand from Chauncey you've done stunt flying. Since we're going to demolish the W-44 after this flight, show us what she can do. Crash her, and you're doing us a favor."

"I'll try not to crash her with me in it," Johnny laughed.

He accepted the envelope and handed it to Coffey. "Mr. Landley, if Coffey approves the plane, I'm ready to go."

Landley stood back as Coffey stepped forward. He climbed onto the wing and leaned into the cockpit, pretending to show something to Johnny. "The fuel injection should work over two hundred miles an hour," he whispered. "But--"

"I know," replied Johnny. "And I know why they chose me to test the W-44. If anything happens to me, it won't be in the *Chicago Tribune* tomorrow morning. Take fifty dollars and bury me, and give the rest to my momma." Johnny stepped up on the wing and looked over his shoulder at the white owners. "I'll be okay," he called out and settled into the cockpit. "As crazy as this might sound, I want to fly this beautiful creature flat out and not care if I've pushed her too far."

The Hispano-Suiza engine whistled, growled, and settled into a steady roar. Johnny and Coffey couldn't help but laugh at how lucky they were.

"Have a great time," said Coffey.

Johnny began with a series of snap turns, barrel rolls, and tight loop-the-loops, shaking the W-44 to its bolts and seams. He buzzed the clubhouse at first at two hundred miles an hour. He gave himself enough distance to attempt to go faster and flew past at 325 miles per hour. He then began a steep climb. The brothers, Landley, and the crowd were amazed by the plane's speed and maneuverability.

Willa didn't care for Johnny's flying antics and went back into the clubhouse. Before she could guide a sheet of paper into the typewriter, screams from outside brought her to her feet. She ran to the door and saw Janet gasping, "Johnny's going to kill himself! He's going to kill himself!"

Shielding her eyes from the sun, Willa looked up. She saw the end of Johnny's climb as he stalled the engine and allowed the plane to fall in a spiral to earth.

"What the hell!" said Landley. The bootlegger brothers grinned, delighted with the show.

Janet screamed again. The W-44 was falling end over end.

Inside the cockpit, Johnny could feel the air rushing past the falling fuselage. He used the plane's downward momentum to regain control. He engaged the rudders and ailerons, pulled out of the dive, started the engines, and finished with three barrel rolls. As he repeated the routine, going even higher and faster, Willa took her hand from her forehead and muttered, "He's crazy." She hated when he showed off recklessly like that. She slammed the door behind her.

The bootlegger brothers were pleased with the test. Before getting back in their Cadillac, they spoke to Landley, who then approached Johnny privately. "They want you to know, if you ever want a job with us, we're taking a hangar at Muni."

"What about Coffey? He put that baby together so she could fly," asked Johnny.

Landley shook his head. "There are no colored mechanics where we're going."

"I'm pretty well set here, thank you," said Johnny. "By the way, this plane can take a much bigger engine. Her airframe's solid, through and through."

Johnny strolled into the clubhouse followed by Coffey, Janet, Chauncey, Grover Nash, and the others. He tossed his jacket onto the coatrack.

Willa stopped typing. "You know, Johnny, you've heard the saying about old pilots and bold pilots?"

"You mean that there are no old bold pilots?" he replied. "So?"

"The designer of the W-44, Jimmy Wilkerson and his brother are dead because they did crazy stuff like what you just did. If you want to kill yourself, at least have a good reason for it." She threw a newspaper at him. "Read that," she said angrily. Janet and Chauncey exchanged glances.

The headlines of the *Chicago Defender* read: "Negro Aviators Charles Alfred Anderson and Dr. Albert Forsythe Complete Round Trip from Atlantic City to Los Angeles." A smaller headline read: "Pair plan to island-hop to South America—and back."

Johnny handed the newspaper back. "It's been done. Anderson's got a rich doctor to bankroll him. What do you want me to do?"

"We have three licenses in this room," Willa countered. "Eight of the forty-three Challenger Aero Club members have licenses. We can send a squadron of planes wherever."

"Well, maybe not a squadron but three or four planes," corrected Coffey.

"What about flying a squadron from Chicago to Tuskegee? Has anybody done that?" asked Janet. Everyone turned to her. She shrugged. "Well, can you imagine?" she asked. "Four planes flying over Jim Crow from Chicago to Tuskegee, Alabama?"

"And do it in one day," added Johnny. "Willa could fly one, Coffey in the Curtis, me in another, and Grover, a teenage kid, if he finishes that plane of his on time. That would make the papers," said Johnny. "If we do it in June, that'll be the tenth anniversary of my graduation from their mechanics program."

"And after that, we'll set up a regular service from Tuskegee to Chicago and call it the Chitlin Airways," joked Chauncey.

Willa scowled and smacked him lightly with the newspaper.

"How much money will it take?" asked Janet.

"It depends if we can get a loan of two additional planes," said Willa. "With tarmac fees, services, and gasoline, maybe four hundred and fifty dollars."

Johnny took his envelope of cash from Coffey's breast pocket. He separated four hundred and fifty dollars from the contents of the envelope and handed it to Willa. "Let's do it," he said.

# 28

**f**red Schumacher's Harlem Airfield was part of the growing investment in aviation enterprises in the Chicago area.
Five miles away, "Muni" (Chicago Municipal Airport) landed
huge contracts with United and Braniff for hangars and facilities and smaller contracts with American, TWA, and several
local carriers. The emerging airline companies had hired away
Schumacher's best mechanics.

To stay in business, Schumacher needed someone with
Coffey's credentials. The white mechanics not hired by the airlines either lacked experience or certification or had criminal
records. Those left behind resented Coffey, Johnny, and the
rest of the Challenger crowd. They watched as Coffey took
over an entire hanger and got first call on Schumacher's best
equipment.

Opinions began to change when a few of the more ambi-
tious white students, like Ray Boyd, recognized that Coffey
was a perfectionist and knew more about engines than anyone else at Harlem Airfield. After working for Coffey for three
months, the more capable white mechanics were regularly
hired away by the airlines. In order to keep a flow of employ-
ees, Schumacher made a deal with the Curtiss Wright School to

hire their students. Since Coffey was a credentialed instructor, the students working under his supervision could receive class credit.

Johnny gave three flight classes in the morning and filled in as a mechanic in the afternoon. On two occasions, he took the Curtiss Hawk out at six in the morning and made a flight somewhere for Marcus Lipsky. Coffey didn't want to know details about the cargo. He serviced the plane before and after and knew to the ounce how much gas the Curtiss used. On a regional map Willa had gotten from Hahn Engineering, Coffey calculated that Johnny was flying to Canada. Whatever he carried as cargo weighed approximately three hundred pounds. Coffey kept tightlipped and didn't speculate about Johnny's flights.

For three young regulars—Grover Nash, Harold Hurd, and Simeon Brown—the clubhouse was a home away from home. There was the cool, graceful Willa and several of her attractive young friends to look at. As long as they kept their voices down and allowed her to type, Willa let them sit by the stove and drink Cokes.

Johnny came in after a class and noticed the three young men looking unusually quiet. "Something's up," he said, tossing his leather jacket on the coat rack. "How's the project?" he asked Grover.

"We've finished painting today. It's drying right now," said Grover.

"Painted? Oh, man, you guys. Did you really put that big engine in that mosquito of a plane?" asked Johnny. All three young men nodded with proud grins on their faces.

"Yes, sir," replied Grover.

"This, I gotta see," exclaimed Johnny.

"Miss Willa? Would you come out and see the finished Pup?" Grover asked.

"I'd be pleased," Willa said, delighted for them. She put aside her letter writing and walked ahead of Johnny and the young men out to the hangar.

Grover, Simeon, and Harold gathered next to a single-wing monoplane. It was less than six feet high, nineteen feet long, and with wings measuring thirty feet across.

Grover couldn't restrain his excitement. His curly golden-brown hair bounced, and his gray-green eyes glowed. Everyone knew the story of the Bull Pup. Grover's father was white, and his mother was African and Sioux. A white cousin had bought the Bull Pup kit at half price when the Buhl Company went bankrupt in 1931. Grover's cousin made an attempt to assemble the plane but abandoned it when it proved to be too difficult. Grover acquired the pieces for ninety dollars, and Coffey gave him permission to build it in the hangar. The assembly hadn't been easy. Unlike Coffey's Heath Parasol kit, which came with drawings and instructions, the Pup's kit contained only a dia-gram — no instructions — and the Buhl Company was no longer around. The three young men stared at the pieces long enough until, like a jigsaw puzzle, they figured out where each one went.

"It has a small gas tank," said Grover. "But it can cruise at over a hundred and thirty miles an hour."

"It can go fast, just not very far," chimed in Harold Hurd.

"Far enough," said Willa.

Willa examined the Bull Pup and congratulated them on their craftsmanship. Unlike the colorful planes parked around

Schumacher's hangars, the Bull Pup was painted an unappealing flat black. Grover thought it made the Bull Pup look mysterious, like something out of a comic book. The effect was the exact opposite. The Bull Pup looked more like a barnyard bailing machine than a seductive aircraft. Willa smiled and winked privately at Johnny. She wasn't about to say anything negative. The boys were much too proud.

"Well, after Coffey checks her out, do you want to try to fly her to Tuskegee?" asked Johnny.

Grover and his friends looked at one another. "Yes, sir," he said, thrilled by the idea.

❧

That night, Johnny, Coffey, and Willa were the last to leave the clubhouse. They found Marcus Lipsky and the blond woman, Roxy Moss, waiting for them outside. Marcus beckoned for Johnny to step away alone.

"Johnny, you know that last shipment you brought in for me?"

When Coffey and Willa were out of earshot, Johnny turned to Lipsky. "I delivered you one person and luggage in good shape. You said he was a nephew."

"Hear me out. He is a nephew. I put him to drive a milk truck the next morning, and he wrecks the truck ten minutes out of the yard. The next day, he wrecks the truck, but doesn't tell me until the end of the day. We have to throw away all the milk. And the next day, he doesn't get out of the yard before he smashes a headlight." Roxy Moss rolled her eyes. Why was Lipsky taking so long to get to the point?

"Did you fire him?" asked Johnny.

"No, I can't. He's my oldest sister's son. So, in Yiddish, I ask him, 'Why didn't you tell me you couldn't drive a truck?' And he answers, 'I was told to say, yes, to whatever you asked.'"

"Do you want me to fix the trucks?" asked Johnny.

"No, Johnny, I want you to fly in six more relatives. Maybe there's a truck driver among them," said Lipsky.

"Six! I can only fly one at a time, two if they're small. You know, this isn't like flying in cases of champagne. They will confiscate and destroy the plane. I'll lose my license and go to jail."

Roxy finally spoke. "Johnny, it's taken a lot of money and effort to get these people this close. You let us worry about the authorities." Roxy sounded in control. She wasn't the ditzy blonde Johnny had taken for a plane ride the previous year.

"I promise you after this, I won't ask for any more favors," said Lipsky. "Prohibition is over. The Chicago Outfit is going legit. We control eighty percent of the milk market and make a profit. You can have a job as long as you want."

Johnny shook his head. "Too many people will know. I can't do this by myself. People will figure it out. I can't hide six trips to Canada. Coffey services the plane. He'll know. Willa keeps the books. She'll know. We have rentals scheduled and can't just cancel without a lot of people asking questions and wondering. This could take weeks. We have weather to contend with--"

"Let me talk to Coffey," interrupted Lipsky.

"Coffey's a civilian," said Johnny.

"I know what he is," said Lipsky. "I want to talk to him. And the young woman, too."

Johnny signaled for Coffey and Willa to come closer. "Mr. Lipsky wants to have a word with you."

Roxy, wearing a tailored navy-blue suit, was fully aware Willa was giving her the once-over. She spoke before Lipsky. "Mr. Coffey, Miss Brown, we need your help. We have relatives who had to get out of Germany to escape the Nazis. They're Jewish, like us. Johnny here says it will take weeks. We don't have weeks. If our people get caught trying to enter the country, they'll be sent back to Germany. If we can get them here, Marcus can take care of them."

"We need you to service the plane and keep it on the quiet," added Lipsky.

Coffey paced several steps away thinking.

Willa stood her ground and answered, "This is a big favor. This isn't like paying off a border guard to look the other way."

"I understand," said Lipsky. "I'll find another way to get them here if I must. But if you can, help us."

"We can't take a chance. They'll confiscate and destroy our plane. I overheard you say you're legit now. We're legit, too. We can't afford to get thrown out of our place here."

"Hold on a moment," said Coffey. "I'm not saying, no. This is going to cost. We need another plane, a decoy, so no one misses the Curtiss. I have a lead on a disabled Curtiss we can use. It's close enough to pass for our Hawk. It'll take a day to repaint numbers. We can do this in three days. We'll use Robbins Field, what's left of it. You take care of the Crestwood cops and have cars standing by to take your passengers away."

"I want to help, " Willa said. "But it's too risky for us. Too many people can find out. How are we going to hide the eighty gallons of gasoline we're going to need? Schumacher will know something is up."

"I can take care of that," said Lipsky. Mr. Schumacher and his wife have just won a trip to Miami Beach from a Brook View Dairy promotion, right, Roxy?"

"He leaves tomorrow," Roxy confirmed.

"Is there a promotion like that?" questioned Willa.

"Yes, there is," answered Roxy. "Except to win the trip, the contestants, chosen at random, have to agree to go right away. Fred's wife is thrilled. Depending on what you say, they'll go to Miami, or Marcus and I will go as the winning contestants, except our name will be Smith. Johnny will be taken care of, and you'll both be compensated, of course."

"I'll do it, but just pay for the expenses and maintenance," said Coffey.

"I'll do it, but for a suit like Miss Moss is wearing and a hundred dollars," said Willa bravely. It was a crazy amount of money.

"Done," said Lipsky. He shook hands with Willa. Roxy gave all three a kiss on the cheek, and the deal was set.

*Damn,* thought Willa. *I could have asked for more.*

Two days later, after taking the Curtiss for a flight, Johnny returned to the clubhouse on foot. He explained to the curious Schumacher crowd that the Curtiss had had engine trouble. The fact was that the real Curtiss was parked at Robbins Field, while a decoy was delivered in broad daylight and taken into the blacked-out hangar. The doors were locked before anyone could get a closer look.

The white mechanics watched, speculating that the Curtiss was probably damaged far worse than Johnny admitted. One of them wished out loud, menacingly, "I hope this spells the end of Nigras at Harlem Airfield."

Willa guarded access to the hangar. No one was allowed in or out without her say.

Earlier that morning on the radio, just before the *Breakfast with Roxanna* program, a male announcer warned that a member of a notorious Shelton Brothers gang had escaped from Joliet Prison. The announcer said the escaped prisoner was believed to be heading home to the Little Egypt region of Southern Illinois. Drivers were asked not to pick up hitchhikers. Roxy made calls to Joliet Prison and confirmed that there was a prisoner unaccounted for. The manhunt focused to the south, and a lone Curtiss Hawk could come and go unnoticed out of Robbins Field to the northeast.

Johnny had flown this route north for Lipsky before. He followed the Sturgeon Bay Peninsula to its end and then veered thirty degrees west. Below, he could see large fish in the clear water of Lake Michigan. If he ever had the time off, he thought, he would like to return to this place and fish.

At ten in the morning, Johnny circled a dirt airstrip on the Canadian side of Sturgeon Bay. He unloaded gasoline cans and refueled the plane, as six people—two children, two women, and two adult men—slowly emerged from a shack next to the strip. Each person carried a small suitcase, and no one spoke English. The men didn't know what to make of the black pilot, but after a moment, Johnny conveyed a sense of urgency. He gave them a note from Roxy explaining his assignment.

"I'm making four trips." He held up four fingers. "Two today and two tomorrow," Johnny said slowly. The six people stared back.

He looked at the plane and indicated there was only one seat for a passenger. He pointed to a woman and a child and then to the seat behind the pilot. He mimed the plane flying away. Then he pointed to the second woman and child and repeated the mime. By the time he pointed to the first man, they understood what he meant. He then pointed to his watch and indicated it was 10:30 a.m. He pointed at his watch again and held up four fingers. "I'll return at four o'clock," he said slowly.

"*Vier uhr*," said one of the men.

"If that means four o'clock, we're set." He motioned for a woman and a child to climb in. With tears and trepidation, the first woman and child boarded the plane. He returned at 4:20 p.m. and made the second run.

The following afternoon, when he took off with his last passenger, he left behind sixteen empty five-gallon gas cans by the side of the strip.

Around 3:00 a.m., the decoy plane was secreted away from the Harlem Airfield hangar. The real Curtiss landed moments after daylight. The hangar doors were thrown open, and when the white mechanics arrived and the Schumachers returned from their Miami vacation, no one could say a word because nothing was different or out of place.

The following morning at 6:00 a.m., Roxy Moss, who hosted *Breakfast with Roxanna*, breathlessly announced on the air that the escaped convict story was a false alarm.

She knew, even before the prison officials knew any of the facts, that the inmate had hidden in a hand-dug pit inside Joliet Prison for two days. Unable to make good on his actual escape, the prisoner came out on his own. Coincidently, Brook View Dairy sponsored *Breakfast with Roxanna*.

Johnny never divulged what he received by way of compensation from Lipsky. A few days later, a messenger service delivered a garment bag with Roxy's navy-blue suit and a hatbox. A note attached said, "May the suit bring you the same good luck it brought me. The hat comes with it, Roxanna Moss."

Other than reimbursement for expenses, Coffey never asked for anything from Lipsky. Johnny heard that the German relatives were taken to Los Angeles to work in the motion pictures as extras, where Roxy had a cousin in the casting department at Universal Pictures.

# 29

Willa received a prompt and enthusiastic response to her request to land a squadron of planes at Tuskegee Institute. Assistant to the president, Dr. Frederick Patterson, wrote that the arrival of four Chicago aviators and their planes on May 22, 1934, the school's commencement day, would make for a truly special occasion.

Willa approached Fred Schumacher and other pilots for leads to airfields where they could refuel en route. Black aviators couldn't get service at most airports below Kentucky and not all that many north of the Jim Crow laws either. Willa made arrangements with two colleges, one manager of an airstrip, the proprietor of a large farm with a paved runway, and the owners of a dirt runway near Bowling Green, Kentucky, that had an above-the-ground gas tank. The colleges, Indiana State College and Fisk University, did not have airfields but had places to land, and fuel would be available. Coffey plotted the seven-hundred-mile zigzag course across Illinois, Indiana, Kentucky, Tennessee, and Alabama.

Meeting with Willa to prepare a course outline, Johnny brought out dozens of dog-eared pages of handwritten notes he'd made while a student at Curtiss Wright.

"I don't need an outline to teach. I have it all up here in my head," he said confidently.

"Let me see those," Willa said, putting out her hand. "Patterson can't read what's in your head," she said, leafing through his notes. "He needs a proposal that says what you'll teach, what equipment you'll need, how you're going to do it, and how much it's going to cost. And you have to say something about where the graduates will find jobs once they've been trained."

Johnny shook his head. "Why? Aviation is the future. Everybody knows that!"

"Forget the future. It's the way things are done, now. After we land, there's a whole rigmarole we have to go through. There'll be a chance for photos. We'll speak to the students, watch the commencement, and then have dinner. The following morning, we'll talk business. That's when we'll give Dr. Patterson the proposal with you as instructor."

"And when will I know if something is going to come through?" asked Johnny, irritated by what sounded like tedious formalities.

"Who knows? A decision isn't going to be made while we're there," answered Willa. "It's academia." She leafed through Johnny's notes. "The proposal is our excuse for the flight. You have what looks like notes from your classes. That's good as a sample of what'll you'll teach, but it's not enough. The fact that we show up in four airplanes and have our pictures taken for the newspapers--and bring publicity to Tuskegee--means you, Coffey, Grover, and I are on the map. Dr. Patterson, after due deliberation, will have to give us an answer--which will probably be that the timing isn't right, or he supports the idea, but the school doesn't have any money."

"Then why bother?"

"Are you getting cold feet?"

"No," Johnny moaned. "I bring my commercial licenses. That should be enough."

"We're doing it because we *can*," she said, emphatically. "We're four licensed pilots flying over the Jim Crow laws like they were nothing more than fences and ditches."

"If that's the reason, why do I have to write a proposal?"

"All right. Forget it. I'll take your notes and see what I can do," said Willa. "I have to get back to work."

Johnny was financing the flight, so whatever was frustrating him wasn't going to bother Willa. The flight was going to happen. Her mind raced with the details. A while back, she'd framed an ad for a flight suit, but that was two moves ago. Willa recalled that when she'd moved into this current flat, she'd stored a box of classroom books and personal items in a shed behind the building. The building super said he had the only key and the box would be safe. Unlocking the door, she found her box stinking of mildew. Looking up at the roof, she could see the sky where shingles had rotted. The spring storms had soaked everything. Her books were warped. Her wedding photo with Wilbur Hardaway was streaked with dark stains. She found the ad for the woman's flight suit and popped it out of its frame. On her way upstairs, she dumped the box with the wedding photo, wobbly picture frames, and books into a trash bin.

The flight suit was madly expensive. Withdrawing a hundred and sixty dollars from her savings, Willa ordered an all-white ensemble: leather jacket, jodhpurs, midcalf boots, and matching aviator's cap with goggles.

Acquiring four planes proved more difficult than anyone had anticipated. The Curtiss Hawk and the Bull Pup were certain. Coffey had sold the Heath Parasol to a young man from Indiana, who promptly crashed it. Citing insurance restrictions, Schumacher claimed his planes weren't covered outside Illinois and Indiana.

One plane owner, Asa McAllister, a ruddy-faced accountant and owner of an older Jenny OX 5 biplane, claimed he was immune to bigot politics. "Take her," McAllister told Coffey. "Do what ya gotta do to make her ready." The OX 5 assured them of three aircraft, and Willa would be flying one.

If Willa had learned anything from Willie "Suicide" Jones, it was that she had to boldly, even shamelessly, promote the event. She called Mack Chevrolet and arranged to borrow a limousine. When she and Simeon saw the loan car, the thought crossed her mind that it looked very similar to the cream-colored convertible driven by the rich bootlegger brothers. As Red Mack walked them out on the lot, Simeon, dressed in his Sunday suit, got behind the wheel. Red Mack held the passenger door open for her. "When this is over, I want you to come to the radio station and visit with us on the breakfast show."

"I'll do that," she said, sliding into the car. Red closed the door and waved her off the lot.

On the surface, in her new white flight suit, Willa looked confident enough to conquer the world. Inside, in the pit of her stomach, she felt queasy. She forced herself to focus on the deluxe amenities on the dashboard, the deco radio, a chrome-plated ashtray, and a mother-of-pearl flint-style cigarette lighter. She opened the glove compartment and found an empty glass half-pint flask. She laughed. It was the same car the bootlegger brothers had brought out to Harlem Airfield.

Simeon drove her to the offices of the *Chicago Defender*, where she swept into the newsroom and aimed straight for the office of the editor, Enoch Waters. She marched in with her head held high, like her imperious old boss Ursula Miller had urged her. Typewriters went silent. The office staff craned their heads to get a look at the show as she knocked on the editor's open door.

"Are you Enoch Waters?" she asked.

The middle-aged man copyediting the next day's stories lifted his eyes just enough to see over his reading glasses. "Yes, who wants to know?" Seeing the attractive young woman, he removed his glasses and unconsciously smoothed his pencil-thin moustache.

The entire pressroom stopped working, stepped away from their desks, and silently converged outside Enoch's office. By some predetermined pecking order, they sorted out their positions, leaning over one another to hear and see.

"I'm Willa Brown, and I'm an aviatrix," she said.

The usually garrulous editor couldn't think of a witty retort. Like the rest of the men in the newsroom, she had his attention.

"This coming Tuesday, four of us will be making a flight in three airplanes from Harlem Airfield in Oak Lawn, Illinois, to Tuskegee, Alabama. If you want a scoop that will excite your readers, you'll be out there at five in the morning with cameras to cover this historic event." She turned so that the staff outside the door could hear. "Imagine: Chicago to Tuskegee, three planes in one day."

"So why are you…"

Before Enoch could finish, Willa, whose energy lit the room, handed him a press release. Enoch grinned helplessly and glanced at the expertly prepared release.

Willa turned to include everyone in her presentation. "We're going to propose that Tuskegee start training students for a career made for the future, aircraft engine repair."

"The hell, you say," said Enoch, picking up half a cigar from an ashtray and lighting it. As the smoke swirled around his head, he thought, *If this gal is for real, it's a triple whammy of a story. Beautiful, poised, and professional, Willa Brown, aviatrix.*

⤜⤏

At 4:30, on the morning of the flight, Asa McAllister's plane was missing, and he was nowhere to be found. He'd skipped out leaving behind months of unpaid Harlem Airfield tarmac fees and a large maintenance bill owed to Coffey.

"Some accountant," grumbled Coffey. "I put twenty-six dollars in parts into his engine."

Willa's face felt hot. Her breathing came in short, rapid breaths. All the preparations, the press releases, logistics--she felt nauseous. Enoch Waters, Janet, Coffey, and Johnny were silent.

"I'm sorry," said Coffey. "Why don't you--"

Willa waved for him to stop talking. She walked to the clubhouse with Janet following a few steps behind.

"Please," she said to Janet. "I need to be alone." She entered the clubhouse and locked the door behind her. Grabbing the first object she could put her hands on, her coffee cup, Willa smashed it on the cement floor — and instantly regretted it; she liked that cup. She looked about for something else to throw.

Her typewriter? No, she needed that. Coffey's clock? It wasn't hers to break. Frustrated, furious, and humiliated, she began to sob. Half choking and coughing, she forced herself to stop. She caught a glimpse of herself in the mirror above Chauncey's cash drawer. Her eyes red, mascara running, and hair a mess, she took a deep breath and wiped her tears. Ten minutes later, she emerged, composed, hair in place, makeup perfect. The flight would take place as scheduled, she told Enoch. She would stay behind to monitor the journey.

Coffey had prepared a meticulous flight plan. Each pilot had a map with the roads, rivers, and towns they would use as guides. He included a small compass, the map coordinates of all fueling stations, alternative emergency stops, sunset and moonrise times, and instructions on what to do if they were separated or lost.

"I'm sorry," he said to Willa, handing her a copy of the flight plan. "Go in my place."

"No, this is Johnny's anniversary event, and you're the mechanic. If anything goes wrong, you have to be there," she answered and waved at him to go on. "Next time."

Willa spoke to Grover Nash's parents, assuring them that he would be safe. Privately, she said to Grover, "Don't take any chances." She kissed her fingers and touched the Bull Pup. "Coffey will keep an eye on you, so do what he says." Grover nodded and started the Bull Pup. The engine turned over instantly, reassuringly. Grover's parents stood nearby, nervous and proud.

Coffey had tuned the Curtiss Hawk and Bull Pup to peak form. The 5:00 a.m. departure took place with flashbulbs popping and a crowd of about thirty. Janet made certain she was in every photo.

Coffey had calculated the Hawk needed three stops and the Bull Pup five. They would cruise at one hundred and ten miles an hour and arrive at Tuskegee, Alabama, by noon.

Joining Enoch Waters at the office of the *Chicago Defender*, Willa took on a documentary role. Contacts at the refueling stops were asked to make collect calls to the *Defender's* office when they had information about the pilots. Instead of Enoch or one of the staff taking the calls, Willa sat by the phone and charted the sightings on a map of the eastern half of the United States.

"If I were out there piloting one of those planes, it would never occur to me that it was dangerous," she told Enoch. "But looking at a map gives me goose bumps. We were out of our minds."

The flight went smoothly until the two planes were a half hour outside of Nashville. Menacing thunderheads accompanied by lightning forced the two planes to veer off course and miss a refueling stop for the Curtiss. According to Coffey's contingency plan, they made an emergency landing at the first safe space within miles, a golf course.

Johnny and Coffey stepped out of the Hawk and watched Grover follow them and land. When the Bull Pup's engine shut off, the continuous drone of cicadas surrounded them. Insects buzzed in the hot air. The old-growth hickory forest bordering the fairway showed no signs of wind movement.

At the far end of the golf course, people began to spill out of the rust-red brick and ivy-covered clubhouse. Golfers running in their direction slowed when they saw the aviators were black. They approached slowly, half crouching as if they expected the biplane to explode.

"It's all right, folks," said Coffey. "The storm near Nashville put us off course. We're low on gas. As soon as we refuel, we're gone."

The manager and someone who could have been a bodyguard escorted Coffey to the clubhouse. He was taken to the kitchen phone, where he called the local aviation gas distributor.

The manager, dressed in fashionably draped slacks, a polo shirt, and two-tone shoes, could have been a movie star. Every sandy-colored hair on his head was perfect, and his chiseled chin gave him the air of social gravity.

When the fuel truck arrived, the driver took one look at the pilots and climbed back in the cab. "I ain't selling no gas to *Nigras*," he said to the club manager.

The manager climbed on the running board and spoke heatedly into the driver's ear. "If you want to keep your job, prominent members who do not approve of *Nigras* on their golf course will make sure this day is your last as delivery man." The driver stepped out of the truck.

"Fine, I brought out forty gallons. I want thirty-five dollars," said the driver.

Coffey coughed. Gas usually sold for less than fifteen cents a gallon, twenty-five cents, a highly inflated amount, was what he'd expected to pay. He had the money, but he could only take on ten gallons. "I'll pay it," he said.

"Like hell," whispered Johnny. "He's holding us up. I'm not paying thirty-five dollars for two dollars and fifty cents' worth of gas." He turned to driver. "I'll take it all. Load it in."

Coffey retrieved a small suitcase from the Curtiss, pulled out a white dress shirt, and began tearing it into long, thin ribbons. He went into the forest to gather sticks approximately two feet long. He paced out the longest stretch of fairway and placed the sticks twenty yards apart. When he finished, he said to Johnny, "The math isn't in our favor."

"Thirty-five dollars," said Johnny. The grins on the white golfers' faces made his stomach knot.

Coffey held up a handful of grass leaves and let them fall.

"There's no wind. We need a fifty more yards of runway or a decent headwind. Two hundred and fifty pounds of fuel... I'm a hundred and forty-five pounds. You're a hundred and fifty. We can't do it."

"I can't let them win this," Johnny said. "We're going to make the noon reception in Tuskegee, and I'm not going to leave anything behind for these yokels."

"There's a mowed field about a half mile from here. I'll meet you there, but you wait until those ribbons on the sticks start to move," said Coffey. "It was a new Arrow shirt, cost me a dollar ninety-eight."

With his own weight off the plane and a five-knot breeze, the Curtiss could clear the clubhouse and the hickory grove at the end of the fairway.

"Wait until a breeze makes the strips flutter, okay?" asked Coffey. Johnny nodded.

Once in the cockpit, Johnny didn't wait. The strips of cloth hung motionless. He taxied to the far end of the course, revved the engine to its max, released the brake, and roared down the fairway. The takeoff appeared solid with better-than-expected ground speed. He was airborne. From the ground, it looked as though he would clear the clubhouse––except for one unusually tall chimney. The right aileron clipped the very top of the chimney, making a dull clunk and sending bricks flying. The aileron broke away, trailing the plane like a kite tail.

"That's gonna cost ya," said the manager to Coffey.

The plane rapidly lost airspeed. The wing snagged on a hickory tree and made a slow-motion cartwheel, ending up upside down in a cotton field. Johnny wasn't hurt, but the plane's wings were broken.

Coffey ran up to the plane, appalled. When he reached the Curtiss, the trees began to sway as a late-morning zephyr finally swept across the Tennessee landscape.

Coffey stalked away. He wasn't talking. Grover arrived and put his hand on a broken wing that was held together only by the canvas skin; the first four feet swung like a gate.

"It's done for," said Grover.

Johnny sat down on the earth, his head still spinning.

"Are you hurt?"

"Yeah, my pride," muttered Johnny. He picked up a clod of earth and threw it out into the cotton field.

"Take the Bull Pup," offered Grover. "Walking over here, I've been thinking, I can't fly on by myself. You have to go. It's your class reunion. You do it."

Coming to his feet and dusting off his trousers, Johnny glanced in Coffey's direction.

"Come on, go," said Grover. "I'll talk to Coffey. He'll understand."

"Thank you," Johnny replied. He ran back to the Curtiss and reached under the seat for his cardboard suitcase. Coffey sat on a stump looking in the other direction.

"Tell him I'll make it good," said Johnny. With that, he ran across the road to the field where Grover had landed the Bull Pup and took off.

Coffey and Grover sent a telegram to Willa requesting additional funds to pay for the damaged chimney and to hire a truck to haul the battered Curtiss back to Chicago.

# 30

J ohnny mulled over his choices. He'd blown it and now felt obligated to do something to keep the flight from becoming a total disaster. He needed a stunt! But the plane he was flying wasn't the impressive Curtiss Hawk, capable of a hundred and seventy miles an hour. He was in a homebuilt Bull Pup, painted a flat, stovepipe black. He pulled out the flight plan with Coffey's directions.

What Johnny was concocting wasn't a first-time fantastic stunt—although a fourteen–hundred-mile roundtrip in less than twenty-four hours in a homebuilt monoplane, needing to refuel five more times with no running lights or instruments was certainly a stunt, albeit a really harebrained one. He reached into Coffey's envelope and to his surprise found a pencil with a sharp point. "That Coffey," he said out loud.

Using the back of the envelope to calculate, he figured that if he took off by 1:00 p.m. from Tuskegee, and if everything went right, he could be in Chicago around eight that evening. With an 8:20 sunset, he had a large enough window of visibility. If, for some reason, he were delayed, there would be a half hour of twilight and then a nearly full moon. For the last five miles to Harlem Airfield, he'd follow the lights on Highway 7. The idea was insanely dangerous. If he could get Willa to help, he could do it.

Johnny circled the Tuskegee campus. He'd spent four years in the buildings below. There were many more cars near the main building and only one horse-drawn buggy. Otherwise, everything looked the same. He saw a young man waving and pointing to the baseball diamond. An excited student reception committee gathered around home plate. As he landed, he saw the students running in his direction. He waved desperately for them to clear away from his path, but they waved back and kept coming. The Bull Pup had no brakes. He gave the engine one last burst of gas to gain ground speed, managed to change direction, and then cut the motor. When he'd finally rolled to a stop, a young woman rushed up and handed him a bouquet of flowers. A class officer hurried away to inform Dr. Patterson.

Dr. Patterson took a precious twenty minutes to make his appearance. He shook Johnny's hand. "Congratulations, young man." He looked to the northern horizon and asked, "When will the others be here?"

Johnny shrugged. "We could only come in two planes. "We...had mechanical troubles outside Nashville. I'd like to use a phone, right away, sir. I'll pay for the call. It's urgent."

"A photographer's on the way," Dr. Patterson insisted, holding on to Johnny's arm. "There he comes." Two hundred yards away, a photographer exited the administration building carrying a tripod and a wooden four-by-five view camera. Johnny squirmed impatiently as the photographer carried the heavy equipment all the way out to the baseball diamond. After setting down the tripod and leveling the camera, the photographer ran back and forth measuring distances and adjusting the aperture on the lens. He ducked under a black cloth and waved for them to do something. Johnny climbed aboard the Bull Pup, shook Dr. Patterson's hand, scrambled from the cockpit and began running toward the administration building.

"The students have planned several events for you this afternoon," called Dr. Patterson.

"No time, sir. We're trying to set a round-trip record, Chicago to Tuskegee in one day!" Johnny shouted.

Dr. Patterson frowned. "Dr. Moton isn't feeling well. He wants to say hello. So, don't go running off."

He stopped and reluctantly went back. "Yes, sir," he said, handing over the proposal for an aircraft mechanics program. "But I have to make this call," he begged. "I'll be back before Dr. Moton gets here. He sprinted to the administration building, leaving Dr. Patterson and the students with no idea what was going on.

The dean's secretary immediately connected Johnny to the *Chicago Defender*. She placed the collect call and handed Johnny the phone. "Willa, you heard what happened?" he half shouted into the phone. "Yes, I'm fine. I think I can do a round trip and at least do something worth putting in the paper. If I can take off in fifteen minutes, I can return to Chicago by eight at the latest." He listened for a moment. "If it's later, I know it'll be dark. The moon is near full, and if you can set some trash cans on fire alongside the runway and get about a dozen cars, I can land." He listened again. "I'll use the same airfields to refuel—but check on them for me. I'll be at my first refueling stop in about two hours. I know...I know...It's crazy. You'll do it?"

The dean's secretary still had no idea what was going on, but she was excited because Johnny was excited.

Back out at the baseball diamond, Dr. Robert Moton, Tuskegee's president, appearing frail and using a cane to steady himself, waited alongside Dr. Patterson.

"John, I see you're up to your old antics." Dr. Moton chuckled. "What is it now?"

Johnny knew Dr. Moton well. While a Tuskegee student ten years earlier, he'd repaired the president's automobile several times. He'd also taken the car for an unauthorized test drive with a young woman and was arrested by the local white deputy sheriff. Johnny smiled and shook Dr. Moton's hand. "Good to see you, sir. We couldn't get all the planes we needed, so we've changed plans. I'm doing fourteen hundred miles in less than twenty-four hours. It's the future, sir."

"In what? This contraption? I've seen faster-looking potbelly stoves," said Dr. Moton.

"Yes, sir, that's why it's going to be one for the books." Johnny climbed back into the Bull Pup and started the engine, taxied away from the crowd, and in a moment was gone.

Dr. Moton turned to Patterson, shaking his head. "Damn fool's going to kill himself."

Willa still had her copy of the flight plan. It took a dozen phone calls for her to alert the refueling stops. At his first stop, she left a message for Johnny telling him that the fourth airfield was closed. All attempts to reach the proprietors had failed.

Willa called Red Mack to tell him that Johnny was trying to set a round-trip record and they needed twenty cars to illuminate the runway. All eligible drivers, including Marie St. Clair, Harold Hurd, and Simeon were recruited to drive cars out to the field.

The third refueling stop was the dirt runway in Kentucky. Someone from the farmhouse came out on the porch and waved. However, no one came to help. Johnny pumped his own gas and left cash in a coffee can next to the tank. Moments later, he was in the air again.

When he got hungry, Johnny gloated for an instant that Coffey might have overlooked an important detail––there was nothing to eat. There were two bottles, one with water and thankfully, an empty milk bottle. He'd needed the empty bottle since before Tuskegee, but because he knew the container was there, he waited until he had a long stretch to fly and then he brought out the milk bottle and relived his bladder.

He had noticed earlier that a construction flaw caused the Bull Pup to drift to his right as it flew. Earlier, on the way to Tuskegee, without really thinking about it, he had automatically compensated to stay on course. On the return, mundane details like that became important. Using long, straight roads below as his guide, he constantly had to correct for the drift. The wind could also affect drift, but he had no way of measuring wind speed and direction. Using his watch and the compass to "dead reckon," he measured how much he went off course in the period of a half hour. It was approximately eight degrees.

As Willa had warned him, the fourth field was closed. He circled the deserted airfield and continued to his next refueling stop. Flying slowly to conserve fuel, he could see that the cars on the farm roads below traveled faster. He looked at his watch. It was nearly seven, and the shadows were getting long.

One half mile from the fifth and last refueling stop, the engine sputtered and went silent. He was out of gas. Johnny landed on long stretch of country road. Without the incessant aircraft motor, the silence was oppressive. Johnny was an hour behind schedule and famished. He would likely lose forty-five minutes of daylight walking to the refueling stop at Indiana State College. Fortunately, students waiting to refuel the Curtiss had seen him go down and soon arrived with enough gas to get him back to the campus. After refueling and swallowing a candy bar offered by one of the students, he asked if anyone had something that could work like a small pendulum. One young man had a brass key chain with an eight ball on the end. "I'll send it back to you," promised Johnny. He hung the key chain from the choke knob and drew a vertical pencil line on the dashboard, corresponding to the angle of the chain.

Johnny pushed the plane to its top speed of a hundred and twenty miles an hour and followed State Highway 7. He banked the plane and saw that the eight ball at the end of the keychain swung appropriately. At least he could tell when his wings were level. This crude setup, along with the compass and flashlight were his only instruments.

The full moon rose and peeked in and out from behind dense clouds. He watched the gathering clouds as they changed hues. Finally, all the colors drained from the sky and the moon became obscured for interminable minutes. He realized during the dark intervals that for a pilot, this was as bad as it could get. With no visual reference points on the ground and only his crude instruments, he had increased his chances for failure and possibly death. He made half-hour steering adjustments to compensate for drift.

During a dark interval, the Bull Pup brushed a treetop, sending a jolt of adrenaline though his body. He flew higher. Then he saw a horizon; the moon appeared, and he saw he had reached the end of a weak weather front. The moon reappeared, but as Johnny scanned the landscape, no road lights or towns were visible. For the next twenty minutes, he flew over forests and fields and nothing else.

Finally, the highway lights came into view. He hoped it was Highway 7. More than two and a half hours late, he had no idea what waited on the ground. He followed the lights on the road until he recognized Harlem Airfield. As he circled the airfield, to his relief, he saw people running from car to car turning on the headlights. As he began his approach, with the cars spaced exactly twenty yards apart, the entire stretch of runway was illuminated. Red Mack's radio station had a man standing by the pay telephone to announce his arrival. A photographer from the *Defender* raced out and caught Johnny climbing out of the Bull Pup.

The following morning, Enoch Waters made the most of it. "Pilot Flies over Jim Crow!" shouted the headline in the *Defender*. A smaller headline read: "Amazing! 1,460 Miles in Less Than 18 Hours in an Experimental Aircraft. Is This the Future?" Willa had written those headlines.

If Willa had any hard feelings about not being part of the flight, she didn't show it. Coffey and Grover returned two days later in the truck hauling the Curtiss. Coffey couldn't help feeling resentful. His best friend had ignored his advice, crashed their plane, become a celebrity, and was now spending a great deal of time with Willa.

# 31

Nearly every issue of the *Chicago Defender* contained articles about the activities at Harlem Airfield, usually accompanied by photographs of attractive women standing by an airplane. Black newspapers across the country readily reprinted Enoch Waters' pieces. No one noticed that while the young women in the articles were different, they wore Janet's leather flight gear and goggles in every photo, Willa and Janet being the most photographed.

Smaller community newspapers, such as the *Mobile Beacon*, relied on big-city newspapers like the *Defender* for access to national news stories. As a reporter and editor, Enoch Waters's articles were well known in the race circuit. Most of his pieces dealt with injustice or tragedy. Enoch had traveled the South reporting on the appeal trials for the Scottsboro Boys, nine black teenagers accused of raping two white women. Even with significant evidence that the young men were innocent, the trials had concluded with harsh convictions for all. In the two years following the Scottsboro Boys' arrest, violence against black men rose dramatically. Sixty-seven black men were murdered at horrific public lynchings, including two of the innocent Scottsboro boys. Few of the pieces about black pilots in Chicago qualified as national news, but smaller newspapers published them because they brightened the society pages.

It was Johnny's coverage that probably drew the most readers, since they at least qualified as public interest articles. Congressman P. H. Moynihan, who represented Chicago's Second Congressional district, nominated twenty-eight-year-old John Robinson for a commission in the Army Air Corps. Enoch knew Moynihan was up for reelection, and the gesture was an attempt to win support from black voters. But the nomination had particular resonance because Johnny was qualified in every way to be an army pilot, except that he was black. In barbershops and beauty parlors, Enoch's pieces had people asking the questions he'd raised: "Why can't black pilots join the military? There are black doctors, black infantrymen, black truck drivers. Why not black aviators?"

As an unexpected result of Johnny's articles, the *Defender* started receiving three or more letters a day from young women across the nation inquiring about Johnny's marital status. Was he dating Willa? Since they had been photographed together on two occasions, the readers wanted to know. Enoch printed two or three of the best letters every week. The thought crossed his mind for a fleeting moment that he should probably do and say nothing about relationships because readers were projecting their own interpretations on the photographs. Enoch wrote that so far as he knew, there was no romantic link between Johnny and Willa. By the time that denial made the social page, no one believed it, and circulation went up. In the following days, letters piled up, demanding confirmation of the nonrelationship. One letter writer passionately claimed she alone was Johnny's real and only true love. This went on for several weeks, and

Enoch made no attempt to put an end to it. During the entire gossip episode, Coffey's name never made it into print.

A week after the botched flight to Tuskegee, Johnny did his best to patch things up with his friend. He sought Coffey out and found him working on the Curtiss.

"I wouldn't have done what you did," said Coffey, without looking up or breaking his concentration on stretching a piece of canvas across the wing frame. "You should be dead. That was three crashes." He took a hammer from his back pocket and began to tack the canvas in place.

"Come on; it was only my second. If I had waited for a breeze, who knows?" said Johnny.

"If you had waited twenty minutes, we could have flown out on that ten-knot breeze." The sharp banging of the hammer made Johnny wince.

"Maybe. Or we could have waited until sunset. The breeze didn't last." Coffey hammered louder, Johnny raised his volume. "By the time I started the engine and warmed it up, that breeze would have been gone. Who knows? Then we'd be three guys in two airplanes taking two days to fly to Tuskegee. Setting a record in a mosquito like the Bull Pup—that's a story."

"Go sell that baloney down the street! You could have idled into next year with the gas you had on board." Coffey finished hammering. He looked up. "What about the mess you left behind?"

Apart from the unpainted canvas covering the multiple restorations, the Curtiss looked ready to fly.

"I made a mistake. I know," said Johnny. He handed Coffey a can of combination primer, paint, and sealer called *dope*. Coffey opened the can and began painting the raw canvas.

Sensing that Coffey wasn't about to stop work to have a conversation, Johnny picked up a brush and joined in doping the unpainted surfaces.

"Back there in that field," Johnny said. "I saw their snickering faces. I got angry. Spur of the moment, I saw that takeoff in my head and knew I could do it. I was trying to save the event. I wanted to show those bastards."

"I wanted you to show those bastards, too," said Coffey. "Except Grover and I were left behind, humiliated. For thirty-five dollars of gas, we're now in debt for nearly nine hundred. They stuck it to us on that chimney."

A clatter of giggling and foot shuffling drew their attention to the door. Three young women were waiting to speak to Johnny.

"I'll make it good. I couldn't have done it without you," whispered Johnny. "You're the master mechanic. You made the Bull Pup safe in ways Grover will never know. But I know your work. I used your flight plan. I knew about the tool kit under the seat. And when I needed a pencil, I had one and a flashlight. From now on, everybody's going to know." Johnny turned to the waiting fans. "Ladies, this is the genius who lets me fly, Cornelius Coffey, master mechanic and aviator."

The young women giggled and applauded. Coffey shook his head, embarrassed.

Coffey was too busy to stay angry. As well as continuing with his regular duties at the clubhouse and maintaining the Schumacher School airplanes, he'd been hired as the first black instructor to teach at the Curtis Wright School of Aeronautics.

Everywhere he went, Johnny was besieged. When would he make another stunt-flying exhibition? The few people who had actually seen him test fly the Wilkerson W-44 enhanced his reputation as a daredevil pilot. But Johnny had no a follow-up plan. He didn't even have the same access to the Curtiss he'd had before.

As soon as the dope dried, the Curtiss was booked solid. Johnny wrote to Dr. Patterson at Tuskegee Institute inquiring about his proposal to teach aircraft mechanics. Weeks passed with no response.

⁓

Enoch purposely stopped printing the letters that came from teenage girls, and except for some poor soul who repeatedly sent letters claiming that she was Johnny's one true love, the letters stopped coming. One letter did come as a surprise. Opening an oversized envelope hand stamped with a diplomatic seal and embossed with a Lion of Judah in gold leaf, Enoch found a letter from the Ethiopian ambassador, Dr. Melaku Beyan, requesting an introduction to the pilots at Harlem Airfield.

On the appointed day, Enoch Waters appeared at the clubhouse with a tall man about thirty-two years old with the bearing of an aristocrat. Willa, Coffey, Johnny, Janet, Enoch Waters, and Fred Schumacher gave Dr. Beyan a tour of the Harlem facilities. What interested him were the airplanes and the maintenance areas. He noted with satisfaction that Coffey was an instructor at the Curtis Wright School and that both Johnny and Coffey were certified mechanics and aviators.

"That's perfect," Dr. Beyan repeated several times.

After Johnny and Willa put on an air show, Janet Harmon hosted a reception in the hangar, where the youthful ambassador addressed the group in his carefully enunciated English.

"Thank you for this opportunity. I am here to propose a special relationship. And with what I've seen today, I am greatly impressed. You have here a training ground for an industry that I believe is necessary in my country, Ethiopia. My government owns over twenty aircraft that can be put to use immediately. All that is needed to set up a commercial airline service are pilots and mechanics, the very elements Chicago can provide."

Dr. Beyan didn't have to do a lot of convincing. The Chicago aviators were well aware that outside the United States, especially in the Caribbean, black pilots routinely flew commercial aircraft.

"We have a man from Trinidad, Colonel Hubert Julian, who has consented to head the venture if I can provide mechanics and additional pilots."

Everyone had heard of Hubert Julian, the first black man to fly solo across the Atlantic in 1929, two years after Charles Lindbergh. In 1930, he had passed through Chicago with a barnstorming flying circus called The Five Blackbirds. Julian had the reputation of being an unabashed self-promoter and a bit of a con. He had been out of the headlines for at least three years, so Dr. Beyan's mention of his name came as a surprise.

"Our government has received inquiries from France and Germany. However, the emperor is looking for an African presence like yourselves," Dr. Beyan continued.

"Thank you," said Willa. "But how would this work?"

"Let me advise you that at the moment, there is no airplane service to Ethiopia. When I write a letter, it will go by diplomatic mail on a ship to our embassy in France. It will then be taken by courier on a ship to Djibouti, then by modern train up the mountains to Addis Ababa, and finally delivered to the emperor, his Royal Highness Haile Selassie. I will put the highest priority on the correspondence, but understand, getting my letter to Addis Ababa could take six weeks."

After the visit by Dr. Beyan, neither Johnny nor Enoch heard a word from him. Willa wrote to the Ethiopian Embassy thanking Dr. Beyan for his time but received no reply.

After five months passed with no word from Dr. Beyan, the Challengers pursued other projects. Congressman Moynihan's letter asking for Johnny's commission in the Army Air Corps was published in the *Congressional Record*. Enoch Waters dutifully wrote about it, though after Moynihan lost his bid for reelection, nothing further came of it.

At the Challengers' November meeting, Waters reported on what he'd learned about Dr. Beyan.

"I'm afraid I don't have much. The Ethiopian Embassy is a part-time operation. Our young doctor's apartment is listed as the embassy address. And he is a medical resident at Johns Hopkins," said Waters.

"What does that mean?" asked Willa. "Is he legit?"

"Maybe. He is a member of the Abyssinian royal family, which is quite large." Waters shook his head. "I think the doctor means well, but who knows? There are a lot more questions than answers."

By December, the Ethiopian ambassador's visit was out of everyone's mind. For Coffey, the winter's first hard frost was something he'd looked forward to. He'd finished work on his cold-weather carburetor. When all other aviation activity was at a standstill, Johnny taxied the Curtiss Hawk out of the hangar and onto the runway. The crew in Schumacher's building hurried to the windows when they heard the sound of an engine. The temperature was far below freezing. Fred Schumacher saw the plane take off, put on his overcoat, and trotted over to the clubhouse.

"Why is your plane flying, and none of my engines will turn over? It's eighteen degrees out there."

"Outside of your heated office, it's eighteen degrees. It's even colder in the hangars. I'm testing a new carburetor," answered Coffey, leaning back on his chair.

"What brand? I want one for all my planes."

"No brand. It's a test prototype." Coffey opened a desk drawer and took out a something wrapped in a clean cotton cloth. He unwrapped a carburetor and handed it to Schumacher.

"Your design?"

"Yes."

"What are you going to do with it?"

"I've licensed it."

"Who's going to produce it?"

"BO and F Manufacturing."

"I've heard of them." Schumacher laughed. "BO and F means 'Back Order and Forget.'"

Coffey laughed. "So, you know Glenn Cartwright's joke. He's made me an offer. BO and F makes the molds for many brands of carburetors."

"And you've got a patent for this?"

"Yes, pending," said Coffey, taking back his prototype, "Glenn's starting production on the Curtiss model now. We still have to do tests."

"As soon as you start manufacturing, I want one in all my planes," said Schumacher.

Coffey rewrapped the carburetor and put it back in the desk drawer. "You'll be the first. Count on it," he said, closing the drawer.

It had always been Coffey's intention to use his earnings to buy his own airplane. With the one thousand eight hundred dollars he'd received as an advance against royalties for the carburetor, he purchased a secondhand Stearman Model 75 trainer with dual controls. It needed work, but what else was new? Coffey felt like a twelve-year-old with a new toy. He eagerly looked forward to the end of his workday so he could get back to replacing the engine and reworking all the control mechanisms. When he finished, he owned one of the best training aircraft available anywhere.

Enoch Waters finally wrote a profile of Coffey for the *Chicago Defender*, including a photo of him and the new plane. Waters called Coffey an inventor, pilot, and entrepreneur. Several aircraft manufacturers licensed the cold-weather innovation for their carburetors, but not all. The bigger companies worked on their own cold-weather designs. They carefully scrutinized Coffey's patent application and borrowed from European engineers working on the same problem. They subsequently patented their own designs--and the big-time lawsuits began. Coffey and BO&F Manufacturing found it too expensive to compete with the big companies. Fortunately, they'd made some money, just not as much as they'd hoped.

In late December, Dr. Beyan reappeared at a meeting of the officers of the Challengers Aero Club. An astonishing couple accompanied him, Zema, a tall, elegant woman dressed in a flowing traditional dress in the yellow, green, and red colors of Ethiopia, and her husband, Dr. Melku, the acting Ethiopian consul in Chicago. After formal introductions, Dr. Beyan announced that he was there to hand deliver the official invitation from Emperor Haile Selassie for John C. Robinson and Cornelius Coffey to come to Ethiopia and begin the process of forming a commercial airline service. "The embassy has no funds for your passage, but once you are in Ethiopia, you will be guests of the emperor," said Dr. Beyan.

Later that week, at an emergency meeting, the Challengers' officers proposed a plan. Because Coffey was needed at home to continue training mechanics and pilots, Johnny would lead the way. He would assess Ethiopia's needs and make arrangements for the pilots, mechanics, and support teams soon to follow. Janet advanced Johnny the money to travel to Ethiopia.

# 32

I n January 1935, Johnny took the train to New York and booked passage to Marseille, France, on the *SS Flyderborg*, a Danish merchant ship. The vessel took twenty days to cross the Atlantic and enter the Mediterranean. From Marseille, he caught a rusty passenger boat to Beirut, Lebanon, stopping at larger cities along the way. Boarding a ferry to Port Said, Egypt, he continued through the Suez Canal into the Red Sea and the port city, Djibouti, Ethiopia. The final leg found Johnny in a first-class cabin on the "modern" train to Addis Ababa. The locomotive and cars had been used in France before the Great War of 1914. From the train, Johnny saw mud huts and children herding goats. Camels standing near the tracks, if startled, could run faster than the train. A single track stretched through a vast desert and then twisted and rocked up mountainsides seven thousand feet above sea level to Addis Ababa.

As the train chugged into the capital, Johnny sensed his journey was more than a visit to a faraway land. He had traveled back in time. Walking out of the station, he saw men in robes wearing scimitars in their belts. While a few automobiles were parked near the station's entrance, camels, horses, and donkeys were common transportation. The high mountain air smelled of cinnamon, cloves, and manure. *I'm back in ancient times,* thought Johnny.

"Mr. Robinson! Mr. Robinson!"

Johnny turned to see a young man in an officer's uniform running in his direction. "Mr. Robinson, I am honored to meet you. I am Lieutenant Abebe Kafele." The young man's accent was so strong it took a moment for Johnny to decipher what he'd said. Young Kafele had an earnest smile and a firm handshake. Feeling definitively out of place in an extremely foreign land, Johnny immediately liked the young officer.

"Mr. Robinson, I am assigned as your translator and guide. You have been registered at the European Hotel where you will find food much like you are accustomed to. I am also your driver. Where would you like to go first?"

"I want to see the aircraft," said Johnny. "That's why I'm here."

Lieutenant Kafele took Johnny's luggage and placed it in the boot of a green Mercedes government car with an Ethiopian insignia of a lion painted on the car doors. Once out of the government and business districts, the streets became dirt roads. The automobile's tires bounced in and out of the deep furrows rutted by animal-drawn wagons.

Reaching the outskirts of Addis Ababa, the young officer escorted Johnny to a long building that looked as if it were designed to stable horses and wagons, not a fleet of airplanes.

What he found was disheartening. Six damaged Junker F8s and eight Fokker fighters, all World War I vintage, lined up like neglected corpses. The Fokkers, considered Germany's finest pursuit fighters during the Great War, were deteriorated beyond repair. The Junker F8s hadn't been flown in two or three years. Johnny could only imagine what he would find when he opened the engine blocks. He'd brought along a set of hand tools, but nowhere did he see any provision for maintenance and repair of aircraft: no winches, ladders, or tools. The runway was nothing more than an open field used for public assemblies.

That night, Johnny settled into the European Hotel. The decor was spare and clean, and the floors tiled. The bathroom was down the hall, its toilet a challenging six-inch hole in the floor. When he went downstairs for dinner, he noted the respect he received from the hotel staff and the aloof indifference of the Europeans.

Several of the European guests looked like businessmen; two were a bit more rough and ready. Judging from their boots and heavy jackets, they could have been pilots, but their hands looked too clean to be those of mechanics. Lieutenant Kafele had told him there was a French pilot in Addis Ababa. Since the men in the heavy jackets ignored him, Johnny returned the favor.

Johnny spent most of the first night staring out over the city and wondering what he could do that the Europeans couldn't do. The following morning, he hiked out to the warehouse and went over the Junker F8s carefully. By the time Lieutenant Kafele arrived, Johnny had finished the inventory. He knew he could restore one aircraft, and there was a fair supply of spare parts on hand for backup.

"What's going on?" he asked the lieutenant. "I was under the impression some planning had been done and all that was needed was a person like myself to start the freight and passenger service."

The lieutenant looked pained. Trained by his position not to speak negatively, he apologized and said, "I am only a small cog in a big wheel. I don't have all the answers."

"I'm here at the invitation of Haile Selassie. When can I meet him?" asked Johnny.

"In due time. The emperor is at his retreat by the sea."

"I'd like to start restoring one of the Junker F8s," said Johnny.

"I will get you permission to proceed, but it will take a few days," answered the lieutenant.

Johnny learned that in Ethiopia, a few days meant weeks. It now made sense why Dr. Beyan could go nearly six months without a word and then not feel the least bit apologetic when he appeared with Selassie's invitation.

In the meantime, Johnny found a local blacksmith shop with wooden pulleys and ropes. Using a part of the barn he felt had the strongest support beams, he created the semblance of a hangar. Lifting the engines out of the planes, he could then pull the fuselage away so he could work on the motors.

It took three weeks before Lieutenant Kafele received clearance for Johnny to proceed. By then, he knew exactly which parts he needed and swiftly began cannibalizing the Junkers. Amazingly, the dry mountain air had preserved the wood and metal. The engine in one of the Junkers was in almost-new condition. Within a week, he had cobbled together a working plane.

"Where did you learn to work so fast?" asked Kafele in amazement.

"Fixing milk trucks."

"Do milk trucks fly in America? I studied in London. Milk lorries do not fly there."

"In Chicago, sometimes they do, depending on the milk." Johnny laughed.

Not getting the joke, Kafele smiled anyway.

The finished Junker was a four-seater capable of carrying a fair amount of cargo. If there was no cargo, additional passengers could sit on the floor. After the plane was restored and painted, it looked impressive. Of all the aircraft manufactured during World War I, the Junkers were probably the most modern in appearance. Unfortunately, the F8 was not one of them. It had a single wing above a boxy, wedge-shaped aluminum fuselage. The Junker F8s were respected as highly efficient aircraft, but they looked like boxcars.

Emperor Haile Selassie finally came out to the stable to watch Johnny fly. He didn't say anything. He simply watched from the shade of a large umbrella held by a member of his retinue. Later that day, Johnny was informed that the emperor had been pleased with the demonstration. Six weeks later, a millisecond in 1935 Ethiopian time, the emperor offered Johnny a commission as a colonel in the Ethiopian Army and issued him an Ethiopian passport, citizenship, and a salary. The pay and position were immediate, but before being commissioned a colonel, he had to wait for an official ceremony, which would come after instruction in Ethiopian history and culture.

During all the time he had been in Ethiopia, Hubert Julian's name had not been mentioned. Johnny finally confronted Lieutenant Kafele. "I thought Colonel Julian was supposed to be the head of the Ethiopian Air Force."

Kafele bowed his head and replied, "Mr. Julian is a *persona non grata*. He lost his commission because he crashed a new de Havilland Gyspy Moth biplane on the day of the emperor's coronation. The flight was supposed to be a demonstration of our modernity. The emperor was humiliated in front of the world's dignitaries."

"We were told by Dr. Beyan that Colonel Julian was in charge," said Johnny.

"Dr. Beyan lives in Washington. Because of his studies, he wasn't present for the coronation. As much as the emperor is concerned with progress, news travels slowly."

"Three years?"

"No one wanted to mention the humiliation."

Johnny's letters back to Chicago were upbeat, yet cautious. He wanted to keep everyone engaged, but before there was any commitment of Chicago aviation talent, Ethiopia had to order more planes. Letters from Willa pressed him for details; she wanted to know when hiring could begin. If getting permission to restore a Junker F8 took weeks, the process for buying a new aircraft was even slower. A French company was ready to take the order, but the proper models had to be selected and approved by officials who knew little about aviation. Johnny wrote that it might take as long as a year before Ethiopia saw a new plane. What he didn't mention in the letters was what he saw at the hotel and government offices; he counted seven new men at the hotel who were definitely pilots. They didn't speak to him, but when Johnny was in the lobby, they watched him intently.

⁂

One of Lieutenant Kafele's duties was to instruct Johnny about Ethiopian culture. There were no formal classes. On their flights over the Ethiopian landscape, the lieutenant pointed out that a battle took place here or a peace treaty was signed there. The Ethiopian kings could trace their lineage to the Queen of Sheba and King Solomon of the Bible. Ethiopian historical paintings resembled children's drawings to Johnny, and he said as much to the lieutenant. Kafele explained that the paintings were intended to appeal to children so they could learn the history of their people.

Whenever he could, Johnny pumped Abebe for information about the government bureaucracies and operations. Learning that if he wanted anything, he had to petition in writing, Johnny wrote a letter requesting to start flying service from Addis Ababa to Djibouti. The lieutenant translated the request into Amharic, the language of Ethiopia.

Johnny and the lieutenant were no longer on a formal basis. The name Abebe was so close to Abe, that Johnny shortened it. Abe called Johnny something that sounded like, "Colonel Ja*chonn*."

"Close enough," said Johnny.

Johnny, curious about new men appearing at the European Hotel, asked, "What's going on there, Abe? I see pilots showing up. There are seven, by my count. Today, I was at the ministry to receive my pay, and I saw officials, who usually sit on their butts all day, rushing around like their pants were on fire."

Abebe looked sheepishly guilty. "I'm sorry for that. That has nothing to do with you. Things are happening which forced us to change our plans. We think--the *emperor* thinks--we might have to go to war. I gave your petition to the emperor requesting to start a flight service. He read it. You will receive a reply from him granting you the exclusive right to begin a mail and shipping service to Djibouti. The answer is yes; you are to build an airstrip in Djibouti near the postal office and customs building."

Johnny probably should have asked Abe about the possibility of war, but he was too pleased by the challenge given to him. It did strike him as unusual that his petition had been approved overnight. The creaky wheels of government were suddenly turning as if they'd been lubricated. The royal decree gave him a small budget, and with that, he hired a tractor with a grading blade in Djibouti. He did a lot of the tractor work himself until he realized he was depriving a local man of the job. He had the man scrape out a flat area near the Red Sea. He contracted Djibouti workers to construct an adobe building to house the new shipping office. A postal clerk was assigned to accept packages both into and out of Djibouti.

The first few weeks of flying mail and passengers from Addis Ababa to Djibouti were plagued with misunderstandings, most having to do with what Johnny saw as a conflict between honesty and bribery.

"I'm being hit with handling and security fees--bribes," complained Johnny.

Abe spoke without apology. "These are not bribes, as you say. What you must understand is that all business negotiations are based on long-standing, even ancient, traditions. In London, I had to leave a gratuity for the waiter who served me. How is this different?"

"But everyone is on the take--even the clerk who's on the payroll."

"It's the way honest men are kept honest," said Abe.

# 33

I n June 1935, the Sunday air shows resumed at Harlem Airfield. Willa promoted them with flyers tacked on telephone posts, a newspaper article in the *Defender*, and a week of very important radio mentions by Roxy Moss. Willa booked the Flying Hobos, a flying acrobatic clown act, the first week and Willie "Suicide" Jones the following week. Her first two Sundays drew twelve hundred people. She programmed the big acts after demonstration flights by the local pilots. Only Willa and Lola Jones had licenses and performed; however, Marie St. Clair and Janet Harmon were introduced as student pilots. Grover Nash, Coffey, and Dale White were the male participants. Dale White, the quiet young man from Indianapolis, put the Curtiss through a choreographed flying routine. He rocked the plane back and forth as if he were skating through the sky and followed that with swirls, slow barrel rolls, and descending spirals.

As he watched, Suicide Jones leaned over to Willa and said, "I'm going to steal that routine. I can get a public address system to play the 'Blue Danube Waltz' while I do what he's doing, and the ladies will love it. Kiss that boy for me."

Local police were present to maintain order and control traffic, and Fred Schumacher got a piece of the gate. Roxy Moss, promoting her radio program, served ice cream cones from the Brook View Dairy ice cream cart.

Janet had shown up wearing her flight suit, although it was ninety degrees and really too warm for leather and a silk scarf. Willa assumed Janet was dressed like that to show she was part of the team. But after the show, as Willa settled accounts at the end of the demonstration day, Janet paced, obviously discontented.

Coffey pretended not to notice and logged the hours the planes had flown. Chauncey didn't look up as he closed out the grill. They didn't want any part of Janet's moods.

"You got something to say?" asked Willa.

"I had people come today to see me fly. I've flown that plane. I could have done it."

"You don't have a student license. If anything bad had happened and the authorities found out about it, Coffey would lose his credentials."

"It's still my plane…"

"That doesn't mean you can fly in front people who could shut us down. Janet, all you have to do is take your flight test with Coffey; that's all."

"Now that Johnny's in Africa…" Janet started and stopped herself. "What's going to happen with the Curtiss payments? Coffey has a new plane he's using for training. The Curtiss isn't earning a cent."

"Janet, that's not true," responded Willa. "Have we missed a payment? Do you think we're deserting you? The Curtiss is the heart of the Challengers' bylaws."

"Well, I want to know," said Janet. "Am I covered?"

"What's wrong? You know better than anyone else that the Curtiss Hawk is the responsibility of the members. Are we in agreement about that?"

Janet ground her teeth and muttered an acidic, "Yes."

"The Curtiss is booked for the next three months at rates that will allow us to make double payments on the loan. I know you had to make payments while the Curtiss was being repaired. We did the best we could."

"With John gone, I feel we lack leadership."

"Janet? Coffey is in charge. He's accountable for every-thing," Willa shot back. "If you'd come to the meetings, you'd know what's going on. Is this about not being part of today's program, or is it about the money?"

"Absolutely, it's about the money. Without my money, none of this would be possible. I should get some consideration."

With that, Coffey stood up. "Janet, your money bought us a plane. It was brave and smart of you. You're right that your money has gotten us here. However, we make the payments, and the reason we're allowed to use your plane is because I have the licenses making it legal. That's why I'm here."

"If you're going to use the Challenger facilities for your new plane, you have to hand over those earnings to the Challengers."

"Janet, that's where we disagree," said Coffey. "My own plane is licensed to me and not the club. I believe I should be able to keep the earnings from my own airplane. I pay rent on these facilities, and the Challengers are my guests. You take classes at discounted rates, and considering the low Challenger membership fee, it's a great deal." It wasn't often Coffey let himself go. "Remember eighteen months ago when the storm wrecked the Curtiss?" he continued. "No one took a salary until it was fixed."

Frustrated, Janet sat down. He was right. No one was trying to take advantage of her. She'd taken flight instruction exclu-sively from Johnny. That was her choice. Coffey's no-nonsense teaching style intimidated her. She'd taken one lesson with him after Johnny left. He demanded she go through the standard checklist and flight protocols that Johnny had always done for her. Coffey said, "Don't be afraid to break a fingernail. It's either short nails or your life…And after so many lessons why are you still carrying the checklist?…You should have the protocols memorized so they're second nature…"

Chauncey saw an opening to lighten things up. "Hey, guys, I have an idea. What if there was this daredevil parachute finish? I read about how in France, they have contests to see who can hit a spot on the ground using parachutes."

"You know somebody that will do it for nothing?" asked Willa skeptically.

"I've taken lessons and have a parachute rig; I've learned to pack it myself. I can jump next Sunday and promote the contest for the following week. The fella I got the parachute from can't come out this weekend. He's available the following week. He'll do it. I'm certain."

Willa, normally very cautious, trusted him. "You pack your own parachute?"

Chauncey grinned. "Yes." After all, he was the son of a famous poet, and he had his own parachute and flight suit.

"What do you think, Coffey? He has his own gear."

Coffey nodded.

Among the new visitors to Harlem Airfield were Willa's ex-husband, Wilbur Hardaway, and his new wife. The Hardaway sisters and their boyfriends were already regulars. Willa's reunion with Wilbur was amicable. She recognized Wilbur's second wife as the ginger-haired teen from Roosevelt High School. Of course, she was no longer a teen. She wore dark-colored clothing similar to the other Hardaway women. Wilbur, for his part, had settled down. He never ran for reelection as alderman, but he did become a successful real estate broker in Gary.

For the last event on the Sunday schedule, Willa piloted the parachute jump. Stepping out on the wing, Chauncey shouted above the engine noise, "I hope this works! I've never done it before!"

"Wh-*what*? Are you crazy?" Willa shrieked. "Get back in the plane," she ordered. "Forget this fool idea. Get back! Your mother will kill me...Stop! Get back inside!" she screamed so hard she hurt her throat.

Chauncey jumped.

Willa's mouth formed the word, "Stop," but nothing came out. Her eyes wide with panic, she watched him fall. In seconds, he became a speck and she lost Chauncey in the mottled background. She could feel the blood leaving her face. This was the end of the Challengers, her flying career, and everything she held dear. Unexpectedly, the parachute blossomed white and round. Her panic abated somewhat. Chauncey landed and raised his arm, accepting the applause from the spectators. High above, Willa closed her eyes in prayer.

After the show, she cornered Chauncey in the clubhouse, her voice so hoarse she could only whisper, "You moron! What was going through your thick skull surprising me like that? I should have Coffey throw you out of here for this. We don't take unnecessary chances! Never. Never. Never. And we don't do anything here without permission from Coffey. If anything goes wrong, he's responsible. If he loses his license for your stupidity, you hurt everybody. And what do I tell your mother? I let her precious son jump out of a plane? You lied to me. You said you'd had lessons."

"I'm sorry," said Chauncey. "I did have lessons…well, one. I learned how to land. I figured jumping was the easy part."

Coffey entered the clubhouse. He'd heard a good part of what Willa had said.

"Willa's right," said Coffey. "We don't take chances. Flying is dangerous enough without adding risk."

Chastened, Chauncey's eyes fixed on the floor. "I'm really sorry. I thought it would be a great surprise, a new gimmick for the air show. I promise I won't do anything again without your permission. Let me stay."

"You can stay as long as you keep that promise," replied Coffey, crossing his arms emphatically. "So, tell me, what was it like jumping from an airplane?"

"Euphoric." Chauncey's eyes brightened. "I could hear the plane in the distance. The people's voices below were so clear. And for a few wonderful moments, I thought I heard the sound of the universe."

"You guys are nuts," Willa whispered hoarsely as she left the room. "You know that? You're nuts."

The following morning, a photo of Chauncey holding an armful of parachute silk appeared in the *Chicago Defender*. The parachute jump became a regular routine at the Sunday air shows, with Chauncey adding a terrifying theatrical twist. He'd jump from the plane, open his parachute, and descend gracefully for several hundred yards. Then he'd unbuckle that first parachute and let it dramatically slip away. He was falling without a parachute! The crowd screamed in terror. For five or six seconds, his arms flailed wildly. Then, just as dramatically, he'd open a second seat parachute, and a collective sigh of relief would rise from the crowd.

# 34

Colonel Robinson expanded the flying service from the weekly mail to Djibouti, by adding a similar service from Addis Ababa to Adwa on the border of Eritrea with a stop at Gonder near Lake T'ana Hayk, the source of the Blue Nile. On the rough terrain below, this five-hour flight would have taken a month or more by camel.

He and Lieutenant Abe flew past centuries-old churches and monasteries carved out of the base of mountainsides. They also were among the first to see the breathtaking waterfalls of the Blue Nile from a plane. The depth and width of the panorama, the massive flow of water feeding two of the world's greatest rivers, made him feel like a witness to a force of nature.

Maps were few and sketchy. Only major mountain ranges and rivers appeared, while numerous significant geographic features and villages went uncharted. The terrain wasn't the predictably well-mapped Illinois landscape with all roads and towns marked. One could easily lose orientation over the vast forests and endless, unchanging deserts. The magnificent buttes of the mountain range in Lalibela were instantly recognizable. The peaks, ten to fourteen thousand feet above sea level, were nearly always shrouded in clouds. The valleys were such a labyrinth that if a cloud obscured a key landmark, Johnny could get hopelessly lost. He had to plan his course through the mountains, because he couldn't fly over them. Ethiopia was twice the size of Texas. If he went down, it could be months, even years, before anyone would find him.

Two rivers, the Blue Nile and the Tekeze Wenz, were his major landmarks. At a village by a wide bend in the Blue Nile, the entire population ran out to wave at his weekly flyovers. In respect for their turnout, Johnny circled the village and dipped the Junker's wings before continuing his flight. Occasionally, he'd drop mail or government announcements. The children would race for the package. The child retrieving the sack had the honor of waving at him, and Johnny would dip the Junker's wings.

As an officer with a commission, he was assigned a squad of twelve men and a sergeant from the motor pool to serve as his aircraft mechanic crew. Lieutenant Kafele was not under his command, but he was nearly always at Johnny's side translating. Under Johnny's supervision, the men disassembled and reassembled several of the Junkers in the stable. He had them name all the parts, and with the lieutenant's help, he created a dictionary. All usable parts, especially tires, were removed from the Junkers, wrapped in cloth, cataloged, and stored in a dry room.

He often ferried generals and government officials to regional meetings. With Lieutenant Kafele at his side, Johnny felt the uneasy sensation that his every decision and action was being judged. Without any advance notice, Emperor Selassie sent a tailor to the hotel to measure Johnny for uniforms. His epaulets were woven from gold thread made especially for the military elite.

He soon learned that his custom-made uniforms were prepared for a reason. Lieutenant Kafele delivered Johnny's first official orders. Emperor Salassie planned to take a six-day tour of his country by airplane and wanted Colonel Robinson to be his pilot. Lieutenant Kafele provided the itinerary listing the towns and villages the emperor wanted to visit.

Sitting next to Johnny where he could see his domain from the air, Emperor Haile Selassie asked, "I understand you're loquacious. Why are you so quiet with me?"

"Sir, I don't know how to address you. I've discovered it's difficult for me to say, 'Your Highness.'"

"I'm not offended. You may call me, sir. That is how you should address a superior military officer. Is it not?"

"Yes, sir."

"You're a thoroughly modern man, Colonel Robinson. But you're still not an entirely free man. Perhaps that will come while you're here."

Lieutenant Kafele and a general sat in the two additional seats behind the pilot while the emperor's bodyguard huddled on the floor with the baggage.

With this tour, Johnny became a celebrity in Ethiopian society. As an officer in the army, he was required to wear his uniform in public. People buzzed, "There goes the emperor's trusted pilot."

On Johnny's visit to a village near Lake Abaya, an elder with a long beard and dressed in ceremonial robes signifying his high position in the community offered Colonel Robinson a dowry of seventy goats if he would marry one of his three daughters. Lieutenant Kafele declined for Johnny, saying that while the colonel was honored by the offer, he was occupied with his duties to the emperor.

Later, Johnny, joking with the lieutenant, said, "I liked the oldest daughter. How old do you think she was?"

"Sixteen. Probably younger. Of course, then you'd have to marry them all. You can't break up a set. And I'm afraid you'd have to live as a herder by Lake Abaya because the girls know nothing outside their tribe."

"As good as it sounds, I'm a city boy."

Back in Chicago, Janet Harmon organized investment support for the Abyssinian Air Transport Service—AATS, as the venture was called in Illinois.

Johnny's letters were short on details for Enoch Waters's *Defender* articles, so he had to elaborate liberally. When Johnny wrote that he had started a route to Djibouti, Enoch wrote that the Abyssinian Air Transport Service would soon start service to all major cities in the Middle East. Johnny's letter that a small mud-brick building had been built to house shipping and travelers became, in Enoch's prose, news that an international airport was under construction in Djibouti. Mail poured in from all over the United States from black and white pilots and mechanics expressing interest in traveling to Ethiopia.

In October 1935, Janet arrived in Ethiopia to bring good news about investors. She had put together a group of wealthy black entrepreneurs who saw an opportunity of getting into aviation outside the United States' borders. Johnny met her at the train station. Their entrance into the European Hotel was an occasion. Guests came out to see the American woman arriving for a visit with the emperor's personal pilot. Hotel staff hustled to take her luggage to her room.

She noticed that Johnny was even more self-assured than before. He spoke enough Amharic to order food and drink sent to his room, and to Janet, he looked delicious in his uniform.

"Appearances are very important here," he told Janet privately as they walked up the stairs. "We're being watched, and the royal family will hear all the details. So we have to — you know — behave."

"Johnny, what are you talking about? Aren't we having dinner in your room?" she whispered hopefully.

"Yes, and at all times, there will be a servant present providing for our every need," he added.

Unlike the sparsely furnished room Johnny had had when he first came to the European Hotel, this suite was decorated with hand-carved, locally made furniture. Janet opened the doors to the balcony and looked down. Squat mud-brick dwellings spread like a maze below, and except for an occasional two-story building or a steep hill, they continued to the horizon.

"It's like being in biblical times," she said.

"That's what I thought, too. It takes getting used to," he replied. "Ethiopia condones slavery."

"Slaves? What do you mean?"

"People are owned. They usually work as servants or concubines."

"My, I didn't know. Is it awful? I mean, it's so beautiful here. We're near the Equator, and it's only seventy degrees. You have a view of a city that's three thousand years old."

"Three thousand years is probably how long they've had slavery. It's part of the culture. Occasionally, I hear women screaming at their slaves, as if they were trash, not much different from a white foreman I met when I was a kid. I haven't seen anyone lynched, but I don't see everything. It could be like some say back home, 'Spare the rod and spoil the slave.'" Reflecting for a moment, Johnny then took out his wallet. "I want to pay you back for the trip," he said, peeling off twelve one-hundred-dollar bills. There was a precision about everything he did.

Janet felt she was watching a completely different person. "John," she protested, "I didn't expect you to pay this back now. It's part of the investment package. I have a presentation to make. She reached for her purse and took out a contract bound with blue paper. "This proposal represents a hell of a lot of work. I have fifteen thousand dollars to bring over a pilot and a mechanic, with tools that will work for the Abyssinian Air Transport Service. They will work under your direction, as the vice president of the AATS."

The meal arrived. Johnny took the contract and placed it on the bench next to him.

Two male servants laid out the plates of food: minced cucumber, white flat bread, yellowish beans, and a stewed meat. The aromas were completely alien to Janet.

"What is that?" she asked.

Johnny tore a piece of the white flat bread and took a piece of lamb and handed it to Janet. "This is mitmita, sort of a lamb stew," he said.

"Oh my. This is so piquant and so good. What's that flavor? Not like any lamb stew I've had before," Janet said, trying to cozy up.

Quickly indicating with his eyes that the servants were watching, Johnny went on, "The spiciness is from some hot African chili peppers, cardamom, cloves, cumin, and different herbs. The ingredients vary depending on the cook. It's always different. That way, you don't get tired of it. The rest of the country should be that creative. It's crazy. I got permission to start the airline service overnight, but business takes forever. You've heard of people set in their ways? Ethiopia is frozen. Everything takes forever."

"What about the French planes?" she asked.

"Probably won't happen. They're buying aircraft from individuals. I've seen a Beechcraft Staggerwing and two Potez 25s. My translator tells me they're preparing for the coming war. And considering that over the last few months, there have been French and German diplomats snooping around and meeting with government big shots, I don't know what's going to happen."

"You mean all this work we've done is for nothing?"

"No, we're in a good position. I have permission from Selassie to operate a flying service. I'm his personal pilot, and he trusts me. He speaks English, so I don't have to go through interpreters. I think we just have to take it slow."

"What happens next?" she asked. "Do we get to be alone?"

"After dinner, I'll escort you to your room, and this man will stand guard at your door all night," said Johnny, indicating a tall, stoic-looking man in uniform. "He's a sergeant in the elite guard. They protect the royal family."

"Am I in danger?"

The sergeant didn't speak a word of English. He nodded when they looked his way.

"The guard is traditional. You're in no danger. It's the way things are done here. You're my guest and therefore a guest of Ethiopia."

"I've come a long way," she said in a lowered voice. "You mean, we can't be alone, not even for an hour?"

"Not even for a minute."

She looked at Johnny and then at the towering sentry waiting to guard her room. She rolled her eyes. What a waste.

At dinner the following evening, Lieutenant Kafele interrupted the meal with news that the Italian Army was poised to invade. "Ethiopia is at war," he said.

"What does that mean?" asked Janet.

"It means the Ethiopian government can no longer guarantee your safety. You will have to leave Addis Ababa on the next train."

"Does John have to leave as well?" Janet asked hopefully.

"I'm a colonel in the army. I want to stay."

Early the next morning, the lieutenant drove Janet and Johnny to the train station. The train had the capacity for two hundred people. Five times that many were lined up to leave. Members of the elite Ethiopian guard were stationed to maintain order. Janet was escorted to the front of the line and allowed to board the train ahead of the Europeans. Kafele found that a white businessman was already occupying Janet's compartment. Johnny noted the incredible deference given to the lieutenant by the elite guard. They snapped to attention in his presence and on his orders immediately carried the businessman's luggage to third class.

"I'll be fine in third class, Madame. I didn't mean to take your compartment," the man called back as he left.

Johnny put out his hand to shake Janet's. She cocked her head and looked at him as if to say, "Are you serious?" She threw her arms around his neck and kissed him on the lips. The lieutenant averted his eyes.

# 35

Willa carried the day's mail into the clubhouse and was surprised to find Coffey working on his flight logs. "What's up?" she asked. "I thought you were at Curtiss Wright today."

"It turns out, it's not a full-time job," he replied, not looking up. "I fill in for instructor Niels Hoffer on occasion, but I'm not guaranteed a steady salary."

"What changed?" asked Willa, putting down the mail and her purse.

"Curtiss Wright thought that since Johnny and I were eager students, they'd have a flood of colored applicants. But any guy today who can pony up over nine hundred dollars paid in advance doesn't want to be a mechanic. They told me yesterday that Curtiss will only consider hiring me full-time when they have ten colored enrollees."

Willa spread out the mail on her desk. She could tell by Coffey's set jaw that he was hurt. She opened the mail and added the contents to a nearly three-inch-high stack of letters. She'd read every résumé and letter of interest for work in Ethiopia. Most of the applicants were eager to find jobs but didn't have money for training.

"Coffey, I have a proposal," she said. "Leave your logs for a minute." She pointed to a chair next to her.

"I thought you were against marriage," he said, trying to disguise his gloom.

"Sit. I'm not thinking about a wedding. It's these letters. People want training, and I'm thinking how your job at Curtiss Wright isn't helping our cause here. If you have the certificates to train pilots and mechanics, why not do it here?"

Coffey glanced around the room, as though he thought she were talking about the clubhouse.

"Not here in this room," she went on, "but out in the hangers where the real work takes place. And instead of charging one giant sum in advance as Curtiss Wright does, we charge for training by the hour like we do for flight classes."

"We already have classes with the Challengers."

"The Challengers' charter only allows for amateur flight instruction. As a school, however, we can train and certify pilots and mechanics — the way you taught me."

"We'd be competing with Curtiss Wright. Their name stands for something."

"Your name stands for something. Right now, white mechanics on Schumacher's payroll who work under your direction get part credit at Curtiss Wright. They're handing over part of their paychecks to Curtiss Wright, and Schumacher pays you. You have the certificates."

"What about Schumacher?"

"Nothing changes here at Harlem Airfield. You still work for Schumacher. He continues to pay you. His arrangement with Curtiss Wright stays the same. Things wouldn't be that much different, except we would have classes in the hangars weather permitting--or at the high school. Classes will all take place on weekends and evenings. I'll take care of recruiting, the licensing paperwork, and the bookkeeping. We have a staff—and they might actually get paid. Marie is a good backup for me. And you have plenty of help — Dale, Chauncey, and even me — ready to step up for six bits an hour."

Without needing any further convincing, Coffey said, "If I do this, I have to quit Curtiss Wright. What are we going to call this school?"

"The Coffey School of Aeronautics, natch."

Willa quickly set about registering the name and incorporating. And just from applicants in the Chicago area, she immediately recruited four students. Within three weeks, her roster had expanded to eight. She designed instruction like traditional college sessions — two one-and-a-half-hour sessions a week and two sessions on Saturday. For the majority of the students, this worked out well. If a student missed a session, the class hours had to be made up. Make-up classes became the important second tier of Willa's plan. They were structured as individualized sessions, and if Coffey couldn't teach them, Dale White, Chauncey, or Willa would cover what students missed.

Willa instituted a weekly staff meeting on Thursday afternoons to go over assignments for the busy weekends. At the second meeting, Marie St. Clair, Lola Jones, Dale White, Chauncey, Harold Hurd, and Willa's brother Simeon received their first pay envelopes from the Coffey School of Aeronautics. The amount may have been only two or three dollars, but it was enough that the unmarried staff decided to catch the bus to midtown Chicago and go on a fun, safe, and flirty outing to the Bijou Theater's nine-cent movie night.

To publicize the school, Coffey made a few demonstration flights. He really wasn't keen on public speaking, and honestly couldn't take time away from his duties at Harlem Airfield. Enoch Waters needed someone to promote, and Willa was the natural second choice. Having spent many hours in front of bored high school students, she knew how to engage an audience. She sparkled during the public appearances and became a must-see attraction when she toured Midwestern cities.

Willa made a point of scouting the locations of her appearances before the crowd assembled. On a trip to Cleveland, Ohio, witnessed by Enoch Waters, she actually flew there once for practice and returned a second time an hour later for her appearance.

Enoch Waters didn't like to fly, but since circulation went up every time he featured Willa, he made the trip holding tightly to the grab bar with one hand and his precious Graflex press camera with the other.

She purposely arrived early, put on dingy mechanic's overalls over her flight suit, and as the public arrived, pretended she was the aircraft's mechanic, and told visitors about the features of the Stearman. Fifteen minutes after the flight was scheduled to take place, she ushered the crowd to a safe point away from the plane. She then boarded the Stearman on the opposite side, out of the public's view. What the gallery couldn't see was that once in the cockpit, Willa shed the overalls and took off to perform a fifteen-minute flying routine. When she landed and stepped from the Stearman wearing that striking white-leather flight suit. The crowd was duly impressed. She made a pitch for the Coffey School and then took dignitaries and potential students for rides.

As she was returning from the promotional tour to Cleveland, the plane developed a fuel leak in flight. Willa could smell the gasoline. The engine sputtered and went silent.

"What's wrong?" shouted Enoch.

Willa signaled for him to calm down. "It's nothing. We're going to be fine," she called back.

"The propeller stopped. Don't we need the propeller?" he shouted, alarmed.

"We're fine," she called back. "See that farmhouse over there? We're going to land in that field." They were still more than two thousand feet in the air.

In his panic, Waters looked over the opposite side but saw no farmhouse. The plane swooped down, gliding lower and then lower, until it bounced hard, coming to a stop in the middle of a fallow field. The weeds and grasses were knee deep.

"Where are we?" he asked as he climbed out of the cockpit.

"I think we're about twenty miles south of Carbondale," answered Willa. She helped Enoch step down off the wing.

"Little Egypt?" said Enoch straightening his suit jacket. "We're in Little Egypt—we might as well be in Georgia."

"We'll be fine." She opened the engine compartment. "The fuel line came loose. All I need is a wrench and a screwdriver. We'll be out of here in no time. Let's look in at that farmhouse."

All Enoch could see was grass, sky, and a house and barn a quarter of a mile away.

"This part of Illinois is still the South," he said warily.

"Enoch, you've been to lynching trials in Alabama. You've looked lying murderers in the eye."

"Yes, but I never dropped out of the sky on a strange house looking for trouble," he said.

"Relax. We're not looking for trouble. We're looking for a wrench and a screwdriver."

Walking out of the field, Enoch noticed that his trouser legs were covered with burrs. He madly slapped at the stubborn burrs.

In the distance, they could see two men running toward the farmhouse. The men reached the porch and stood with their hands on their hips waiting for the aviators. Enoch stopped batting at his trouser legs, straightened up, and fixed his tie. Willa in her white aviator's outfit and Enoch in his business suit made for a surreal vision walking out of the prairie.

To Enoch, the vision they were approaching had its own bizarre reality. The farmer's overalls and hat and his teenage son's clothes and hair were covered with thousands of bits of hay. Only their noses and mouths were free of hay, and the bandanas around their necks explained why. Willa knew exactly why they looked that way; they had just stepped away from a bailing machine. But to Enoch, the hay only made the scene more sinister.

"I'm Willa Brown, and this is Enoch Waters of the *Chicago Defender*," announced Willa, smiling, as they approached the farmhouse. "We had engine trouble and could use an adjustable wrench and a twelve-inch screwdriver, if you could be so kind. I hope this isn't an inconvenience."

The farmer's wife stepped out from behind the screen door. "You folks come on in and sit. I'm Hanna Borstad. This is my husband Olav and our son Anders. Olav and Anders have to stay outdoors; otherwise, I'll have hay on the furniture. Come in." She opened the door. "Anders, you get the tools they need, and, Papa, brush yourself off and come in for some coffee."

"Pleasure to meet you, Mrs. Borstad, Olav, and Anders," said Willa. "This is Enoch Waters of the *Chicago Defender.*"

"We don't want to be a bother," said Enoch picking more burrs from his pant legs.

"Bother? An airplane lands in our field, and two aviators come to my door," said Hanna. "You sit a while. I'll have something to talk about at church this Sunday."

Hanna ushered them into the parlor and served them coffee and buttermilk biscuits with honey. Her husband came in, his clothes brushed off and his hair wet and combed.

"I'm pleased to meet you," said Olav, accepting a cup of coffee from his wife. "Anders is coming with the tools you need. How'd you come to be in Southern Illinois?"

Anders arrived moments later, his clothes also brushed off. Willa was telling his parents about the Coffey School and why she was flying from city to city.

When she finished, Anders said, "The tools are on the porch."

"Thank you, young man. Please excuse me, Mr. and Mrs. Borstad. This shouldn't take long."

Once out by the Curtiss, Anders hovered over Willa's shoulder as she worked on the engine.

"You can fix airplanes?" he asked.

"Can you fix the tractor?" she asked back.

"Sure."

"Well, then you can fix airplanes, too. It's a little more complicated because we have to keep records of how many hours we run an engine. Otherwise, with a few classes, you could fix planes."

"Do you need the field cleared a little? I can bring out the tractor and mow a runway for you. You won't have so much drag."

Willa looked at him. She had a live one, a bright young man with energy and imagination. "That would be tops," she said. "If you let me drive the tractor, I'll give you a ride on the plane."

"Willa, we need to get back," said Enoch. "People will get worried."

Too late, Anders was fifty yards away sprinting to retrieve the tractor. Willa cleared the weeds for a runway and then invited the entire family to sit in the cockpit. As Mom and Dad watched anxiously, Willa took Anders up for a ten-minute flight. The young man's excited eyes were as large as silver dollars when they landed.

"Mom!" he shouted from the passenger seat. "I could see Carbondale and Cairo at the same time. They're twenty miles from here—in opposite directions."

As Anders stepped down from the plane, he asked Willa privately, "Is your flying school for colored people only?"

"No, we have people like you, too," Willa replied, laughing.

"When I'm eighteen, I'm coming to Chicago. I'm going to learn how to fly."

The farmer and his wife politely declined her offer for a ride. Willa handed Enoch his camera and said, "Get a picture."

# 36

On an overnight stop at the border city of Adwa near the Eritrea border, early morning explosions startled Johnny from sleep. After pulling on his pants, he scrambled to the roof barefoot. In the glaring sunrise, he saw two large single-winged aircraft bombing the defenseless city. Two biplanes followed close behind, strafing civilians as they ran from houses and buildings into the street. Hotel guests and locals hurried toward the Red Cross hospital. When the Italian aircraft turned and began their second run, the Red Cross flag became the target. The building took a direct hit, and the survivors were strafed. The dead and wounded were scattered along the rubble-filled street. Soldiers in uniform shook their ceremonial scimitars helplessly at the planes.

As Johnny put on his shoes and grabbed his gear, he recalled that Abe had told him the Italian colonizers had been kicked out of Ethiopia at the Battle of Adwa in 1896. Since the city was defenseless, the bombing was apparently punishment for merely existing.

Keeping his eyes on the skies, Johnny ran to his plane. The Junker was partially protected by a stable and had not been discovered by the Italians. Except for his own sidearm, his plane was unarmed.

"Thank you, Coffey," he called out loud. "Always leave the aircraft ready for the next flight."

He had a full gas tank and quickly took off. He followed the Italian planes from below and behind, then slipped into the blind spot behind one of the bombers. By staying under the Italian's wings, he was able to rise within twenty-five yards of the plane he was shadowing and fire his revolver at the pilot. The only effect his bullets had was to make the Italians fix their machine guns on him. He executed a hard backward dive to avoid their guns. One of the nimble Italian biplanes broke formation to pursue his much slower Junker.

Johnny pulled the Junker into a climb as high and as fast as he could until the Italian plane had him within range. He then stalled his engine and went into freefall dive toward the maze of canyons below. "*Bravo!*" said one of the pilots on the radio. "*Egli morirà, o dire gli Etiopi siamo qui.*" The pilots laughed at the man trying to shoot them with a pistol.

Landing safely in Addis Ababa, Johnny saw his interpreter, Lieutenant Kafele, stepping out from under an umbrella and hurrying out to meet him.

"Abba Tekel would like to speak with you," he said. Abba Tekel was a family name for Haile Selassie. Only close relatives used it.

"What's with the 'Abba Tekel'?" asked Johnny, as they drove to the palace. In the past, Abe had only referred to Emperor Selassie in formal terms.

"He's my grandfather," said Abe.

"You're my translator," said Johnny. "You should be an ambassador."

"That will be my destiny. But what good is a future of service if I can't have adventure to look back on?"

"Any intelligence officer could have checked me out; why you?" asked John.

"After Hubert Julian embarrassed Abba Tekel, he wasn't taking chances. He wanted to know all about you. He put his life in your hands. It was my honor to tell him that Colonel John Robinson was a man of high moral character, a master of his craft, and is the man he appears to be, trusted here and at his home in Chicago."

Johnny had never been beyond the front office in the government's headquarters to receive his pay, but now he and Abe were escorted to a large room in the main building. Surrounded by senior officers, Selassie looked up and motioned for Johnny and Abe to approach. The emperor listened intently to the details of the attack on Adwa.

"As best I could, sir," said Johnny, "I wrote descriptions and aircraft numbers. Two bomber aircraft and two Fiat fighter biplanes."

"You are my pilot," Selassie said. "We have military pilots to fight the Italians. You and your plane are too valuable to me. It was foolish to try to shoot the Italians with your sidearm. Don't do it again. I will remember this."

"Yes, sir," chuckled Johnny. "But if I am attacked, I have no way to defend the aircraft."

After consulting with one of his senior officers, Selassie said, "You have my permission to install one fifty-caliber machine gun, which you may use to defend yourself — not that it will do you much good. My order for you is to stay out of harm's way."

There weren't many places a gun could be installed for effective defense. Behind the four passenger seats, a person of short stature could stand in the cargo area and fire a machine gun. It was no surprise that even though any enlisted man could have done the job, Abe, now a captain, volunteered to test the machine gun. During the tests, they discovered that the plane was not designed to attack targets on the ground. To do that, the Junker had to go into a steep dive and then pull away, leaving its broad underbelly exposed. If they tried to strafe from the side, the Junker's slow speed made it vulnerable. It was no match for Italian antiaircraft guns or warplanes.

For the next two months, Johnny and Abe ferried supplies to the front lines and carried reports to Selassie on troop movements. The only commercial service Johnny was able to continue was the once-a-week Addis Ababa–to–Djibouti route, flying two hundred pounds of mail and freight and diplomats on their way to the League of Nations at The Hague.

⤟

As Johnny entered the hotel lobby, a slender European in a businessman's khaki jacket waved him over. "Josef Jobim," he introduced himself. "The pilots have a private get-together, and I would like to invite you to join us for a drink on Saturday."

Johnny wouldn't wager on the matter, but Jobim's Portuguese name didn't jibe with his accent, which was probably German. He also wore kid gloves, a rather odd affectation, Johnny thought.

On Saturdays, the European pilots rented a suite and whatever took place in that room was not for the eyes of the local authorities. Johnny found that the gathering was nothing more than an occasion for them to drink and unwind without servants or minders watching them. Major Josef Jobim was in charge. He allowed all pilots to enter, accepting whatever name they gave. The two pilots from Finland said their *noms de guerre* were Laurel and Hardy.

Johnny pointed at them and asked, "Who's Stan, and who's Ollie?" The flyers shrugged. They didn't speak English, but they'd seen American films.

Johnny guessed Jobim to be in his late forties. He had thinning, sandy-gray hair and blue eyes. His pale skin was blotched from prolonged exposure to the sun. He still wore gloves as he held up a bottle of Hennessy VSOP and poured him two inches' worth into a ceramic cup. "Colonel Robinson, you are too young to have flown in the European War. What makes you a colonel?"

"Nothing at all qualifies me except I'm licensed to fly any type of aircraft, single and multiple engine. I'm certified to fix engines—all kinds. I've heard that some of you are aces. I haven't done anything like that. But here we sit. Here's to flight." He held up his cup and took a drink.

Jobim translated, "*In die flucht.*"

Several men joined in raising their cups. A German pilot glared at him in a way Johnny recognized from home. "Tell him to go to hell," Johnny growled. "I'll drink to him anyway." He raised his cup.

"I respect that you are an accomplished pilot," said Jobim. "However, your baptism by fire was inexcusably stupid. A Colt thirty-eight, six-shot pistol against a fifty-millimeter cannon? You should have kissed your arse good-bye. You were lucky. You did the smart thing by staying alive and reporting what you saw. Dead men are useless. However, your information we can use. What did you see?"

The pilots who spoke English came closer to listen.

"The two bombers were twin-engine beasts. I've never seen anything like them before. They didn't waver from their bombing run. Their escorts were two Fiat CR32 biplanes. Once I saw how fast they were, I turned tail and ran." The pilots laughed.

"Don't get us wrong. We're laughing because it's the exact same thing any one of us would have done. There is no heroic bravado among us," said Jobim. "We get paid well for the mischief we create. You fix engines?" He looked at the other pilots.

"I'm sorry; I can't service your planes. I have my own assignments. I assumed you brought your own crews."

"We have a few. But they don't know everything. You say you are certified to fix anything," said Jobim.

"If you have the parts, I can fix anything," answered Johnny.

"We don't have parts for everything, but with your help, we can make do," said Jobim. "We have resources."

"I have my own crew service the Junker, local soldiers with auto-repair skills. They're not top-of-the-line aircraft mechanics, mind you. They can refill your tank and change your oil. A few can do minor repairs, if you direct them. Language is the problem—not theirs, yours."

"We have six French Potez biplanes thirty kilometers from here. We're expecting more. We can deliver parts that might be of use to you. If we can use your facilities, the hangar you laid out with your crew to maintain our planes, we might have a chance against two bombers and two fighters."

"I'll have to clear it with Captain Kafele," said Johnny. He swirled his drink and put it aside. He felt obligated to do something. "It's probably in every one's interest we work together, don't you think?"

Jobim and his pilots proved resourceful. When they flew in a new plane, it was loaded with food, spare parts, tires, and alcohol. With the new supply of parts, Johnny was able to resurrect another Junker and two Fokker fighters. A Heinkel transport and three de Havilland Gypsy Moths were flown in from Jerusalem. At its peak, the Ethiopian Air Force had eighteen antique aircraft compared to the fifty-five warplanes the Italians brought for the invasion.

The mercenary pilots in support of the Ethiopian infantry had several early successes. Using the landscape to their advantage, they came in low and surprised the Italian columns. The advantage didn't last. The Italians had truck-mounted fifty-millimeter antiaircraft guns. Over the next several weeks, the Ethiopian planes one by one were torn apart and the pilots failed to return from their missions.

The rugged Ethiopian terrain was the Italians' most formidable enemy. Ethiopian roads turned into camel trails, and only high-axle trucks could continue. The Italian infantry was easy prey for snipers and guerrilla attacks. Facing a potential stalemate from a nation with more camels than guns, the Italians resorted to genocide. Along with mortars, bombs, and other munitions, they brought deadly mustard gas.

Dropped from airplanes, mustard gas canisters exploded on hitting the ground. Breathing the fumes burned the lungs, causing a slow, agonizing death. The best equipped, elite Ethiopian army units were reduced to a trail of corpses.

"These are war crimes," said Abe. "And militarily, it's insane. Their own troops are going to pass this way. Where mustard gas lingers, it kills."

By dropping leaflets from the plane, Johnny and Abe warned villagers to evacuate their homes.

"When can they return?" asked Johnny.

"Maybe never."

"What if the villagers can't read?" wondered Johnny aloud.

"There are usually several people in each community who can read," answered Abe. "Nonetheless, it is a concern."

At the village by the bend in the Blue Nile, they were too late. The crumpled bodies of men, women, and children were sprawled along the river's edge.

"No," cried Johnny softly. He could imagine the children running to be the first to find the containers.

"These were civilians," Abe said solemnly. "They exterminated them like vermin."

In April 1936, as the Italian army approached Addis Ababa, three Ethiopian planes flew out to stop the advance at the Entoto Pass, sixty kilometers from the capital. Their mission was to slow the Italians by a day, maybe more, so the Ethiopian leadership could escape into exile. Two planes had the mission; the third, Johnny's Junker, was only along to observe and report the results of the skirmish.

The two fighter planes, a Potez and a Gypsy Moth, attacked the Italian column from different directions. Abe and Johnny saw how the mercenary pilots picked off units that pulled aside from the main column and were without antiaircraft protection. The Gypsy Moth got lucky and scored a hit on a truck loaded with diesel fuel. The massive explosion sent up a huge cloud of black smoke that in effect gave the Italians cover. The antiaircraft guns were able to reposition from near the front of the column and began firing from inside the smoke screen. The Potez and the Gypsy Moth were shot down. For all their sacrifice, they hadn't stopped the advance.

As the column neared a narrow pass, Abe saw an opportunity. "If we can destroy the first trucks, we can stop them," he said.

"Won't they just push the trucks off the road?"

"Not at that point. There's no place for them to go. There's no outlet for fifteen kilometers in both directions."

An attack on vehicles in a narrow pass meant Johnny had to come in from above and then pull away.

The antiaircraft guns were not yet in position as they made the first run. The Junker took a couple of hits but nothing serious. Johnny couldn't hear the sound of the gunshots, but the bullets hitting the airplane's frame made an unforgettable "ping" followed by the whistling sound of air blowing across a hole. Abe's gun strafed the first truck but didn't stop it.

"Again! We have to do it again!" he shouted. Johnny turned the Junker and started a second run. His approach was steeper, allowing Abe a better angle. The timing and angle were good. Abe made direct hits on three trucks. One truck containing munitions exploded and stopped the column completely. As the Junker banked, it became completely exposed to antiaircraft fire. Bullets passed through the aluminum fuselage as if it were paper. For several seconds, the Junker disintegrated around them. Johnny felt a burning sensation in his right arm. He tried to bend his elbow, and the rush of pain nearly made him pass out. "Abe!" he shouted. "Abe, I need help!" There was no answer. The machine gun had gone silent.

For the final twenty kilometers, Johnny screamed with pain every time he needed to use his right arm. Part of his radius bone was exposed, and he could see the muscles moving when he had to change altitude. After landing the Junker in Addis Ababa, he tied a tourniquet below his bicep. He found Abe hanging limp in the cabin. Johnny surmised that Abe had been wounded on the first run and had tied himself to the gun with his belt in order to keep firing. He cut the belt with his knife and lowered the emperor's grandson to the floor.

As Johnny walked away from the Junker, he had no idea if what they had done had been successful. His mission had been to observe. Instead, he had gotten Abe killed.

# 37

Chauncey answered the phone when Dr. Melaku Beyan called from Chicago's Union Station. He wanted to know if the Challenger officers could be available in about an hour. He had news from Ethiopia. Willa and Coffey were in the hangar. Chauncey phoned Janet and left word for her to come to Harlem Airfield immediately.

Willa, Coffey, and Chauncey waited in the clubhouse as Dr. Beyan stepped out of a taxi and paid the driver.

"Whatever he's got to say, he certainly looks diplomatic," said Chauncey. Dr. Beyan wore a dark business suit, tie, vest, gloves, and a gray homburg hat. Stepping into the clubhouse, he removed his gloves and then his hat, put the gloves inside it, and cradled the hat in his left arm.

"I am in Chicago to speak at the university about the situation in Ethiopia, and I received several cables that I thought I should tell you about in person. I fear the news is not good. Colonel John Robinson was reported missing and presumed dead," Dr. Beyan said straight out.

"How do you know?" Willa's voice wavered.

"It is not definitive. After the surrender of Addis Ababa, communications have been nil."

"So, what proof is there? You're in DC. John is in East Africa," said Chauncey.

Willa held up her hand. "Chauncey, please."

"I have to believe he's alive," said Coffey.

"It's possible, but not likely," said Dr. Beyan. "The reason we know anything at all is because Colonel Robinson was accompanied by his liaison officer, Prince Abebe Kafele, who was killed on the same mission. The cable said there was blood found on the pilot's seat, and the aircraft was badly damaged. Eyewitness accounts relate that Colonel Robinson's heroic actions before the fall of Addis Ababa allowed the emperor and staff to leave the country. After the capital fell, the Italians did not take prisoners. Haile Selassie sends his deepest regrets."

Coffey stoically clenched his jaw. Willa couldn't help tearing up. She leaned into Coffey's chest.

"When will we know anything?" asked Chauncey.

"The emperor has moved his headquarters to Jerusalem. I now receive cables from him frequently," said Dr. Beyan. "As for the capital, Addis Ababa, it's not likely we will hear anything for weeks. The other news is that the emperor has requested that all plans for the Abyssinian Air Service be held in abeyance until the invading forces in our nation are expelled, and at such time, we will resume our collaboration."

"They didn't find his body, so how can they be sure?" asked Willa. She dabbed her eyes with the cuff of her sleeve. Outside, they heard Janet's car grind to a stop on the gravel.

"What's going on?" she demanded, bursting through the door.

"He's missing in action," said Coffey.

"There was chaos when the capital fell," said Dr. Beyan. "Colonel Robinson's body may never be found."

"No!" Janet trembled. Her deep-throated sobs moved Dr. Beyan, who took out a handkerchief and wiped away his own tears.

⤚⤙

When Janet married her second husband two weeks later, many assumed she did so to lessen the heartache. No one knew the fellow, but Chauncey learned the man was an undertaker who owned several funeral homes.

Willa packed up all the Abyssinian Air Transport Service materials and stored them in back of one of the hangers. The Ethiopian adventure was over.

Life in Chicago went on. Willa convinced the school board that aviation was no longer a hobby. Using statistics provided by her professor and mentor Dr. Miller, head of the Commerce Department at Indiana State College, she demonstrated how over the past several years, Chicago Municipal Airport, "Muni," had become the busiest airport in the world with over sixty thousand flights in 1935.

Willa continued to teach typing and business math, but under her direction, students in an auto-shop class took apart a small aircraft engine and learned the names for all the parts. Willa's key selling point to the board of education was that if the graduates from her high school class passed a proficiency test, they could qualify as apprentices with the aircraft mechanics union. A school board member reminded her that none of these unions currently had black members.

"Yes, sir, that's true," Willa replied. "And the aircraft industry will continue not hiring colored mechanics as long as there are no well-trained colored applicants. I've spoken to the mechanics' union organizer, Norman Kuppers, and he said they're willing to try taking our graduates, but he doesn't know how the workers will accept our kids. I told him I think it's easy to dismiss someone who isn't there. It's harder to discriminate when the person works next to you and knows how to do the job."

At the next meeting of the Challengers, the clubhouse filled to standing room only with members wanting to hear what was to be done about Johnny. Coffey was adamant that no memorial should be discussed until there was more definitive proof. "He's missing," said Coffey. "That's all we know."

"But we should have a plan," injected Janet. "I mean, he's the president of the Challengers, and he's not here to make final decisions on the club, or my plane."

"Let's table the discussion about Johnny's memorial for later," replied Willa. "Just because Johnny's not here, doesn't mean we can't talk about what's happening now with the Challengers." She looked around the room. Most members seemed in agreement.

"I think things with the Challengers are falling to pieces," said Janet.

"No, that's not true," Marie St. Clair spoke up.

"Janet, we all feel badly about Johnny," Willa responded. "But we're doing as well as can be expected. As you know, the payments are current on your plane. Whether Johnny is here or not, we have to look to the future, and that was the next order of business today--even before we heard the news from Ethiopia. And that's why Enoch Waters is here."

Enoch Waters took the floor. He lit his stump of a cigar and waited a moment to feel its focusing effect on his brain. "I just got back from Washington where I interviewed Roy Wilkins for an article I'm writing on black unemployment. He'd heard about Johnny--and he asked me, by the by, how things were going with jobs in aviation. I told him about the Challengers and the Coffey School of Aeronautics. He was curious because our good friend Chauncey here has been working with the new general counsel for the NAACP, Thurgood Marshall. They're looking for a case where a fully qualified aviation mechanic is denied employment because of his race. Isn't that true?" Enoch asked Chauncey.

"I didn't know that," added Janet.

Several others in the room chimed in, "I didn't know, either."

Chauncey nodded. "It's not a secret. We've only started to look. There's no question that the shops are all white, but we haven't found an applicant who can make a case--not yet, anyway. The Coffey school will soon have its first graduates with enough hours of real experience to qualify as journeymen."

"Back to my reason for being here. It turns out there's independent colored participation in aviation around the country," Enoch continued. "And most activity only receives local publicity at best. Roy Wilkins suggests that what's needed is a coordinated national effort that can represent Negro aviation interests in Washington, state and city governments, and at the local airports."

"What would that be?" asked Marie.

"It would look like a national organization. We invite every colored pilot, mechanic, and student interested in aviation to join a national Negro aviators' association. The reason for existence would be--*jobs*. Did you know that government departments, like the post office, are getting their own airplanes, meaning pilots, mechanics, and support staff? These are government jobs that should be open to everyone."

Willa followed. "We also need an advisory board of some of the best minds we can find to help guide our efforts."

"Who will be the officers of this new national organization?" asked Janet.

"Until we actually have a national convention and elect officers..." Willa looked around the room. "...We're the officers."

Chauncey spoke next. "Thurgood Marshall can help make introductions for us. There's a good chance that William Hastie and Roy Wilkins will lend their name to a masthead, but they can't serve as board members."

Willa looked at Chauncey as if he had finally soloed.

Closing the meeting, Willa called for a vote on a date three months later for a memorial for John Robinson. It passed unanimously. The formation of a National Negro Airmen's Association was listed in the minutes as the subject for the next meeting.

# 38

John had left Captain Abebe Kafele stretched out respectfully on the Junker floor. He knew the royal family would send a search party for him. As he staggered back to the European Hotel, the city was preparing for the invasion. Private dwellings and stores were shut. Merchants moved wagonloads of inventory to safer places. Families walked, rode donkeys, and pulled human-drawn carts to the provinces where they might find shelter with relatives. Johnny knew that an Italian victory was inevitable. Once the Italian army cleared the mountain passes, they would meet with little resistance. The best-armed Ethiopian units had been destroyed by poison gas. What remained were scattered units of the regional guards being assembled to meet the advancing army. On his trips with Emperor Selassie, Johnny had admired the regional guards — gallant tribesmen with their feathered helmets, animal-hide robes, spears, and leather-covered shields. Until he saw the devastating casualties, he had assumed the bows and arrows, spears and swords were ceremonial, and not their actual weapons against Italian machine guns.

The few guests remaining at the hotel were anxiously awaiting transportation and ignored him. The manager announced that the next train, if it came at all, would arrive the following morning.

Josef Jobim, the mercenary pilot, saw Johnny enter the lobby, bleeding and holding his arm.

"Come up to my room, and I'll take a look." Jobim patted Johnny on the back so they appeared as if they were comrades-in-arms on the way upstairs for a drink.

Jobim had been a competent mercenary officer, as far as Johnny could tell. There were always more pilots than planes, and he made assignments on the basis of a pilot's success. When the number of planes diminished, he shipped excess pilots out of the country.

Inside his room, Johnny saw that Jobim's duffle bag was already packed. He opened the bag and brought out a compact medical kit and a bottle of brandy.

"We have to take care of ourselves," he said, uncorking the bottle of brandy and handing it to John. "Take several big draws of this…Yes, *big*."

Johnny leaned back in a chair and took several large swigs. He put down the bottle and realized his left hand was inexplicably shaking.

Jobim filled a pitcher with water and carried it out to the terrace. "I'll be right back," he said. The room had a balcony with an exterior fireplace where servants prepared tea. Jobim poured water from a crockery pitcher into a kettle. He placed the kettle on the iron shelf above the embers and added several sticks and dry kindling, and in seconds, the flames lapped at the kettle.

As the alcohol took effect, Johnny's left hand stopped trembling. Jobim returned and sat facing him. He took the injured arm and turned it right and left. The pain was so sharp Johnny gasped.

"I've seen worse," said Jobim. "You have tears in the bra-chioradialis and the carpi radialis. I don't have morphine. I can sew you up. It won't be perfect, but considering everything, it's the best available. How far away are the ground troops?"

"I don't know. If we're lucky, a day, maybe two."

"When the Italians get here, we're dead men," said Jobim, removing his gloves and rolling up his sleeves. The skin on his hands and forearms was pinkish and wrinkled with burn scars. "What happened to Laurel and Hardy?" Jobim asked, preparing a needle and thread.

"I saw them go down. Are you a doctor?"

"A medical student before the war. What are your plans?"

"I'll get to Djibouti and out of here," said Johnny.

Jobim left his surgical setup ready and went out to the balcony. He carried in the kettle of boiling water. "I have to let it cool so it doesn't burn us. This will only take a few minutes. Be warned. It's has to be hot enough to kill microbes."

Five minutes later, Jobim poured a stream of hot water over the cut. He examined the injury and poured again. Johnny flinched and gritted his teeth. For an instant, the hot water stung, and then the arm felt numb. Jobim washed his hands with the remaining water, and once his hands had air-dried, he picked up the needle and thread.

John winced as Jobim began stitching his arm.

"Head for Egypt. Tunisia and Algeria are safe. If you catch a boat from Port Said to Tunis or Algiers, you'll bypass Libya. Libya is Italian. If they suspect because of a wounded arm that you were part of the Ethiopian war business, you could get shot. Burn your uniform. Spanish Morocco is a question mark. Unfortunately, that is the fastest and cheapest place to cross to Spain. When you get to Cadiz, ship out to Havana or New

York, whichever comes first. If you have to go through Libya, become an American," said Jobim. "A big stupid American. Tell them you sell toothpaste and smile your gorgeous white teeth at them."

"If my arm wasn't being sewn up, I'd slug you for that remark," John said, laughing.

Johnny stared at Jobim's scarred hands as they carefully closed the wound. Noticing his patient's curiosity, Jobim offered, "I was shot down in 1917. The petrol tank exploded. The skin is fragile; that's why I have to wear gloves." He looked up. "Go home and don't come back. Africa is not ready for the likes of you." He finished sewing, cut the thread with scissors, and poured brandy over the wound.

"Yow!" John flinched, jerking his arm loose from Jobim's hands. "Oh, jeez, that hurts worse than the stitching. You kill for a living. What do you know about what Africa is ready for?"

Jobim ignored the question. "Your arm will be stiff for a while. As soon as it heals, put it to work as much as you can tolerate. You have a small tear to your lateral epicondyle, and because of that, your arm will hurt like hell for some time. Take a clean bedsheet and make enough bandages to last a month. I'll order some honey from the hotel kitchen; use it to cover the injury. If you don't want to die of blood poisoning, wash the wound with alcohol twice daily; then slather it with honey each time. Keep it covered with a clean bandage until you get to a hospital." Jobim took a drink and offered it to Johnny.

"No, thanks."

"Most of the places you're going you won't find any of this." Jobim held up the bottle of brandy and then wrapped it in a pair of trousers and stuffed it back in his duffle bag.

"Take as much booze as you can carry. You can drink what you don't use, and if you get hungry, the honey can carry you for a good while."

"Where are you headed?" asked Johnny, his arm still stinging from the alcohol bath.

"Spain. The army generals want to take down the elected Socialist government. It's best we not travel together. I'm wanted in several countries, and you're not. Guilt by association, you know."

"How do you know all this?"

"It's my business to know. Whichever side has planes and money will be my employer."

"It doesn't matter to you whose side you're on?"

"It mattered once." He shook his head. "My country lost, and I learned that when all the bodies were buried and the tears of the widows had dried, the same rich bastards were in charge. The politicians changed; the aristocracy remained the same."

John joined the exodus of Europeans and Africans escaping the invasion. The overcrowded train had two breakdowns and took three days to make Djibouti. He walked to the one-room office and airstrip he had built. There was no sign of the postal clerk. Inside the office, the counter and furniture remained intact. His intention was to destroy anything the Italians could use. He couldn't bring himself to destroy the furnishings. Perhaps a looter could sell the two chairs for a few Ethiopian cents. He did set fire to anything with his name on it and cleared any signs that the airstrip was anything more than a road under construction. A major seaport for several thousand years, with more recent Ottoman and French occupation leaving their imprint, Djibouti was a graceful and entertaining city to visit. There were sufficient hotels. However, conscious that someone looking for a reward might recognize him, he stayed in the office several nights until he caught a boat going north.

Before he left in May 1936, Johnny heard that Addis Ababa had been bombed extensively, and the city surrendered.

❧

Traveling as an American businessman in civilian clothes, he walked and hitchhiked his way across North Africa. His Western clothes often brought truck drivers to a stop to offer a ride. He took trains and buses when possible. He had started with nearly a thousand US dollars. Where he could, he exchanged his dollars to the local currency, and learned that a small bribe could get him through border crossings and customs without having his luggage opened. He had packed his Ethiopian officer's uniform and didn't want it confiscated. To his surprise, his arm healed in less than two weeks, but as Jobim had predicted, it constantly hurt like hell.

Something had changed in him in the last year and a half. He sat where he wanted and walked where he wanted without giving his actions a second thought. He saw bitter poverty everywhere as well as immense estates with wealthy African owners. In rural areas, the larger mass of humanity, while poor and black, looked healthy. They wore traditional robes, so he was the curiosity. Children stared at him. His height and his clothes made him a standout from the refugee flow.

In the major cities, the European presence existed behind protected compounds with polished military guards. White diplomats in dark suits were trailed by male secretaries, and their wives dressed as if they were on display. The power behind the power, Johnny concluded.

Cairo, Tunis, and Algiers were ancient cities with medieval fortifications standing near European-style colonial structures, next to modern office buildings. As long as he had to play the tourist, he decided he might as well enjoy it. The guides in Tunis and Algiers charged only a few cents, but in all, he was running low on money. In Algiers, he found the American Embassy locked with no note about when it would reopen. In Spanish Morocco, a guide told him about ancient Carthage and that the port of Ceuta was where Hannibal had crossed the Mediterranean with his elephants in 200 BC. The guide took him to a point where he could see the port city jutting into the Mediterranean. A seventeenth-century Spanish castle guarded the port below. Ceuta, near the Straits of Gibraltar, was where he was to board a ferry for Spain.

His hotel was near the port on a street called Avenida de los Reyes Catolicos (Avenue of the Catholic Kings). In the morning, he walked to the piers and nearing the ferry, he sensed something was not right. Ports were normally noisy with passengers, cargo loading, and venders selling bread and dried fish. There was none of the hustle and bustle of a vessel about to cast off.

The guard at the ferry asked for his passport, glanced at it briefly, gave it back, and motioned for him to join the other travelers camped in a nearby warehouse. From a far corner of the hall, a man motioned furtively for Johnny to step outside.

It was Jobim. He wore his familiar tan jacket, a Panama-style hat, and his gloves, looking every bit a businessman. He took out a pack of cigarettes and offered one to Johnny. He refused.

"Take the cigarette, and offer me something that looks like a cigarette in return," he said. "We're just two strangers trading smokes." Jobim struck a match and lit their cigarettes. "How's the arm?"

"It's healed, thank you. Hurts so much it's hard to sleep."

"It will get better, but I can't tell you when." Jobim made a gesture pretending he enjoyed the cigarette Johnny gave him. "The port is closed until further notice," he said in a lowered voice. "It's best you not stay here. The Spanish generals have begun their offensive here in Morocco. Italy and Germany have pledged to support the Fascists."

"Where should I go?"

"Get back to Algiers."

"I was there. The embassy was closed."

"Sit yourself in the doorway, if you must. Someone will come and inquire about you."

Nearly out of money, Johnny backtracked to Algiers where he found the American Embassy open. He couldn't enter because there was a small but noisy crowd of embassy workers and visitors blocking the entrance. The atmosphere was festive.

He approached a white staffer in shirtsleeves. "What's going on?" he asked.

"Jesse Owens won three gold medals, and he's going for his fourth in the four-by-one-hundred meter relay," said the staffer. "We're waiting for a cable with the results now. The race was scheduled thirty minutes ago. You're an American? Have some lemonade," he said, pointing to a table in the courtyard with glasses of lemonade.

Johnny had forgotten about the Olympics. "So, that's today," he said, feeling he had to say something. Of course, Johnny knew all about the world-record-holding sprinter from Ohio State.

"I wonder what that Hitler will think when his master race gets beaten by our Negro," said the man in shirtsleeves.

Johnny was going to say something but held his tongue. He helped himself to a glass of lemonade.

An excited young woman appeared in the doorway waving a sheet of paper. "Attention everyone. The Americans won the four-by-one-hundred-meter relay, making four gold medals for Jesse Owens. Bravo!" The small gathering applauded.

After the brief celebration, the embassy reopened for business. Johnny cabled Coffey for money. It had been eight weeks since he'd disappeared.

⁓

Willa was in the middle of one of her typing classes when Coffey knocked on her classroom door and motioned for her. As she stepped into the hallway, she saw Coffey's eyes red and teary, with a crooked smile on his face.

"What's wrong?" she asked, worried.

"He's alive."

Willa screamed.

# 39

C offey sold his Stearman to Schumacher for a bargain fifteen hundred dollars and wired the money to the American
Embassy in Algiers the following morning.

From Algiers, John boarded a merchant vessel that took
him to Perpignan, France. He crossed the European peninsula
at the narrowest part, the French side of the Pyrenees. He hitchhiked and took buses to Bayonne, France, and booked passage
to Portsmouth, England, and then to New York.

Still reeling from his experiences since the fall of Addis
Ababa, Johnny wasn't prepared for what happened. Upon
docking in New York in September of 1936, the celebrities and
socialites on the ship assumed the large crowd assembled outside the customs building was for them. As they left customs
and passed through the mass of people, the crowd's attention
remained silently fixed on the doorway. When Johnny exited
customs, a cry went up and scores of American and Ethiopian
flags waved madly.

Willa and Dr. Melaku Beyan met Johnny and turned him
toward the waiting crowd. Willa hurriedly explained that his
adventures in Ethiopia had been written up in race newspapers
all over the country. "You're a hero," she said.

"How?" he asked.

Dr. Beyan, accustomed to speaking in public, hushed the crowd by raising his arms. "We welcome home Colonel John C. Robinson of the Ethiopian Air Force and personal pilot to His Majesty, the Conquering Lion of the Tribe of Judah, Haile Selassie."

The throng cheered.

"What's going on?" asked Johnny.

"I'll tell you on the plane," she whispered. "Just say, 'Thank you. It's good to be home.'"

"Plane?" he said, dazed.

"Yes, you and I and Dr. Beyan are flying TWA to Chicago; we'll be there this afternoon." She took him by the arm. "Just wave. They're here to see you."

John waved. "Thank you. It's good to be home." Another cheer continued until he was inside a waiting limousine.

"Do you still have your uniform?" asked Willa.

"Yes," said John.

"Put it on when we get to the airport." Willa looked at Johnny's shoes. They were badly scuffed and had holes in the soles. "Driver, stop at the first shoe store you see." Willa bought him a new pair of brown wingtips.

What he experienced in New York was only a preview. That evening, twenty thousand cheering fans greeted Colonel John C. Robinson in the park across the street from Chicago's Grand Hotel.

"I don't know this many people," joked Johnny nervously.

"They know you," said Enoch Waters.

Janet and her new undertaker husband, a short, balding man in his late forties, squeezed onto the platform by Johnny's side next to Willa, Enoch Waters, and Coffey. The Challenger crowd, Johnny's students, and Fred Schumacher and his wife were there. Marcus Lipsky and Roxy Moss waved.

The local ward alderman presented Johnny a proclamation from the mayor of Chicago declaring it Colonel John C. Robinson Day.

Dr. Fredrick Patterson, the new president of Tuskegee Institute, holding a copy of the proposal Johnny had given him two years before, announced the school would begin fundraising immediately for an aviation program with Johnny as director.

Dr. Beyan spoke of the valiant fight going on against the Fascist Italian occupation. In closing, he asked Johnny to stand. "His Majesty, Haile Selassie, has cabled me from Jerusalem. He has bestowed upon me the privilege of presenting to Colonel John C. Robinson, in recognition of his honorable, distinguished, and courageous service, the Order of Menelik II." He placed a gold medallion, attached to a green, yellow, and red ribbon, around Johnny's neck.

On Dr. Beyan's signal, several large Ethiopian flags were unfurled and brandished. A cheer spread through the crowd and grew louder as Colonel Robinson stepped forward and waved. Marcus Lipsky managed to get close to Johnny. He pointed to Roxy Moss. "She wants to put you on the radio. Your girl, Willa, has the phone number," he shouted into Johnny's ear. Johnny nodded as if he understood what was going on. The faces of people he knew––but who hadn't crossed his mind in nearly two years––were vying for his attention. He was in a fog.

Willa did have Roxy's phone number, and early the next morning, a car came by the Grand Hotel to take Johnny to the radio station. Willa had had his uniform cleaned and pressed overnight. His brown wingtips were polished to a high shine, and he found new socks and underwear in his shoes. He looked distinguished as he entered the studio. Red Mack pumped his hand.

"I gave this man his start," boasted Red.

Before she introduced Johnny, Roxy Moss reminded listeners, "This special interview with Colonel John C. Robinson, the hero from Abyssinia, is made possible by Brook View Dairy and all their wonderful milk products and, of course, by Mack Chevrolet. Isn't it time you drove a Chevy?"

# 40

As Johnny entered the clubhouse, he felt grateful for the room's familiar smoky scent. Coffey and Willa had arrived only minutes before and were waiting for him. Johnny took off his hat and sat down at his old desk—now covered with receipts from the café, since Chauncey had taken it over in his absence. Coffey opened the windows, airing out the place. Willa sorted through the mail and waved a stack at Johnny.

"These are for you, marked personal. And this one is from Tuskegee Institute. It's not for you, but it's about you. It arrived yesterday addressed to the Challengers, so I opened it. They've sent out a national press release soliciting donations to establish an aviation department," said Willa. "It says, 'Famed alumnus John C. Robinson will be joining our faculty as an aircraft engine mechanics instructor.'"

"Do you still want to teach at Tuskegee?" asked Coffey.

"That was two years ago. I suppose if that's the best offer, I'll take it. As for now, I'm just glad to be back in Chicago. I ran an air service for eleven months. I'd like to fly commercial planes."

A knock on the door came as a surprise. They weren't expecting anyone. Dr. Beyan opened the door and leaned in.

"Dr. Beyan, come in," urged Willa.

Coffey crossed the room to offer his hand. The doctor carried his suit jacket in his arm, and his shirt had wet sweat circles in the armpits.

"Nice to see you, Doctor Beyan," said Coffey. "Did you just walk from the bus stop? It's ninety degrees out there."

"Yes, greetings, everyone," replied Beyan as he laid his jacket over a chair and fanned himself with his hat. Our embassy has no funds for my travel anymore. It's only two kilometers from the final stop."

"Let me get you something to drink," said Coffey. "I believe there are some cold soft drinks. What would you like?"

"Just water, thank you. That would be very helpful." He nodded toward Willa and Johnny. "It's so good to see you, my dear friends. My assignment now is to gain support for the cause of Ethiopian liberation. Tomorrow, I will be at Trinity Abyssinian Church. Please come, Colonel Robinson. You must speak for Ethiopia. You must tell Americans that Abyssinia is their friend. You are part of us now."

Johnny smiled. "I'll do what I can, sir. You have to understand this is not Ethiopia. Here, I'm only a pilot and a mechanic. I have no official position."

"Understood," said Beyan. "But you have the respect of your community. That stands for something."

"I have friends who might be interested. May I invite them?" asked Willa.

Dr. Beyan accepted the glass of water. "Thank you, so kind. Of course, you may invite whomever you wish. And Colonel Robinson, no, sir, you are not here to represent Ethiopia. But you can speak for her courtesies."

The following evening, Johnny, Willa, and Enoch Waters drove to Trinity Abyssinian Church and met with Dr. Beyan.

Approximately thirty people, black and white, were gathered in the basement meeting room, all looking forward to meeting Emperor Selassie's personal pilot. Their friend Oliver Law was there with a young woman. He introduced her as Emily Dalrimple, his fiancée. Willa had heard that she was daughter of the president of the local Communist Party. She shook hands with Oliver and hugged Emily. Johnny thought that Oliver's fiancée had a very sweet face, but she was dressed so conservatively in a black suit with the skirt nearly down to her ankles that she looked like a schoolmarm to him.

The pastor of Trinity Abyssinian introduced Dr. Beyan, who began with an impassioned plea for the United States to support Ethiopian independence. He concluded his remarks by referring to a cable from Haile Selassie.

"For the time being, the emperor has ended the hostilities of what he calls 'the most unequal, most unjust, most barbarous war of our age.' He has chosen exile in order to prevent further bloodshed and so that he may work for the restoration of our nation's independence. The League of Nations must not recognize the Italian territorial presumptions gained by deceit and arms. They must sanction the Italians for war crimes in violation of the international agreements. In 1896, Ethiopia became the only African nation to expel a colonial power, and we will do it again. They may claim Rome as their heritage, but we are the descendants of King Solomon and the Queen of Sheba. We shall prevail."

Dr. Beyan received a smattering of respectful applause.

Johnny wasn't comfortable speaking about political matters. He cared about Ethiopia, but he felt that whatever he experienced there had not made him an expert. The people in attendance appeared to know so much more about world affairs than he ever could. He wanted to say, "I'm a pilot. I fix airplane engines." Instead, when Dr. Beyan asked him to stand, he said, "I'll take questions and see if I can give you an idea of what I saw in Ethiopia."

Oliver's companion Emily spoke first. "What did you do there, Colonel Robinson?"

"I was just trying to stay alive," he admitted. "I wasn't part of the military Ethiopian Air Force, not until the last month. The plane I flew was a boxcar compared to the Italians' flying war machines."

"I mean, why did you go to Ethiopia to begin with?" Emily followed up.

"I originally went to start a Middle Eastern air service out of Addis Ababa. I started with one aircraft, flying from Addis Ababa to Djibouti round trip once a week. Then I expanded to Adwa, which is to the north, once a week. I also made trips to the provinces. I was kept busy."

Dr. Beyan stood up and added, "Colonel Robinson was Haile Selassie's trusted personal pilot. He has been much closer to the emperor than anyone in government. We had eyewitness observers on the ground who reported on Colonel Robinson's last mission. He prevented the capture of the emperor and allowed the government time to evacuate the capital."

There followed a bigger round of applause and subdued calls of "Bravo."

"Did you really see combat? Was it exciting?" a teenager asked.

Johnny thought. "On two occasions, I was in combat, and it was the most terrifying thing I've ever done."

"What about the atrocities? Are they true?" Oliver Law's question was rhetorical. The moment Johnny nodded affirmatively, Oliver continued, "This is the beginning. This can only escalate when men like this Fascist Mussolini believe that 'might makes right.' In Spain, a democratically elected Socialist government is fighting for its life. War in Europe is inevitable."

"I can't believe another war is coming," said a white minister. "It's inconceivable. There were a million and a half casualties at the Battle of the Somme, four hundred thousand dead. That's madness. Cooler minds must prevail."

"War will come because industrialists will make a profit," argued Oliver. "Look at Ethiopia. Her coffee plantations, seaside resorts, and precious minerals are there for the taking. John Robinson, why don't you come join the fight against the Fascist overtaking of Spain? Thirty-five of us are leaving to join the Abraham Lincoln Brigade."

"I'm not ready to go back," admitted Johnny. "I just got home."

An elderly Asian man tapped his cane on the floor. Heads turned. "He is right," he said. "War is already here. The real threat is from Japan. It has already invaded Manchuria and is bombing Nanking as we sit here talking. The Philippines, an American protectorate, will be next."

Emily spoke up. "We should be focusing our efforts on the injustices here at home. How can people claim this is a free and just country when lynching continues without prosecution? Just this month, there have been three public murders."

Johnny found all the opinions persuasive. It was a different world to come back to. The mention of lynching brought to mind the mile after mile of dead children, civilians, and soldiers — memories he had hoped to forget. He closed his eyes and forced himself to recall the waterfalls of the Blue Nile and the rising mists, as the debate continued in the Trinity Abyssinian Church basement.

Regrettably, Dr. Beyan didn't have much luck organizing in Chicago. At that meeting at Trinity Abyssinian Church, he had in the audience Communists, Socialists, Wobblies, a CIO labor organizer, ministers, schoolteachers, college students, and a few cranks. When the minister passed the hat, only seven dollars and thirteen cents had been contributed toward Ethiopian liberation. After Dr. Beyan returned to DC, Johnny received an occasional letter from him. By necessity, however, the ambassador wrote that he had to restrict his activities to New York City and the capital.

When Enoch wrote about Johnny's recollections at Trinity Abyssinian Church, he was stunned by the letters he received calling Colonel John C. Robinson a liar. The letter writers didn't understand how the Italians—people like the corner greengrocer or the famous recording star Enrico Caruso—were enemies. After that strong negative response, Waters toned down mention of the Italian atrocities. *Fascism* hadn't entered the American vocabulary, and Ethiopia was half a world away.

# 41

A week later, on a hot Sunday afternoon in early October 1936, over ten thousand demonstrators against the Italian occupation of Ethiopia gathered in Chicago's Grant Park. Oliver Law, his shirt wet with perspiration, stood on the reinforced awning over a Woolworth's store directly across the street. As the crowd fanned themselves with folded copies of the *Daily Worker*, he spoke out against Italian war crimes.

At the far edges of the crowd, panicked screams caused everyone to turn. A phalanx of two thousand police marched into the crowd, striking at anyone not scattering. Two cops were hoisted onto the Woolworth awning. Rushing Oliver, they forced him to his knees with blows from their billy clubs. One of the officers handcuffed him roughly, and only after the pleading of a white pastor and his wife was Oliver removed from the awning without further injury. At the opposite end of the park, thugs threw rocks at the demonstrators, sending them back in the direction of the charging police.

In the aftermath, *The Chicago Defender* and *The Daily Worker* published articles in defense of Oliver, while the major dailies, *The Examiner* and *The Tribune*, played down the massive demonstration. A conservative editorial writer blamed the "Grant

Park Riot" on Communist agitators and their "union stooges." After numerous witnesses vouched that he had not instigated the violence at the demonstration, the charges against Oliver Law were dropped in December.

As the civil war in Spain garnered headlines, support for Ethiopia faded. And as Dr. Beyan had said, Emperor Selassie had ceased military resistance. No more lives would be lost for Ethiopia. For Italy, Ethiopia was a *fait accompli*, and now Spain became the great humanistic cause.

In January 1937, Oliver Law and a group of American men willing to put their ideals into practice prepared to sail to Spain. They intended to join the Abraham Lincoln Brigade in support of the democratically elected Republican government against Franco and the military.

At the reception for the departing men, Johnny admitted he wasn't inclined to fight and possibly die for Spain. "My loyalties are with the nation that treated me with dignity and rewarded my service." He knew that wasn't what Oliver and the men shipping out wanted to hear. "Salassie made me a colonel, and I was responsible for his life while he was in my plane," he said. "If I am going to fight, that's where I will go."

"I respect your experience, John," said Oliver. "I respect what you say, but I spent eight years in the US Army. I had ambitions to be an officer. I have the qualifications and a degree. When I couldn't get promoted beyond corporal, I resigned. You know I abhor the war crimes in Ethiopia, but I can't fight for a monarchy."

Johnny shook his head. "It's different for me."

"For God's sake, John," Oliver went on, a bit irritated, "Ethiopia condones slavery. How can you defend that? In Spain, the Popular Front has won an election, and now the Fascists in

Germany and Italy have stepped in to overthrow a duly elected Socialist government. This is the fight of the twentieth century. It's about whether the monarchists, the militarists, the capitalists, and the church will continue to exploit people for their own obscene benefit, or whether the average Joe has a chance at a decent life. That's it," he added forcefully.

"I don't know about that. You're good, though," said Johnny. "If I hadn't made up my mind, you could probably talk me into going."

Oliver smiled. The two men shook hands and embraced.

"*Buena suerte*," said Johnny. "That's all the Spanish I know."

⸺⸺

For the time being, war wasn't Johnny's lot. Financially, he ended 1936 fairly well. He had over twenty-six new students paying ten dollars each for an hour-long class. He was taking in two hundred and sixty dollars a week, and after paying the plane rentals and tarmac fees, he kept a hundred twenty-five dollars. January and February were predictably slow, but there wasn't a spring recovery. He was down to a half dozen students, who paid discounted rates because they were Challengers. Nationally, the economic depression had deepened. Johnny heard about the rise in unemployment, but he didn't think it would touch him. It hadn't touched him in 1929. By March, his cash flow had reversed. He wasn't breaking even.

He finished a lesson with Marie St. Clair one Thursday afternoon; she was anxious to get back to the clubhouse because it was movie night and all the gang would be there. As they walked into the noisy room, Johnny couldn't find a place to sit and fill out his paperwork. Coats were piled on his chair.

Chauncey Spencer, Dale White, Simeon, Lola Jones, Marie St. Clair, and Harold Hurd were about to start a meeting with Willa for weekend assignments.

Johnny resorted to finishing his paperwork outside with the café customers. He took the flight forms to the café window and passed them to Chauncey.

"Make sure Willa gets these," he said.

Chauncey detected Johnny's annoyance. He leaned out the window and called, "Hey, Johnny. It's nine-cent movie night. A bunch of us are going to see a Charlie Chaplin flick later. Want to come?"

Johnny shook his head. "Thanks, I'm done here for the day. I'll see you tomorrow." He walked away, putting on his flight jacket. In one motion, he mounted his motorcycle and started the engine. The tires spit dirt and gravel as he sped from the parking lot.

Thursday movie nights had become a tradition for the part-time Coffey School staff. The unmarried staff went to the movies as a group on nine-cent night.

More than the average filmgoer, the Coffey School staffers were eager to see the latest newsreels, especially anything featuring aircraft. Pathé, Fox Movietone, and The Eyes and Ears of the World regularly supplied weekly features of odd-looking aircraft, wing walkers, a flying car, and, of course, the reigning women media stars, Amelia Earhart, the first woman to solo across the Atlantic, and Jackie Cochran, holder of the women's national speed record.

In addition to the news and a cartoon, depending on the length of the feature presentation, the two-hour program was filled out with short entertainment pieces, *Pete Smith Specialties* or promotional bits.

The short film that accompanied the one-week run of Charlie Chaplin's *Modern Times* at the Music Box Theatre was a commercial for Germany's transatlantic fleet of rigid-frame dirigibles. Chauncey guffawed, and several others in the audience who saw the ironic juxtaposition laughed as well.

The narrator said that the *Hindenburg*, flagship of the German Graf Zeppelin fleet, was scheduled to return to the United States in May.

Over shots of the *Hindenburg* in flight, the narrator intoned, "For eight years, these mountain-sized dirigibles have provided regular service from Berlin to London, Madrid, Rio de Janeiro, Havana, Miami, *and New York City, by way of Lakehurst, New Jersey.*" The last was part was delivered with an exaggerated Bronx accent.

Harold Hurd leaned over and whispered to the group, "That's the same airship that Max Schmeling took last year." No sooner had the words left his mouth than the infamous boxing footage of Max Schmeling knocking out Joe Louis in 1936 appeared on the screen.

"The twelve-round knockout shocked the boxing world," continued the narrator. "Louis had an unbeaten record of twenty-seven wins, nineteen by knockout, and no losses. The Max Schmeling match was supposed to be a warm-up fight for Joe Louis."

The newsreel continued with Schmeling stepping into the frame with the *Hindenberg* in the near background. His hair perfectly combed and wearing a white plush robe with an embroidered German Eagle crest over his heart, he smiled and wiped his forehead with a towel, as if he had just returned from a workout. Then he waved good-bye to America and boarded the *Hindenburg*.

The narrator noted, "Schmeling's return to Berlin on that record-setting nonstop flight of two days was ordered by the German Ministry of Education and Propaganda."

As several people in the audience hissed, the narrator added that the record was set in an atmosphere of unparalleled luxury, as seen on the screen in the images of the art deco dining room and the stylishly attired passengers sipping champagne. The last shot featured the ground crew untying the rope moorings and the *Hindenburg* rising into the sky, a swastika boldly emblazoned on its tail.

On the bus ride home, Simeon wondered aloud, "That means an airship leaving New York early on Monday morning will get to Berlin Wednesday morning. Beats ocean travel by three weeks."

Marie St. Clair and Harold Hurd looked at Chauncey, the group's acknowledged know-it-all. Dale White and Lola Jones, sitting a row behind, leaned forward to listen.

"Well, they set a record. Two days." Chauncey chuckled. "Normally, the *Hindenburg* takes seven to ten days to get to Berlin. They stop in Madrid, London, Paris." He hit his fist into the seat. "Damn, think about it. Those bastards. The ministry of propaganda sent the *Hindenburg* just to rub our noses in Joe's loss. And then the damn bastards set a record getting Schmeling back to the Rhineland. The damn thing is a lumbering flying hotel and cruises under thirty-five miles an hour. As you can imagine, it's very expensive. They must have pushed their engines to eighty miles an hour on the return trip and got lucky with the high-altitude winds Wiley Post talked about."

"What's that?" asked Marie.

"You know, Wiley Post? He was the first man to fly around the world. He noticed as he was flying west to east that his actual speed was faster than what his instruments said. He had high-altitude tailwind."

"Is that the end of ocean travel?" Marie wondered.

"Pretty much," replied Chauncey. "But it's not the *Hindenburg* that's going to end it. You're the pilot here, Dale. What say?"

Dale White looked up. "Coffey says Douglas, Boeing, and other manufacturers are designing airplanes that can go three thousand miles without refueling. They'll be able to fly above twenty thousand feet, carry more than a hundred people, and with one stop to refuel, will get passengers to Berlin in less than a day with a crew of eight."

"The moment that happens, passenger ships will become museum pieces," said Chauncey. "The few remaining paddle wheelers on the Mississippi will take tourists on trips to remind everyone when cotton was king and slavery made it profitable."

"That I'd like to see," chimed in Simeon.

"By the way, who liked the movie?" Chauncey asked, changing the subject.

"I liked the movie but didn't understand the ending," said Marie. "Where are Charlie Chaplin and his girlfriend going? They don't have a job or a house. He's dressed like a tramp. They have nothing."

"I liked it, but wasn't it like four or five short movies put together?" suggested Dale.

"Where were they going? They have no food. They could starve," persisted Marie.

"We're not supposed to know," Chauncey replied. "They're walking to their future, and no one knows what the future holds. The happy ending is that they're doing it together. It's called an ambiguous ending, very modern."

"I don't like it," said Marie. "I think it's a sad ending. People with nothing are walking toward a lot more nothing."

～

Newsreels the Coffey School crew saw that year included a January 1937 piece about Howard Hughes. He was shown grinning and giving a hearty thumbs-up after setting a cross-country record flying from Burbank, California, to Atlantic City, New Jersey.

In March, freelance cameramen caught Amelia Earhart's vulnerable smile on her visits to several American cities before she began her attempt to circumnavigate the globe. Footage of Hughes's thumbs-up gesture and Earhart's bashful smile was filmed, processed, edited, duplicated, shipped, and shown in all major American cities within two or three days.

In April, Pathé brought news of the bombing of a town in Spain by German airplanes in support of General Franco and the Fascists. Most American audiences had never heard of Guernica, a market village in Northern Spain.

"The bombing was meant to bring the Basque opposition to its knees," intoned the narrator, "but the Popular Front fights on, with victories in Madrid and the north."

As they watched the footage, the Coffey School gang's thoughts were on Oliver Law.

In May, Fox Movietone had the exclusive and tragic footage of the *Hindenburg's* infamous crash as it docked in Lakehurst, New Jersey. Different camera angles showed the dirigible in flames as its metal frame melted and collapsed to the ground.

All through the fiery imagery, a man's voice screamed, "This is terrible! It's one of the worst disasters in the world! Oh, the humanity…"

In July, Amelia Earhart's plane missed a stop at Howland Island in the South Pacific on her attempt to fly around the world. Week after week, the news services used whatever footage they had of Earhart as the narrator gave updates on the search for her and her navigator, Fred Noonan.

Even though they didn't all agree she was due her acclaim, Willa, Marie, Lola, and Janet were keen to hear any news about Earhart. At a Challengers meeting to plan the first National Negro Airmen's Association conference, Janet complained, "Jackie Cochran is the better pilot, but Earhart's got that husband who raises money and puts deals together for airplanes. What I wouldn't do for someone like that. Know what I mean?" Out of view of the men, Janet moved her loose fist up and down suggestively. Marie was scandalized. Lola laughed.

What didn't make the newsreels but brought the Spanish war home to Harlem Airfield was a cable that arrived stating that on July 7, 1937, Oliver Law had been killed at the Battle of Mosquito Ridge. At the time, he was the commanding officer of the Abraham Lincoln Brigade.

# 42

Twice a year, Willa contacted area high schools to promote careers in aviation for bright students and athletes. Like a professional baseball scout, she spoke with their teachers and coaches. She visited the homes of the prospects and gave the parents a pitch for the Coffey School.

Aviation careers were a tough sell. Academically successful students were not interested in aircraft engine repair. And even if the young person expressed a strong interest in learning to fly, mothers who had invested years nurturing a boy to manhood balked at the idea.

"Didn't that woman Bessie Coleman die in a plane crash?" the mother of a promising student asked.

"Mrs. Lowery, it's much safer today," replied Willa. "Bessie's plane was obsolete when she flew it. It's nothing like today's advanced aircraft."

"James is sixteen, and he's graduating this May from high school. He's tired of school and doesn't want to go to college. He doesn't know what he wants to do when he grows up," said the mom.

"I want to learn how to fly an airplane," said James.

"That's not a career," replied Mrs. Lowery firmly. "I want him to go to college and become something."

"I think both of you should come to a meeting we're having about the future of aviation. It's in three weeks at the Michigan Street YMCA. It's free. There'll be ten, possibly fifteen, pilots there from all over the country. One is a doctor who flies his airplane to see his patients in rural Kansas. Another is a dentist from Milwaukee. Another is schoolteacher. The Coffey school offers free classes that apply toward gaining a mechanic's license—which is a great way to learn an aircraft inside and out. You get the free mechanics classes through the school district."

"What about flying lessons?" asked James, glancing at his mom.

"We do that, but they're not free." Willa looked him straight on, eye to eye. "You have to have a decent job to be able to afford flight classes. They're ten dollars an hour. And you'll need twenty hours of classes before you qualify for a beginner's permit. Once you get your basic pilot's license, you'll need a good job to pay for the airplane rentals. So, Mama, he's got to get an education if he wants to fly. And we'll be discussing the National Negro Airmen's Association strategy to get our pilots admitted into the Army Air Corps as officers."

Willa could tell that for sixteen, James was immature. But it was a pleasing quality because he wasn't afraid to speak. She'd met with his high school track coach and learned that he had top grades and was running the 220-yard and the 440-yard races with competitive times. Although he wasn't setting any records, he was the school's top runner.

"He's a natural athlete," his coach told Willa. "If he would only apply himself, he'd have a scholarship to Ohio State."

"But when can I fly?" asked James eagerly.

"Flying lessons? Until you're eighteen, you'll need your mom's permission."

Mrs. Lowery took a deep breath. A two-year delay sounded better than having to make a decision that day. "Maybe," she said.

"I'd like to attend the conference," said James.

Mrs. Lowery nodded. Willa gave them a press kit and membership information for the first ever NNAA conference. James grinned as if he'd just won the Irish sweepstakes.

⬱

At the final planning meeting for the National Negro Airmen's Association in January 1938, Janet complained, "We're pretending we're a national organization, even though all the members come from Chicago. What if no one shows up?"

"Well, we're going to be a national organization even if the only new member is the dentist from Milwaukee. He's our only prepaid registration. California said they would be here. And there's the doctor from Kansas, who seems anxious to participate. We'll wait and see. We still have a week to go. Enoch Waters of the *Chicago Defender* and Claude Barnett of the Association of Negro Press have given our effort a national profile," she reported. "It's up to us to make it real."

On the day before the convention, almost all registrations were from local members, while only two came from outside Chicago. At 6:00 a.m. the next morning, as Willa and Coffey arrived to set up for registration at the Michigan Street YMCA, they were met in the lobby by a bald, exuberant bear of a man pacing impatiently. He wore a tailor-made Western-style jacket and bolo tie. He stopped and confronted Willa and Coffey. "I'm Doctor Porter Davis from Kansas City, Kansas," he said.

Porter A. Davis, MD, was of Kiowa, African, and Irish descent. His green eyes sized Willa up. He came ready to engage, talk aviation, and take over the proceedings. Catching Willa with an armful of handouts and class information, he blurted out, "What's on the agenda for today?" as though he were speaking to an assistant.

Willa laughed cheerfully. "Let me set up a table, and then we can talk," she replied.

"Did you drive in or did you come through Muni?" asked Coffey, setting down his boxes.

"I flew my own plane, landed at Harlem Field. The young man at the clubhouse told me the meeting was here."

"Yes, sir. That was Chauncey Spencer. We'll start around eight o'clock, if that meets with your approval," said Willa.

"That was Chauncey? He didn't introduce himself. I know his mother's writing. Can I help carry something?"

"No, sir. Relax. We have everything under control," said Coffey.

"I've come a long way. I don't want to be part of a rinky-dink affair. You fellas better be for real, or I'll expose you as scoundrels."

Willa appeared shocked. Coffey stopped what he was doing and faced Davis.

"I understand you fly a de Haviland 3, a good plane for short stops. You can land about anywhere. Is that right?"

"You know the de Haviland?" asked Davis.

"I know you had to stop at least two times when the de Haviland should have made it on one tank of gas. Right?"

"How'd you know that?" asked Davis.

"Because the de Haviland has a problem with its fuel system. As long as you're making short hops, you won't notice it.

Once you go over a hundred miles, the engine sounds like it's choking for fuel, and your tank is half full, right? Let's just say it's a specialty of mine. I can fix it. You're a doctor, true?"

Dr. Davis laughed. "Yes, sir…"

"I won't tell you how to set a broken arm, and you don't test me about engines."

"Your analysis does resemble my symptoms," Davis replied, laughing. "I stand corrected. You know my plane."

After Willa set up the registration table and prepared coffee, she cornered the doctor. "The military and government agencies hire over five thousand civilian aircraft mechanics, airframe specialists, and pilots," she began. "A good percentage of those jobs are open to qualified Coffey School graduates. And our graduates can exceed their test threshold."

She retrieved her briefcase and showed him a stack of letters of support. "The most recent letter is from Congressman Everett M. Dirksen wishing the NNAA success at our conference."

Throughout the first day, forty-three pilots from sixteen states arrived. Janet, in charge of facilities, was both excited and frustrated with the turnout. There weren't enough chairs, and the rooms she reserved were too small. They had to move the opening meeting to the gym in order to handle all the attendees. James Lowery and his mother were there, as well as all the Challengers, friends, and guests. Initially planned as a one-day event, the conference was extended to an entire week in order to give everyone the opportunity to tell his or her story. There were doctors, dentists, schoolteachers, lawyers, postal clerks, and everyone committed to the goals expressed in the NNAA press release. Not all the participants were African American. Seven new members had been denied training in their home states because of their Jewish, Mexican, Caribbean, Native American, or mixed-race backgrounds.

Chauncey Spencer proposed dropping the word *Negro* from the National Negro Airmen's Association. In a unanimous vote, the name was changed to the National Airmen's Association of America (NAAA).

On the final day, Dr. Davis and Willa presented the mission statement to the group. The NAAA's chief goal was to lobby Congress to include qualified individuals, no matter their sex or race, to become Army Air Corps aviators. Johnny was elected the first president; Coffey, vice president; Willa, secretary-treasurer; Dr. Davis, sergeant at arms; and Janet, parliamentarian.

# 43

At six in the morning, Johnny rode his motorcycle into the parking lot at Harlem Airfield. The only activity he could see was Chauncey setting up the café for the day. Stepping away from his motorbike, he saw there was no sign of his student's automobile. He leaned into the clubhouse and called out to Chauncey.

"No, sir, no one's been here; no one's called," he said over his shoulder. "You're the first to arrive."

Chauncey hurriedly brought him a coffee and cleared off Johnny's desk by taking away the café's bookkeeping.

"Willa will be here in a minute," said Chauncey. "Hang around a bit."

Johnny grunted what sounded like, "Thank you." He kicked his chair toward the window and sat staring out. This was the second student who had stood him up that week.

When Willa entered the office, she could tell Johnny was in a funk. She glanced at Chauncey, who unobtrusively shook his head.

"Hey, let's go outside," she said. She retrieved something from her desk drawer and grabbed Johnny by the arm, leading him outdoors.

They walked fifty yards to the hangars. Willa swung a door back revealing a new Cessna Airmaster with a single wing above the cabin, a plane that had the reputation of being one of the most reliable aircraft of the day.

She handed him the keys. "It's new," she said. "Coffey prepped it for Schumacher. I was going to take her up, but you should do it. I'll have my chance later. We'll talk when you get back. I'll log you out for 6:15 a.m."

Johnny's dark mood lifted immediately as his focus became the new interior of an aircraft only two weeks from factory delivery. There wasn't a speck of dust or a mar on any surface. The leather pilot's seat lacked that faint stench of hundreds of hours of human habitation. Johnny looked over the checklist. The Cessna's record showed hours logged while the engine was in the factory and later as part of flight tests. Coffey's signature at the bottom of the forms indicated that the Cessna was in factory condition and that he had accepted the delivery.

At 6:30, Johnny sped down the runway and felt the tires lift from the tarmac. Flying the Airmaster was like remembering that you could ride a bicycle. For new pilots, the controls were clear and logical. For experienced pilots, the controls were instantly responsive. A hard turn felt solid and controlled. The gas tank was full, the sky was clear, and the Airmaster was a pleasure to fly. He made a corkscrew flyover above Harlem Airfield and disappeared.

⥲

When Johnny entered the clubhouse later, Willa could tell that he felt better. She took him outside again and walked along the parking lot.

"You need to go to Tuskegee and show Patterson you're serious about teaching," she said. "I'll set up some meetings for you. You'll be asked to speak to the students, things like that. You'll do fine."

It was understandable why Johnny wasn't keen on traveling south. Chicago wasn't perfect, but in comparison to the American South, the Windy City was a haven. He knew Willa was right about making a personal contact with the Tuskegee administration.

The train ride to Tuskegee made clear how different his life in Ethiopia had been. At Chicago's Union Station, he boarded the train cars at the rear like the other black passengers. He wore a new blue serge suit, white shirt, and tie. Carrying a small cardboard suitcase, he felt like a preacher. He could have sat wherever he wanted, but if he sat in the newer, less-crowded cars in front, he would have had to move to the rear cars when the train reached Jim Crow Kentucky. By then, all the best seats would be occupied.

At Tuskegee, President Patterson and the office staff received him warmly. On Dr. Patterson's desk was the proposal for the aviation mechanics classes that he'd sent a month before.

Johnny attended a dinner with the faculty, spoke to the assembled students on Sunday afternoon, and had a formal appointment with Dr. Patterson on Monday morning. Dr. Robert Moton, the retired past president who still had an office in the main building, joined in greeting him. Before Dr. Patterson said a word, Dr. Moton asked, "John, you came by train?"

"Yes, sir."

"Not setting any records today?" Moton pursued.

"No, sir," said Johnny, knowing he was being teased.

"This is an excellent opportunity," Moton said, "turning our auto shop into an aircraft engine repair facility. Why, we can start this fall. The students are very excited."

"Well, no, sir. Your auto shop is for automobiles. You'll still need that. The fact is I couldn't get a decent-sized truck in there, much less an airplane."

There followed a long silence. Apparently, Dr. Moton had been under the impression that not much more was needed for an aircraft engine repair workshop than was required for an auto shop. Johnny thought the old man must not have read the proposal or had forgotten that planes were significantly larger than cars.

"Aviation mechanics requires special facilities," said Johnny. "You have to have an enclosed hangar. The shop has to have portable working platforms, sturdier pulleys and winches, special tools, and a basic airstrip. How else will you get planes in for repair and maintenance? I've made a down payment on a Piper Cub. It's only four years old, but it went through some bad times and needs work. After the students repair the engine and the frame, we'll have a Tuskegee airplane. Imagine being able to travel to Chicago or Washington DC without having to put up with Jim Crow."

Dr. Moton shook his head. Johnny wondered if he was disagreeing with him or finding the idea of a Tuskegee plane too far-fetched. "Dr. Moton," said Johnny, "the last time I came to Tuskegee, I landed on the baseball diamond."

"I don't recall," said Dr. Moton.

Dr. Patterson stepped in. "Please believe that Tuskegee's commitment is real," he said, trying to set any of Johnny's doubts to rest. "What, uh…what will this new facility cost?" he asked, clearing his throat.

"The whole operation could cost between five to six thousand dollars. That's for a working maintenance hangar and a stretch of runway; a six-acre stretch could work. We have plans for everything."

Patterson smiled and replied, "We can do that."

Dr. Moton nodded, but Johnny couldn't tell if Dr. Moton was in agreement or was falling asleep.

⤙⤚

When Johnny's returning train arrived at Cairo, Illinois, the first stop outside Jim Crow country, passengers moved from the black-only section into the front cars. Though he'd traveled on the same route eight or nine times over the years, this time, Johnny felt an emotional jolt when the train crossed the Jim Crow border. It was another humiliating reminder of where he now lived. He felt unbalanced by nostalgia and missed the daily routine he had had in Addis Ababa before the war.

In Chicago, the everyday struggle to make ends meet began to grind him down. He reached out to other contacts for work. Marcus Lipsky was legit now and didn't need an off-the-books mechanic, and the on-the-books white guy didn't get anything close to what Johnny had been paid. "I can use a milkman, but that's not for you," said Marcus.

Even Fred Schumacher could sometimes make a remark that would put him on edge. As Johnny checked in at the main office at the Schumacher School for mechanic work, Fred cracked, "John Robinson, the Abyssinian war hero. What can I do for you?"

The way Schumacher said, "Abyssinian war hero," as if it were a risible epithet, disturbed Johnny. He ignored the remark and said, "If you need any help with the Muni maintenance contract, I'm available."

"Sure, John. Things are real slow. You know, it's just oil changes and scheduled stuff. Are you sure you want to do that?"

"Work is work," said Johnny.

"Okay, I'll put your name on the list, but until you get your own tools, I'm going to have to deduct for rentals. You'll find the schedule on the bulletin by the pay phone."

# 44

The following Thursday evening, Johnny sat alone in the clubhouse. The single crowd had gone to the movies, and even Willa and Coffey had left for the day. Johnny allowed the evening to overtake the room and didn't turn on the lights. His last student at least had the decency to show up and tell him that he could no longer afford the classes. Johnny had the use of the clubhouse, but it didn't feel like it was his anymore. Chauncey ran the café. Willa, with her trainees, did all the scheduling and bookkeeping, and Coffey ran the shop. There wasn't enough work for Coffey, much less for two master mechanics.

Workspace was at a premium, because out-of-work white mechanics hungering for a job camped out in all the hangars. Even as Johnny got leads for repair work, there wasn't enough long-term space available to him.

Tuskegee had always been Johnny's fallback plan. Johnny knew he could do a good job for them. He'd begun to plan how he would organize classes. He hadn't actually made a down payment on a Piper Cub trainer, but if he didn't make a move soon, there was a chance he could lose the plane. Weeks passed. Dr. Patterson should have sent a letter of confirmation. Johnny began to feel that he'd been used.

❧

As he locked up the clubhouse, his head was a jumble. Normally, a night ride on the motorcycle would clear his mind. The dark, unlit streets forced him to give his complete attention to the moment. He had to know the road and anticipate hazards. On most evenings, the cool night air blowing across his face made him forget. That night, the ride didn't clear his brain. At ten o'clock, he ended up in Janet's driveway. She'd recently divorced her second husband and had extended an open-ended invitation for Johnny to drop by whenever he wanted. She lived in a transitional neighborhood, and even at that late hour, the white neighbors noted his arrival.

"Don't mind them," she said. "They're nosy. Tomorrow, they'll be over here asking, 'Who was that handsome man on the motorcycle?' Would you like something to eat? A beer? Anything?"

"Thank you, no."

Janet sat on her long, plush sofa and patted the cushion next to her. "Did you hear from Tuskegee? You'll have to move there if they give you a post, won't you?"

"It *ain't* going to happen."

"Don't use that word. You know I hate it."

"All work has slowed down," replied Johnny, slumping down beside her. "I'll have to make adjustments because I sure can't continue like this."

"You can move in with me," she said, putting an arm around his waist and snuggling closer. "There's room."

Johnny kissed her cheek. "I'm okay. I just mean even repair work is slow."

Janet stood, took him by the hand, and led him down a hall to her bedroom.

"What will the neighbors say? Didn't you just get rid of an undertaker husband? Shouldn't there be a mourning period?"

"Stop that," scolded Janet. "You should be the one running the Coffey School." She stopped at the side of a four-poster bed with a maroon satin bedspread. She pushed him down on his back and straddled him. "You have all the flying experience, the war experience. It's not fair," she whispered.

"I don't want Willa's job. She's good at what she does. There's just not enough work," Johnny replied, aware that saying anything positive about Willa would spark Janet's jealousy.

On cue, Janet sat back up. "Why do you always defend her?"

"Willa can defend herself. I'm complaining, and for that, I'm sorry." He rolled out from under her and lay on his back. "I know the world is changing. What kills me is that it's not changing fast enough. I'm all right. I have irons in the fire. I'll be okay."

Janet curled up next to him. "If there's anything I can do to help, you know I will. I know my way around money, property, and business."

"Yes, but all your customers are elderly, sick, or dying. They don't have anyplace else to go. Flying lessons and plane maintenance are not on top of the list for living."

"Johnny, let's not talk. Don't you want to kiss me?"

Even as he kissed Janet, he knew that the only constant in his life was Willa. He could count on her to book and organize public appearances. As his students dwindled, she made sure he had use of the Curtiss Hawk at no cost so he could give flight instruction.

Johnny missed having his own workshop like he'd had in Addis Ababa. As much as he enjoyed Janet's generosity, he didn't want to go into business with her. He did have leads for repair jobs, and he knew that if he had his own shop, he could take on the work and conceivably start his own school.

When Dr. Beyan visited Chicago in 1936, he had introduced Johnny to an Ethiopian couple who ran a restaurant out of their living room. Johnny arranged for the couple to prepare a traditional meal and invited Willa to an evening of music and Ethiopian food. What he didn't tell her was that they'd be alone.

A tall woman dressed in a flowing green silk robe opened the door for Willa.

"I am Zema. Are you here for Colonel Robinson?" asked the woman, speaking in an East African accent.

"I am," answered Willa, impressed by this tall woman's elegant bearing. She'd seen Zema before with Dr. Beyan.

Willa was led to a room where the meal was ready and the lights were low. Zema closed the door, leaving Willa and Johnny alone.

"Johnny, this is what? It's a house and a restaurant?"

Johnny shrugged. "We're guests of the acting Ethiopian counsel." Willa noted the tapestries on the wall portrayed historical scenes.

"Do you know the stories that these wall hangings represent?" she asked.

"Some of them. I'm told they're hundreds of years old and priceless."

An odd plunking rhythm came from another room. "Is that music?"

"It's a begena. It's like a harp. It can be quite soothing."

Willa winced as if she'd bitten into a lemon.

Without saying a word, Johnny pulled her to him and kissed her. To his surprise and pleasure, Willa kissed back—deeply, fondly. Her purse slipped out from under her arm and fell to the floor. Her lips and breath matched his. After an extended silence, Johnny whispered, "Marry me."

Willa pulled away. "You know that I'm living with Coffey," she said.

"I understand you don't sleep in the same room."

"That's none of your business, is it?" she snapped.

"I thought...yes...but that kiss."

"No. I'm not about to marry anyone."

"What was that...what we just did?" he fumbled.

"Johnny, it was a mistake. Forget it happened," she said kneeling to retrieve her purse and belongings. "I can't stay. I have work to do." She stood and straightened her jacket, and before he could think of anything to say, she was gone. The door slammed behind her.

Confused and humiliated, the next day, Johnny walked away from Harlem Airfield––leaving a note that said he could be contacted at Chicago's Municipal Airport, care of Dr. Efran Landley.

# 45

Johnny's departure from Harlem Airfield shocked everyone. Coffey went to Johnny's apartment but didn't find him in his room. His rent was paid, but the landlady hadn't seen him, either. The corner of the hangar where he kept his motorcycle and tools had been cleared out. No one had seen him for three days.

Entering the clubhouse, he asked Willa, "What's happening with Johnny?" She shook her head and kept typing.

Although Janet stayed in touch because of the payments on the Curtiss Hawk, she generally made herself scarce. When Chauncey phoned her, she claimed to have no information regarding Johnny's whereabouts.

Chauncey made several attempts to reach him through Dr. Efran Landley. The phone rang and rang with no answer. It was as if he didn't want to be found.

Nor did Johnny attend the following meeting of the NAAA. The guest that evening was Dr. Miller, Willa's commerce department professor from Indiana State. Dr. Miller drove onto the Harlem facilities, with Willa as his passenger. Steering to the far side of the parking lot nearer the Schumacher buildings, he braked to a stop, turned to Willa, and said, "You know,

I'd hoped you'd go to work for the Chicago Public Schools." Stepping out of the car to take in the view, he continued, "But you never listened to my advice. Which is probably the smartest thing you could have done."

Willa smiled, got out of the car, and joined him. "I do work for the Chicago Public Schools, and I work here," she replied.

"You work as a teacher, not an administrator. However, this is impressive," said Miller. "Six hangars, at least fifteen aircraft, and ample office space."

"Dr. Miller, I don't run the whole operation. Everything you see belongs to Fred Schumacher, who owns Harlem Airfield. We rent the house on the other side of the parking lot. You drove past it."

Dr. Miller glanced toward the wood-frame ramshackle clubhouse. It certainly wasn't much to look at, but he didn't let on.

The professor was neither a famous name, nor an aviation expert; consequently, only half the local NAAA membership showed up to hear him speak. As Willa finished introducing Dr. Miller, Janet slipped into the room. She nodded to everyone and with the back of her hand, signaled for Willa to continue.

"Dr. Miller has brought some information he believes can be useful to us," said Willa. "Dr. Miller?"

Dr. Miller stood, gathered several pages of notes, and coughed to clear his throat. The members' casual posture gave away their low expectations. His right eyebrow appeared shorter than his left, as if he had a habit of picking at the outer edge when he concentrated. He had gained a paunch since Willa had last worked for him setting up the commerce library. His suit jacket didn't close in the front, and he didn't impress anyone. It had been Dr. Miller who called Willa and asked if he could make a presentation to the club. Though she could hardly have turned him down, she was beginning to wonder if she'd made a mistake.

"I have been reading the *Congressional Record*," he began. His fingers absently tugged at his eyebrow. "And I've been following the discussion on preparations for the coming war."

"Coming war? What war?" asked a surprised Marie St. Clair. Everyone turned to her. She shrugged, as if to say, "I didn't know."

"I know this may sound alarming," continued Dr. Miller, "but here are the facts: Japan has invaded Manchuria, Korea, Indonesia, and Malaysia. They'll soon control all commerce in the East. If they isolate the Philippines, a US protectorate, they'll control eighty percent of the world's rubber and have access to oil. This may seem far away and have nothing to do with us. However, reports say Japan's military is large enough to worry about. And then there is the German participation in the Spanish Civil War. Observers tell us that Germany has rebuilt its military, especially its airpower. And for what purpose?"

"What about the Munich Agreement?" asked Chauncey. "Doesn't that give Germany what it wants?"

"You're better informed than most Americans. Giving Germany a piece of industrial Czechoslovakia is like giving a starving tiger a tiny scrap of red meat. It will only make it hungrier. After the last war, the German people suffered inflation, starvation, and national humiliation. They feel oppressed, and Hitler is taking advantage of that. He has convinced German-speaking people in Austria, Poland, Romania, and Hungary that they will have space for the German culture to thrive. He's called it *lebensraum*, 'living space.' National pride is at stake. Germany has massive intellectual and manufacturing resources. They have coal. They have iron. They need oil to truly become a world power. And the only way they will get it is by military means."

"How do you know all that?" asked Janet sharply.

"Good question. It's my business to know business, and like it or not, war is business. I also know because I have contacts in Germany, and they tell me that thousands of young men are being trained as pilots. It's no secret."

"What does that mean for us, Dr. Miller?" asked Willa.

"I'm getting to that." He pulled out a set of clippings from the *Congressional Record* and handed them to Simeon. "I need those back, but pass them around, read them. It's called the Civilian Pilot Training Act. Congress is proposing that private flight schools, like the Coffey School of Aeronautics, provide training for young men in case the United States is drawn into a war. This will create a pool of pilots with a basic knowledge of flying. When the act goes into effect, it will pay flight schools to provide seventy-two hours of ground training and forty-five hours of flight training. And it will pay students a small stipend while they're getting trained. The Coffey School has the credentials and access to facilities to qualify. If this isn't what you've been working for, I don't know what is."

The room became silent, as if all had taken a collective breath. Dr. Miller produced another clipping and passed it around.

"There's a good chance you could receive Waco UPF-7 aircraft as trainers, and you would probably know better than I what these are. The Waco trainers are army surplus. The army bought twelve hundred of them. Today, they're obsolete in terms of the military standards. Still, if the school can maintain them, you can have them on loan to teach young men to fly. As an educator, I see the wisdom of it. Rather than the army putting terrified young men in the pilot's seat, why not find young men with an enthusiasm and talent for flying?"

For the next two hours, the Challengers barraged Dr. Miller with questions. Some, like Janet, were skeptical. Most were excited by the possibility.

As hard as it was for everyone to believe, it was true. Congress was actually going to fund flight schools and pay young men to learn to fly. Over the next several days, Willa verified Dr. Miller's information from several additional sources. Chauncey's friend and the new NAACP legal counsel Thurgood Marshall sent a telegram to Chauncey. "Not only is Dr. Miller's information correct," Chauncey read from the telegram. "Thurgood says the legislation is on the 'fast track' for funding."

Dr. Porter A. Davis, from Kansas, called Willa and Coffey long-distance to pass on the news. "Full speed ahead!" he shouted over the phone. "Full speed ahead!"

Johnny, riding his motorcycle up the coast of Lake Michigan to the end of the Sturgeon Bay Peninsula, had no idea about the excitement back at Harlem Airfield. He'd seen this lonely stretch of wilderness from the sky when he'd flown to Canada to bring back champagne and Jewish refugees. That spit of land and pine trees had been the landmark where he'd turned west thirty degrees. Seeing schools of big silvery fish feeding in the shallows of the dark-blue water, he had promised himself he would return one day.

The absurdity of his journey crossed his mind many times as he left the paved road, and had to push and carry the motorbike over craggy ridges. He rode where he could, until he reached a point between the pines and the rocky glacier-scraped shore-line. The water was so clear he could see brook trout darting to the surface and a three-foot walleye cruising by deep below. The lake's glossy sheen stretched before him toward a sharp horizon, dividing water and sky. The greens and blues were brilliantly distinct from the dusty Chicago hues. He built a small fire, caught a trout for dinner with a hand line, and ate his dinner from the frying pan. After washing his utensils, he took out a green wool army blanket and went to sleep under the stars.

# 46

Marie St Clair and Lola Jones settled into the first row of balcony seats at the Portage movie palace. Holding popcorn, Chauncey and Dale White followed close behind Dorothy Fox, an attractive sixteen-year-old new flying student with a pale complexion and straight, raven-black hair. Chauncey and Dale vied for who would sit next to her as Marie and Lola looked on amused.

"Come sit on the other side," Marie said to Dorothy. She patted an empty seat she'd saved for her next to the aisle. "Let those goons sit by themselves." The lights dimmed as the Pathe's crowing rooster appeared on the screen introducing the *News of the World*.

The first image featured a crowded Yankee Stadium with a boxing ring where the pitcher's mound should be. Joe Louis and Max Schmeling climbed into the arena and along with their handlers gathered around the referee.

The narrator's excited voice introduced the segment. "The anticipation at sold-out Yankee Stadium ran high as Joe Louis and Max Schmeling met for the second time. Hollywood and politics gathered ringside as Clark Gable and Mayor Fiorello La Guardia waited for round one." The camera panned the decked-out celebrities in the first row as the bell rang. For the next two and a half minutes, the newsreel ran with only the sound from the boxers and the crowd.

The bout began with Louis and Schmeling trading punches up close, shoulder to shoulder. Louis, sensing an opening, unleashed a powerful right hook, knocking Schmeling off balance. Seeing his opponent drop his guard, Louis pounced like a leopard. He pounded Schmeling with three machine-gun left jabs and a hard right. Pinned against the ropes, Schmeling turned his body to avoid the onslaught. A right hook caught him in the lower back that buckled his knees. He cried out in pain and grasped the ropes.

The Coffey School crew had heard the fight on the radio only days before and knew how it would end. They'd specifically come that evening to see this footage and sat motionless. Dorothy gripped the armrests. Tears streamed from Marie's eyes. Lola held Dale's hand so tightly he winced.

The referee stopped the action long enough for Schmeling to let go of the ropes and face his opponent. His body crooked with pain, Schmeling put up his guard.

With a precise left jab and a powerful right cross, Louis knocked him to the canvas for the first time. The referee paused the fight as Schmeling scrambled to his feet. He gamely put up his fists, as another vicious right caused his body to give out for the second time. Schmeling took a bit longer to rise to his feet. The referee shook his gloves and stood away. Louis struck again with a single lightning right to the jaw. Schmeling collapsed and pitifully squirmed on the canvas. His manager rushed to his side and stopped the fight.

Marie and the rest jumped to their feet, cheering so loudly the usher had to signal them to hold it down.

The next short feature began with shot of a Lockheed Vega taxiing for a takeoff. "Women want to learn to fly." Over the footage of a woman pilot in the cockpit, the narrator's tone had a lighter quality, as opposed to the deliberate "voice of God" style used in serious segments. "As men are being trained as possible candidates for the Army Air Corps, hundreds of women across the country want to take their place along with their brothers in the Civilian Pilot Training Program."

The blond, attractive Jackie Cochran, holding a trophy, appeared standing in front of her record-setting Republic P-47, a stubby, single-winged airplane with a giant engine. The narrator spoke as if he were interviewing her, "Jackie Cochran, holder of three world speed records for flying, wants to fly for the US Army. Tell us why, Jackie."

Jackie, squinting at the movie lights in her eyes, said, "I want to join the US Army Air Corps. But if the Army won't let me, I'm going to Canada or Great Britain where I have all the right credentials and experience to help with the war effort. Ladies! Get trained and get flying. Our country needs us."

The woman seen earlier piloting the Lockheed Vega winked and gave the camera a big "Howard Hughes–style" thumbs-up, as if she'd actually heard Jackie Cochran's advice.

The Lockheed Vega, accompanied by comical sound effects, bounced to a shaky landing, stopping suddenly, ending with its nose down on the tarmac and tail in the air. "Lots of luck, Ladies. You're going to need it." The narrator added derisively, "And remember, any landing you can walk away from is a good landing."

The audience roared.

"Baloney," said Marie so all nearby could hear. "That wasn't even the same airplane. Why do they always show women as bad drivers?"

The following morning, as Johnny awoke on Sturgeon Bay Peninsula, his back ached deep inside. The blanket he'd slept in was wet with dew and hadn't been much of a cushion against the rocks. His fire was out and the coals cold. His clothes smelled of smoke and the great outdoors, and he was fairly ripe as well.

Johnny peeled off his shirt and dropped his trousers. He walked barefoot across the sharp stones to the water's edge, jumped in the icy lake, and screamed. Rubbing his armpits briskly, he retreated to the shore. The rocks felt doubly sharp as he gingerly tiptoed back to his motorcycle, shivering. Without a towel, he wiped away as much water as he could with his hands and then dressed in a clean pair of pants and shirt. He pushed, carried, and rode his motorbike back to the road, arriving at his apartment after midnight. Then he fell into bed and slept for the next twelve hours.

At the next meeting of the NAAA, with all members present except Johnny, Enoch Waters, editor of the *Chicago Defender*, passed around that day's newspaper with an article featuring Willa in a flight suit with her photo captioned, "Ready to Join the Army Air Corps." Dr. Porter Davis was present, having flown in from Kansas earlier that day. He took one of the *Defenders* and held it up.

Willa waved away the paper. "They'll teach a dog to fly before a fully qualified woman becomes an army pilot."

"You joke, but there's a major effort by women not only to be included in Civilian Pilot Training," Enoch responded, "but to join the Army Air Corps. A congressional staffer told me they've had over twenty thousand applications from women and hundreds more coming in every day."

"This will embarrass the old boys at the Pentagon, so they'll have to accept the Coffey School students," quipped Dr. Porter. "Let's get to it, folks. Who calls the meeting to order?"

Coffey stood and patted the doctor on the back. "Before we start, we have several items of business to clear. Marie St. Clair goes first."

Marie waved her clipboard toward the group. "A quick announcement: we need everyone who hasn't paid his or her dues to do so tonight. We have to pay for the lawyer and the incorporation costs this month."

"I'll cover the legal and incorporation," offered Dr. Davis. "What's the next business?"

"Well," said Coffey with a chuckle, "the secretary-treasurer will make a note of that. The next announcement is that Willa and I have completed the Civilian Pilot Training application and sent it in. We're waiting for a reply. In the meantime, Willa and Chauncey have been putting together national support."

"It's all Willa," Chauncey spoke up. "I just do what she tells me."

Willa stood. "Chauncey knows everybody, and I mean *everybody*, we need to know."

Chauncey shook his head.

"Don't be modest, young man," said Dr. Porter. "We have to go after Congress high and low."

Willa continued, "We're trying to have Eleanor Roosevelt pay us a visit through Chauncey's mother's contact, Dr. Mary McLeod Bethune, from Florida. I've written to Dr. Bethune, and she has returned my letters, but I don't know her personally like Anne Spencer does. We also have advice from Thurgood Marshall of the NAACP. We have letters of support from six congressmen, including Congressman Everett Dirksen, who is a Republican member of the Armed Forces Committee. Congressman Arthur Mitchell, Anne Spencer, W. E. B. Du Bois, and Langston Hughes have written letters. The national Negro press is behind us. Can you say something about that, Enoch?"

Enoch Waters stood. "The national Negro newspaper service has hired me to write a weekly column with an emphasis on colored participation in the armed forces by both men and women. Willa will be doing four one-day excursions that we'll cover. Our big push is a five-city tour by two of our young men with a key stop in Washington DC. Chauncey Spencer and Dale White will meet with a dignitary worthy of the venture, someone on the Senate Commerce Committee that will fund Civilian Pilot Training."

Willa immersed herself in the politics, meeting frequently with black political and intellectual leaders to gain their support but also meeting with local Republican precinct captains, church auxiliary officers, and parent groups. She made well-publicized flights to Detroit, Indianapolis, Terre Haute, and St. Louis. If she thought the army would train dogs to fly before a woman was commissioned as a pilot, she didn't act like it. She advocated so persuasively that she had a following of women, black and white, ready to join the Army Air Corps.

Anne Spencer's contact, Dr. Mary McLeod Bethune, was a member of Roosevelt's black cabinet, advising the administration on matters important to Negro Americans. She wrote a personal letter to Eleanor Roosevelt, with a copy to Willa, asking the first lady to add a visit to the Coffey School while on her tour of the Midwest.

Planning for Eleanor Roosevelt's visit was temporarily set aside, however, to make way for an even more important guest. Joe Louis, Heavyweight Champion of the World, with only a week's notice, agreed to visit Harlem Airfield. Enoch Waters pulled off a major publicity coup by promising Louis's manager, through Marcus Lipsky, that Joe would get a ride in a new Cessna Airmaster with Haile Selassie's personal pilot, Colonel John C. Robinson, at the controls. Any concerns Joe's manager may have harbored about his boxer's safety were set at ease knowing Colonel Robinson had flown a head of state. He had Lipsky's word for it. Naturally, all the possible publicity angles swirled in people's minds. Enoch envisioned newsreels in movie houses across the country. *Time* and *Life* magazines would run photo stories.

Willa had Johnny's uniform cleaned for the occasion. Johnny's Ethiopian experience felt so distant it now seemed reduced to a dry-cleaned uniform hanging in his closet. He dug out his scuffed flying boots and brushed a decent shine on them.

He rode his motorcycle to Harlem Airfield early to go over the preflight checklist and, he hoped, visit with his friends. Except for Schumacher's staff, the clubhouse was deserted. The weather appeared to be the reason. Dark skies and churning clouds above were massing, not diminishing. By 7:00 a.m., a blustery rainstorm with frequent thunderclaps and lightning brought all air traffic to a standstill. Harlem Airfield closed. Johnny called Enoch, "This ain't going to happen over here. Even if they lift the shutdown, it's not safe."

Enoch knew it was impossible as well. "We were so damn close. Damned rainstorm. Come on down to the high school, and we'll get a photo of you meeting Joe Louis."

"My part is over. It's Coffey's and Willa's show now."

Joe Louis's visit to Wendell Phillips High School was awkward. He posed with Coffey by a large metal lathe. The champ's expression made it clear that he had no idea who or what he was standing next to. An overflow crowd waited in the auditorium.

Louis signed autographs and repeated over and over that they should finish school. Willa tried to get him to say more. "Joe, can you tell us what it was like to win the heavyweight title twice?"

The Brown Bomber was uncomfortable speaking off the cuff. "It felt okay," he said softly. His shoulders rolled forward as if he were embarrassed by the attention.

"Would you ever consider becoming a pilot?" urged Willa.

Lewis looked surprised by the question. "I'm a boxer," he replied. The champ appeared greatly relieved to see three men with umbrellas come to hurry him to the waiting limousine. It was still raining hard.

The event wasn't the smashing success Enoch Waters had hoped for. Joe in an airplane would have meant newsreel cameras. It wasn't a total loss, however. After all, he had a photo of the heavyweight champion of the world standing next to Coffey. The photo of Louis and Coffey appeared in every black newspaper in the country the following week.

# 47

About noon on a sweltering day in July, Army Captain Eugene Dugosh arrived at the clubhouse without calling ahead. The thin-faced, ramrod-straight investigator from the Pentagon had the look of a skeptic coming to expose the Coffey School of Aeronautics. By luck, Willa was present and Coffey was nearby; otherwise, he would have found the clubhouse padlocked.

"What would you like to see?" asked Willa.

"Show me your setup," said Dugosh briskly.

"Our setup? We have a schedule right behind you on the blackboard, if you want to see that." She directed him to the chalkboard with times for classes and plane bookings. "You've come on a Wednesday, and as you can see, between twelve and four thirty, we have nothing scheduled. Normally, I'm at Wendell Phillips High School at this time. All of our flight classes are in the early morning, and our ground training is in the afternoon, after school and after work. Saturday and Sunday, we're booked all day. Cornelius Coffey, the license holder, is doing maintenance in the hangar. If you'll come outside, I'll introduce you."

The midday sun blasted the pavement. Four students from the Schumacher School approached. "Is the diner open for lunch?" asked one.

"Chauncey should be here to open up. You're early," Willa answered, signaling with a toss of her head to a shady spot where they could wait. "Stay in the shade, and if he's not here in fifteen minutes, I'll open up the grill."

Willa took the captain around to the hangars and training spaces, where Coffey was in the middle of an oil change. He looked up from the engine. "Almost through here. Be with you in a sec."

"That's Cornelius Coffey," said Willa.

"What is your relationship with Mr. Coffey?"

"We're business partners."

"Are you married?"

"No."

"But you live together. You both give the same address as your primary domicile."

"We're roommates. We share the rent."

Dugosh took several steps toward the plane Coffey was servicing. "Where do you get the training planes?" he asked.

"We rent the Curtis Hawk from the Challengers Aero Club. We also rent planes from Fred Schumacher. It's in the application," she answered.

Coffey capped the engine and carefully wiped his fingers until he was certain they were oil free. He held out his right hand.

Willa studied Dugosh, but he gave her nothing: not a smile, nod, or grunt of approval.

"Would you like to see our planes?" asked Coffey, leading Dugosh out of the hangar. "I restored this Stearman 75 trainer. We have a lease-purchase deal with Schumacher. It's powered by the new Pratt and Whitney engine. Since Boeing took over the company, it's quite interesting what money can do. Can I show her to you?"

"Not necessary," said Dugosh. "I just want to look at your vehicles." Strolling down the line of planes staked down on the tarmac, Captain Dugosh looked more like a tourist in a museum than an aviation inspector.

"Vehicles? I don't think he knows anything about aircraft," whispered Coffey.

Willa nodded. "He was more concerned about where we live and if we're married."

"What did you say?" asked Coffey.

"I told him we weren't married and said we shared an apartment as roommates. What was I supposed to say?"

"It's the truth."

Back in the clubhouse, Willa opened the logs to show the captain how the pilots' hours were entered. "Everything is described in our CPT application," said Willa. "The office is small, I'll admit. But we also rent a hanger with a repair shop. We have full access to the Harlem Airfield runways and the control tower. Wendell Phillips High School provides us with classroom space. If we need additional instructors we can get them from Schumacher School. The Coffey School meets all the requirements to qualify for the Civilian Pilot Training Program."

"Probably so," said Dugosh.

Chauncey arrived for his afternoon shift and opened the grill for the four students waiting outside the diner window. "What can I get for you?" he asked the captain, putting on his apron.

"Nothing," replied Dugosh.

"I can get you a gin and tonic with ice. It's hot out there. We don't have a liquor license, so I can't charge you for it."

"Well, it *is* warm out there," said Dugosh, running his fingers across his chapped lips. The captain sipped his drink slowly, making his gin and tonic last.

An hour later, Dugosh had loosened up a little. "I'm an army lawyer, and I do research for my boss in the army's legal department," he said. "How did you meet each other? I mean, get involved in flying?" he asked Willa.

"I was working as a waitress at Walgreen's when I heard these two fellows, Cornelius here and John Robinson, boasting that they had an airplane. I told them to show it to me or just pay the check and be on their way." She laughed. "It was put up or shut up. And they surprised me. They had a cute little Heath Parasol. Do you know what that is?"

Dugosh shook his head and finished his drink. The ice was gone.

"It's a kit. It looked like a kayak with a long beach umbrella above."

"It did not," Coffey protested good-naturedly. "Don't malign the Parasol. It was a very efficient little plane. It was for one person. My version flew fifty-five miles an hour and had a range of two hundred miles."

"I'm not maligning," Willa said fondly. "Parasol means umbrella. She was a sweet-looking airplane, and she hooked me. And that's how all of this started."

That tidbit of information, along with all the activities of the Coffey School diner, found its way into a report Captain Dugosh prepared for the Pentagon's congressional liaison officer evaluating the applicants for the Civilian Pilot Training Act.

The congressional committee hearings on the CPT applications were held in the old Supreme Court hall in the capital building. Since the Supreme Court had moved to its own

building, a good portion of this august hall now stored dis-
carded furniture and congressional archives. The committee
used a quarter of the dais and about half the room. The elegant
fluted ceiling and the attorneys' tables still gave the space an
impression of substance.

When it was the Coffey School's turn to be reviewed, Enoch
Waters took his place at the front table before the dais.

Already seated at the table was Colonel Parker Hudspeth,
representing the army, and his investigator, Captain Eugene
Dugosh. Hudspeth opened a dossier and addressed the congressmen. A polished political player, who was offering his
appraisal on hundreds of applications, began perfunctorily, "I
rate this application poor. The director, Willa Brown's career
begins as a domestic and a waitress." He snorted. "She did a
short stint as a schoolteacher. She is divorced. Her marriage
ended due to what her attorney called 'uncontested grounds.'
She currently operates an unlicensed diner at Harlem Airfield,
which serves alcohol. She strongly advocates for the inclusion
of women in the pilot training program."

Elwin Biggs, a congressman from Alabama, removed his
glasses. "Ah've read this report. If the waitress from Chicago
thinks she's qualified to run a government flight-training program, she's delusional."

Furious, Enoch Waters stood up. "That's outrageous. This
is a session to solicit public support for individual applications. Qualifications matter! What Mrs. Brown did in the past
or that she occasionally cooks meals for students at the Coffey
School or serves alcoholic beverages for guests is not important.
She has a college degree in vocational education, holds a US
Department of Commerce commercial pilot certification, has
instructor ratings, gives flight instruction, adheres strictly to

all documentation, issues evaluations, and completes the voluminous paperwork as required of a professional flight school. Why aren't you asking about her business partner, Cornelius Coffey? He's one of the most respected flight examiners, senior mechanics, and flying instructors in the region. By eliminating her, you eliminate him. Is that what this is about?"

Waters pointed to a stack of applications in front of Colonel Hudspeth. "There isn't a person, male or female, colored or white, in the entire United States applying for a contract that comes close to matching their combined qualifications," he insisted. "And you know it's true, even if you won't admit it. The Coffey School's letters of recommendation include Dr. Bethune, Congressmen Everett Dirksen, Arthur Mitchell, retired Congressman Oscar De Priest, Judge William Hastie, college professors, artists, writers, legal professionals, the superintendent of Chicago's public schools, Niels Hoffer from the Curtiss Wright School, and Fred Schumacher, owner-operator of Harlem Airfield. They all say these are honorable people worthy of the responsibility."

Enoch opened his briefcase.

Congressman Biggs leaned forward. "Isn't it true that the waitress is living with a man who is not her husband?"

"You'll have to ask Willa Brown yourself." Enoch Waters slammed his papers down on the desk. He swept everything into his open briefcase. "If there are no more questions, I ask to be excused."

"Mister Waters, I have one more question," pursued Biggs. "There's an application here for the John C. Robinson School of Aviation. What can you say about that school?"

Enoch stopped. He turned to the sour-faced congressman. This was the first he'd heard of Johnny's CPT application.

"Colonel John Robinson has proven that the Negro has no fear of heights and combat. He is fully qualified in all phases of mechanics and flight instruction. He is among the best." With that, he turned and left the chamber, knowing that Congressman Biggs's playacting was far from over.

# 48

ꞏꞏ **W**hen were you going to tell us?" demanded Willa.

"Willa, I just got in from Washington last night. I was going to tell you now," offered Enoch. "Janet was waiting for me outside the *Defender's* office this morning. She wants me to write an article about the Robinson School of Aviation and the CPT Program."

"You can't possibly," Willa said.

"I learned about Johnny's CPT application yesterday morning," Enoch explained. "I didn't know I was going to get waylaid by Janet this morning. Willa, I have to write about him. He's good copy. People want to read about the Ethiopian war hero and what he's doing. I read their application. They're relying on Johnny's reputation and Landley's PhD. Clearly, they're competition. But they have no political support and Landley has only a basic pilot's license. Janet is listed as project manager, and she has no aviation license; her experience says she runs five nursing homes, manages two large rental properties, and has a financial interest in three funeral homes. The application did have a letter of support from Dr. Melaku Beyan, the acting Ethiopian ambassador, and a handful of letters came from colleagues of Efran Landley."

"That sonofabitch," Coffey whispered angrily. Willa had never heard Coffey ever say anything harsh about anyone and certainly never curse. "You write what you have to write; I don't want to know about it," said Coffey.

"What happened between you people?" asked Enoch.

"I don't know what's wrong with Johnny," said Willa. "We're all barely hanging on — and we've tried to keep him employed, but if we aren't making any money, there's nothing to share. He's got to figure out what he wants to do now."

"Willa and Coffey, you know where my heart is," Enoch pleaded. "I'm in a bind. I can't ignore Johnny. Just between us, I don't think he has a chance."

"What else came out at the hearing?" asked Coffey, changing the subject.

"The Pentagon hates women, and they dislike you, Willa, particularly. They can't have a woman, especially a colored woman, proving she's equal to them. And it is not that you are not equal to them. It's that they are not equal to you."

"What did they say?" asked Willa.

"I've never given your living arrangements a second thought. For Christ's sake, why didn't you just say you were married?"

"Because we're not."

"I'm not saying it's right or fair, but Congressman Biggs puts a lot of fire into his fake outrage. Women's groups will write letters. Ministers will rail against adultery."

"Adultery? Damned hypocrites!" said Willa, angrily. "Men can have wives and two or three girlfriends and that doesn't keep them from running a flying school. I can name names."

"Listen to me…" Enoch pronounced each word deliberately. "I…know…it…is…not…fair…It's about whether you want the CPT contract," he said emphatically.

"Why can't we leave things the way they are?" Coffey grumbled. "I could get a couple of girlfriends." He regretted the weak joke the moment it left his lips.

"You don't have time for this one," Willa snapped.

"Do you want the CPT contract?" insisted Waters. "If that's what gets you in the game, what's to lose? In France, this marriage would be a business arrangement."

The following Wednesday, a justice of the peace arrived at Harlem Airfield carrying a briefcase. He set up a portable podium. Willa grabbed a secretary from the Schumacher School off the street and lassoed the owner of BO&F Aircraft Supplies, who happened to be making a delivery. When the secretary offered to borrow a camera from the Schumacher School, Willa said, "Thank you, no. Let's just do this." The vows were read in the clubhouse with no one else present.

Enoch became furious when he heard the news. Willa and Coffey had gotten married, and he had no photos. "Wasn't it you who said, 'Take a picture'?" he shouted. "This is the kind of story that sells newspapers. You hate me."

"I don't hate you," she replied. "I just wanted to get it over with. Here's the signed marriage license. What else do they want?"

"You have to give me something. One picture," demanded Enoch. "One picture that I pose."

Reluctantly, Willa agreed to one photograph.

Enoch posed Willa as a happy homemaker wearing an apron, standing in front of the stove. She hated the image, but it resonated with married women. The issue spiked the sale of the *Defender* for the week.

# 49

The visit by First Lady Eleanor Roosevelt had been scheduled for 10:00 a.m.; however, by noon, the Coffey School staff, Fred Schumacher and his wife, Enoch Waters, Challenger members, and friends were waiting in the shade of one of the hangars. At twelve thirty, two gleaming black Cadillacs with police motorcycle escorts roared into the parking lot. Willa, Coffey, and the school staff hurriedly lined up outside the clubhouse.

A husky Secret Service agent bounded from the second car and opened the passenger door to the first Cadillac. Dr. Bethune, a stout woman with a shock of white hair, emerged first. The Secret Service agent held out his hand and helped Mrs. Roosevelt from the car. As they walked along the newly graveled pathway to the freshly painted clubhouse, the first lady and Dr. Bethune chatted privately as if they were best friends on an outing.

As Mrs. Roosevelt neared Willa in the receiving line, she hooked her arm and brought her close. "Why don't you lead this tour?" Mrs. Roosevelt commanded softly.

On entering the clubhouse, Chauncey offered the guests iced lemonade. He knew from his mother that Dr. Bethune grew her own lemons and was a connoisseur of lemonade. While drawing the first lady's attention to the credentials on the wall, Dr. Bethune took a sip and glanced over her shoulder at Chauncey. She approved. An entire wall inside the clubhouse had been dressed for the occasion with Coffey's many licenses and certificates and Willa's commercial pilot's license and college degree.

The entourage proceeded out of the office onto the tarmac. Positioned in front of the hangar were five aircraft lined up for Mrs. Roosevelt's inspection.

Wherever Dr. Bethune, Mrs. Roosevelt, and Willa went, two Secret Service officers followed a few steps behind. Everyone else had to stay at least ten feet back. Enoch and a photographer trailed as closely as they could.

Fifty yards away, Schumacher students and ground crews lined up to catch a glimpse of Mrs. Roosevelt.

"Mayor La Guardia is building a huge airport in New York City," remarked Mrs. Roosevelt to Willa and Dr. Bethune. "Think of the mechanics and people needed to service the airplanes. That's going to be big. You wait and see."

"And they'll need pilots, too," added Enoch Waters.

Mrs. Roosevelt turned, saw Enoch, and motioned for him to come closer. He eagerly stepped forward, only to have her hand him her empty lemonade glass. Dr. Bethune gave him her glass as well. Enoch took the glasses and sullenly retreated to the clubhouse. "Take lots of pictures," he grumbled to the photographer.

"What do you train for here?" Mrs. Roosevelt asked Willa.

"Here, we have flight instruction. Coffey is certified to qualify a person from basic to commercial ratings," Willa answered. "At Wendell Phillips High School, where we will go next, we train the mechanics who fix and maintain these planes. Would one of your bodyguards like to go for a flight?" Willa didn't expect the Secret Service agents to accept. It was simply an offer.

Mrs. Roosevelt pushed the younger and huskier of the two agents toward Willa.

"This one would love to go," said Mrs. Roosevelt. "He told me so."

"Sure," said the agent, grinning. "Where's the pilot?"

"I'm the pilot," said Willa. "Let's go, big guy." She took the agent by the arm and led him to the Stearman 75. Although the young man looked uneasy, he gamely climbed into the passenger seat, a grin disguising his terror.

"It's a tight fit," he said.

"There's a belt; put it on as tightly as possible across your middle. Have you done that? We won't take off until you do. Whatever you do, do not loosen the belt until we are back on the ground. Hold on to the steering wheel. It's disconnected, so it doesn't control the plane. Understood?"

The agent tightened the seat belt and nodded.

Simeon ran from the hanger and secured a shoulder harness on the agent, which made the young man's eyes flash even more fearfully.

Climbing into the pilot's seat, Willa shouted over her shoulder, "Hold on! You'll enjoy this!" As she started the plane and taxied out for a takeoff, the agent held on to the disengaged second steering wheel, his knuckles a bloodless white.

With a deafening roar, the Stearman sped down the runway and became airborne. Willa circled the field once, executed a barrel roll and a loop-the-loop, and then circled the field once more before landing.

The moment the agent's shoes touched the tarmac, his knees turned to rubber. Willa steadied him by gripping his arm. "I've never flown before," he admitted. "But that was better than any carnival ride I've ever took, lady."

At their next stop, Wendell Phillips High School, wherever the visiting dignitaries looked, they saw a fully integrated school, with men and women, and black and white students and instructors.

As Dr. Bethune and Mrs. Roosevelt were being hurried to the town cars at the end of the visit, the first lady stopped and motioned for Willa to come close. "I'm sending you a young man, Charles Alfred Anderson. He needs a commercial license," she said. "Apparently, no one in the capital will certify him. Take care of that for me, please."

Mrs. Roosevelt entered the car, and the door closed before Willa could say, "I know who you're talking about."

Four Chicago motorcycle policemen formed an escort, racing ahead to intersections to stop traffic as the two-car motorcade proceeded to its next appointment.

Everyone knew whom Mrs. Roosevelt meant. The famous black aviator Charles Anderson had crossed the United States twice and set a Los Angeles–to–Washington DC record for a two-engine aircraft.

Willa and Coffey didn't quite know what to make of the visit. For his part, Enoch was pleased. He'd gotten over the first lady's snub. After all, he had his lead article and a couple of excellent photos for the next issue of the *Defender*.

Although major Chicago papers had to report that Mrs. Roosevelt visited Harlem Airfield, beyond that, there was no mention of the Coffey School of Aeronautics. Nor was there a single photo or any follow-up story in the white press.

# 50

**B**efore the Civilian Pilot Training Bill was brought to a final vote, the congressional subcommittee writing the law voted to allow women to participate in civilian pilot training—on a ten-man-to-one-woman ratio. No matter how well women scored on CPT tests, they would not be accepted into the Army Air Corps.

Willa had known she never had a chance to become an army pilot. Still, the news made her angry. Coffey caught her staring out the window.

"Are you crying? It was all about PR; you said so yourself," Coffey said.

"I know it was all a fantasy for *The Defender*." She took a deep breath. "You know what, though? I couldn't have made myself go through all that hell if I didn't believe I could make it as an army pilot."

"Of course, you could. If it makes you feel better, you're too old. The cut-off age is twenty-six. Even if they accepted women, you're what? Thirty-three? You're over the hill."

Willa laughed. "You bastard." She turned to him with tears in her eyes and embraced him.

Willa continued making appearances. She was always a big draw at county fairs and church picnics. Now she traveled to promote the accomplishments of the younger male pilots.

In Detroit, she and Coffey were present when Challenger protégé Grover Nash became the first black pilot to fly a US Post Office mail route.

Willa diligently promoted the Chauncey Spencer and Dale White flight from Chicago to Cleveland, Washington DC, and Tuskegee and back to Chicago, even as the trip became a nightmare to plan. Again, no one would loan or rent a decent plane to two young black men. They needed nearly three thousand dollars, an enormous sum, to pay the airport fees, gas, living expenses, and the rental of one ancient Lincoln-Page biplane. The venture received a two-hundred-dollar donation from Dr. Porter Davis. Anne Spencer gave her son, Chauncey, one thousand dollars, adding a stop at Lynchburg, Virginia, to the itinerary.

Sitting at her desk, Willa complained to Marie and Chauncey, "We've announced a date. Thurgood Marshall has arranged for Roy Wilkins and a couple of members of Congress for a photo. And I don't know if we can put a plane in the air. We're going to have egg on our faces."

That evening, after Willa locked up the clubhouse, she found Bernie Coco, the Southside numbers racketeer, waiting in his car. She'd seen him once, years ago, at Coffey's shed, during the Heath Parasol days. He still drove an expensive car and dressed impeccably.

"Can we take a walk?" he asked, without a "hello" or "how do you do?" They walked along the runway until they were out of earshot of people sitting outside the clubhouse. He stopped and handed her a box of candy.

"This is for you," he said.

Willa opened the box enough to see an envelope with cash.

"What do you want for it?" she asked. Willa knew these guys. There was always an angle.

"Nothing. This isn't just my money. The other donors want to be anonymous," said Bernie. "I've known about you since 1933. You've always been a straight-up person. Let's say, there are people who want to see you make it."

Bernie wasn't much for conversation. He turned and left, leaving Willa to wonder what had just happened.

"Thank you!" she called after him.

⌀

On the day of the multicity flight, Enoch Waters and a photographer came out to Harlem Airfield and posed Willa, Chauncey, Dale, and Coffey standing in front of the Lincoln-Page.

Dale was the official pilot and Chauncey the navigator. Although they would take turns flying, Dale was unquestionably the better pilot. One hour out of Harlem Airfield, Chauncey thanked all the powers that existed in the universe that Dale was at the controls when the Lincoln-Page's crankshaft snapped. The engine raced, but the propeller stopped turning. Chauncey glanced around in a panic. Dale looked over his shoulder and waved to him that all was fine. Dale shut down the fuel, killing the engine, and then banked the plane toward a freshly mowed pasture and glided to a safe landing.

The following morning, Coffey brought out a new crankshaft and repaired the biplane in a farmer's barn. Chauncey and Dale continued on their five-city tour. In Washington DC, they were met by Senator Harry S. Truman and Congressman Everett Dirksen.

"Sir, could we take you up for a ride?" Chauncey asked Senator Truman.

Truman laughed. He wasn't about to climb into a flying coffin. He put his arm around Chauncey's shoulder and walked him toward the plane. "No, sir, but if you've got guts enough to fly this creaky antique," Truman said, putting a hand on the Lincoln-Page, "I've got the guts to go to Congress and demand to know why you, as US citizens, can't serve as army pilots."

Charles Alfred Anderson, the young man Mrs. Roosevelt referred to the Coffey School, arrived on the coldest day in January 1939.

Willa invited Charles into the office and sat him in a chair near the wood-burning potbelly stove. Slender with a boyish face, he took off his coat and tossed it over the back of the chair.

"That's a long walk from the curb to the door," he said.

"It must get this cold in DC," said Willa.

"No, this weather has a meaner bite to it," replied Charles, rubbing his palms together. "Well, here I am. Nice place you have."

"It works for us," said Willa. "You're a big name for the Coffey School. The whole staff will want to meet you."

"So, you need a commercial license," said Coffey. "Let's start at the beginning. How did you learn to fly?"

Charles laughed. "Self-taught. I nearly killed myself on my first try," he said. "I misjudged the field, and I couldn't get lift before I ran out of runway. I slowed, but with no brakes, mind you, the darn thing kept rolling and rolling until I ran smack into a tree, I flew out of the cockpit and broke my collarbone. I told my mother I fell off the roof. I couldn't confess that I banged up my plane and nearly killed myself the first time out. She already hated that I'd bought the darn airplane. To top it off, I had borrowed five hundred dollars from her employer to buy it. I hid the plane in a garage under a tarp until I could replace the propeller."

Charles warmed his hands by the potbelly stove and laughed. "I was crazy," he finished. "How did you buy your first aircraft?"

"I didn't exactly buy a plane," answered Coffey. "I had some plans and leftover parts from unfinished Heath kits, and I built it. It took a year and a half."

"And it flew?" Anderson asked. "What did you use for an engine?"

"A twelve-hundred-cc Ace in-line four-cylinder motorcycle engine, and it flew for about two years until it came apart in midair," said Coffey. "We're lucky to be alive."

"I operate a sightseeing service in Washington DC and take tourists and big shots on flights over the Potomac River and the capital. I need the commercial license to make me legal."

Over the next two months, despite the cold weather, Charles got in enough flight hours to finish his requirements for a commercial pilot's license. Coffey rated him as an excellent pilot and instructor.

As a parting gesture, Anderson gave Willa a set of flying gloves with a note that read, "You'll need these when you fly high." And to Coffey, he gave a leather briefcase. The salutation said, "For your meticulous notes."

Even Marie St. Clair, who had only spoken to Anderson, received a bouquet of flowers. As Anderson drove off the Harlem lot, Marie said, "That man has the finest manners of anyone I've ever known. He gave me flowers. Nobody ever gave me flowers!"

# 51

The following Friday morning, a slender white man wearing a dark business suit and holding a briefcase knocked on the clubhouse door and entered. Marie St. Clair, sitting at Willa's desk, stopped her typing and looked up. "Can I help you?" she asked.

"I'm from Congressman Dirksen's office. I'd like to speak with Mr. and Mrs. Coffey."

"If you mean Mr. Coffey and Mrs. Willa Brown, they're sitting outside," she said and led him to the back exit.

Coffey immediately recognized the congressional aide as Virgil Bentley, the missionary's son he'd tutored years before at the Curtis Wright School.

"Been awhile," said Coffey, giving Virgil a hearty handshake. "What brings you here? Willa, you remember Virgil?"

"Welcome, Virgil. It's good to see you again."

"I should have called," Virgil apologized. "But I didn't want to say anything over the phone. They're likely listening."

"Who's listening?" Willa asked concerned.

"Let's just say that some people out there know what we're talking about when we use the phone. Word will be out on Monday, and I thought you should know before it's official.

It is my duty and pleasure to request you write the language for the Civilian Pilot Training (CPT) Act of 1939 allowing the Coffey School to participate in government-sponsored aviation training. You will provide seventy-two hours of ground school classes, followed by fifty hours of flight instruction. All other Negro CPT programs will take place at six college campuses. The Coffey School is the only independent school selected."

"You want me to write what?" asked Willa, incredulously.

"What you will do with your CPT contract."

Coffey sat down. Willa stopped breathing. She caught herself and inhaled deeply. "This really is a surprise visit. You mean it's going to happen?"

"Immediately. Congress wants results right away."

"What about the Robinson School?" asked Willa.

Virgil shook his head. "It's a test, understand? The army would like to see all civilian pilot training fail and be abolished, obliterated like you never existed. You've been a particular barb in their shoe." He laughed. "You have many friends in high places. The first lady asked about your proposal. Congressmen Dirksen and Wilson and Senator Truman have made calls on your behalf. And besides the stack of letters in your support, this fellow, Dr. Porter Davis, from Kansas has been a one-man army to get you funded."

Willa, her mouth dry, was feeling a bit lightheaded and went over to the café window to ask for a soft drink from the cooler. "Can I get you something?" she asked Virgil.

"How about a hot dog like you used to make? The best times I had in aviation were the two Sundays out by that old shed you had, Cornelius. It's lucky no one got killed. Remember when John tore the engine out of that homebuilt of yours?"

"Remember?" coughed Coffey. "That was not my best memory."

Willa brought Virgil a hot dog with onions and pickle relish. He bit into the sausage and closed his eyes. "It's like coming home," he said. "I can't eat anything like this in Washington, too much pressure. I know my stomach is going to set this hot dog on fire and I'll be up all night. Once in a while, though..." He took another bite. "It's worth it."

"We have that same problem here, Virgil," said Willa. "I'll get you a seltzer."

When a single-story army barracks was towed to the location four days later, the reality began to sink in, and over several weeks, sewer pipes, plumbing, and electricity were installed. Whatever improvements were made to Harlem Airfield to meet training facility requirements also created contracts for a host of local small contractors, craftsmen, and laborers. The Harlem Avenue parking lot was graded with gravel. A concrete sidewalk now replaced the gravel path to the clubhouse, and a flagpole was erected near the main entrance.

Until that moment, Willa's, and everyone else's, work and attention had been focused on winning acceptance as a training facility. Now Willa sat in the middle of an almost theatrical set, surrounded by used metal bunk beds, wooden footlockers, and an unsorted pyramid of mattresses and army-green blankets, towels, and sheets. She sat alone for a long, pensive while. Not only was the Coffey School the only Negro-operated CPT Program not affiliated with a university, Willa was the only woman in the entire United States, black or white, to serve as the director of a fully accredited, government-funded CPT school.

She stood and danced a soft-shoe routine and sang to the tune of "K.K.K. Katy," a popular World War I song. "We... we...we did it. We did it. We did it. We did it. We did it!" She glanced around to see if anyone was watching. All alone, she began a jazzy shimmy, shimmy shake. "We did it! We did it. We did it. We did it. We did it. Yeah!"

*Time* magazine called for an interview! A photographer came to Harlem Airfield and shot dozens of photos of Willa, Coffey, and the airplanes. When *Time* wrote about the award, it ran a photo of Willa looking like a glamorous cabaret singer with a large white hibiscus blossom in her hair. She looked as though she were about to break into song.

The caption beneath the photo identified her as "a waitress from Chicago."

❧

Willa, who had remained in touch with many of the parents of likely prospects for training, began a search for candidates for the first class of CPT cadets. James Lowery graduated from high school at sixteen and now, at nineteen, was a premed biology major at Chicago Northeastern University. He'd taken a class at the Coffey School in engine repair and had done very well. And though he appreciated the skills Coffey taught him, he didn't want to become a mechanic. He wanted to learn to fly.

Willa visited Mrs. Lowery and her son at their apartment to discuss James's future. "There's no guarantee he'll be accepted into the army," she told her. "He'll get paid what a private in the army makes, and he'll have a pilot's license. That's it. If he's not accepted, he can return to college."

"Everything you said sounds good to me except for the pilot part," replied Mrs. Lowery.

"I can do it all. You'll see," said James to his mother.

Mrs. Lowery was well aware that at nineteen, James could apply or enlist without her permission. She either supported him, or she didn't. She signed the papers.

Willa, arriving at six one morning to open up the Coffey School, found a skinny young man half asleep, sitting on the stoop with his back against the front door. Willa leaned forward.

"The café doesn't open for another hour," she said.

The young man—all legs and arms—immediately jumped to his feet. "Do you remember me?" he asked. "You took me on my first airplane flight."

Willa cocked her head and looked at the young man. It had been several years, but the sinewy muscles and farmer's suntan were familiar. "Carbondale, Illinois. Anders Borstad?"

Anders grinned, glad to be remembered.

"If you've got a place for me, I want in," he said.

"In where?"

"In Civilian Pilot Training."

"Anders, there are CPT programs all over the country. If you have two years of college, you can go anywhere you want."

"Yes, ma'am. But Mom likes you. She'll be able to come and watch me fly."

"You have to take a test. It's not easy."

"I'm ready."

Anders was one of twenty-five applicants who took the entrance exam, along with Dorothy Fox. Tennessee-born Dorothy, "Dotty," as the women called her, had graduated from college in 1938 at age sixteen. A math prodigy with a mind of her own, she chose to learn to fly before continuing with her studies. Admitting to being one-eighth each Native American and African, she nevertheless looked and could easily pass for white — but lived and spoke like an educated Southern-born black.

✆

After Johnny Robinson's competing bid for a CPT contract failed, all attention was drawn to the Coffey School. Johnny's phone stopped ringing. He'd never intended for his application for CPT funds to undermine Willa and Coffey. Johnny had hoped his reputation alone might bring him a piece of the action, but he was wrong.

To add another tier of humiliation, Tuskegee was listed as one of the six black colleges awarded CPT contracts, but Dr. Patterson had made no attempt to contact him.

Chauncey visited Johnny at a small hangar near Muni Airport. He found him alone, working on a battered Piper Cub.

"You know a lot of us have no idea why you left Harlem Airfield. We feel it's like when a marriage breaks up and friends have to choose the wife's or the husband's side."

"It was time to move on," answered Johnny. "There's no reason to choose sides."

"Move on to where? Why don't you go down to Tuskegee and run their program?" asked Chauncey, not aware of Johnny's history with the institute.

"You know that Tuskegee doesn't have an airfield," Johnny replied. "You land on a baseball diamond. I got plenty to do here, thank you."

A few days later, Willa surprised Johnny at his hangar. He pretended he was too busy to give her his full attention. "I'm replacing an alternator on the trainer," he mumbled.

"Coffey called you a son of a bitch," she said, following him.

"That's pretty strong language for Coffey," Johnny replied with his back to her. He retrieved a box from the spare parts closet.

"Isn't that a Weber? Don't you need a Bosch for your Piper?"

Johnny turned and faced her. "Still not cutting me any slack, huh?"

"Slack? Is that what you want?" she replied, mocking him.

"Why are you here?" he asked, walking away. "Did you send Chauncey to spy on me?"

"What? Is it because I didn't marry you?" she replied.

"No, it's because I depended on you," he said facing her.

"And what? Because I wouldn't marry you, you blew a gasket? I didn't abandon you. I'm still here. I should hate you for what you did."

"You used me to build up the Coffey School," he retorted. "You used me."

"I thought we were building something together for all of us," she shot back. "Tell me, who sold a Stearman he'd lovingly rebuilt--in the beat of an eye, so you could come home from Algiers? Is there a man anywhere in the world finer than Cornelius Coffey?"

Johnny knew she was right.

"I don't care if you've paid back every penny you owe him. You will always owe him," she said. "Do you think we were living like your big-time bootlegger swells while you were in Ethiopia? For years, I couldn't afford to pay for a hot dog from my own grill. And I ate them for breakfast, lunch, and supper. Do you know how much I hate those shhh...god...bless... sausages?" Willa took a breath. "Listen, blockhead...we need a chief flight instructor. It's the position we always saw for you. Come back. Give these kids some of that self-confidence of yours."

"Isn't Coffey going to do that? What about you?" Johnny asked, surprised.

"Coffey and I have our hands full with the seventy-two hours of classroom instruction. He'll be in charge of ground training. You're flight instruction, and I'm administration. Someone has to be the lead flight instructor, and that would be you. Can you live with that?"

Johnny paused to think, but nothing came to mind. He closed the engine cover and tossed the alternator box aside—it was empty. "When do you want me?" he asked.

The first class of fifteen cadets came from all over the Midwest and South. Dorothy Fox was the youngest. James Lowery was nineteen. The oldest was twenty-five-year-old Elroy Meeks, who had a degree in dentistry from Florida A & M. At twenty-one, six-foot-four-inch Quinton Smith was a senior at Northwestern University where he played football.

The other cadets included two graduates of Howard University. Howard also had a CPT program, but as Midwesterners, they chose to stay close to home. There was also a literature major, Westley Tappen, from Prairie View A & M in Texas. Three were graduates of Tuskegee Institute, one with a degree in veterinary medicine, and two white men, twenty-three-year-old Mitchell Rosen, an engineering graduate from the University of Chicago, and Anders Borstad, the young farmer from Carbondale, with two years at Southern Illinois College. All the cadets signed agreements that they would be willing to join the Army Air Corps at the completion of their training.

The Coffey School was issued four training aircraft, Waco UPF-7s, to use to qualify the student pilots. Virgil Bentley explained to Willa that in the clever way budgets were prepared, these planes were part of the money Congress was contributing to the CPT program. Even though the Army's Waco aircraft were obsolete, they represented cash, at least on paper. The same applied to the barracks, towels, sheets, and scratchy toilet paper. The army used the actual money it received from Congress to update its own airplane fleet.

To be close to the school and the cadets, Willa and Coffey moved into a house trailer parked on the grounds of Harlem Airfield. They spent hours at the cramped trailer kitchen table working out a schedule. The classroom work was spaced out over six weeks, and the entire course would take ten weeks. Most black colleges were not ready to begin CPT training immediately, so their start dates were postponed.

At Tuskegee, with no aviation facilities, the process of getting underway took longer. While the army may have dumped their surplus equipment on CPT contractors, such as the Coffey School, Tuskegee would have none of that. It was asking for new construction. Negotiations for a hangar, office building, and runway dragged on.

The first week of class at the Coffey School was rocky. One hangar didn't provide enough space. Classes were held outside in brisk weather until Schumacher could clear out a second hangar for them to use. Chauncey, Dale White, and Marie St. Clair served as office staff. Simeon Brown and Harold Hurd were all-around utility help. With Willa in charge, by the end of the first week, meals were ready on time, toilets were fixed, used school desks were set up in the second hangar, and a laundry service was created. They'd pulled it together.

# 52

In May 1940, Dr. Efran Landley and the two bootlegger brothers returned to Harlem Airfield. This time, the brothers were not decked out like the Douglas Fairbanks pretenders of the past but looked suitably professional, wearing conservative Brooks Brothers navy-blue double-breasted suits, black wing-tips, and gray fedoras. They introduced themselves by their first names, Warren and Davis. Previously, they were only known as the Buckley Brother Number One, Tall, and Number Two, Short. They hung back allowing Landley to do all the talking.

Since they'd asked for a private meeting, Coffey sent everyone home early. Landley, dressed like a college professor in an off-the-rack brown suit and a bow tie, shifted uncomfortably as his bosses craned their necks toward the café, expecting Chauncey to appear with a pitcher of martinis. Landley loosened the knot on his bow tie and then opened the shirt button at the neck.

"I'm glad you can meet with us," said Landley. "We have an offer to make. It has to be confidential because we're in competition with several contractors."

"What is it?" Coffey and Johnny asked almost simultaneously.

"We're building a prototype of the Wilkerson Model W-44, which we're now calling the Apache. We want you to inspect the construction so it passes. We've leased an empty truck barn near South Branch Road for the next six months. It has every-thing—moveable scaffolding, overhead winches, lifts, what-ever we will need."

"You want me to be an inspector? I can't do that," said Coffey.

"Not as an inspector, but as master assembly supervisor. You drew the plans for what we have of the Apache."

Coffey shook his head. "Can't do it. I have my hands full here."

"We'll take care of anything you need. We can get that instructor from Curtiss Wright, Niels Hoffer, to fill in for you if we have to."

"You can do that?"

"He's the one who recommended you for the job."

"How many people are going to be involved?" asked Coffey. "That's a big job."

"A hell of a lot of work," said Johnny, adding his two cents.

"We'll have a crew of five to assemble, along with another six assembly helpers. These are top guys laid off from Northfield Aircraft. They've signed away their souls and tools to us. We have our own mold maker, and we've contracted with a cast-ing company. We're using a cast aluminum alloy for the frame and the skin. We're going to need some finesse at the end. Mr. Coffey, that's where you come in. We'd like you to design and build the engine mounts for whatever engine we end up using and whatever else needs designing. Mr. Robinson will be our test pilot prior to the delivery."

Johnny, clearly interested, nodded.

"I have a full-time job," said Coffey.

"We know that," said Landley. "We also know you'll get a break after your cadets take their finals. And as I said, we can back you up."

Landley whispered avidly, "We've seen plans made from a captured German Messerschmitt Bf 109. We think we have a better design, even better than the Curtiss P-40 Tomahawk. We have contracts for both of you. We'll pay you, Mr. Coffey, three thousand dollars with an added bonus of another thousand if we win the competition. And fifteen hundred for you, Mr. Robinson, for what we believe will be about a dozen test flights."

Landley opened a briefcase and handed them their contracts.

"I trust you, Mr. Landley," Coffey spoke softly so the Buckley brothers couldn't hear. "What if this doesn't work out? My time is limited, and I'm needed here. I feel...I can't sign anything that's selling my hide to those two swells, know what I mean?"

"Yeah," grunted Landley.

"I'll shake your hand, and you have my word. You know my work."

Landley took a deep breath and glanced at the two brothers. "Don't sign it," he whispered back. "I don't want it to come to that. There's a check here for one thousand dollars. Take it. And if at anytime, you feel you have to walk away, you'll relinquish all future payments and bonuses. Agreed?"

Coffey felt conflicted. "You can get Niels Hoffer to step in for me?"

"It will only be to fill a few days, maybe a few weeks, as a substitute. We've talked about it. It can be done."

"I don't know." Coffey looked at Johnny, who shrugged as if to say, "It's up to you." The three and possibly four thousand dollars was a powerful incentive. Coffey extended his hand and agreed to start as soon as the current class session ended.

The cadets were respectful of Johnny and his experience. In between classes, he would entertain them with stories about Ethiopia and how he tried to shoot down an Italian bomber with a revolver.

Away from Johnny and the classroom, each cadet had his own story to tell about going up for the first time with Johnny, who didn't make it easy. In case cadets suffered from motion sickness while in the air, Johnny provided them with a bucket. "Whatever you do, don't let go of the bucket," he'd warn them.

Then he'd execute stomach-churning turns, dives, and pull-ups, testing the cadets' fortitude. At the end of their first flight, he would do a barrel roll. If the cadets vomited, the contents of the bucket went everywhere, and he made the poor students clean up after themselves.

"I gave up my lunch up there," said Quinton Smith. "I had vomit on the wing above me, on the floor, across my lap. I was out there with a bottle of apple cider vinegar cleaning until lights out."

"I threw up," said Dotty Fox. "But I wasn't going to let him beat me. Knowing he was going to do the barrel roll, I let gravity take care of me. Who else did that?" Several men held up their hands.

"Liars," said Quinton. "I saw you guys out there with the vinegar."

"The man is sadistic," said Tappen, the literature major from Prairie View A & M.

"What about you, Lowery?" asked Dotty.

"I don't get airsick. I love the sensation of motion," bragged James. After seeing a maneuver done once, he was trying it himself. He could do a tight loop-the-loop and a snap turn and roll just as Johnny had demonstrated.

Tappen jotted down short paragraphs about his flying experiences in a leather notebook he kept in his back pocket. "Someday, I'm going to write a book about you guys, and Dotty, too."

"Sure, Tolstoy," cracked Elroy Meeks, the dentist from Tuskegee. "Someday, you'll make us all famous."

Dotty couldn't stand being the third to solo. But the selection for who would go first was determined by a lottery. She was the fifth slip of paper out of the hat, but two of the men failed to muster the courage to go up alone. This included the football standout from Northwestern University, Quinton Smith. Dotty was shorter than the men, and the cockpit suited her. She steered steadily down the runway and was in the air without a wobble. She followed that with a picture-perfect landing.

On a football field, Quinton Smith may have had the agility of a dancer, but he froze when it came to the man-machine choreography of flying.

Johnny did everything he could think of to help Quinton find his feel for flying. "The kid freezes," he told Willa. "If he doesn't solo, it will be too bad. He's a really bright young man. I'd hate to see him wash out."

Willa took Quinton's next flight class. The dual-control Stearman 75 was the largest plane they had. At six foot four, Quinton had to squeeze himself in carefully.

"Can you reach everything?" she asked him, standing on the wing.

"Yes," he replied.

"Then taxi out to the runway. Can you do that?"

"Yes, ma'am."

"Have you made a takeoff before?"

"No, ma'am."

"You've had plenty of hours' practice. You're going to do it now."

"What if we crash and I kill you?" he asked, perspiration beading his forehead.

"I'm not a fool. I'm not going to let that happen," Willa answered. "We have dual controls," she said climbing into the seat behind the pilot. Quinton rolled the plane out to the end of the runway and turned for takeoff.

Willa could see him gripping the steering wheel so tightly the blood vessels on the back of his hands were visible. "Loosen your grip!" she shouted. "You're not going to lift the plane into the air with your arms. The propeller and wings are going to do that for you."

Quinton half turned and nodded.

"I'm holding the steering wheel with you," she continued.

The plane sped down the runway and was lifted early by a five-mile-an-hour headwind. "Easy, easy, easy. Okay, we're in the air. You've got it. Slowly bank to the left. There…Wasn't that easy?"

"Yeah, but you had the wheel, too!" Quinton shouted, looking more at ease.

"No, I didn't," she said and gave the dual wheel a spin. It's not connected." The plane made a hiccup. "Relax!" she shouted. "Now, enjoy your flight."

# 53

C offey visited the warehouse four times a week after his work at the Coffey School. He never saw the Buckley Brothers around that location again. But into the third week of his break, the assembly was far behind schedule.

"What's the matter?" Coffey asked, cornering Landley. "Only one or two casts are coming in each week. That's not fast enough if you plan to finish in five months."

The workers didn't mind; they were paid whether they did anything or not. On the warehouse floor, five aluminum-alloy ribs sat mounted like a dinosaur skeleton exhibit.

"What gives?" demanded Coffey.

"I really can't talk about it," said Landley in a lowered voice.

"Do you know how many hours I work every day?" asked Coffey. "I can't spin my wheels here. I have too much to do. When you have something for me to work on, let me know; otherwise, I'm getting some shut-eye." He started to leave.

"Wait," called Landley. "Let's go outside." He closed the door behind them. "The Buckleys have a deal pending with a big aircraft company. Right now, they're waiting for the deal to close, but the company wants to see the prototype before they put up the money. I'm stuck here in the middle."

"Well, I'm not in the middle. If the bootlegger brothers won't turn loose of the cash to do this right, they can finish the Apache—or whatever they call the W-44—without me. I can't speak for John, but considering the history this plane had before we got to it, I wouldn't recommend he fly it, either."

"Let me make a phone call. Wait a moment. Please." Landley scurried back into the building and climbed the stairs to the mezzanine office with observation windows all around. When he returned, his sullen expression made it plain he didn't have good news.

"They're incensed that you're walking off the job," he grumped. "We will finish the W-44—I mean Apache—without you."

Coffey felt his face flush. "Those stingy bastards," he blurted out. "You know what makes me angry? I know I can make the W-44 better and faster. Frankly, I don't need the headache of two tightwad millionaires trying to do this cut-rate." He stalked off. "I thought they were big-time players."

The next morning as Coffey was shaving, Willa called him to the phone.

"Have you reconsidered?" Landley asked, expecting Coffey to ask for a pardon. There followed a long moment of silence.

Coffey shook off his morning cloudiness. "What's to reconsider? I'm glad to be free of the responsibility. I spoke to John. He's out, too. We're going full speed over here."

Landley briefly muffled the telephone and whispered to the brothers, "He's not interested."

"What's he want?" demanded the shorter brother. "Double the goddamn pay."

"What will it take to get you back?" asked Landley. "We'll double the pay."

"Let me think," Coffey wiped away the shaving soap from his face. "Put me completely in charge, and I'll build their damn plane. Double the pay is fine, but they better start shooting out the castings. No castings, no deal."

"They're looking into that. I assure you. It's being taken care of. Come on in. I have something for you to read."

The following morning, Landley gave Coffey the specifications provided by the British Purchasing Agency. Coffey spent several hours sitting in the office with the observation windows, poring over the details of size, speed, fuel capacity, payload, and maneuverability. When he finished, he came out and handed the specs to Landley.

"Those bastards. Your bosses know the W-44 is exactly what the Brits want."

"Yes," admitted Landley.

"I want those cheap bootleggers to deliver the frame right away. Next week. I don't care if they have to buy the casting foundry, which isn't a bad idea. The deadline is four months away, and they've already pissed away three weeks."

"It's not entirely wasted, " said Landley. "We have gotten some work accomplished." Coffey surveyed the assembly floor and saw the workers napping on the scaffolds or playing cards on an overturned wooden crate.

"It's not going to be cheap anymore," advised Coffey.

Coffey's race may have been an issue with the assembly workers at the start.

"Gentlemen," he called out to the room, "we're going to have a production meeting. Gather around."

The card players stopped what they were doing, but only to glance peevishly in his direction.

Coffey put down his notes and placed himself in the center of the warehouse floor where he could see everyone. "I'm going to build an aircraft like none of you sons of bitches have ever seen before," he said forcefully.

Several men bristled at having their mothers called bitches.

Coffey didn't care. "If I seem a little beside myself today, it's because I have a little over four months to make something that's going to make history. If you're not going to be my crew, let me know right now. I will find another crew fast. Isn't that right, Mister Landley?"

"We have contracts," one of the workers called out.

Coffey couldn't tell who said it. "I said, I will hire another crew today. Isn't that right, Mister Landley?"

"Yes, sir, Mr. Coffey. You are in charge," Landley said from behind the crew.

"Shall we get started then?" said Coffey, going back and picking up the plans and notes.

The poker players tossed their cards, and the rest climbed down off the scaffolds. They slowly gathered in a semicircle in front of Coffey. Over the next week, Coffey pretty much showed the crew that he knew everyone's job and could probably do it better and faster.

The Buckleys didn't buy the casting company, but they went into full production. They brought the molds back to the warehouse for storage. The castings for the different parts of the plane still had to be deburred and precisely tailored to fit together. The staff grew to over forty craftsmen and assistants. Sheet-metal workers hand shaped the outer aluminum bodywork, polishing the panels so the plane looked like it had a single aerodynamic skin.

As the workers began to see the beauty of the aircraft's design, they started to share a pride in the work. They competed to finish their tasks ahead of schedule, while meeting Coffey's exacting standards at the same time. Coffey didn't give many compliments. "If you're still getting your pay envelope, then you're doing okay by me," he had said early on. But when he said, "Good job," he meant it.

Designing the modifications for the retractable wheels was the kind of problem Coffey thrived on. Hunkered over his worktable, he'd occasionally make a sucking click with his teeth when he was frustrated and hummed a low, tuneless accompaniment when his ideas were working. He built models and tested the mechanisms over and over until he was certain all possible snags were worked out.

Late at night, in silent moments alone, Coffey could envision what the W-44's designer Jimmy Wilkerson saw: a lightweight and extremely sturdy aircraft with a low drag underbelly, wings shaped and positioned for increased performance, and an engine incorporated into the total sleek design. Even as he finished his part in the production phase, Coffey knew that the W-44 could handle a much more powerful engine. The Harrison J-39 liquid-cooled engine Landley had ordered was adequate for the job, but Wilkerson had designed the plane for a much larger racing engine.

"Get an engine with more oomph; it will boost performance by at least twenty-five percent," he told Landley. "The frame can take it. This is a really beautiful machine."

"Can't afford it. They have to keep the unit cost down if they want to win the order," said Landley. "None of our competitors can use a bigger engine."

"You're putting a motorcycle engine in a racecar. Couldn't you see the new Rolls-Royce Merlin engine in this?"

"Yeah, but it's not in the budget."

Johnny's first two days of test flights gave him a good sense of the Apache/W-44's performance. At top speeds, she felt a like a bullet, though still basically skin, frame, gas tanks, and motor with no baggage. To compensate for the missing weight of two fifty-millimeter guns, ammo, bombs, and navigation equipment, Johnny and Landley strapped in sandbags.

"That's a hellava lot of weight," said Landley.

"She taxis smoother loaded down," replied Johnny.

As Coffey and Landley watched, the plane took off without laboring and flew through stress performances appreciably better than anyone had expected. Altitude tests were made in five-thousand-foot increments, starting at ten thousand feet — nearly two miles high. At eighteen thousand feet, the engine developed an intermittent sputter, and as it climbed past nineteen to twenty thousand feet, the motor coughed and died.

Johnny thought he could hear his heart beating in the silence. He leveled out the flight, pulled on the choke knob, and punched the ignition switch. The starter growled, but the engine refused to grab—it wasn't getting any fuel. After several failed attempts to start the plane, Johnny noted that terra firma was approaching quickly. He glanced around for a place to land. There were too many houses in one direction and too many trees in the opposite. Finally seeing a stretch of road with light traffic and no phone lines, he made one last attempt to start the engine, and it fired up as if nothing were wrong.

Back on the ground Coffey gave the engine failure his best guess. "She probably can't suck enough oxygen at twenty thousand. And by the time you began your approach, gravity stabilized the carburetor." Coffey turned to Landley. "We need those carburetors I made for the original W-44."

"They're gone. Destroyed, I'm afraid," said Landley. "Even if we had them, they were for a different engine."

"I know," said Coffey pensively. "There were a couple of design ideas I need to think through again. To go faster and keep a steady mix of oxygen and gasoline firing in the chambers, Wilkerson used a combination of mechanical and electrical innovations––like no one else makes. I need to see them again."

"We do have your notes and drawings, if that would help," offered Landley.

Coffey laughed. "Yes, that would help."

With only three weeks until the British Purchasing Agency deadline, Coffey spent his time designing and making molds for a supercharger, a device that forced compressed air into the firing chambers. He used the crew to deburr and polish the castings and tested them in the warehouse under controlled conditions.

Coffey choose three of the finished super carburetors slightly different in design. Each unit was mounted on the plane and tested on the ground and in the air. Johnny reported that without putting a lot of stress on any of the superchargers, they essentially performed the same.

With only two days to the British purchasing deadline, Coffey selected his favorite of the three units, and Johnny took the W-44 for its final supercharger test run.

"If this works, we're home free," said Landley. "If it doesn't, the W-44, I mean the Apache, will be out of the race."

"You know where to send my money," replied Johnny, climbing into the cockpit.

Fully loaded, the Apache cruised at three hundred and fifty miles an hour at an altitude of twenty-five thousand feet, faster and higher than the Messerschmitt Bf, the Mitsubishi Zero, the British Spitfire, and the Curtiss Tomahawk.

After the tests, Coffey asked Landley, "What happens now?"

Landley shook his head. "We're out of here. We're anonymous. The corporation that's taking over the Apache has their own engineers, and they'll take all the credit for our work."

"Not even Wilkerson gets credit?"

"Especially not Wilkerson. Why do you think they changed the name to the Apache?"

Even though the Apache lacked gun mounts and was skeletal in all other respects, the British agents were impressed enough with the potential range of six hundred miles, the plane's appearance, and its speed and maneuverability to undertake its own test flights.

In January 1941, the British test pilots wrote: "The performance exceeds specifications. The Apache is recommended for purchase." Great Britain's first order was for one thousand five hundred of the new fighter plane.

The North American Aviation Company announced that its design team had won the contract to deliver a new fighter plane to the Royal Air Force. A review of their contract revealed that the Buckley brothers didn't have naming rights. A purchasing agent, whose name no one can recall, took the suggestion of one of the British test pilots literally. "The aircraft is not the warrior," the pilot had said. "Our British lads are the warriors. And they ride into battle on a rugged Indian pony, a Mustang." The new acquisition became known as the Mustang P-51 Pursuit Fighter.

# 54

I n the time that most colleges took to complete one class, the Coffey School had graduated two. For the final hurdle to completing the Civilian Pilot Training program and becoming fully qualified candidates for the Army Air Corps, the Pentagon required all CPT graduates to pass a demanding written exam. In June 1940, Willa sent postcards to all graduates announcing that she would conduct a one-day review of the classroom material in preparation for taking the test. When she arrived at 7:00 a.m. Saturday morning to unlock the door to Wendell Phillips High School, thirty-two of the thirty-five graduates were waiting to take the review.

Colonel Hudspeth, the Pentagon's congressional liaison, who had delivered the negative Coffey School report before the Commerce Committee, in an interview with a gaggle of reporters, was quoted as saying, "This test will end the presumptuous ambitions of that willa-nilly waitress from Chicago." The laughter that echoed in the congressional hallway prompted the sergeant at arms to open the door and motion to the colonel to hold it down.

A week later, a representative from the army administered and monitored the test in a Wendell Phillips classroom. The students were quiet, trying to go over one last time in their minds the most difficult parts of their training. After the exam, Lowery felt too confident. "I didn't like it," he said. "It was too easy."

Tappen, the writer, disagreed, as did most of the others. "There was always a right answer and a close second on the multiple choice," he complained.

Dorothy Fox also found the test too easy, but when asked by Meeks what she thought, she begged off. "It was so-so."

A month later, the scores were posted at the Pentagon and a copy sent to Congress, as well as to the participating CPT contractors.

Willa proudly made expensive photographic copies of the page and posted them outside the front door. That first day, Willa could hear the whoops and shouts of success, because not only had no one failed, as a group, the Coffey School cadets scored in the ninetieth percentile, placing them in the top tier of all flight schools and colleges in the country. Willa wasn't surprised that nineteen-year-old James Lowery and eighteen-year-old Dorothy Fox had scored in the top 2 percent of the thousands of people who had taken the test nationally.

The day the test results were published, thousands of qualified young black, Latino, Asian, Native American, and Jewish men had suddenly become eligible for army flight training. The army had run out of excuses to exclude them.

Several months later, white Coffey School cadet Mitchell Rosen wrote to Willa that he had graduated from army flight school and was now a second lieutenant in the Army Air Corps waiting for his assignment. It gave her a moment of reward and a measure of painful resignation, as well. Mitchell Rosen was smart and good, but he wasn't the top of the class. She heard that colored cadets with even better skills were told that since there were no segregated aviation facilities, there was no place for them. They were welcome to join the service units as cooks and laundrymen. A few graduates were angry about the army's policy; most laughed it off as same old Jim Crow. They had been trained as pilots and it hadn't cost them a cent.

Anders Borstad, the farm boy Willa had taken up for an airplane ride when he was seventeen, asked to speak with Willa. "I'm going to enlist in the Royal Canadian Air Force," he confided. "My uncle, mom's brother, was executed because he represented the carpenters' union in Oslo, Norway. The government has sided with Germany and Fascists."

"What's your mother say," asked Willa.

"She doesn't want me to go, but I feel that this is family." Anxious to see action, Anders enlisted in the Royal Canadian Air Force and became the first of the Coffey School graduates to face combat in Europe.

Chauncey, Marie, Lola, and Dorothy Fox were the regulars for the Thursday movie nights. There were others who came, but they weren't as committed to the weekly ritual. The movie they saw that evening was *Mr. Smith Goes to Washington*. Everyone liked Jimmy Stewart and his gangly antics, but it was Gene Arthur's scratchy voice and world-wise persona that appealed to everyone. Besides the main attraction, the newsreels held equal or even more interest for the Coffey School crowd. Pathé News brought images of the ever-expanding war in Europe. The narrator spoke in the punchy style, hitting key words for emphasis. "As predicted, Germany was not satisfied with the small piece of industrial Czechoslovakia it appropriated last year. Since then, Poland, Norway, France, and Yugoslavia have fallen to what German propaganda calls *blitzkrieg*, lightning war." Images of German soldiers posing in front of the Eiffel Tower were shown. "Now, Germany's appetite appears to be for Russia. With the breakdown of diplomatic talks between Russia and Germany, Hitler has ordered a three-pronged invasion of the Soviet Union."

An ominous military drumbeat sounded as the newsreel featured images of tanks rolling and soldiers marching superimposed over a map of Germany and Russia, which was being pierced by animated trident prongs. "What does this all mean?" added the narrator. "Only the mind of Adolf Hitler knows." Hitler and an escort of high-ranking officers stood on a reviewing platform. Stone-faced, the *fuhrer* nodded approvingly as scores of German military aircraft flew in formation overhead.

The next image was filled with hundreds of American flags waving at a rally in view of the White House. "John Q. Public is still undecided as to what should be done about Germany," the narrator went on. "Opposing American involvement in the European war, the America First Committee gathered this weekend in Washington DC." Demonstrators carried antiwar signs as aviation hero Charles Lindbergh addressed the rally. "To express his opposition to American intervention, Colonel Charles Lindbergh submitted a letter to President Roosevelt resigning his commission in the Army Air Corps."

The newsreel footage depicted reactions at the DC rally to Lindbergh's speech. Some in the crowd booed as others cheered. An America First member holding a sign reading,

"Stop Warmonger Roosevelt," looked comically stunned as a grandmotherly looking woman grabbed his sign, ripped it in half, and slapped his face.

As they exited the theater, Marie was concerned. "What if Congress listens to Lindbergh? Germany acts like it wants everything. Italy has taken Ethiopia, and this Mussolini guy and Hitler are now pals. When is the *blintzkrieg* going to stop?"

"*Blitzkrieg*," Chauncey corrected. "It doesn't make any difference what the newsreels say about the isolationists. Congress has expanded the CPT program to include more colleges and flight schools—not less. Marie, the side having a technological advantage wins wars. The long bow was superior to the sword. The Colt six-shooter was superior to the bow and arrow. *Blitzkrieg* is nothing more than attacks on countries with more horses than tanks. I don't like the idea of a war. People die, and people suffer. I'm afraid it's gone too far. Whoever makes the decision about going to war is going to take us to war."

"I don't want to believe that," said Marie. "It's too cynical."

"Chauncey, sometimes a question is rhetorical," said Dorothy Fox. "You don't have to give us a history lecture every time someone thinks out loud." She exchanged looks with Marie and Lola Jones. Chauncey occasionally went on too long.

# 55

**E**noch Waters waited outside the hearing room as congressmen met in a closed session. The question before the committee was not whether the army would train black cadets, but where. The debate Enoch had listened to rehashed a lot of the old thinking that for many whites justified that the position of officer in the US military was an honor reserved for the sons of wealth or for young white men with exceptional talent. To the conservative members, this made sense; pilots were, after all, entrusted with an aircraft valued at more than forty thousand dollars. The handful of liberals on the committee argued that the Coffey School had proven beyond a doubt that their cadets were equally qualified and responsible. They pressed for the establishment of a racially integrated army facility at Harlem Airfield, which met all the requirements for runways, hangars, and support facilities called for in the guidelines.

Colonel Parker Hudspeth, the army's congressional liaison, also waited in the hallway for the committee to adjourn, and seeing Enoch, he stubbornly made no effort to keep his voice down. "There's no chance in hell we'll give a contract to the waitress from Chicago."

Virgil Bentley, Congressman Everett Dirksen's aide and Coffey's friend, exited the meeting. "Mr. Waters, they're wrapping up in there. Walk with me a bit," he said to Enoch privately. "Here's the outcome. The president of Tuskegee Institute, Dr. Frederick Patterson, has offered a pasture forty miles from the college as a location for a training base for black aviators."

"Tuskegee doesn't meet the requirements," whispered Waters. "There's nothing there."

"The committee has approved funding for an entire military base to be built from scratch: hangars, barracks, airstrip, mess hall, headquarters, everything in that pasture in Alabama," divulged Virgil.

Enoch knew that an isolated training base in the segregated South probably sealed the deal. It was a bad piece of news to bring home, because Willa, Coffey, and the school staff felt certain they were in the running. None of the colleges had anything equal to the talent and facilities available in Chicago.

Two days later, coinciding with the public announcement that the training base was to be in the Deep South, Eleanor Roosevelt paid a visit to Tuskegee Institute. In a symbolic gesture of support, she went up for a well-publicized flight with Charles Alfred Anderson, Tuskegee's new chief flight instructor.

A photo of the first lady sitting in an airplane behind Anderson appeared on the cover of the *Chicago Defender* the morning after Enoch Waters returned from Washington DC. He brought copies of the newspaper to a Challenger meeting that evening and passed them around.

Chauncey pushed the newspaper back into Enoch Waters's hands. "Just because you tell us Anderson got his commercial license here at the Coffey School, doesn't make it right," he complained. "It's not supposed to be this way. The Coffey School is integrated. Isn't that what we've been working for?"

Enoch shook his head. "It's politics, Chauncey. You know that! It's not what we wanted, but Mrs. Roosevelt has made her decision. It was probably the only choice she had."

"What did the NAACP have to say about it?" asked Willa.

"Roy Wilkins calls it half a victory," answered Enoch. "In other words, half a loaf of bread is better than none. Even though it will be a segregated unit, our young men will be trained as pilots and become commissioned officers and gentlemen."

"In the goddamn segregated South!" said Chauncey angrily. "What kind of message does that send to the young men?"

"We're funded, Chauncey," said Willa firmly. "This is what we've been working for, right here. We're not going to change the way we do business."

"If they learned to fly here, I know they can make it there," said Johnny. "If our young men have to be two times better than whites to be considered equal, we push them to be ten times better."

The Coffey School became a full-time operation, obligating Willa to resign her teaching position with the Chicago public schools. Young women from her high school typing and book-keeping classes took part-time jobs to help with the additional paperwork. Willa had a hard rule that the young women had to dress professionally and not fraternize with the cadets. She quickly learned that the fraternizing rule was ridiculous since the presence of so many single young men made the low-paying part-time positions premium employment for young women. And naturally, it was the young men who did the fraternizing.

As the first class of black Army Air Corps trainees got underway at Tuskegee, Alabama, over 50 percent of the officer candidates were Coffey School graduates, including the now twenty-year-old James Lowery.

# 56

On a cold, gray Sunday afternoon in December, Chauncey was taking his new girlfriend, Joanne, to the early show at the Music Box Theatre when they saw a crowd gathered in the doorway of the Dyno-Electric vacuum cleaner store.

Johnny was having a beer with friends at Hilly's Tavern when a man ran in from the street and waved to the barkeep, "Hilly, turn on the radio, quick!"

Coffey sat at the kitchen table in the trailer he shared with Willa working on a carburetor. Willa was ironing her skirts and blouses and Coffey's shirts for the following week while listening to the Paul Whiteman orchestra performing live from the Belvedere Hotel Ballroom, when the music stopped suddenly and a man's voice announced, "We interrupt this program to bring you a special news bulletin..."

As Chauncey and his girlfriend neared the vacuum cleaner store, they heard, "The Japanese have attacked the military base at Pearl Harbor Hawaii by air, President Roosevelt has just announced. The attack has also been made on all naval and military activities on the principal island of Oahu. We go now to Washington..."

That moment, for those who heard the broadcast, became indelible. Everyone would remember where they were and what they were doing the moment they heard the news of the bombing of Pearl Harbor. For the next several days, the nation would remain close to a radio.

Chauncey and Joanne, sensing that the news was historic and probably life changing, talked late into the evening, made love, and spent the rest of the night clinging to one another.

Joanne joined Chauncey at the clubhouse the following morning to stay apprised of developments. Chauncey made general introductions. "Everybody, this is Joanne Marbury; she's the youngest professor of economics Howard University has ever hired. I met her at my mother's house last time I was home. This is our boss, Willa, and then there's Marie, Dorothy, Lola, our benefactor Janet, Cornelius Coffey, the other boss, and the part-time staff––Patty and Rita."

Joanne smiled shyly. "Pleased to meet everyone." Her presence in the clubhouse was unprecedented. Away from Harlem Airfield, Chauncey may have been a bit of a flirt and certainly a good-time Charlie. However, he never dated any of the staff. He treated the young women at the school as if they were sisters. Now Marie, Lola, Dorothy, and the part-timers saw an attractive, well-dressed young woman sitting at the counter making "goo-goo eyes" at their handsome grill cook/scholar and—infuriatingly—hanging on Chauncey's every word.

Around noon Chicago time, Chauncey and Joanne sat at the café counter holding hands, as President Roosevelt was about to address a joint session of Congress.

"The mood in the gallery and legislature is somber," intoned the radio announcer. "This speech is being simultaneously broadcast on all radio stations in the country and by short wave to American ships at sea and military bases abroad."

Simeon had caught the bus to downtown Chicago intending to buy a new pair of shoes at the Thom McAn shoe store. As he walked past Schultz's Bespoke Tailors, and the National Shirt Shop, all storefronts were tuned to the radio. He could go from shop to shop and not miss a word. Clusters of people gathered around radios or stood motionless in doorways, listening.

The announcer introduced, "The President of the United States." There was no applause, only the sound of a nation holding its breath.

"Yesterday, December 7, 1941, a date that will live in infamy," President Roosevelt spoke in a slow, deliberate cadence, "the United States of America was suddenly and deliberately attacked by the naval and air forces of the Empire of Japan. The attack yesterday on the Hawaiian Islands has caused severe damage to American naval and military forces. I regret to tell you that many American lives have been lost. In addition, American ships have been reported torpedoed on the high seas between San Francisco and Honolulu. Yesterday, the Japanese government also launched an attack against Malaya. Last night, Japanese forces attacked Hong Kong. Last night, Japanese forces attacked Guam. Last night, Japanese forces attacked the Philippine Islands..."

At the Coffey School clubhouse, at Hilly's Tavern, at Schumacher's office, at Roxy Moss's radio studio, at stores on North Broadway, and in kitchens, living rooms, and workplaces throughout the United States, Americans were stunned by the cold-blooded efficiency and the enormity of the attack. Less than an hour after the speech, Congress declared war on Japan. By dinnertime, Americans learned that Germany and Italy had declared war on the United States. The world was at war.

# 57

"They're trying shut down the school," argued Chauncey. "Why else would they draft every one of us?"

"Chauncey, you're all the right age and you have talents. You and Harold are aircraft engine mechanics. Dale's a flight instructor. Simeon and Grover are licensed pilots."

Coffey and Johnny were deemed to be too important to the war effort to be inducted. The Coffey School draftees went on to perform their military service with distinction as staff, mechanics, or flight instructors at Tuskegee.

If the army's raid on the Coffey School's male staff was intended to cripple the school, as Chauncey had suggested, it didn't work. The vacancies created openings for a new crop of eager young men and women, willing to work longer and harder. The attack on Pearl Harbor had had a galvanizing effect on the US population, and the Coffey School was no different. Marie St. Clair, as office manager, provided continuity by keeping the work roster filled and showing the new staffers and part-timers the ropes around the café and the hangars.

In 1942, the Civilian Pilot Training program became the Wartime Training Service. The army exerted more control over training, and many low-performing CPT schools were cut. Because of the caliber of their graduates, the Coffey School continued to produce young men already in possession of a basic pilot's license or a mechanic's certificate. As part of the Wartime Training Service, Coffey, Johnny, Willa, and all the cadets were obliged to wear the uniforms of the Civilian Air Patrol (CAP). Willa became the first black female CAP officer, achieving the rank of captain. She was photographed in her CAP uniform and became the model for the black Miss Coca-Cola.

In June of 1943, the postman delivered a large envelope from Congressman Dirksen's office. The congressional aide, Virgil Bentley, regularly barraged the school with newspapers and articles of interest, so Marie was in no hurry to open it. The part-timers, Patty and Rita, hung over her shoulder hoping there was a letter for them. They'd given cadets the clubhouse address because their parents wouldn't allow them to receive mail from men at their homes.

Expecting to find a copy of the *Congressional Record*, Marie was surprised when out slid a copy of *Stars and Stripes*, the Army's newspaper. Virgil had attached a note on page eight, pointing out a short article and a photograph of three pilots, lieutenants in the all-Negro 332nd Fighter Group now in North Africa. One of the young officers was definitely the Coffey School graduate, James Lowery. Willa had recruited him. Coffey had taught him the physics and mechanics of flight. Johnny had taught him to fly. Marie knew him well—quite well. Even though she was twenty-three and he was nineteen, she had secretly dated him. The article described how the three pilots had received the French *Croix de Guerre* for victories in combat missions against German aircraft over France.

Virgil's note read: "This is confirmation that American colored pilots are flying combat missions. You've done it." Marie jumped up.

"We've done it!" she exclaimed. She tuned the radio to a station playing music. Glenn Miller's "In the Mood" was just starting. She grabbed Coffey and tried to dance, but his feet didn't cooperate. Johnny did a few steps with her, but his heart wasn't in it.

Patty and Rita clapped as Willa danced with Marie until the music ended. The next song, "If I Didn't Care," by the Ink Spots made Marie stop dancing. In tears, she returned to her desk, made the sign of the cross, and put her hands together.

Patty and Rita rushed to her side. "Marie, what's the matter?" asked Willa.

"I don't know. I just thought that instead of dancing, maybe I should be praying for them."

Johnny felt relieved Marie had ended the celebration. Privately, the news of this significant milestone made him gloomy. He envied the young cadets and their future. And as much as the Coffey School students admired him, he felt he'd become a parody of himself. He'd told the same tired story about trying to shoot down an Italian bomber with a revolver too many times.

# 58

Captain James Lowery returned home on two weeks' leave in January 1944. He'd seen action in North Africa, Italy, and France, and along with other commendations, he'd won the coveted Silver Star. Lowery paced as he regaled the cadets for an entire class session with stories of his eight confirmed kills, which made him an ace. Johnny sat in the back, silently proud.

"Why do they call you the Red Tails?" asked one of the cadets.

"I'll tell you how that happened. Up there in the sky, flying like a goddamn banshee, it's hard keeping track of your own guys. It was the writer, Tappen, the guy we called Tolstoy, who came up with the idea. He loved to play basketball, and in Algiers, he played with crewmembers from the B17s — he didn't know these men--but they were playing his sport. After the game, while having a beer with a Mexican-American gunner, the corporal explained how the B-17s had blind spots where they couldn't see the enemy coming at them.

"The Messerschmitts know where to hit us," the gunner said, taking a big swig of beer. "They take out the tail gunner or belly gunner first. Then they come at us from below. The *cabrones* pound us like *piñatas*--and they're not wearing blindfolds."

"Our guy Tolstoy came to us and proposed a game plan for what we should do. Guess what it was? It's important." James looked around the room at the hungry eyes of the cadets. "In fighting situations, we're flying anywhere from a hundred to four hundred miles an hour. We're crossing a hell of a lot of map space. First, we needed to know where our team members were at a glance, hence the red tail. Then, like basketball, we go for the ball, meaning the Messerschmitt closest to the B-17s' blind spot. It was just an idea, but on our next outing, we escorted a squadron that had taken a beating in their last two missions. By beating, I mean, *beating*. They'd started with thirty-five B-17s. They were down to sixteen. These weren't milk runs. But Tolstoy's idea worked. When a Messerschmitt zeroed in on the bomber's weak spot, it was vulnerable. That day, the B-17s made their run, dropped their eggs, and didn't lose a plane. There was plenty of action, too. I got two of my kills, and our squadron had a confirmed seven kills total. By teaming, we had an advantage. We kept the fucking Messerschmitts away from our babies."

Several of the cadets laughed nervously.

"So...a whole bunch of them, B-17 officers and crew, came over with cases of beer wanting to meet their Red Tail fighter escorts. They walked into our tent, and they thought they'd made a mistake--maybe they were in the laundrymen's quarters. So, one of them asked, 'Where can we find the Red Tail pilots?' And one of our guys says, 'You've found them. What can we do for you?' Long goddamn pause." Lowery theatrically dropped his jaw in mock astonishment. The cadets bent over laughing.

"Finally, one of bomber pilots says, 'It's an honor to meet you. We were flying the B-17s. Hell of a job you did for us.'" The cadets roared, again.

Willa came into the room and looked at the clock. James Lowery got the cue and began to wrap up his visit.

"You guys pay attention to the colonel," he told the cadets, referring to Johnny. "He'll save your ass a thousand times if you learn what he knows about handling a plane. And just wait until you get into your own P-51 Mustang. With the new Rolls Royce engine, you'll fly four hundred and seventy-five miles an hour. You'll be the fastest, meanest son of a bitch in the air. You're a goddamn killing machine. The colonel knows things about the P-51 Mustang that not even our army instructors know. Pay attention."

Johnny shook his head and waved his hands as if to say, "It's not true."

"What happened to Quinton Smith?" Willa asked. "We haven't heard from him."

"Quinton was too tall for the fighters, six foot four, so he and a batch of tall guys were sent to bomber training. I haven't seen him since flight school. Something fishy happened--I don't know what. And 'Rosie'—you know, Mitchell Rosen? He's in the Pacific on the carrier *Yorktown*. The dentist, Elroy Meeks? Meeks got shot down and wounded. He's okay, though. He was transferred to the medical corps."

"What about Anders Borstad? He used to write, but we haven't heard from him."

Lowery's mood turned serious. "Months before Pearl Harbor, Andy went and flew for the RAF. They've taken terrible casualties. I'm afraid he was one of them."

"Oh, no," whispered Willa.

"I might as well tell you about Tolstoy, the basketball strategist who was going to write a book about us. He and his Great American Novel were lost over Italy. We were stationed in a town three hundred miles away from our target, a beach town called Anzio. By the time we reached the German defenses, we had enough gas for a ten-minute attack. We had to turn tail and fly back if we wanted to save our planes. The Germans were ready for us, too. It was bad. Luckily, we could fly faster and outrun them. Of course, that's not something I'm proud of."

"I'm sorry. We didn't know," said Willa. "They were fine young men." Her eyes moistened recalling the eager farm boy from Carbondale and the studious writer from Prairie View A & M.

Lowery shook off the serious tone. "Now, the reason I know about Anders at all is because of Dorothy Fox! Remember her, Willa? For you cadets, Dotty Fox was in the first class of CPT graduates. If you think that women can't fly, then you don't know Dotty Fox. She's a pistol. She was some kind of math prodigy, graduated from college at sixteen. Headstrong...and knew exactly what she wanted to do. We stayed in touch after graduation. And well, she passed for white in England and lied about her age––she was nineteen and said she was twenty-one. So as I sit here on my butt, she's flying planes to the front with the British Women's Auxiliary Ferrying Squadron, the WAFS. We happened to be in London at the same time and turned a lot of heads when we walked into the officers' club arm in arm." The cadets laughed and applauded not wanting the interview to end. Willa nodded toward the door. It was time to go.

As she walked James to a waiting taxi, Willa looked at her protégé and admired how he'd turned out, full of raw confidence, with a razor-sharp mind, and he was only twenty-two years old. It occurred to her that all of the cadets who had sat in wide-eyed admiration were at least two years older.

# 59

J ohnny searched for any news he could find about Ethiopia.
He read every clipping that Virgil Bentley sent. He accompanied Marie St. Clair, Lola Jones, the part-time staffers, and several cadets to the Thursday-night movies but only stayed for the newsreels.

Once a week, he visited the restaurant where he had proposed marriage to Willa. The proprietors, the tall and elegant Zema and her kind husband, Dr. Melku, the unofficial acting consul for the Ethiopian government in exile, were surviving meagerly. Dr. Melku taught one anthropology class at the University of Chicago, and his small part-time professor's income was likely what kept them from starvation. Johnny couldn't help but notice that the "priceless" antique tapestries were missing from the walls and guessed they'd been sold. Zema told Johnny he could order anything on the menu, as long as it was *Sega Wat*, the lamb stew. On his weekly visits, he was often their only customer.

When Johnny asked if they had heard any news, Zema left the room and returned with a box of letters from exiles living in London and Havana. She sat at his table and with her long fingers opened letters that were months old and had been read over and over, as if one more reading might reveal a coded message of hope. But the couple knew nothing more than what the local newspapers provided, and they hadn't heard from Ethiopian ambassador Dr. Melaku Beyan for over two years.

"I feel forgotten," Zema lamented.

⁂

Fortunes changed when news reports arrived that a combined British and Ethiopian force had expelled the Italian army from Ethiopia. The newsreel footage showed Emperor Haile Selassie's triumphant return to Addis Ababa. For the Chicago folk, this was the break in the clouds they'd been waiting for. Johnny immediately wrote to Dr. Beyan, asking for the reinstatement of the Abyssinian Air Service. He had Zema and Dr. Melku translate the letter into Amharic and mailed off his official petition.

Sadly, several months later, Johnny learned from a *Defender* obit that Dr. Beyan had died a year and a half before. From sketchy coroner's records, Enoch Waters had surmised that during the fierce Washington DC blizzard of 1942, Dr. Beyan collapsed and died of pneumonia while going door to door, raising funds for Ethiopian relief. Once he was dead, his wallet, shoes, and coat were more than likely stolen, and when no one came forward to identify the body, he was declared a "Negro John Doe." His photo was taken, and he was buried in a pauper's grave. Johnny assumed the news of Dr. Beyan's death ended any chance of his return to Ethiopia.

When a new crew of young Ethiopian diplomats arrived in Washington DC to reestablish relations with the United States, they knew little or nothing about John Robinson. Almost all new delegates were sons of prominent Ethiopian families, and they'd spent the last ten years in London. The embassy, a hotel suite near the capital, was nearly always filled with representatives from Trans World Airlines. Enoch told the newly arrived Ethiopian embassy staff what he had learned about Dr. Beyan's death, and arrangements were made for an official funeral.

The one thing that did help Johnny was that restaurant owner and friend, Dr. Melku, had credibility in Ethiopia. Dr. Melku advised the new embassy officials not to disturb Dr. Beyan's mail and to send it all to Addis Ababa. It took several additional months for someone to find Johnny's petition and forward it to Emperor Selassie, who fortunately at that moment had access to the British transatlantic cable system.

In August 1944, nine months after Johnny sent his letter, Marie St. Clair was signing for a telegram from His Royal Highness Haile Selassie for Colonel John. C. Robinson.

Knowing this telegram had to be important, Marie stopped Johnny's class to give him the envelope. He ripped it open and in a voice an octave higher read aloud, "'His Emperor Haile Selassie, the Lion of Judah, is requesting that Colonel John Robinson resume his commission in the Ethiopian Air Force.' My duties are to begin immediately by supervising the preparation of a Douglas DC-3 to fly to Ethiopia."

Johnny couldn't continue. He handed the letter to Willa to finish.

"The telegram says how the plane should be painted green with yellow and red stripes diagonally across the body and how he wants the coat of arms of Ethiopia, the Lion of Judah, in gold-leaf paint on the tail. The telegram says, 'These are details well-known to Colonel Robinson.'"

Johnny took the train to the California assembly plant to supervise delivery and prepare the aircraft for international travel. He found it ironic that as himself, John C. Robinson, he would have stayed in a decent hotel in the predominately black neighborhood in South Central Los Angeles. But with his Ethiopian passport, Colonel Robinson was housed in a private bungalow overlooking the Pacific Ocean in Laguna Nigel, California, a hideaway normally reserved for the titans of industry, movie stars, and royalty. The views of the palisades and the rocky beach below were splendid, and the Douglas Aircraft assembly plant was in Long Beach, a one-hour chauffeured drive away.

❦

At the reception for his departure, Dr. Melku, the now official Ethiopian consul to Chicago, and his elegant wife, Zema, who wore a striking headdress that made her seem at least seven feet tall, handed Colonel Robinson a portfolio of elaborately decorated documents permitting him to travel across oceans, countries, and continents. This time, he wasn't going alone. With him were a copilot and a Coffey School graduate with a master mechanic's license in multiple-engine aircraft. They carried a substantial number of spare parts and enough food and water to take them far beyond Addis Ababa.

Janet and her newest husband made a late entrance to the reception in the Coffey School hangar. Her spouse smiled uncomfortably as Janet pushed her way to the front of the reception line and planted a full kiss on Johnny's lips. After an awkwardly long and passionate smooch, they separated. "Next time I see you, things will be different," she said.

"They always are, Janet," answered Johnny.

Willa followed next in line for a good-bye. She hugged him. When they separated, she touched his face. "We're going to miss you," she said.

"Well, you have plenty of people who can take my place," he answered.

"That's true, but we're still going to miss you." Willa couldn't remember when she'd seen him as vibrant as he was that day—and astoundingly humble, too. She gave him a kiss on the cheek and squeezed his hand. "It's time to pull out all the Abyssinian Airline files. Stay in touch."

"Watch yourself crossing the Atlantic," said Coffey, wrapping his arms around Johnny's shoulders and hugging his dear old friend.

Johnny laughed; half embarrassed, he pulled back from their hug. "Coffey, this isn't 1927, and this isn't the *Spirit of Saint Louis*. People have been flying across the Atlantic for years now. When the war is over, you and Willa have to come and see me. Ethiopia is a beautiful country."

Johnny climbed the stairs to the DC-3 and waved good-bye. Though there wasn't any possible way anyone could have known, this was the last time any of them would see him.

# 60

A week later, Coffey and Willa received a registered letter from the secretary of commerce telling them that Congress was ending funding for the Wartime Training Service (WTS). Enoch drove out to Harlem Airfield to take a look at the correspondence and found everyone in a grim mood. Willa handed him the letter.

"I guess the war is going better than expected," said Enoch, "because the Germans and the Japanese haven't surrendered as far as I know." He read the letter and shook his head. "This change was coming, though. I can tell you as a fact that the army doesn't want any outside training. It wants to do its own recruiting and take command of all flight training from basic to advanced. Early on, they had a few hotdogging pilots, thinking they knew more than the instructors."

"The thing that gets me," said Coffey. "It says here, the army wants the return of the four Waco trainers they loaned us in 1941. I've rebuilt those obsolete crates at least six times. They're not the same jalopies they unloaded on us."

The letter from the secretary of commerce ended by commending the staff of the Coffey School of Aeronautics for their splendid work, but that was that.

Enoch wrote an article for the *Defender* profiling the accomplishments of the Challengers Aero Club, the National Airmen's Association of America, and the Coffey School of Aeronautics. The publicity brought out a dozen or so interested prospects to take a free class, except that they were interested in learning to fly as hobbyists rather than pursuing careers in aviation. Without the monthly checks from the Wartime Training Service, the infusion of new students wasn't nearly enough to cover the overhead for the Coffey School. Overnight, they had to give up the hangar rentals and cut back on tarmac fees.

Willa and Coffey's separation may have come as a surprise to some but not Marie St. Clair. She had known for at least three years that Willa and Coffey didn't sleep in the same room. In public, there was never a cross word or hint of sarcasm, but there was also never a touch or sign of spontaneous affection. Marie thought that maybe they were exhausted from the intense years of working together. They'd become like roommates who'd learned not to get in each other's way.

When the Coffey School could no longer pay her a salary, Willa packed her things to leave. She explained that she needed to be closer to her job prospects. Coffey sat stoically at the kitchen table working on his carburetors and didn't say a word.

Unintentionally, in the grand scheme of things, closing Willa's café might have helped spell the end for Harlem Airfield. For over eight years, at 5:30 in the morning, the café had provided coffee, scrambled eggs, biscuits, and sausages for twenty-five cents, rain, sun, or snow. Even Schumacher had come to depend on it. When the café closed, the entire airport was poorer for it. Coffey had to remove the diner awning with a crowbar, because it attracted too many inquiries.

Activity at Harlem Airfield slowed considerably when the war ended in August 1945, but the operation had been hemorrhaging cash since the end of the Wartime Training Service a year before.

Fred Schumacher found Coffey alone in the clubhouse. Mail was stacked on Willa's old desk, and the place lacked the tidy atmosphere that Willa and Marie had kept up when they ran the shop.

"We're going to have to make the move," said Fred, removing a stack of phone books from a chair and sitting down. "Flight schools are springing up like dandelions after a rain. You can't throw a rock on Cicero Avenue without hitting one of 'em."

"You going to keep your school open?" Coffey asked, not looking up from his log keeping.

"Our antique planes can't compete with Douglas and Curtiss Wright. They're hiring war aces and flight instructors who've taught men to take off from aircraft carriers. I'm done with flying schools. I have the two maintenance contracts, which I can do at Muni cheaper than here."

"What's going to happen with my setup?" Coffey glanced over at Fred, who shook his head.

"Well, you'll take a space in one of the Muni hangars; you're still my lead mechanic. My brother's hot to shut me down. He thinks he can get me out of debt and make a profit by selling the one hundred and forty acres to developers. They're going to build housing for the veterans coming back from overseas."

Fred Schumacher called Coffey, immediately after the property sale went through. Harlem Airfield closed and the buildings and hangars were bulldozed. In February 1946, right after a major snowstorm left Chicago under a blanket of unblemished snow, Willa rode the bus to the end of the line and walked to what would have been the entrance to Harlem Airfield. She'd always enjoyed seeing the clubhouse after a good snow. However, there wasn't a flagpole, bump, or part of a wall left of the Coffey School under three feet of fresh snow. She might as well have been looking out over a frozen lake, and the bare trees in the distance were the opposite shore. Disappointed not to have gotten one last look at the old place, she trudged back to the bus stop.

Schumacher moved his repair and maintenance contracts to Muni, and Coffey set up a workstation and a tiny closet of an office. He had a client list of aircraft owners who wanted him, and only him, to personally service their planes. He became a popular flight examiner, taking pilots up for their proficiency tests.

Willa returned to teaching high school in Chicago. She also applied for a position preparing flight instruction for the navy at the Great Lakes Naval Station. When tax time 1947 rolled around, she realized that the Coffey School still had to file a return, even though they hadn't earned a cent in the last year.

There had been no reason to communicate, and until taxes came to her attention, Willa and Coffey hadn't spoken. She caught the bus to the Muni Airport hangar and told him that they needed to close the books for the Coffey School of Aeronautics.

"Taxes? I thought that was all over in 1945."

"This is for last year, 1946. I talked to Enoch, and he says we have to notify the government that we have closed the school. But first, we have to dissolve the business charter with the state of Illinois. I'll take care of it, but I'll need your signature at some point."

"As long as you're taking care of that, I need a divorce. I'm... thinking...of marrying Lola," Coffey said, hesitantly.

"Lola Jones?" Willa asked, quizzically. "I hadn't expected that. Lola? Well, I did expect someone to snatch you up. You're prime real estate, Coffey."

"Yeah, well, there haven't been a lot of takers."

A few weeks after Willa submitted the papers for a divorce, the Cook County city clerk informed her that they weren't legally married. Their marriage license had never been registered. This posed a legal problem since husband and wife, Mr. Cornelius C. Coffey and Mrs. Willa B. Brown, had signed the Coffey School incorporation papers. Appropriate documentation of a divorce needed to be included to absolve both parties of tax liability.

Willa arranged for a judge to marry them in chambers and then had him execute the divorce documents. All through the wedding and divorce process, Coffey participated sullenly. He signed where he was told to sign and only grumbled after they left the chambers. "I thought our marriage was official."

Willa waited until they were outside the courthouse before she answered, "The army wanted a damn piece of paper. I gave them one. So, what's the matter? I thought you were anxious for a divorce."

"I know it's too late now, but I didn't want you to go. I needed you," said Coffey.

"Why didn't you try to stop me?"

Coffey shrugged.

"You can be incredibly selfish. You know that?" she said. "I thought Johnny was the selfish one, but I was wrong. You never do *anything* that you don't want to do, and when you want something, you live like a monk until you've got it. It's your genius. I admire you tremendously for it. But you can't expect me to be your personal maid. I told you in the beginning, I'm not a house *frau*. If I ironed your shirts or cooked meals, it wasn't because I was your wife. It was part of the job. Where was I supposed to fit in after we lost funding? You continued with your job with Schumacher, and I'm supposed to what? Sit at home--in a trailer? You know that's not me." Willa paused.

Coffey looked apologetic enough.

"Did it ever occur to you to give me flowers? I told you many times how much I liked flowers."

Coffey wanted to say something, but his brain froze. In all the years they were together, he'd never once given her a gift, not a flower or a box of hankies.

"I'm sorry," he said, finally. "I was never any good at those things. Willa, I couldn't have run the Coffey School or done any of the CPT stuff without you."

"And I couldn't have done anything without you. We were a good business match. And for a time, we wanted and needed the same thing."

"I saw you that day you came out to Harlem after the snow."

"You saw me in February? Why didn't you say something?"

"I was embarrassed. The place we had built together was gone. If we were so damn good, why is it gone?"

"Because the war's over, Coffey. We had our turn, and we have plenty to be proud of. We did our part. I don't miss the pressure, though. Remember what it was like every month having to make payroll and pay for rentals? For us, it was life and death. Before the war, for the army and Congress, we were a nuisance. We played by their rules and beat people with a lot more money and power."

"Still, I didn't want it to end."

"I didn't want it to end, either. I intended to visit you and see how you were doing. Then I got a teaching job right off, and no one told me they'd bulldozed the airfield. But whatever came your way, I knew you'd be all right."

"It happened very fast. They're starting construction on the houses as soon as the ground is dry enough. My new place at Muni is more...professional. You saw it. I have to do my own logs, but I can handle that. But since you've gone, nobody does my shirts like you."

Willa laughed out loud and slapped his arm with the divorce documents. "Well, there you go. So Lola's not gifted with an iron. She was never much of a flyer, either, but she's a good person. If nicely ironed collars are the only thing you miss, then we really didn't belong together."

# 61

As the DC-3 circled Addis Ababa, the mechanic joined Johnny and the copilot in the cockpit to survey the changes and damage left by the Italians. Johnny pointed out that the royal residence had been bombed, as were nearly all synagogues and Muslim temples. The houses of the prominent families, as well as large sections of mud-hut neighborhoods, were in ruins. The main thoroughfares were cleared for traffic, but numerous side streets were littered with rubble. Bomb craters made most long stretches of road useless for landing. As he approached the site of the stables where he had rebuilt the Junker F8 in 1935, he found the old barns were gone, and in their place, British forces had constructed an airstrip. A Union Jack along with the national flag of Ethiopia hung above the control tower, which appeared to be empty. Apparently, there was no one to greet them. Johnny landed and, along with the crew, remained by the plane knowing someone would come. Within ten minutes, a jeep appeared at the end of the airstrip and sped in their direction. They were three old colleagues, men who'd served in Johnny's company before the war — men personally selected by the emperor's grandson, Captain Ababe Kafele.

He introduced his Chicago crew to Master Sergeant Danni who should have been an officer, but was the son of a shepherd. Danni and the two other men were all that remained of the twelve-man squad he had trained to maintain aircraft.

"Where's everyone? The tower's empty," asked Johnny, greeting his old comrades.

"It's teatime," said Danni. "The British are unpleasantly punctual and observe a rigid teatime."

<hr />

His arrival in Ethiopia was a return to the frustration of dealing with an inept, corrupt bureaucracy. The old guard may have been steeped in tradition and small bribes, but the new guard was schooled in modern greed and big graft.

The young bureaucrats ignored Johnny and Sergeant Danni as they waited in line with a queue of local petitioners. However, the moment British, Dutch, or American agents arrived, the bureaucrats jumped into action and escorted them into the inner offices. Sergeant Danni pointed out that envelopes with cash were being openly exchanged. The Dutch wanted a coffee monopoly. The Brits wanted any kind of trade they could bring home as a kind of reparation. American agents were after a contract for an airline service.

Johnny could barely cover his hotel bill. The cost of living in the capital had become ridiculously expensive. Additionally, as an American without cash for bribes and escorted by an enlisted man, an English language telegram from the emperor wasn't enough to get him past the gatekeepers.

Trans World Airlines, with already established international routes from the United States to Europe, moved aggressively into the Middle East with ten planes and locked up air service to Athens, Istanbul, Beirut, Cairo, Jerusalem, and Addis Ababa.

Johnny learned about these developments while sitting in the government building's lobby waiting with other petitioners for an audience with Selassie. The preparations for the first ever celebration of the victory over Italy, a new national holiday, became the latest pretext as to why the bureaucrats avoided making eye contact. On the day prior the festivities, the emperor unexpectedly entered through the main entrance. The crowd of petitioners rose to their feet and jostled their way towards the emperor. Office workers rushed to the Selassie's side, forming a protective phalanx. Seeing Johnny sitting in the waiting area. Emperor Selassie waved for him to come closer. He kissed Johnny's cheek and held his hand.

"Colonel Robinson, I thank you for your service. Thank you for the respect you gave to my grandson. And thank you for writing your request in Amharic. It passed through the layers that protect me. Anything written in English, Russian, French, or Hebrew is lost in this wasteland out here," he said waving in the direction of the bureaucrats. "You will resume your commission in the Ethiopian Army, with a command over flight training. I want you to teach our young men to love engines as you do. I'll assign you a staff officer. I hope the sergeant has made you welcome."

"Sir, I request you make Danni my captain and make his tribe proud."

"The son of a shepherd?"

"Is he a free man?"

Selassie grinned warily.

"Done, but don't ask me for more favors."

"Sir, I didn't come back to be a flight instructor," Johnny pressed on. "I am honored. If that's what you wish me to do, I will do it—and gladly. But I came here for the Abyssinian Airline Service. That was in your telegram. Now I fear I'm too late. TWA has everything I came for."

Selassie glared sternly. "Not everything. I give you a monopoly to run the Abyssinian Airlines Service within the Ethiopian borders. From there, we shall see how we can grow."

A moment later the emperor was gone and Johnny was left wondering if what he had just heard was true. The following Tuesday, a message arrived at the hotel that he was to present himself to the bureaucrats and accept his credentials. When he and newly commissioned Captain Danni entered the office, the young men who had ignored them for weeks were suddenly bowing and offering Danni a new wool coat from England and Johnny a thriving coffee plantation in the faraway province in Welega—which was equivalent to accepting the Brooklyn Bridge from a stranger. He accepted, knowing that Welega was a region for herding and not plantations.

The DC-3 Johnny flew to Ethiopia belonged to the government. He was in charge of it and maintained and flew it, but for his monopoly to operate an airline service within the country's borders, he had to have his own aircraft. Janet arranged for Johnny to purchase a war-surplus Canadian-made UC-64 Norseman, a reliable aircraft capable of landing almost anywhere there was a flat strip of land or shallow water.

Johnny never returned to the United States. He remained in Ethiopia and ran the Abyssinian Airlines Service, ultimately operating four aircraft with international flights to Nairobi and Cairo. He had to train local men as pilots and mechanics for his own airline, as well as for Ethiopia's military because, no sooner did an English-speaking and US-trained pilot or mechanic arrive in Addis Ababa, than they were wooed away by TWA, who paid four times what Abyssinian Airlines could pay. Many of these men later returned to the US and found that their international experience was valued by stateside airlines.

Exactly how Johnny died is not known. Some credible sources within the Ethiopian government say he died bringing plasma to an injured pilot. There was a huge public display of national mourning in June 1954, and a casket was buried in the Cemetery of Heroes. However, no witnesses saw his body. There's a second version that says that Johnny died bringing aid to a famine-stricken region of a remote province, at a time when Emperor Selassie was seeking foreign investment by projecting the image of a modern Ethiopia. A Dark Ages–style famine was something the government didn't want the world to see. There's a third version, completely disavowed by the government. For a time, rumors circulated that Johnny's plane had never been found. He was supposedly living as an elder in a remote region in the province of Welega, and the children of his village are now university students at the Sorbonne.

# 62

*April 29, 1972*

Posters of pioneer black aviators decorated the walls of Detroit's grand Ponchartrain Hotel ballroom for the annual Tuskegee Airmen Reunion banquet.

The mood was celebratory, the attire formal. The evening's entertainment, a jazz quintet, riffed on "American Patrol" as World War II veterans, dressed in tuxedos and accompanied by their fashionably attired wives, filed into the ballroom. Many veterans hadn't seen one another in years.

Dr. James Lowery brought his mother, wife, and four children forward to greet the guests of honor. "Willa Brown and Cornelius Coffey, you remember my mother, and this is my wife, Nicole," said James.

"So pleased to see you again," said Willa to Mrs. Lowery. "And a pleasure to meet you, Nicole." Willa glanced at their brood. "So you became a pediatrician?" she teased.

"I'm a vascular surgeon," replied James, without hesitation. "Willa and Coffey, I'd like you to meet my children..."

Before he could finish, retired General Benjamin O. Davis approached and put his hand on Lowery's shoulder. "I'm sorry to interrupt, Captain, but we're running late. I'll be taking the guests of honor from you," he said and led seventy-year-old Coffey and sixty-six-year-old Willa to the dais. The seating place cards read: Willa B. Brown and Cornelius C. Coffey.

There was a third place setting with a single white rosebud placed atop an upside-down plate for Col. John C. Robinson.

Many friends and former students lined up to congratulate the honorees. Willa, wearing a black evening dress, greeted everyone warmly. Coffey, in neatly pressed khaki pants, a crisp striped dress shirt with no tie, and a navy-blue windbreaker, appeared embarrassed by the attention. He wore a baseball cap, which Willa reminded him to remove as they took their seats.

They joined several other guests already on the dais, whose place cards read Janet Harmon Bragg Waterford, Harold Hurd, Enoch Waters, and Chauncey Spencer. All were decked out for the evening.

As General Davis approached the podium, the well-wishers retreated to their tables. The general put on his glasses and opened his notes. "We have honored aviation pioneers in the past," he began. "Bessie Coleman, our collective grandmother."

The audience applauded.

"And my personal friend, Charles Alfred 'Chappie' Anderson. Chappie, thank you."

To rousing applause, Charles Anderson, now a venerable, white-haired gentleman seated at a front table, stood and made a good-natured salute in the direction of Willa and Coffey.

General Davis waited for the applause to subside.

"History is bigger and more complex than an evening like this can reveal. Bessie Coleman inspired a generation of inordinately gifted people who organized in Los Angeles, Washington DC, Kansas City, Oklahoma City, and most important, in Chicago. In Chicago, three individuals — Willa B. Brown, Cornelius Coffey, and John C. Robinson — were at the forefront of the movement to train African-American young men as pilots and mechanics and integrate the Army Air Corps. Their images hang behind the dais, at the center of the gallery of pioneer aviators. Today, we are fortunate enough to have with us some of their cohorts: writer and *Chicago Defender* editor Enoch Waters, and businesswoman Janet Harmon Bragg Waterford, who purchased the Challengers' first plane."

A round of applause gave Janet a reason to stand briefly and wave.

"I welcome my close friend, civil rights activist, pilot, community leader, and ex-parachute daredevil, Chauncey Spencer, whose story is legend, and which we shall save for another night."

More applause.

"And my dear friend, Challenger historian and Tuskegee Master Sergeant Harold Hurd."

A round of applause rang out for Harold.

"Many of you present here today are here because of the excellent start you received at the Coffey School of Aeronautics."

Charles Anderson and many in the audience stood.

"The love and dedication to aviation demonstrated by Willa Brown, Cornelius Coffey, John Robinson, and their associates not only set the standard for us all, they were models proving that an integrated military could exist."

Willa reached out for Coffey's hand, as those around them remained standing and applauded.

Willa rose slowly and made her way to the podium.

"Thank you, General Davis, and thank you to the Tuskegee Airmen committee for this beautiful occasion. Thank you, Enoch, Janet, Chauncey, Harold, and...where's Marie?"

"Over here," she heard from the assembly.

"Thank you, Charles Alfred Anderson. Or do you prefer to be called Charlie? Alfred? Chappie? Or sir? We never knew."

A round of amused applause spread through the room.

"However, before I thank anyone else, I have to say that Coffey is not wearing a tux tonight because he's an eccentric. No, no, nothing of the sort." Willa laughed lightly. "It's because his luggage is in Atlanta. Coffey, we could have made a fortune training baggage handlers instead of pilots."

The audience roared and applauded.

"You may already know that between 1940 and 1944, the Coffey School trained more than fifteen hundred students, and over nine hundred men went on to serve at the Tuskegee Army facility as pilots, mechanics, and instructors. We never had one student death, nor were any of our planes ever damaged beyond repair."

More applause.

"The activity I describe here tonight took place thirty years ago. And I must say that I personally have not gone unrewarded for my efforts. When I read not so long ago that the navy trained their first black woman pilot and her name was Brown, I was so proud." Willa put her shoulders back and lifted her head high. "As I stand at my back window, I can see the planes departing Midway Airport. We used to call it Muni, remember? My heart rises, thinking that today there are women pilots who are at the controls of those magnificent jumbo jets." Willa dabbed her eyes, and her voice cracked. "Yes, I am rewarded."

# Epilogue

On July 26, 1948, President **Harry S. Truman** signed Executive Order 9981 ending segregation in the United States Armed Forces.

⬿

**Cornelius Coffey** continued in aviation as a flight examiner into his eighties. He has an aviation navigational position named after him on the approach path to Chicago's Midway Airport—it's called the "cofi fix."

⬿

**Willa Brown** designed flight instruction for the US Navy for several years. She retired as the head of a high school vocational education department where she promoted careers in aviation. Her navigational intersection on the approach to Midway Airport is called "Wila."

⬿

**Janet Harmon Bragg Waterford** retired a millionaire businesswoman.

❧

**Marie St. Clair** married a student she met a Harlem Airfield. She and her half-black, half-Hawaiian husband worked in small nightclubs performing Hawaiian music. She played the slide guitar, and her husband played the ukulele.

❧

**Chauncey Spencer** worked tirelessly for the integration of the armed forces. After 1946, he served as police commissioner of San Bernardino, California and was the deputy administrator for the City of Highland Park, Michigan.

❧

**Dorothy Fox** returned Stateside after the war. She married a white college professor and earned a PhD in history. She retired as the head of a women's studies department at a Southern university. Her son became a congressman.

❧

The site of **Harlem Airfield** is now a shopping mall. There is no sign or plaque telling of the history that took place on that land.

The End

wanted to get it down before it

disappeared —

CHANGES —

IN 2 lines —